Love So Sweet Collection

5 stories of sweet love and delicious desserts

Love So Sweet Series

Steena Marie Holmes

Love So Sweet Series

The Love So Sweet Series:

I'm so excited to share these short but sweet romances written early in my writing journey. Where the recipe for happily-ever-after contains chocolate, sweet love, and heartfelt apologies. Whether it's a flickering flame from a previous relationship or a secret love that is shared, you'll find it in this series.

I hope you enjoy reading them as much as I enjoyed writing them!

WHO IS STEENA MARIE?

STEENA MARIE HOLMES is the sweeter name of Steena
Holmes, a NY Times & USA Today author with over 2 million
copies sold. The novels you will read under the name Steena
Marie Holmes are heartwarming stories full of sweetness.

Let's Connect!
www.steenaholmes.com
steena@steenaholmes.com

Would you like a free read?

I have two books for you to choose from if you'd like to sign up for my newsletter. I send out one email a month, sharing updates, book sales, what I'm reading and even a delicious recipe I've tried that month.

Choose between Halfway to Nowhere or Stillwater Shores...just click here to join my mailing list!

Dear Reader...

Welcome to my world of chocolate, mountains, romance, and wanderlust. The Love So Sweet series captures all the things I love the most - like second chances, believing in oneself, delicious chocolate and baked pastries, and of course...sweet romance that stands the test of time.

Each of the books in this series are short but sweet reads, stories you can read before bed or while sitting at the doctor's office or even while waiting for your plane to take off.

I have a few hopes for this series...that you enjoy them, that you want to travel to the settings I've placed them in, and that you wish you had a piece of chocolate in your hand as you read.

From my happy heart to yours...

HAPPY READING!

A LOVE SO SWEET
NOVELLA

sweet
MEMORIES
STEENA MARIE HOLMES
New York Times Bestselling Author

Sweet Memories

Happily-ever-after only happens once in a lifetime, right? But what if Prince Charming runs for the hills at the first sign of trouble and leaves you to pick up the pieces?

Coming back from a whirlwind secret wedding, the last thing she expected was for her new husband to run away once they got home.

After months with no word, she especially never expected to fall into his arms during one of her catering events.

What's a girl to do when her heart still goes pitter-patter for a man who ran out on her just after they'd made their forever vows in secret, and now comes back asking for a second chance?

Chapter One

WHEN LIFE HANDS YOU LEMONS, don't bother making lemonade. Tessa scrunched up her nose at the timeless saying. Why was it always about lemons? She'd much rather just throw those suckers away and reach for a cupcake with buttercream chocolate icing on it instead—like the ones on the table in front of her.

"I'm sure no one will notice if you take a small one."

Tessa turned to find her best friend and business partner, Eleanor Paige, beside her. "I'll notice. It'll leave a spot open and then I'll have to rearrange everything to cover it."

She wiped her hands on her apron and took in the scrumptious dessert table she'd just painstakingly created. Every type of chocolate delicacy one could crave was on that table and it was all she could do not to do a little taste testing. The chocolate aroma in and of itself was enough to...

"Tess, here, just a little sample." Ellie popped a salted chocolate caramel into Tess's mouth and winked. "This way you give an honest assessment if any of the guests ask."

O.M.G. Delicious. Pure heaven. The chocolate melted in her mouth while the salt had her taste buds singing the chorus of *Hallelujah*. She didn't even try to speak. No words were necessary. Apparently, Ellie felt the same way as she had a similar look of ecstasy on her face when she bit into her own small caramel.

"Oh. My. Jolly Rancher," she mumbled around the treat. "I could eat these for the rest of my life and die a happy woman." Ellie reached for another piece but Tessa slapped her hand away and gave her a mock frown.

"Don't you dare. These are for the guests who are about to arrive," Tessa glanced at her watch, "any minute now. And," she glanced at her friend, "please, 'jolly rancher'?"

Ellie wasn't one to swear, so instead, she'd add in odd phrasing in its place. Earlier, she'd dropped a tray of chocolate tortes and the glass had smashed all over the place, and instead of the curse word you'd expect, all she yelled was "sweet sugar plum fairy."

She shrugged before reaching into her pocket and pulling out a pack of Jolly Ranchers, watermelon flavored.

"If you're not careful, all that sugar is going to head straight to your hips and butt," Tessa cautioned.

"What? You're saying I can't have my cake and eat it too? Where's the fun in that?" she teased as she held out her notebook. "Everything is ready. The place looks great, doesn't it?"

It really did. The room glistened with sparkling chandeliers and gossamer wall hangings dotted with glittering gems that reflected the lights around the room, while dozens of soft grey linen-covered round bar tables held cream and red rose flower arrangements and small plates of chocolate hearts. Tessa wanted, no, she needed this night to be extra special.

"I'm so glad we decided to go with those chocolate-toned aprons. Our logo stands out quite nicely on them."

Tessa smiled at the servers who milled around the room wearing their new aprons. Yes, they did look quite nice. Her gaze swept around the room as she mentally checked off all the things that needed to be completed before the party could start. Everything was done, but one.

"What's keeping Bob and Jean? They were supposed to be here by now." Tessa pulled out her cell phone to see if perhaps they'd left a message.

"Oh, I forgot." A blush crept along Ellie's face. "They called a little while ago and mentioned they might be a bit late."

"How late?"

Ellie glanced down at her notes and bit her lip. "About thirty minutes give or take."

Tessa's brows rose. Thirty minutes wasn't just a *little* late when the whole night was planned down to the last minute. She glanced at the copy of the schedule for tonight to see what could be rearranged.

"It's okay," Ellie reached out and touched her arm, "I've got it under control. The photographer is going to start fifteen minutes early, the band is cool, and I've already alerted the kitchen. It's all good."

Tessa breathed a sigh of relief. She should have known better than to worry. If anyone could work their magic on last minute changes, it was Ellie.

"Why would Bob and Jean be so late?"

A sly smile crossed Ellie's face. "Maybe they're celebrating a little early?"

A blush crept across Tessa's face. As much as she loved her in-laws, thoughts of them celebrating their fiftieth wedding anniversary early definitely wasn't something she wanted to dwell on.

"I'll go start greeting our guests if you can watch the staff and get them handing out the drinks?"

"Sure, but before you head out to the doors, you might want to change your apron," she called out.

Dang it. Tessa glanced down at the apron she wore and groaned. Icing sugar and smears of chocolate icing criss-crossed the fabric. She undid the ties at the back and balled the apron up before heading to the kitchen to grab a new one.

"Hey, Tess?"

She stopped at the kitchen door and glanced over her shoulder.

"Do you think Jude will show up tonight?"

She'd love nothing more than for him to come home. It had been months since she last saw him. Months full of anger, regrets, and heartbreaks, but most of all, it she'd spent most of that time missing Jude.

Unfortunately, she knew him and knew that short of attending his parent's funeral, nothing this side of heaven or hell would drag him back to her, not when he thought their relationship had been based on a lie.

* * *

Tessa stood at the front door and handed bags to the groups that walked in. She couldn't stop the grin from spreading on her face at the number of people who arrived.

Banff was a small town if you discounted all the tourists who crowded the main street throughout the year to ski or mountain climb. Not much went on without everybody knowing everything and while there were plenty of times she hated this aspect of small town living, tonight was not one of them. Bob and Jean deserved to be showered in love, especially now.

"Oh my, what a pleasant surprise!"

She'd just handed a stuffed bag to an older couple who walked hand in hand. Their reaction to what was in the bag was similar to all the others Tessa had heard as people opened up their gift bags from the Turners.

"I thought we were supposed to be the ones bringing gifts?"

Tessa shook her head at an older man who hesitated to take the bag she offered him. Just take it," she leaned forward and wrapped an arm around the shoulder of George Sauder, and placed a soft kiss on his cheek.

"Now, what am I supposed to do with this?" He grumbled as Tessa hooked the bag over his arm. In his hand was a small box wrapped in a red bow.

George was one of those grizzly old men who complained about everything but would do anything for you at the same time. She had first met George when she was seven years old and had just moved into the house next door to him with her mom after her dad passed away. Whether he liked it or not, George became her pseudo-grandfather.

"You weren't supposed to bring a gift." She'd tried to tell Jean that no one would listen to their request. She thought about all the gifts she'd seen so far come through the door and shook her head. Secretly she was pleased that so many wanted to spoil the Turners. They deserved it.

"It's not every day someone celebrates being married to the same person for fifty years," he muttered. Tessa's smile trembled at his comment. She should be celebrating her upcoming one year anniversary with Jude over a candlelit dinner, but instead, she'll probably end up sitting on her couch, crying through a chick flick while eating take-out by herself.

"Hey now, none of that. Not here and not tonight." George pressed a Kleenex into her hand. Tessa stared up at the ceiling and attempted to blink past the tears that gathered. He was right, this was not the time or place, and she knew better.

"What's in there?" she asked him again in a pitiful attempt to change the conversation.

George glanced down at the box in his hand and frowned. "Never you mind." He stuffed the box back into his coat pocket and ambled off into the main room.

Tessa watched him go before she turned and grabbed more bags. The idea was to give people small gifts that represented who Bob and Jean were as a couple. Jean was known for her journaling and Bob for his gardening, so inside the bags were packets of seeds wrapped in a brown ribbon and a lovely journal with a heartfelt message from Jean on the first page.

As an extra surprise, Tessa had added a handmade card from a local shop with a note requesting the card be filled out with a small message to Bob and Jean and dropped in the basket by the main door during the night. Throughout the event, the staff would offer pens to people if they were needed, as well as help collect the cards.

The card idea was Tessa's own personal gift to them. She didn't know how she would have survived the past few years without their love and support, and she knew there were others in the room who felt the same way.

Tessa wanted tonight to be extra special for them. No. She *needed* this night to be extra special for them. This past year has been so hard on them, and she was responsible for some of that.

If only Jude would come home. Even if he never came back to her, he could at least come home for his parents. If only he knew...

Tessa stopped that last thought from forming. She wasn't going to think about that right now. Tonight was about celebrating the life Bob and Jean had together and praying they'd share many more. That's what she needed to focus on, not the fact that, quite possibly, this might be the last anniversary Jean would ever celebrate.

Chapter Two

HE WATCHED Tessa as she wove her way through the crowd, stopping at tables to talk with couples, even taking a minute or two to dance with a small child on the dance floor. He couldn't get over how beautiful she was. His parched soul drank her in until he felt energized. She was his breath of fresh air, the light that broke through his darkness.

He rubbed his hands down his thighs. Without a camera, they were empty, useless. If he could, he would immortalize her, like this. Elegant. Beautiful. Mesmerizing.

Jude backed away from the door at the far end of the room and went to search for his parents, who'd snuck into one of the closed off rooms in the building to talk. Nothing could have prepared him for the news he'd received when he showed up at his parents' door earlier this evening. Coming to this party was the last thing he wanted to do, but if it meant seeing his mother smile, then he would keep his mouth shut and make sure this was a night she'd remember.

Coming home tonight had been a fluke. He knew he couldn't stay away forever, and in reality, he didn't want to, but he'd dragged his feet in returning—something he knew he shouldn't have done. The only thing that had stopped him from returning right after he left was his pride. He'd reacted foolishly without giving her or Sean a chance to explain anything. Later though, when he'd calmed down and attempted to connect all the dots, there were none.

"You're kidding me, right?"

Jude stopped in his tracks and slowly turned. "Hello, Ellie." He wasn't sure if he should hold out his arms for a hug or present his cheek for a slap.

"I can't believe you actually showed up. Does Tess know?"

Jude shook his head. "Not yet. I wanted to wait—"

"Really? So what's the plan? Surprising her in the middle of your parent's party with a toast about the amazing example your parents are for what makes a marriage work?"

Damn. She might as well have kicked him right in the groin. Leave it to Tessa's best friend not to hold anything back.

"I thought maybe I could grab her attention and maybe go someplace to talk."

He knew by the look on Ellie's face what she thought of his idea. "Okay, okay, maybe not my best idea, but that's all I've got." He stuck his hands in his pant pockets and shrugged.

"Do your parents know you're here?" Ellie cocked her head as she stared at him. Not for the first time, he wished he could read her thoughts.

"That's why they're late. I missed my flight and arrived at their place just as they were leaving. My mom..." His voice hitched up a notch when he thought of how his mother had crumbled in his arms while his father stood by, stoic, on the other side of the screen door.

Ellie surprised him by rushing at him and throwing her arms around him. He slowly raised his own arms and hugged her back.

Of all people, he figured Ellie would be the first to shove a knife into his heart for returning. He figured Tessa would have told her the truth about them, about what they'd done before he'd left so abruptly...but apparently, she either didn't know or didn't care.

"If you ever leave like that again, I'll kill you before you have the chance to return. Do you understand me?"

Considering Ellie's father was a cop and had taught her how to shoot a gun at an early age, he had no doubt she meant what she said.

"I'm here to stay." Jude stared straight into Ellie's eyes and dared her to believe him. He'd do everything in his power to win back Tess, even if it meant starting all over again. She deserved her white knight, and he meant to be exactly that.

He even came prepared to slay that invisible dragon.

"It's not going to be easy, you know that, don't you?" With her arms crossed over her chest, Ellie watched him.

Easy? Nothing about Tessa was easy. She was sweet, endearing, gorgeous, and the smartest woman he knew, but easy? Not his Tessa.

"Will you help me?" Jude fiddled with his hands as he waited for her answer. If anyone knew Tessa better than he did, it was Ellie.

"Will you break her heart again?" There was a calculated look in her eye that had Jude wondering why she even asked.

Will he break her heart again? He'd never wanted to in the first place. He hadn't known what else to do, though. Yes, he knew running away as he did had been a mistake, but at the time, it seemed like his only option.

"I love her. I always have, and that is never going to change."

Seeing her tonight only sharpened that truth inside of him. He'd been a fool to run away. He'd been scared and unsure of how to handle what had happened. He'd been a weak man, and rather than protect himself, he should have done everything he could to protect the Tessa rather than hurt her.

"Just don't forget it." Ellie gave him a satisfied smile before she walked down the hallway and back into the main area.

Her comment had him on edge. He wanted to tell her he never would, but he had a feeling it wasn't going to be as easy as that. Knowing Tessa, he needed to prove himself.

And prove himself, he would.

Chapter Three

"TESSA."

She turned to find Ellie weaving her way through the crowded room.

"Bob and Jean are here."

Tessa breathed a sigh of relief. "Finally! Where are they?" She'd been doing her best to play hostess to the large crowd that had gathered for the party, but there was only so much she could do before people started to question where the guests of honor were.

"They'll be out soon."

Ellie was hiding something. Tessa knew it. It wasn't that her gaze darted around the room and the fact she wouldn't look her in the eye, nor was it the way she fiddled with her fingers as she stood there. Instead, it was the half smile Ellie tried so hard to hide that had Tessa on edge.

"What's going on?"

Ellie licked her lips and fiddled with the pen she'd taken out of her apron pocket.

"Seriously, Eleanor. If there is something going on, I need to know." It was rare Tessa used her full name, but she didn't have time to play games tonight. She needed to get Bob and Jean out here to greet their friends.

"Remember earlier when I asked you—"

"Hey there, gorgeous." Arms snaked around Tessa and squeezed tight. Tessa gave off a little squeal as the air was pushed out of her lungs before she was lifted up off the ground and the back of her neck kissed.

"Put me down, you big lug." Tessa laughed as she attempted to swat at the solid arms holding her.

"Only if you say the magic word," Sean Patterson teased as he tickled her.

Tessa knew her face had to be bright red by now. Why was it that anytime she was around Sean, he had to embarrass her in some fashion? Why couldn't he just leave her alone?

"Want me to tell Mrs. Monroe who really destroyed her prized rose gardens?" Tessa threatened. Within seconds, Sean set her down and backed away. She knew that would work, especially since Mrs. Monroe stood only a few feet away from them.

"I must say Tessa, you worked your magic and transformed this ugly place into a palace. Great job." Sean's eyes twinkled with mirth as he changed the subject.

Tessa looked around her and shrugged. "It wasn't all that bad."

Ellie groaned. "Don't listen to her, Sean. There's a reason this place is rarely used for anything more than seasonal craft shows. It took hours to get it to look this good."

"You know, I've always said you'd be a natural at interior decorating," Sean began.

Tessa didn't let him finish. "And you'd hand feed me clients from all your big multi-million dollar homes, right? No thanks.

Planning their events is enough." She glanced down at her watch. What was taking Bob and Jean so long?

"Well, if that's an option..." Sean teased.

Tessa gave her head a small shake. A draft from somewhere wrapped itself around her ankles, and she shivered. She knew she should have worn a sweater tonight over her black dress.

"You know I'd do anything for you," Sean's voice dropped an octave as he stared at her.

A stone dropped to the pit of her stomach. She didn't want to get into this with him, not here. He was a great friend, but that's all Tessa saw in him. Friendship. Sometimes Sean's teasing went a little too far.

"I tried calling you earlier."

Tessa let out the breath she held, thankful that he didn't continue that line of discussion. She caught the questioning glare from Ellie.

"You did?" Tessa pulled out her phone and scrolled through the latest calls.

"What happened to the girl who never turns her phone off?" Sean wiggled his brows before nudging her with his elbow.

"The chocolate was calling to me," she glanced behind her to the table of chocolates.

"I told you their catering was the best. I can't believe you've never used them before," Sean settled his hand on her back, and guided her through the ballroom and out into the hallway.

"I will now, thanks to you, I already have them booked for three more events."

"What you should do is entice their baker away from them so you'll have exclusive catered events. Especially when you see the place I've lined up for you." Sean grabbed a champagne flute from a server who passed them and held it out to her. She waved it away. She'd wait till the evening was over to have a drink.

17

"We can't afford a baker to be on the payroll. Not yet. And what do you mean?"

"We could if we took over the lease on the bakery next to us. Plus, there's always my sister. Lexi would bake circles around this caterer." Ellie interrupted.

This wasn't the first time they'd discussed this topic, but Tessa wasn't sure if they were ready for this type of expansion. Ellie's outlook was *go big or go home*. Tessa just wanted to make sure they had a home to go to. The last thing she wanted was to expand their Decadent Events to include a bakery and have it all be a flop.

Sean cleared his throat. "What about bringing on some partners?" He toyed with the edge of his glass while Tessa's mouth dropped.

"Sean, I...why..." she shook her head, unable to form a coherent thought. Partners? Where did this come from? She'd known Sean forever it seemed. He'd been like a brother to her for longer than she could remember.

"Why don't we save that discussion for another night?" Ellie wrapped her arm through Tessa's and pulled her close. "I think I see Bob peeking through the doorway down there."

Tessa could almost have kissed her friend. Sean stepped back, and Tessa gave him a small smile.

"Later?" He asked.

She nodded. Later could be anywhere from tonight to next week to even next year. She needed to mull this over, and think about the ramifications of bringing Sean on board as a partner.

She caught sight of Jean in the doorway close to the kitchen. Jean wrung her hands together as she searched the room. Tessa gave her a wave, and the look of relief on Jean's face had her worried.

"Have you talked to Jean tonight?" Tessa asked Ellie out of

the corner of her mouth. Ellie faltered in her step, and Tessa stopped short.

"All right, what is going on?" She asked. Ellie was acting a bit off tonight.

"There's something you need to know," Ellie looked everywhere but at her. Tessa was getting a bit annoyed. She didn't have time to play these games. Either something was wrong, or it wasn't, but if it was going to affect the party in any way, the girl had better spit it out.

"Like what?"

"It's about—"

"There you are." A hand gripped Tessa's shoulder and forced her to turn around. Evie O'Neil held a plate of tarts and almost shoved them right into Tessa's nose. "I was just telling Charlie that these pecan butter tarts are simply divine. My bridge club would love this. I don't know who you have catering tonight, but I have to get the recipe for this. I have to."

Tessa rolled her shoulder to ease out the sudden kink and attempted to be patient with Evie. She was a dear old soul who never took no for an answer, nor understood the concept of personal space.

"Tessa Turner, I insist. I've been trying to get in the kitchen for the past half hour, but I keep getting blocked by one of your servers. If you won't let me bug the caterer, then I insist you do it for me." Evie took a bite of one of the tarts and moaned.

"Now sugar, if you keep doing that, you're going to make me gather up every last tart and hide them," Ellie teased before Tessa could say anything. "Oh, don't you worry, there's none left on the table." Evie's eyes lit up as she chuckled past the food in her mouth.

"Evie, you can't do that." Tessa tried not to act shocked, but it didn't surprise her Evie would hoard all her favorite treats. She made a mental note to have one of the servers stay close to the table to keep an eye on the food. She'd planned for extras, but it was better to be safe than sorry.

"If you give me the recipe, I'll put some of them back." Evie winked at her.

Now how did you say no to someone as cute as her? She was everyone's crazy grandmother, short with wild curly hair and going on eighty-five years of age.

"I'll see what I can do." Tessa leaned in close, cupped her hand close to her mouth, and whispered in the woman's ear.

"That's my girl." Evie toddled off back to her table where her husband sat, and he gave her a high-five. Tessa laughed. They might just be the youngest oldest couple she'd ever known.

"Okay, let's go find the guests of honor and get them out here before all the desserts disappear." She turned towards Ellie and was about to grab her hand but stopped when she saw the way her friend's eyes widened.

"Don't turn around," Ellie hissed, "there's something you need to know first."

A low murmur grew through the room.

"What's wrong?" Tessa's chest constricted, and the palms of her hands tingled. She saw the faces of the crowd around her, the wide eyes, the bright smiles, the whispers while they all looked at her.

"Tessa, it's about Jude."

A lump formed in Tessa's throat, and she had a crazy need to run. Was he here? Did something happen to him, and that's why his parents were late? The room spun around her and her ears buzzed. She reached out to grab hold of Ellie's arm, but she missed and almost toppled over before strong hands gripped her arms and steadied her.

Warm breath teased her cheek as she leaned against a hard body. Heat radiated it and the cold chill she felt earlier disappeared. She could only think of one person whose touch affected her like this, but didn't dare dream that Jude had finally come home.

"Hey, gorgeous."

Tessa melted.

Chapter Four

TESSA TURNED and found herself staring into the same chocolate-colored eyes that filled her dreams on a nightly basis. He was here. Actually here. Part of her didn't want to believe it, and she blinked to see if he was a figment of her imagination.

"Breathe, Tess," the soft timber of Jude's voice washed over her and left goosebumps all along her arms.

"You came back." Once the words were out of her mouth, she wanted to swallow them. She wasn't sure how she should be feeling right now. Joy that the only man she's ever loved, was back? Anger that it took him so long to return? Elation to finally be in his arms again?

Memories of that awful day crept in, and she shuddered. His hands dropped from her arms, and when he stepped away from her she immediately felt the chill between them. A part of her wanted to reach out, to touch him, to gather back some of that warmth, but the other part of her wanted to crush his heart, like he'd crushed hers. Her counselor had warned her of that, and even worked with her on scenarios if something like this ever occurred.

"I couldn't stay away." His words were infused with warmth, but the look in his eyes was stone cold.

She gave herself a mental shake and reminded herself of where they were. Whatever was going to happen, whatever words needed to be said, this was not the time or place. It was bad enough that she'd once again added fuel to the local gossip fodder.

In the background, Sean yelled, "It's about time you two love birds showed up."

There was a smattering of laughter as Jean's face turned bright red, and Bob gave off an exaggerated wink. Tessa glanced over her shoulder and smiled at Sean in thanks. His lips rose into a smile, and he gave a small bow.

"I should have come home sooner, I see." Tessa caught a note of disappointment in Jude's voice.

She didn't say anything. She only looked at him, really looked at him. He looked good, more toned, filled out, if the size of his biceps beneath his dress shirt was any indication. He wore his hair a little longer than she remembered, there were small curls around his ears and collar, and there was a faint scar beneath his chin that hadn't been there before. He fingered the scar, as if to hide it from her gaze.

"You look good."

His brow quirked at that. "Good? That's all you have to say?"

She shrugged her shoulder. "I'm glad you came."

"That sounded almost like a question. You should know me better than that."

"I thought I did," she whispered.

Ellie broke the awkwardness between them by clearing her throat. "Um, hate to break up the reunion, but Tessa..." Ellie cocked her head towards Bob and Jean.

Tessa breathed a deep sigh, straightened her shoulders, and

forced a bright smile on her face. Without a word, she walked away from Jude and toward the people she considered family, and gave them both a tight hug.

"He came home," she whispered into Jean's ear. As she pulled away, she caught the look on Bob's face as he watched his son. Love, happiness, and peace. She knew how much it meant to him to have Jude back. He wasn't alone anymore. He didn't need to deal alone with what was about to hit them all like a tidal wave.

"He still loves you," Jean whispered back.

Tessa just smiled, but she studied Jean's face carefully. The lines beneath her eyes were darker, her face paler, and there was a slight shake to her hands that Jean tried to hide.

All that mattered was that Jude was here for his mom.

Three weeks ago, Jean had gone to the doctor to complain of stomach pain that wouldn't go away. What they all thought was mild food poisoning or the flu turned out to be cancer. Advanced adenocarcinoma, or stomach cancer. And Jean, no matter how much both Bob and Tessa argued with her, refused to accept any sort of treatment. They'd been advised that with chemotherapy, Jean might have a year. Both of Jean's parents had died of cancer, and she refused to end her days as they had. She wanted to live what life she had left on her own terms, in her own house, surrounded by those she loved. Not in a hospital, hours away in Calgary.

"I want you two to get back together." Jean gripped Tessa's hands and squeezed.

Tessa nodded. She wanted that too. "Does Jude know yet?" She hated to ask.

Jean shook her head. "Bob told him. I didn't want him to, I need there to be good memories from tonight, but Bob needed him to know." The wavering smile on her face faltered before

Bob stepped closer and wrapped his arms around his wife's waist.

"What do you say we get this party started, huh? I've been looking forward to these desserts you women keep raving about."

Tessa's eyes widened. The desserts. She glanced over at the table she'd so carefully arranged and realized she'd forgotten all about putting aside a platter for the head table.

"Evie might have eaten all the good ones," Tessa whispered, "that's what you get for being late," she teased while she led the couple to their table.

Once they were seated and Ellie took her place at the podium with the microphone, Tessa wove her way towards the dessert table and did her best to ignore the feel of Jude's gaze when she walked by.

Chapter Five

Jude's smiled tightened as he watched the soft smile Tessa gave Sean. He was still jealous and he hated that. He thought by now he would have dealt with those feelings but apparently seeing them share a moment like that brought all those feelings back.

He needed to address his insecurities if he wanted to get Tessa back.

Tessa wasn't the only one he missed.

Sean had been his best friend, and college roommate, and even agreed to be his best man at their 'official' wedding. Many times these past few months Jude had kicked himself for believing in something that wasn't true.

He'd let his weakness destroy two relationships he valued the most.

He caught Sean's gaze and nodded. Sooner or later they'd need to talk. From the steely look Sean gave him he wasn't sure if they'd be talking over drinks or with their fists.

He knew he brought unwanted attention to himself tonight and he could only imagine what was being said about him.

Jude grabbed a beer off the drink table and leaned against

the wall. If he stayed out of the way tonight, maybe that interest would die down. The last thing he wanted was to steal any of the spotlight from his parents.

Besides, from this vantage point, he could watch Tessa all night. After not seeing her for so long, he could watch her forever and never get bored.

Chapter Six

As the night wound down, Tessa gave a slight nod to Reverend Frank who sat in the corner, then dimmed the lights until only the Christmas lights they decorated the room with shone. A low murmur of excitement filled the air. Many of the guests knew what was about to happen.

Tessa walked towards the front of the room where Bob and Jean sat and didn't even bother trying to hide the smile that filled her face. Bob winked at her before he pushed back his chair and held out his hand to Jean.

"What's going on?" Jean gripped the napkin in her hand and looked from Bob to Tessa and back to Bob.

"Jean, love, just take my hand." Bob sighed as he reached down and plucked the napkin from her hand.

"But what's going on?" Jean's cheeks flushed when she realized the room had gone quiet and everyone listened in.

"Fifty years ago I promised you I'd love you forever. Back then, forever seemed like such a long time, but now, forever only seems like a day. So tonight, I want to promise you my love till the end of time, because honey, you deserve that and so much more." Bob voice cracked. As his smile wobbled,

Tessa brushed away the tears that gathered in her eyes and fell.

Bob walked Jean over to the arbour of lights and roses Ellie had set up in the corner and when Jean caught sight of Reverend Frank, her sob could be heard throughout the room.

"I love you, you silly, silly man." Jean wrapped her arms around Bob and leaned her head on his shoulder.

Tessa sank down in a chair and struggled to swallow past the lump in her throat. She searched the room for Jude and found him in the opposite corner of the room. He looked so handsome with his arms folded as he leaned against the wall. The way he stared at her had her face heating up.

Was he remembering their own secret wedding? The one they flew to Vegas for, without telling anyone?

She looked away before she made a fool of herself. Tonight wasn't about her or them. It was about Jean and Bob, and she tried to focus on the vows they spoke to one another, but memories of the vows she'd made with Jude kept creeping in.

It had been a whim. One minute they were sitting at their kitchen table, arguing over some stupid detail and the fact Jude wasn't listening, and the next, she was packing a bag to Vegas. While she'd been stressing, he'd been planning and arranged for a marriage license and tickets. Their wedding was supposed to be about them, and that's what they were going to do.

It had been a whirlwind of excitement and secrecy, of romance and adventure, and they'd both agreed to keep it a secret, just between them. Their original wedding date was less than six months away, so they'd do the ceremony, have a big party, and no one would be the wiser.

It was all perfect. She wore her white reception dress in Vegas, they drank champagne, she carried a bouquet of pink roses and vowed to love Jude for the rest of her life.

Their wedding back home would have been just as equally

special, with a waterfall as their backdrop, beneath a setting sun, on a walkway full of flickering tealights in mason jars. She would have worn a soft white gown with embroidered flowers, while Ellie would have stood beside her in a chocolate brown knee-length dress.

Instead, they came home, and within hours, Jude had packed and left, the dust flying behind his truck the only goodbye she'd received. She'd been in the bath while he packed and left, never saying a word to her.

She glanced over at him now and wished to go back in time, to erase the past months and start fresh. She wanted that to happen more than anything else in life, but she wondered if it was possible. There was so much distance between them. So much anger and hurt. He'd left her without giving her the opportunity to fix what she hadn't known was broken. And now, with him here, the distance seemed impossible to overcome.

She wasn't sure her heart could handle him leaving again.

Chapter Seven

TESSA PULLED out a chair and sank into it. She moaned as pinpricks of pain blasted through her feet. While heels worked wonders on the calves, they hurt like hell after standing for six hours. She opened her notebook and went over the checklist of items still to complete before she could call the evening a success.

"I never thought this night would end," Ellie complained as she pulled out the chair next to her and leaned back. "I feel like Cinderella, except the stroke of midnight never came, and I've been stuck in this ridiculous dress forever."

"Let me be your Fairy Godmother then. The stroke of midnight came and went. Feel free to turn into a pumpkin at any time." Tessa waved an imaginary wand in the air.

"Nice fairy godmother you are," Ellie complained. Tessa pretended to ignore her. "The caterers are gone, the staff has all been paid, cleaning crew is just about done...did I miss anything? Oh, kicking out Jude...or did you want to do that?"

Tessa played with the pen in her hand. She'd caught the way he hung around, always in sight but never too close. So many times she'd wanted to go up to him but stopped herself from making a scene. Instead, she flittered around the room, talked to different groups, and even danced with a few children to help place a smile on her face. The last time she saw him though, was with his arms full of gift-wrapped boxes on his way to his parents' vehicle.

He never returned.

"What are you talking about? He left hours ago."

Ellie snorted. "You're kidding me, right? Answer me this, why am I still wearing this ridiculous dress? What I wouldn't give for my cargo pants and black tee-shirt. I can't believe I let you talk me into wearing this. Next time, expect a revolt."

"You could have worn the pants, I told you I didn't mind."

Ellie groaned. "Oh sure, say that now."

Tessa shook her head and glanced around the room. If Jude didn't leave, then where was he?

"Hey, what happened with Sean?"

Tessa jerked her head around and stared at her friend. "What do you mean what happened?" She had a mental image of Sean and Jude fighting.

"Whoa, calm down. I just wondered where he went, that's all. I expected him to stick around, help with the cleanup, maybe talk a little more about that whole partnership thing."

Tessa leaned back and crossed her arms. "Do you think it's a good idea? We're doing well, we've got a lot of parties booked, and I had a few people ask to schedule appointments for the upcoming months tonight."

Ellie leaned close and rested her elbows on the table. She stared at Tessa until it became almost unbearable. "You don't want to work with Sean, do you?"

Tessa crossed and uncrossed her legs. "I just don't think we need to rush into anything...let's see if we could swing it on our own, bring your sister on board like you keep mentioning. There's a lot of possibilities." Tessa hedged.

"R-i-i-ight." Ellie nodded. "Are these possibilities falling in our laps just like the partnership offer?"

Inwardly, Tessa groaned. How could she explain it when she wasn't even sure herself why she hesitated?

Was it so wrong not to want to lean on anyone and just do this themselves? When Jude walked out on her, everyone said she was going to fall apart, but she didn't. She proved them wrong.

And now that Jude was home? She'd heard the murmurings tonight. Too many times to count, she'd walk up to a table, and the conversation would stop, and she knew that she was the topic. Again. All thanks to Jude.

And where was he now? He hardly said two words to her after he saved her from falling earlier. Great way to add fuel to the already burning flame. *Twice Spurned*—she could see the headline in the gossip section of *the Banff Weekly*.

"Decadent Events could make it big with Sean's help, Tess, you know that. The level of clients he has...the sky's the limit. Why are you hesitating?"

"Why are you pushing this so hard? Can I at least get a few days to think about it?" She rubbed the back of her neck and rolled her head to work out the kinks.

"Sure, sorry. I know it's not great timing right now, especially with Jude back, but you know my little sister will be home soon from Paris, and I think Lexi would be a great addition to the team. She'd be the perfect pastry chef for us, and I know she'd jump at the opportunity."

"I'm sure she would. But what if she wants to work elsewhere? I imagine it would be hard to work alongside the best patisserie chefs in France and then come home to doing only catered events. I'm sure you sister wants more than this."

Ellie shook her head. "I've already asked her and she said yes."

"You what?"

"Oh come on, Tess. This isn't the first time we've had this conversation. Don't sell us short, that's all I'm asking. Think about it, okay? Hey, you had that vacation planned after this, didn't you? Are you still going to go?"

Tessa shook her head. She'd canceled her vacation to the coast for a week of relaxation after she found out about Jean. She'd forgotten she hadn't told Ellie. Her life had been a bit of a haze since hearing the news. She leaned forward and reached for Ellie's hand.

"I canceled it earlier this week." She swallowed the lump in her throat. "Jean has an advanced-staged cancer and doesn't have much time left. I don't want to—" she couldn't get the words out. She knew Ellie would understand, having lost her own mother to cancer.

"Oh honey," tears filled Ellie's eyes "of course you couldn't go. Oh my...no wonder she looked so tired tonight."

"You caught that too? I hope tonight wasn't too much for her." She had tried to do as much as she could throughout the evening. Among the three of them, herself, Bob and Jude, Jean had received the royal treatment.

"She's stubborn, she won't let this hit her until she's at home and alone. At least, that's what my mom was like."

Tessa nodded. She remembered that. Maybe she'd head over tomorrow with some homemade soup and check in on her. "That's probably where Jude is," she muttered to herself. Of course, that's where he'd be. Why did she think he'd hang around here for her?

A chisel pounded straight through her chest and into her heart as she finally understood why Jude was back. Not for her or for their marriage. He was back for his mother. Of course. All night she'd fought against the hope that he was here for her, that realized he'd been wrong and wanted to make a fresh start.

What a fool she'd been.

"Are you okay?" A concerned look filled Ellie's gaze.

Tessa nodded her head, and grabbed her notebook and pen, stuffing them into her bag. "Of course I'm okay. I'm exhausted, though. I think I'll head home, take a long bath and go to bed." She knew she blathered on, but she could feel the tears well up, and the last thing she wanted to do was break down here.

She was so tired of breaking down, of being weak, of crying her life away.

"Are you happy he's back home?" Ellie's question stopped her.

Happy? Yes, she was happy he was home. Jean needed him. If anything, even if he were only here for his mother, it was worth it. It would be hard to see him, to run into him, but she could handle it. She didn't really have a choice, did she?

"The look in Jean's eyes tonight was worth it. Did you see the way she held tight to his arm and wouldn't let him leave her side for the longest time?"

"And you?"

Tessa gave her friend a sad smile. "He's not home for me, Ellie. It's time I accept things between us are over. You don't just walk away for months with no word and expect things to be perfect the moment you decide to come back." She shrugged and pretended her heart wasn't already in little pieces.

"No, whatever Jude and I had, is over."

Chapter Eight

Her and Jude were over.

She hadn't wanted to believe it, but it was time to accept the truth and somehow find a way to move on.

Just the idea alone makes her nauseous.

Deep down, a small part of her had been hoping he'd realize he'd been wrong, that he over-reacted, that he threw away something worth saving...but she should have known better.

She drove home in a fog, barely noticing the herd of mountain goats that blocked her driveway. These things were the bane of her existence lately. They took a liking to the shrubs she'd planted in the spring and now wouldn't leave her place alone.

A few quick honks of the truck horn and a feeble wind through the herd had her slowly edging up her driveway. She was so intent on the goats that she didn't notice an unfamiliar pick-up parked ahead before it was almost too late.

Jude sat on her side porch deck, while her dog—no, their dog —sat at his feet. Her steps faltered as her heart swooshed at the sight of him.

The smile on his face sent the sleeping butterflies into a frenzy.

She wanted to say something, anything, but the words were stuck on her tongue.

"Did you almost hit my truck?"

She lifted her shoulder in a shrug. "It's a little hard to see."

She nodded her head toward the outdoor lights that were black. She'd been meaning to replace the bulbs, but like everything else, it was on her ever-growing list of to-do's she never had time to focus on.

"I'll pick up some lights tomorrow and get that taken care of," he said.

She wanted to tell him not to bother but stilled her tongue instead. The house, and their dog, were half his, at least for now.

She let out a long sigh. She didn't know why he was here, but she figured selling the property was probably high on his list of things to discuss. She didn't want to sell their old farmhouse. She loved it here. He used to love it just as much.

The silence stretched thin between them until the chirping of the crickets filled the air.

"I'd forgotten how much I loved sitting out here." Jude let out a long sigh and leaned back, anchoring his elbows on the wood behind him.

Tessa turned towards him and looked him over. He looked like hell warmed over, if she were to be truthful. His hair was messed, there were dark circles beneath his eyes, and his twelve-hour stubble had hints of grey she'd never seen before.

That shocked her more than anything.

"It's peaceful." She climbed to her feet. "I don't know about you, but I could do with either a beer or coffee with Baileys. Would you like either one?" She stopped him when he went to get up. "Stay, enjoy the peace.

"Coffee would be great. I've got a long night ahead of me."

So he was leaving, heading back into the city or wherever he was living now. Guess that answered that.

She grabbed her bag and pushed open the house door, hoping he hadn't noticed the disappointment on her face.

"You should keep it locked," Jude said.

It took her a moment to realize he was talking about the door. Tessa shrugged. "Why? Rusty's here to protect the place." They'd never locked their house door, Why start now?

"Being all alone out here isn't safe," Jude muttered.

Tessa glanced over at the shotgun she kept by her porch door. She was safe enough.

She dropped her bag on the kitchen table and took in a deep breath. Jude was here. Really here. All the words she'd wanted to say to him disappeared except for the one phrase she uttered to herself over and over in the middle of the night.

I still love you.

It didn't matter anymore, did it? Too much time passed. Too much water beneath the bridge and all that.

For months she'd wished to go back in time and do what she could to fix things, but how do you repair something you didn't know was broken in the first place?

She brewed his coffee, straight black, and then made one for herself, adding double the amount of Bailey's she normally would, before she carried the two cups outside.

Her hands shook a little as she nudged the door open. Jude jumped up and reached for his coffee before stepping to the side. Rather than sit back down on the stairs, Tessa headed towards the wicker patio set she'd picked up at a garage sale the other weekend. She didn't ask Jude to join her, but assumed he would.

When he hesitated she gave him a soft smile. "I won't bite, I promise."

The glow from her kitchen window illuminated Jude's face

as he climbed the stairs and sat down in a chair. Rusty ambled his way over and, with a small jump, plopped himself down beside Tessa on the two-seater with a sigh. He stretched himself out so he could rest his head on Jude's knee.

"I think someone's happy to see you." Tessa sipped her coffee while she watched Jude lean forward and pet their dog.

"I hope he's not the only one," Jude said.

Tessa had a hard time swallowing. What did he just say?

"I know it's sudden and that I don't deserve a second chance, but…" His shoulders slumped as he rested his elbow on his free knee.

He wanted a second chance.

Everything inside of her wanted to shout yes, but she kept quiet and looked out over the dark yard. She had a feeling there was more that needed to be said. Explanations, apologies…on both sides. But, how did you get past the fact that he just up and left with no contact, no word?

She realized he'd been hurt, but did he ever think of what his silence and absence did to her? To them?

A second chance. A war between her head and her heart commenced.

Right at that moment, her cell phone rang. Tessa winced as the recorded sound of Sean's voice filled the air. He'd set his ringtone of her phone ages ago, and she'd never changed it.

Probably a mistake on her part, especially from the hardened look that settled on Jude's face.

"Does he call this late at night often?"

Tessa gave him a sidelong glance as she reached for the phone. "He's probably just calling to make sure I made it home okay." In all honestly, she appreciated that he did.

"That's … nice of him." Jude's lips tightened.

"Yep, it is."

It was wrong, she knew it, but she let his recorded ringtone play out. It was Sean singing *"You Are My Sunshine"* to her in a silly voice. It always made her smile to hear it.

"What's up?" She clicked the answer button on the phone and put it on speaker.

"Just making sure you made it home in one piece."

Tessa glanced over at Jude. "Sure did. The mountain goats are eating those bushes again. Would you ask your gardener for ones that they don't like next time?"

The sound of Sean's chuckle filled the air. "Sure can, doll. Anything for you. Sleep tight, okay?"

Tessa smiled. For years, they'd said the same thing to each other, *sleep tight* rather than goodbye at the end of the day. "You too." She clicked the end button and set the phone down beside her.

"Why didn't you tell him I was here?" Jude asked, sounding an awful lot like he was jealous.

"Cause it didn't matter. Does it?"

And that's how easy it was to get to the root of all their issues.

Chapter Nine

HE COULDN'T LOOK at her.

Did it matter? Good question. For him, the answer was an easy one.

His facial muscles spasmed as his jaw tightened.

It mattered enough that he'd left.

It mattered enough that he'd once questioned Tessa's love.

It mattered enough that he'd...

He'd what? Made the worst mistake of his life? Destroyed any relationship with the only woman he'd ever love? Left his family?

He'd been a fool. Plain and simple.

Coming here tonight had been a whim. He'd joined his parents at home and couldn't stop pacing. Eventually, his dad told him to go clear his head, and for some reason, that led him here.

He'd sat on the porch for a long while, trying to figure out what to say when she pulled up. If she pulled up.

Everything he knew he needed to say, everything he knew he should say, it all disappeared the moment she sat beside him.

Them being together, even in the silence, felt right. She felt that too, didn't she?

No. He couldn't make assumptions. Somehow, he had to fix this between them, because he knew, without a shadow of doubt, he couldn't live without her.

He knew that the second he drove away from her, but his pride wouldn't let him pull over.

Then there's the whole Sean issue. Seeing him at the party had been one thing. But listening to his voice on her phone irked him way more than it should.

Jude took a sip of his coffee and set it down on the porch floor. When he'd first walked into the party earlier, and he saw her, it was hard to be silent. The need to be with her, by her side, holding her hand, overwhelmed him. And when she'd almost fallen, and he caught her, there was an instant connection, a heat that radiated between them.

It took everything in him to leave her alone, but it was the one request his mother had made before they left the house that night. Tessa didn't need him to get in the way.

Tonight was her night to shine, to show their friends and family what she could do. To prove herself and her company.

A horrible gut feeling gnawed away at him when he discovered how he'd made life difficult for Tess by leaving. He'd had no idea. But what did he expect when he had never bothered to contact her?

"Why come home now?"

"I should have come home a long time ago." The answer ripped from his soul, bearing all his scars, if she even noticed them.

She didn't believe him. He could read that right away. She leaned away, arms crossed, and wouldn't look at him.

He didn't blame her. How could he when he'd been the one at fault?

He'd been a jerk in so many ways. The ink wasn't even dry on their marriage vows, the glow from their secret wedding not yet dimmed, and what did he do at the first hint of trouble? He ran.

He'd been a coward.

"I mean it, Tessa. I should have come back a long time ago." What he should have said was he should never have left.

"And yet you didn't. I wonder why?" Tension flowed from her in waves. She was mad, and she had every right to be. "I made a list of the possible reasons why you'd leave me like you did. Want to hear them?"

He wanted to say no. He wanted her to stop and let him explain, give him the chance to apologize, but then he realized that he didn't deserve it.

He deserved everything she threw at him and more.

"At first, I thought it was some emergency, that someone from your past needed you, and you were in such a panic, you didn't think to say goodbye. Then I thought maybe you had cold feet and realized we'd just made a huge, terrible mistake, but you didn't know how to tell me." She paused, holding her two fingers in the area.

"Then I thought maybe something horrible had happened, and you wanted to protect me from it. Like you were dying or something ridiculous, but I realized that couldn't be it." Her voice hitched, just slightly, but enough that he caught it.

"It was in the middle of the night I realized what the real reason was. Or what I figured was the reason, considering you never said anything to me. You were jealous of Sean and thought we were having an affair." She glared at him, as if challenging him to deny the truth.

He wouldn't. He couldn't.

"Am I right?" She challenged him to admit it. She deserved that much from him, and yet, all he could do was shake his head.

He was a coward. A fool. An absolute jerk. He knew that down the bones, and yet, he couldn't say the words.

She was right. One hundred percent.

While she'd been having a bath, her phone lit up with messages from Sean. Despite knowing their past, and understanding their bond as childhood friends, a stupid idea got stuck in his head that she loved Sean more than him. The idea of confronting her, of revealing his fears, scared him more than knowing the truth.

He saw the dejection on her face. The sadness from his silence.

"Believe what you want to," her voice was a mere whisper now, but he heard all the pain, anguish, and tears in her voice. "All you had to do was ask, and I would have told you the truth." She wrapped her arms around her body.

Jude rubbed his hand over his face. This wasn't going the way he thought it would go. But then, what did he expect? For her to throw herself back in his arms because he realized he'd let the best thing in his life slip through his fingers due to his own insecurities.

Maybe he needed to say the words. Actually, there was no maybe to it. He needed to say the words. But he knew there was something she needed more.

She'd once told him she didn't need words, just actions.

She knew he loved her because he'd shown her. She'd had others say the words, then betray her without a second glance, so she stopped trusting what was said and believed the actions instead.

He had come home with a plan to show her again how much he loved her, a plan he knew would work. Except, the longer they sat there, the more he wondered if he'd been mistaken.

Who was he to decide what she needed or even wanted?

"I believe you. I do." The pleading in his voice was raw. Sean didn't care. "I made a mistake by leaving and not trusting you, but I won't do that again."

Tessa stood up and stared at him. He could read the words in her eyes and knew he was too late. When she walked back into the house without saying a word, his world dropped beneath his feet.

"Tessa, please."

He wanted her to stop, needed her to stop, but she kept on, moving from the kitchen to the living room.

He stopped in the doorway, not knowing if he was welcomed inside or not. Even though the house was theirs, when he walked away, he walked away from assuming he'd be welcomed back inside, too.

She grabbed the hand-knit blanket from a chair and wrapped it around herself.

He should have realized she was cold. There was a nip in the air tonight, but he hadn't noticed it.

"Jude, it's been a long day, and I'm tired. I just want to soak in a hot bath and then go to bed. Can we do whatever this," she drew a circle in the air between them, "is, tomorrow?"

He could tell by her voice it was more than just about being tired. Disappointment laced her words.

"I'm sorry, I should have thought...my mom said the same thing, about the bath." He pinched the bridge of his nose.

"Is your mom okay? I thought I'd take her some homemade soup tomorrow." Tessa's shoulders slumped, and she sank down on the couch.

Jude edged his way inside and toward the bookshelf, looking at the images. Hope stirred in his heart as he saw the photos. Of them, of his family...maybe it wasn't too late.

"Jude?" Tessa asked again. He set one of the frames back down on the shelf and turned.

"I think she's okay, but I don't know." He shrugged. "She looked really tired and...not herself. Dad thinks tonight was too much for her."

"It probably was, but I understand why she didn't want to cancel it. I still can't believe..." Tessa's voice trailed off, and she leaned her head down on her knees.

Jude wanted to go over and put his arms around her and hold her, but he didn't.

He knew if he did, he'd lose it, and he wasn't ready to really process the news of his mother's cancer. He didn't think he'd ever be ready.

He couldn't accept that there was nothing they could do, and he didn't understand why his mom wasn't getting the help that was available.

There had to be something...anything... He clenched and unclenched his hands to relieve some of the tension in his body, but it didn't help.

When Tessa looked up at him, and he caught the way the tears pooled in her eyes, his heart broke, and even if he had wanted to, he couldn't stop himself from going to her and placing his arms around her.

She melted into his touch, and when she rested her head against his shoulder, the tension in his body finally disappeared. This felt right. This was what had been missing in his life for the past few months. This. Her.

He leaned his head down on hers, and they just sat there, close to one another, and let the silence wrap them in a bubble.

He'd tried hard not to think about this house while he was away. They'd picked it out together, having fallen in love with its rustic look and peacefulness. He loved coming home after a long day of cooking at the Banff Springs Hotel. It was his sanctuary, and he'd missed it more than he thought possible.

He noticed Tessa hadn't changed much in the room. There

were a few new framed prints on the wall that, knowing her, looked like they might be from a local artist, but other than that, it looked pretty much the same.

The coffee table in front of him was the only thing new. The base of the table was a wine barrel with a weathered slab of wood on top, stained to match the barrel. It was quite an interesting piece of furniture, and he liked it. It suited Tessa.

He caught sight of the paper and envelopes on top of it. He recognized the letterhead, and as he read the few words visible on the top of the pages, his heart sank.

Was he too late? Had she given up on them already? There was one word in particular that stood out to him.

"Um, Tessa. Is there something we need to talk about?" He leaned forward, forcing her to lift her head from his shoulder as he reached for the envelope on the table.

"You want a divorce?"

Chapter Ten

THE SILENCE in the room loomed. Tessa bit her lip while Jude sat there staring at the papers in his hand.

How did she explain this?

She was tired and emotionally spent, and Jude was no better. She understood now why he was here. He needed someone to talk to, someone to help him understand what was going on with his mother, someone to help dull the pain.

Her eyes closed as that thought sent shivers down her body. Dull the pain through sex. How many nights had she spent dreaming about having him back in their bed, of being held by him in the middle of the night, knowing she wasn't alone anymore?

Too many.

Those empty nights had nothing to do with what was happening to them right now, though, and she - they - needed to remember that.

"Tessa? Is this what you really want?"

Did she really want that?

No. She never did.

"I haven't heard from you in months, Jude. What did you expect me to do?" She curled her legs beneath her and sighed.

She'd had the envelope from the lawyers' office in her purse for over a month and finally took it out today. She'd opened it, pulled the papers out, and then thrown them on the coffee table, not ready to deal with them yet.

She'd totally forgotten about them until now.

Jude pushed himself up from the couch, dropped the papers back on the table, and stood there. She could see the questions in his eyes, but she didn't have the energy to deal with them. Not tonight.

"You're right. I was just...surprised, that's all. I'd hoped..." His voice trailed off, and he rubbed the back of his hair.

Tessa wanted to get up and wrap her arms around him, but she didn't. "Why are you here, Jude?"

"My mom—"

"No," Tessa stopped him. "Why are you here? At the house? Why were you waiting for me?" She leaned her head against the couch and watched him.

"I..." his shoulders deflated, "I don't know. Maybe because I've missed you."

Maybe he missed her? No, that won't cut it.

"You saw me tonight at the party. You had plenty of opportunities to talk to me, but you never did. So why come out here, at night?" She kept at him, needing to know the truth.

Was he here for his mom, for comfort, or was he here for her? She wasn't dumb enough to believe he'd come back to town for her, for them. He'd had three months to do so if that was the case. Still, there was a part of her that wanted to hope that he'd come out here for her and her alone.

"I needed you Tess," Jude admitted.

She could see how hard it was for him to say it. But she didn't care. She thought about all the times she'd needed him over the past few months. All the times when she could have used his support, his trust, his love.

So instead of giving him what he needed, she closed her heart and shrugged. "I'm tired, Jude. It's been a long day." It came across as cold as she intended it to be. Maybe that was wrong. Maybe she was being too harsh, but she wasn't in the mood to play these types of games, not tonight.

She ignored the way he dug his hands into his jeans, or the way his shirt stretched across his shoulders as he pushed them back and nodded. One look into his eyes and she found herself staring at the floor, otherwise, she'd lose whatever strength she had to push him away and protect her broken heart.

She'd held onto the memories of their love, the belief she had that he would come back home to her. She had swept up the broken pieces of her heart when he walked out their door and held onto them, praying for him to come back home and put her back together.

He never did.

He didn't come back. He didn't call. He didn't reply to any of her text messages either. He ghosted her, his own wife.

When they should have been enjoying their secretive married life while throwing the biggest party around, she was instead nursing a broken heart with only Ellie and Sean for support.

No. It wasn't fair of him to expect her to be there for him now, even though she saw the way he was crumbling inside.

If that made her a cold-hearted witch, then so be it. It was time to start looking out for herself, to start protecting her heart that had once belonged to him.

"Can I ... can we maybe go for coffee tomorrow?"

Her will almost broke then, at the hesitancy in his voice. She didn't have the strength to say anything, so she just nodded and watched him walk away.

"You were amazing tonight, by the way." He paused just before he was out of sight and looked over his shoulder at her.

"Thank you," she whispered.

The screen door banged closed behind Jude, and Tessa listened to the sound of his vehicle as he drove down her driveway. She hated the sound, knowing that this time it was definitely her fault he drove away.

Clutching the blanket tightly around her, she headed to the bookshelf where Jude had stood. She knew he'd noticed that she'd taken down the photos of them as a couple and replaced them with other images. Did he recognize them? Did he see them for what they were worth?

Jude was an amazing photographer, a hobby she'd often tried to get him to take to the next level. But he always claimed the camera was his getaway once he stepped out of the kitchen. She picked up the picture of the bridge she'd recently set there and smiled as the memory washed over her.

Jude's parents owned a cottage higher up in the mountains, and that's where they liked to spend their free weekends whenever possible. A Chinook wind had rolled in, and the air had a taste of summer in it. They found this bridge on one of the mountain paths they'd explored. It was their backdrop for an afternoon of lovemaking. Jude had covered her eyes with a soft, satin cloth that caressed her face, and made love to her amongst the fragrant spring flowers. Blinded, Tessa had learned to rely on her other senses while Jude teased her with kisses.

A shiver ran along Tessa's skin as she remembered the feel of a blade of grass as it danced along her skin, the sensation of the wind as it blew across her body while Jude feathered her thighs with a flower and kissed his way from her toes to her lips.

She knew her cheeks were flushed as she stared at the picture in her hand. How could something so wonderful fall apart in so little time? That was something she had never really understood. Their marriage was to have been built on trust, friendship, and love. But all it took was a text message taken out of context ...

A scratching sound grabbed her attention. With a sigh, she replaced the photo and headed over to let Rusty in.

Now that Jude had seen the papers, she needed to decide what to do with them. Would she ask him to sign them, or would she tell him she'd made a mistake? For months all she'd wanted was for him to return home, to come back to her.

Now that he was actually here, she wasn't so sure anymore.

Chapter Eleven

"Why didn't you call me?" Jude reached across the breakfast table for his mom's hand.

He didn't like how she looked today. Her feet scuffled the floor like an old woman as she made him breakfast, refusing to allow him to help, claiming it made her feel coddled. Since when did having him cook for her feel like coddling? She used to like watching him work in the kitchen.

"I didn't want you to worry. Your father has that covered."

"Of course, I'm going to worry. You have cancer, Mom!" Jude's teeth ground together as he tried to understand her logic.

She actually had the audacity to roll her eyes at him. "I know I have cancer, dear. You don't need to remind me." She patted his hand before picking up her fork and taking a bite of her plain scrambled eggs. "Now, why don't you tell me what your plans are to woo your wife back?" She chewed on her eggs with slow precision, as if she were savoring each bite.

He sat there in stunned silence. How did she know? When had she found out? Did Tessa tell them?

"Did you really we wouldn't have figured it out? Jetsetting

off to Vegas at the last minute? Come on, Jude, we're old, but we're blind." Her tsk-tsk-tsk had him give her an impish grin.

"Did Tessa tell you?"

His mom shook her head. "No, and we've never let on that we figured it out either. We figured one of you would eventually tell us...guess late is better than never."

The frown on his mother's face, combined with the exhaustion he could see in her eyes, ate at him.

He should have been here. He should have been a shoulder for his parents to lean on. He'd failed them as a son.

Just like he'd failed Tessa as a husband.

"I'm sorry." There was nothing else he could say. He was sorry for not being there. Sorry for not calling, for not letting them know where he was, and sorry for causing so much hurt and worry.

He had no illusions about the type of man he was. Not was. Had been. He wasn't that man anymore.

He refused to run away again when things got bad. He couldn't explain his actions any more than to say he'd been a fool and he was sorry.

"I know you are, dear. But you can only say the words so many times before it becomes meaningless."

Jude sat back in shock. His mother wasn't normally this frank with her words.

"Oh, son, you're a grown man now who deserves to be told the truth instead of coddled. Just say what you mean and mean what you say. Isn't that what your father has always said?" She turned to give his father a soft smile as he entered the kitchen.

"Welcome back, son." His father patted him on the shoulder. Jude watched as his father placed a kiss on his mother's cheek before pouring himself the last bit of coffee left in the pot.

Jean's cheeks were a soft pink as she smiled at him. "Back to my original question. How are you going to woo my daughter-in-law back?"

"I was ah, going to say I'm sorry," he paused at his mother's look, "and tell her I still love her." Jude knew that sounded lame, but he didn't really have any other plans.

"How about admitting you were a fool?" His father added.

"And for being such an idiot for leaving her alone," his mother said.

"And for running rather than dealing with whatever imagined issue that had you all in a panic?" His father continued.

"Okay, okay," Jude held up his hands in surrender. They were right. Of course, they were right. It was obvious his parents were practicing tough love this morning.

Not that he didn't deserve it

"It would probably help to mend ways with Sean as well," his dad muttered before taking a sip of his coffee.

Jude's figured his father would bring up last night.

By the time Jude pulled into his parents' driveway last night, Sean had been shooting the breeze with his father out on the front porch. One look, one brief warning to behave, and inside his father went, while he and Sean stood there, staring at each other.

Sean finally broke the uncomfortable silence between them when he threw a punch. Jude didn't move, didn't flinch, didn't do anything but let the punch land.

He'd deserved it.

He kept quiet while his best friend reamed him out a good one, calling him every name in the book and telling him he didn't deserve Tessa's heart.

Jude agreed with him. He didn't deserve it, not for what he'd done, but he was hoping Tessa would still give him a chance.

"We did, last night."

His dad only chuckled. "I'm not sure who that boy loves more, you or Tessa. Last night solved nothing."

"If there is something you both want to say, feel free." Jude tried to keep the sarcasm out, but he knew it didn't work.

"Son, in life, you need to learn to roll with the punches. If you can't do that, then be prepared for us to reteach the lesson. That's what parents are for."

"I can roll, Dad," Jude muttered as he kept his gaze downwards.

"Then you never would have left."

"I said I was sorry." The words burst out of his mouth before he could stop them.

What was wrong with him? He knew it wouldn't be easy coming back home. In fact, he expected it to be worse. He was the proverbial black sheep, not just in his family but in the town now. He expected to be shunned, look down upon, and talked about behind his back.

But, if truth be told, he expected to have at least one person at his back.

Again, he should have known better.

"We don't doubt that," his mom reached over and covered his hand with hers.

"So why the tough love?" He felt like a school kid right about now.

"It's because we love you that we're not making light of what happened. You left us, Tessa, your job, all without a word. And instead of letting us know what was going on, you kept silent for months. You could have been dead for all we knew!" Tears glistened on his mom's lashes, and guilt scored his heart, leaving open wounds he wasn't sure would heal.

"But you did know. I left you a message on the home phone." He ignored the way his parents shook their heads. "I know I should have called afterward, but ... I didn't know what to say." He turned to stare out the kitchen window and watched the leaves blow in the early morning air. "I was foolish and humiliated that I'd run like that. I wanted to come back right away, but...my pride got in the way. Then I got a job in Calgary and figured the least I could do was work on my own issues before I came home to work on the ones I'd left behind."

"The one that said you needed time?"

Jude turned in his seat. "I think that's what I said."

His mother shook her head. "Jude, telling us you need some time does not explain anything or calm our fears. You didn't say where you would go, for how long, or even why. We had to piece that last little bit together on our own."

"I made a mistake," Jude admitted. No amount of excuses would make up for his cowardliness.

"It takes a grown man to admit that. Now, what do you plan on doing to bring that daughter of ours back into the fold? I can only handle so many awkward moments." His father narrowed his eyes before winking.

Knowing this awkward moment between them had passed, Jude breathed a sigh of relief. He'd spent all night thinking of how to prove to Tessa he'd never stopped loving her and that he'd made a huge mistake.

"Well," a smile grew across Jude's face, "I have a plan..."

Chapter Twelve

TESSA DRUMMED her fingers on the table as she watched the minute hand on the kitchen clock tick slowly by.

It wasn't like she was sitting here trying to waste time, right? Not like she had anywhere to be, or anything.

So why was she still here, feet rooted with something between fear and anxiety?

She eyed the container of homemade chicken soup and biscuits she'd made earlier and wondered for the hundredth time why she was doing this.

Jude was a chef, for pete's sake. He could surely make his mother some homemade soup.

Her cell phone vibrated on the table beside her.

> Delivery arrived. You might want to check it out. Just sayin'.

A small thrill shot through Tessa at Ellie's text. She knew exactly what had come in that delivery.

> Be right there. Keep your hands off them till I get there!

No promises.

Tessa chuckled. She knew Ellie wouldn't touch the chocolate treats that had arrived. At least, Tessa hoped she didn't.

She placed the chicken soup and biscuits in a bin, grabbed her purse off the old china cabinet she'd discovered at a flea market, and headed out towards her truck.

"Keep an eye on the place, okay, boy?" Tessa called over her shoulder to Rusty, who rested his head on his paws while sunning on the porch. He woofed in reply.

Normally she liked to take the day after an event off and let Ellie hold down the fort and take care of things, but today wasn't just any regular day.

Today was *the* day for a special delivery, one she'd been waiting on for months.

Earlier in the year, she'd stumbled across a website that personalized chocolate gifts. After having sampled several chocolates from different venues and realizing they were all the same, she got excited when she recognized the name of this chocolatier.

She'd met him at the local chocolate festival held in Banff a few years ago. He'd been the featured guest, and she'd managed to win tickets for a private tasting for both her and Jude.

She smiled just thinking about that private tasting. It was a night she would never forget.

The most decadent chocolate she'd ever tasted had been displayed on crisp white platters, with white-gloved waiters ready to help serve them. The evening had been perfect. They'd sampled wines paired with different samples, laughed over private jokes, and by the end of the night, Jude had kneeled before her and asked her to marry him.

The ring he presented to her had been served on a silver platter and made especially for this night. The plate held a box made out of chocolate, a box with exquisite detail that had been hand painted with edible gold. Inside the box nestled the most beautiful engagement ring with a chocolate diamond in its center.

Even now, as she glanced down at her ring, the memory of how perfect she'd thought their life had been overwhelmed her. How could she have been so wrong?

Tessa shook her head to dispel the memories and thought about Ellie's text.

A few months ago, she'd found Paul's new website and had contacted him to order some personalized chocolates. She wanted to have her own stand at this year's chocolate festival to highlight Decadent Events as a premier event planning company. She'd worked with Paul to have their logo on some signature chocolates. She envisioned a long-lasting relationship with him in regards to her catered events, now all she had to do was convince him to provide treats that were just meant for Decadent Events.

She made her way into downtown to Beaver Street to park by her office. Thanks to Sean, she'd managed to secure a location off the main avenue.

As she crossed the road, she took a look at the empty store beside her and thought about the suggestion made by Ellie last night. It would make sense to open a bakery beside them, one that was part of Decadent Events.

Perhaps she could convince Paul Ormand to keep a display of his chocolates in there as well. She knew the only reason the store hadn't been leased out yet was due to Sean. From the looks between him and Ellie last night, they both had to be in on this plan.

Why they hadn't hooked up yet was beyond her. She knew Ellie had a secret crush on Sean. She'd had one for years. She'd once asked why Ellie had never taken the initiative and asked

Sean out instead of waiting around for him to do it, and she'd all but been told to mind her own business.

Since then, she had tried to stay out of it.

As Tessa looked at the empty store beside her, she knew she'd give in and let Ellie talk her into it.

This would be Ellie's master plan, and along with her sister Lexi, it would need her passion to make it work. But Tessa would be her biggest supporter. After all, it had been due to Ellie's support that Tessa had even managed to get Decadent Events off the ground and running.

Jude had left just as she signed the final papers with Sean for the office space, and if it hadn't been for Ellie, Tessa would have wallowed in self-pity and depression with no anchor.

Ellie had been that anchor. Ellie and Sean.

Satisfied with this decision, Tessa pushed open the door to Decadent Events, ready to share the news with Ellie, but she stopped in her tracks.

Seated on top of her desk at the side of the showroom, was Jude.

Tessa's stomach dropped at the sight of him. He wore dark ripped jeans and a plain black tee shirt, and his hair was tousled as if he'd run his hands through it too many times. There were faint dark circles beneath his eyes, and the stubble on his face only enhanced his rugged good looks.

She wanted to rush over to him and place her arms around him. She knew last night must have been hard on him, and she wanted to be there for him.

Guilt had eaten at her in the middle of the night for turning him away. She should have let him stay longer, talked about his mom, and helped him deal with the news.

She should have told him how much she still loved him.

Except, this morning, when Tessa awoke, she knew she'd

61

made the right decision. As much as she still loved Jude, she needed him to explain to her why he left her as he had.

That's all she needed.

She thought about the papers she'd stuffed into her purse and wondered again if asking him for a divorce was the right thing to do.

Maybe that was why he was here.

"Where's Ellie?" First things first. She had to see about this delivery, and then she would deal with why Jude was sitting on her desk.

"In the back going through some invoices from last night." Jude pushed himself off her desk but kept his arms behind his back.

"I didn't expect to see you here." Tessa walked around him and dropped her purse on her chair. She glanced around the room for the boxes from the delivery, but didn't see them anywhere. Maybe Ellie took them to the back.

"Ellie told me she sent you a text." He turned towards her.

Tessa shook her head. "No, well, yes, she sent me a text, but not that you were here. She told me a delivery had arrived." Her voice faltered as Jude brought his arms out from behind his back. In his hands was a vase of fresh-cut flowers.

"This delivery?" He set the vase down on the desk and turned it so that the card lodging in between some flowers faced her.

Tessa was caught off guard. She reached for the envelope, her gaze never leaving his, and pulled out the small card.

"My parents asked me to drop it off personally."

Thank you for making our anniversary a night we will always remember.

"But, I was bringing her some soup and biscuits."

Jude shrugged. "Mom was tired when I left. Dad was

drawing her a bath, and then she was going to have a nap. And our fridge is full of leftovers from last night."

So, in other words, they didn't want or need her soup. Tessa's shoulders sagged.

Now that Jude was home, was she not needed? Was it going to be awkward to have her around now?

Bob called her his true daughter, and Jean had promised she'd always be a part of their family, no matter what happened between her and Jude, but...

The thought that she might have lost her family now that Jude was back almost killed her.

She sank down in her seat and struggled not to let her devastation show. The last thing she wanted was for Jude to realize how much this hurt her.

"But, soup is probably the only thing her stomach could handle right now."

Tessa forced a smile on her face and knew Jude only said that because he caught her reaction.

"Thanks for bringing the flowers. They're beautiful." She set them down on the corner of her desk and then sat there, unsure of what to say. She straightened some of the displays on the shelf, centrepiece ideas as well as various gift displays.

When they'd set up their storefront, the idea had been to visually wow their potential clients with ideas on how they could create their own event.

So far so good.

Although, with the fall coming, it was time to change the look a bit.

"Tess?"

She turned and faced Jude.

"Ellie mentioned you normally take the day after an event off."

She nodded, unsure of where he was going with this.

"If you already have plans, I understand, but I was wondering if you'd like to spend the day with me." He cleared his throat and glanced at the ground.

Did she hear him correctly? Spend the day with him?

"As in coffee?" That had been the original plan last night. That's what she was prepared for. Coffee. In a crowded coffee shop where they might snag a table and actually hear one another.

A coffee shop where they weren't known, and no one would be watching them.

Coffee that would only last an hour, if things went well, and less if the topic of the divorce papers came up.

"And dinner," he continued. "Maybe we could play tourist and walk through the stores like we used to."

"I'd love that." The words came out before she had the chance to stop herself. It was as if her heart, instead of her mind, took over.

She knew she'd said the right thing the moment Jude let out a long sigh and smiled.

Maybe today wouldn't be so bad after all.

"I know you have a lot of questions, and I promise to answer them. But before that happens, let's enjoy our day, like we used to when we would pretend to be tourists. As if we didn't have a care in the world. Is that okay?"

He wanted to go through the day ignoring the large pink elephant between them? What would they talk about? Life before he walked out on her?

How could they ignore the fact he'd destroyed their marriage, and she still had no idea why?

Chapter Thirteen

WHETHER IT WAS summer and the tourists were here to hike the trails or winter and it was ski season, there was nothing quite like walking down the main street in Banff with the towering Cascade Mountain in front of you.

When Tessa and Jude first met, it had been quite accidental and all thanks to the view of the Cascade Mountain range.

Tessa had stood with a group of friends, attempting to take a photo of them with the mountain in the background. Jude walked up and offered to take the photo so that she could be in it and then offered to point out various sites within Banff that they didn't want to miss.

He showed them the best fudge shop situated off the main avenue, a doorway that apparently led to nowhere, and he even offered to be their tour guide on their quest for haunted locations.

While all the other girls in their group fawned over Jude, Tessa kept her distance. It wasn't that she didn't like him, but rather because she became tongue-tied anytime he spoke to her, which was unusual for her.

A few hours later, when they were about to part ways, Jude

had pulled her aside and asked if she'd like to go out for a hike one day. They'd fallen in love on that mountain path the following weekend.

"Where would you like to go first?" Jude asked as he held the door open for her.

Tessa glanced behind her to find Ellie standing in the back doorway with a huge smile on her face.

"I heard there was a new cafe just opened up on Bear Street by the Ski Shop. Apparently, they have amazing chocolate croissants."

Jude grinned. "Apparently? You mean you haven't checked it out yet?"

Tessa shook her head as they walked side by side. Her body naturally wanted to lean into him, to have him put his arm around her, or to link her arm through his.

She found herself clutching the straps of her shoulder bag and focusing on the pavement ahead of her instead. "Not yet."

They walked in silence, taking in the sights around them and squeezing through the crowds that gathered at the corner of Banff Avenue.

"It's busier than I'd expected," Jude grumbled when he had to sidestep past a group of giggling teenagers.

"It's the weekend for the Farmer's Market," Tessa reminded him.

Jude rolled his eyes and grinned. "How could I forget? This is the first year I haven't been corralled by Mrs. O'Neil to help set up the booths."

Tessa didn't stop the smile from spreading across her face. "Evie's a hard one to say no to, that's for sure."

"Did you see all the desserts she snuck into her bag last night before she left?"

"I caught that. I ended up offering to box them up for her

and gave her the name of the caterer so she could order more." Tessa shook her head at the memory.

They turned the corner onto Bear Street and made their way to the cafe. It wasn't difficult to find since there was already a line up out the door.

It was while they were waiting that Tessa decided to broach the subject of his leaving her even though she knew he'd asked her not to.

"Where have you been these all this time?"

Jude shuffled his feet and looked everywhere but at her for a few moments. "I went to Calgary," he finally admitted.

"Calgary?" He had been that close? Whenever she thought about where he could be, she imagined across the country, not in the city less than an hour away.

"I crashed with an old culinary friend, and he got me a job at the Paliser Hotel until I figured things out."

"Was it as great as you always talked about?" Tessa bit her lip to stop from asking him why he just didn't come back home to the job he already had.

Instead, she focused on the fact that they were surrounded by virtual strangers and tried to keep her tone light.

Jude shrugged. "I enjoyed working under the executive chef there, but it was no Banff Springs Hotel."

"When do you go back?" The thought of his leaving again made her sick to her stomach.

"Tomorrow." He moved to her other side and let her walk through the door of the cafe ahead of him.

Tomorrow.

He was leaving tomorrow. Of course, he was. Probably right after signing the divorce papers too. She should have known.

She gripped her purse tighter and thought about the divorce papers inside. This was it then. They were really over. Her heart shattered into minuscule pieces, but she kept a smile on her face.

All she'd done for the past bit was pray for just one more day with him. One day when everything was perfect, and they still lived in their little happily-ever-after-world that she'd believed in. This apparently was an answer to prayer, so all her questions could wait.

If all she had were the next few hours of playing tourist with him, of once again living in her dream world, then she'd take it.

After that, she'd come back down to the real world.

Her heart might lie in pieces, but she'd be damned if he would know that. She'd changed since he'd disappeared. She wasn't the girl he'd married. She'd started her own company and made a name for herself as an event planner. She was no longer the girl content to be at home wishing to do something with her life. She'd done it, and she planned to do more.

He didn't know that girl, but if she had her way, he would.

"Where to next?" Jude looked at her. She read the question in his eyes. "Once we get our coffee. Where do you want to go next? Walk up town or head down to the falls?"

They used to have a routine when they were "tourists" in their own town. They'd grab a coffee, walk the avenue, enjoy a beaver tail pastry smothered in butter, cinnamon, and brown sugar, and then head down the trails till they reached the falls.

She thought of one photo on her bookshelf, taken as the sun set over the mountains, with the glow on the water. She loved it. But she really hoped he didn't want to go there this time.

His lips pursed. "I didn't bring my camera, so how about we just walk downtown and go into stores?" It was like he could read her mind. "I kind of wanted to see if I could find an angel figurine or something for Mom."

Tessa reached out and touched his hand. Call it habit. Instinct. A bond that could never break.

She tried to pull away, but Jude gripped her hand and wouldn't let go. He stared down at her, with a questioning look. He must have found the answer because he laced his fingers through hers.

Tessa's world was on kilter right now. She didn't know what to expect from him. He was leaving tomorrow; he was walking away from her once again. His words all said one thing, but his body language said another. Did he feel the pull between them too?

"Jude, I—"

"No, don't say anything. Let's just enjoy the day, enjoy being together again. I know you have a lot of questions, and I have a lot of explaining to do, but right now, let's just enjoy this." He squeezed her hand. "Let's just enjoy us. Please?"

Tessa swallowed the words she wanted to say. He must have known she wanted to distance herself from him, to protect herself, her heart. Why did he want to play this charade that their life was perfect again when they both knew it wasn't?

She pulled her hand from his, grabbed her coffee, and held on tight. She led the way out of the cafe and onto the sidewalk. She shielded her eyes from the bright sun's glare and fought to remain calm.

When Jude was beside her, she turned, closed her eyes, and took in a deep breath.

"I can't do this. You want to pretend that nothing's wrong, but I can't. I just can't." Tears pinpricked her eyes, and she blinked them away. "I can't pretend that you didn't break my heart, that you didn't destroy something that I thought was so perfect." She turned so she no longer faced him and let the tears trickle down her face. "I can't pretend that our marriage isn't over. I just can't."

Chapter Fourteen

IF HE HAD THOUGHT today would be easy, the tears on Tessa's face proved him wrong.

He'd been a fool to think his idea would work. His mother had warned him earlier that Tessa wouldn't be able to ignore the past, but he hadn't wanted to listen to her.

He'd hoped that by spending the day doing the very thing they used to love doing would help. He'd assumed that he could show Tessa just how much he loved her, just how wrong he'd been without saying the words right away.

But he knew what they say about assuming...

When she turned from him, it was as if she were turning away from them. And he couldn't handle that. He wouldn't let that happen. He'd fight for them if that's what it took.

"I was a fool. A fool to stay away so long when I knew the second I drove down our driveway that I needed to turn around. I was wrong, and I made a mess of so many things."

He caught the way her shoulders slouched at his words, and he reached out and touched her shoulder.

"Let's go to the park and talk. If you want to walk away from me afterward, it's okay." He took a step towards her. "But be warned, I'll just follow you. I know I was an idiot, and I know that there's nothing in the world I can say that could force you to forgive me, but please, let me try?"

He could read the questions she didn't ask. Everything she wanted to say to him, he could read in her eyes. He always could. She was like an open book to him.

It was why he'd left the way he did. He couldn't handle seeing the truth, or what he'd thought was the truth, when he confronted her.

"Okay," she said.

It was only one word, but it was all he needed to hear.

He reached for her hand again, and instant relief hit him when she entwined her fingers with his. Maybe he had a chance after all. Maybe he hadn't destroyed things as badly as he'd feared.

Maybe she'd accept his apology and give their marriage another chance.

They walked along in silence, and Jude struggled with what words to say. He didn't want to screw up and say the wrong thing, but he also knew she needed answers. She deserved to know what an idiot he was, the real reason behind his leaving, and how his pride got in the way.

"When did you find out about your mom?" Tessa asked as they waited at the crosswalk.

"Yesterday. Trust me, that wasn't the homecoming I was expecting." He blew out a puff of air and pushed the memory of learning about the cancer from his mind. He didn't want to think about what the future held. He knew it was bleak, and he couldn't imagine a world without his mom in it.

"What do you mean, yesterday?" Tessa pulled her hand from his and held on to her cup. Her brows knitted together as her lips thinned in anger.

71

"That's why they were late arriving at the party. Dad thought I should know before we left for it."

Tessa's head shook. "No, your mom promised me that she would tell you the next time you called. She promised me, Jude." She glanced up to the sky while he stared at the pavement below his feet. "You did call, right?"

Damn. He shook his head and waited for what was about to come. He didn't expect the punch to the arm, nor did he expect the strength behind the punch. He rubbed the area she'd hit and winced.

"How could you not call your mother? Your own mother! I get that you left me, but your parents? What were you thinking?"

The walk sign lit up, and they crossed the street. Jude didn't reply, he didn't think Tessa expected him to. He let her lead them to a bench in the park, and he sat down while she paced in front of him.

"Honestly, Jude, I can't believe you would do that to your parents. Do you know how hard this has been for them? It's tearing your father apart, and your mother refuses to listen to reason. She won't take the treatment being offered to her. She's dying before our eyes, and you haven't been around." Her nostrils flared as she stared at him. "You haven't been around." She choked on those last words as tears fell down her cheeks.

Jude held out his hand, and she grabbed it. He pulled her close and then gathered her in his arms as she sat down beside him.

"I'll never forgive myself, Tess. Never," he whispered and rested his head against hers. He'd made a mess of too much in his life, and knowing he could lose his mom was the worst.

"Why did you leave?" He heard her whisper against his shirt.

This was it. The moment of truth.

He didn't know what would be more painful, talking about his mother or why he left. Both things ate him up inside. Both tore him apart until he wasn't sure what was real anymore.

There was no easy way to say it.

"I thought you were in love with Sean."

She pulled back from his arms and gave him a look full of disbelief.

"What?"

He swallowed and placed his hands in his lap. He stared out over the grass and watched the crowds of tourists swell around them. Maybe they should have gone someplace a bit more private.

"Your phone had gone off while you were in the bath, and it was a message from Sean. He said how he couldn't do it anymore, couldn't keep the secret and that he'd never been more in love with you than he was then, after he got your phone call." His heart thudded from speaking the words out loud.

If he could go back in time, he'd never pick up her phone. He'd never read that message. He'd rather live in the dark, believing she loved him, rather than knowing the truth.

Or what he thought had been the truth.

He'd felt so betrayed in that moment. By both Sean and Tessa. He'd reacted in the moment, and regretted it ever since.

Jude turned to look at Tessa and read the truth in her eyes. The truth he'd been afraid to see that day.

"I don't remember that message."

Jude dropped his head. "I deleted it."

Tessa sighed.

He glanced over at her, and the look in her eyes this time changed.

"So you just left. No questions asked? You didn't want to hear my story? Give me the benefit of the doubt? I thought you

73

knew me better than that." Resolution filled her voice, and it worried him more than he wanted to admit.

In all the scenarios he had built up in his mind, never had Tessa been resolute. Angry, disappointed, maybe. Forgiving and open possibly. But never resolved, not like this.

He knew Tessa when she was resolved. She went hardcore, no holds barred. Nothing would or even could stop her. And that's what worried him now.

Would his apologies not matter? Would she look behind the words to see the actions, to see the fear that crept up from their past?

Would she give him a second chance?

Chapter Fifteen

Tessa took a sip of her coffee and worked on processing Jude's words. Not just what he said, but what was behind them. He'd left out fear. Fear of something he'd never been able to face. It made sense, somewhat.

"Sean does love me, and I love him." She would never deny that. Ever.

But she didn't love Sean the way she loved Jude. She never had.

She'd thought Jude understood that. She'd thought they had gotten past this issue among the three of them. Apparently not.

Tessa and Sean had been friends from childhood, old souls that connected from the get-go. They had melded together like a brother and sister. They fought like it too. But never had Tessa viewed Sean as anything but a really good friend.

"But Sean is a vanilla cupcake with plain buttercream frosting on it. You're the decadent fudge cupcake with a rich chocolate frosting covered with ganache."

When Jude's eyes lit up at her chocolate reference, she knew he understood.

It was the same phrase she'd used in her wedding vows - the one of his being the decadent fudge cupcake.

All she'd needed from him since the day he left was an explanation of why. That was it.

She needed to know if it was something she'd done or if it had been his own decision.

She'd always been afraid that he had realized he'd never loved her.

She never once thought he had the same fear.

"Sean does love you, you know. It was plain for everyone to see last night."

Tessa shrugged. There wasn't much she could do about Sean's feelings. They'd had this talk over and over. What mattered to her was that she loved Jude more than anything else. Sean knew that. He'd always known that.

"It doesn't matter how Sean feels. What matters is that you didn't trust me enough." She angled towards him and laid her hand on his forearm. "You didn't trust in us enough." Jude nodded. At least he didn't bother to deny it.

"Sean told me about the talk you guys had the night before we left for Vegas. How all it took was for him to say one thing and you went berserk and punched him in the face. You never let him finish, because you'd already assumed you knew what he'd say." She said.

Surprise registered in Jude's gaze.

"That's why you suggested we elope, isn't it? Because you were afraid that if I knew how Sean felt, I'd have doubts about us." She turned from him and stared out toward the mountains.

She'd always known how Sean felt. Always knew he'd harbored feelings for her. She also knew he didn't love her the way she loved Jude.

"I was scared," Jude admitted. When she finally looked at him again, his head was buried in his hands.

"Why didn't you come to me and ask what was going on?" She asked. "The answer would have been so simple, it is simple."

For weeks before Jude's disappearance, Sean had been trying to talk Tessa into what she was doing today, event planning. As one of Banff's high-end realtors, he often had requests from his clients for recommendations, and while he would volunteer Jude's name as a chef for their small gatherings, he'd come up with a brilliant business plan.

Tessa could organize the actual events and Jude would cater.

Tessa's immediate response had been no.

That all changed with a simple comment from Ellie. She'd been the one to plant the seed, saying that if she didn't find a job soon, she'd have to move away since Lexi's culinary school costs were more expensive than she originally expected.

Ellie was her best friend, and Tessa didn't want to consider the idea of losing her.

Tessa didn't need to work. After her parents' death from a head-on collision with a truck a few winters ago, she had more than enough money in the bank. And Jude more than made enough to support them both as one of the top culinary chefs for the Fairmont Banff Springs Hotel.

So she casually mentioned the idea of going into the event planning business to Ellie, who jumped all over it, and the rest was history.

"I wanted to surprise you once we returned from Vegas. I called Sean and left a message that I'd be coming into town to sign the lease, but I wanted to tell you first. That was all. He had a big client who had just bought the Bell mansion, and they wanted to host a fundraiser there but needed an event planner. He probably said he loved me because I just made him a ton of money for agreeing to start this venture." Tessa shook her head in exasperation.

Of all the ridiculous thoughts and fears that she'd experienced since he'd left, finding out he left because of a stupid text message cut the cake. She didn't know whether to hit him or hug him.

"Why didn't you let me explain?"

When Jude stood up and paced in front of her, a tiny seed of worry made its way into her heart.

"I was afraid. I've always been afraid that there was a little part of you that loved Sean more than me. Stupid, I know. But it was always there."

Tessa knew that. She'd always known that. "Do you still think that?"

Jude dropped down to his knees and looked at her. After a few moments, he shook his head.

"No. But I wouldn't blame you if you did. You deserve better than me."

Tessa nodded. He was right. She did. She deserved someone who loved her with all his heart. Who trusted her completely. Who put her first in his life.

But then, if she had someone like that, she'd feel like she was on a pedestal. And she didn't want that. She wanted a man to love her with all his heart, no matter his fears.

She wanted someone who would walk along beside her, hold her hand when he was scared, snuggle her close when she needed comfort. She wanted someone who would understand her and love her in spite of her shortcomings and someone she could love in spite of his.

Someone like Jude.

"You should have come back sooner. If not for me, then for your mother."

He nodded. "I know. Trust me, I know. But I couldn't think

straight. All I could focus on were Sean's words, and when I landed that job at the Palliser, it became easy to lose myself in cooking."

"You've had months to focus."

"I know."

"You could have called."

"I know."

Tessa stared into Jude's eyes. He wobbled a bit, still on his knees, and eventually, he pushed himself to his feet, but he never took his gaze from hers.

At least he didn't try to give excuses. He could have, and she might have even believed him. But she was glad he didn't.

"I was stupid, Tess. I was an idiot for not calling you, for not turning around the moment I realized I was making the biggest mistake in my life. I was scared."

She thought about the papers in her bag. Why wait till tonight? Why not get it all out in the open and see where things went from there?

She opened her purse and slowly pulled out the envelope. Jude caught the movement and placed his hand over hers.

"Please don't," he moaned.

"I have to." She watched Jude's hand fall away. He sank down on the bench beside her and dropped his head into his hands.

"I didn't know what else to do," she tried to explain. Yes, Jude left her first. He gave up on them before she did. But, she was just as much at fault, because in the end, she gave up on them too.

"I don't blame you," he muttered.

"But I do. In our vows, we said forever, through the good and the bad. I promised you I'd never give up, that I would fight for us even when there seemed like there was nothing left to fight for."

Jude took her hand and squeezed. "You did nothing wrong. I was the one who left. I don't blame you for not waiting for me, for wanting to move forward with your life." He let go and reached for the envelope. He withdrew the sheets and read them, taking his time before he reached the area for his signature.

"Do you want me to sign this?"

Did she? In her heart, she knew the answer.

She still loved him.

They didn't have the foundation both their parents had. Not yet. But she wanted that.

Yes, his leaving almost destroyed her, and if it weren't for those around her, she wasn't sure how she would have gotten through being alone. Yet, she had survived. And she knew that if she asked him to sign the papers, she would survive once again.

But she didn't want to merely survive.

She wanted to thrive, to live with love in her heart. And she loved Jude, enough to forgive him and give them another chance.

She reached for the papers and turned to look deeply into Jude's eyes. With one swift motion, she tore the papers in half and laid them on her lap.

"No, I don't want you to sign them. I want us to figure out how to make our marriage work." She let out a long breath. "I also don't want you to return to Calgary tomorrow. I want you to stay here. With me."

Jude's brow furrowed. "I'm not returning to Calgary."

"Yes, you are, you told me so yourself." She was sure that's what he'd said.

Jude shook his head. "No, no. I go back to the Springs Hotel tomorrow. I managed to get my old job back. That's what I meant."

Tessa blinked in surprise. Of course, that's what he meant. She shouldn't have read into his comment like she had. A smile bloomed across her face before she jumped up from her seat and reached for his hand.

"You know, the last time we played tourist was before we were married. Come on," she pulled him off the bench, "we'd better get started before the crowds get to be too much. Besides, we need to give ourselves enough time to head to the market. I'm in the mood for a good home-cooked meal."

"Home cooked, huh?"

Tessa nodded. "Think you could handle that? I mean unless you'd rather eat the soup that I made for your mom."

Jude shook his head before he pulled Tessa close.

This was what she'd dreamed. This. Being held close, tight against his chest, with his arms around her. Hearing his heartbeat beneath her ear and knowing she was safe.

She was back where she belonged. Her husband had come home. No more sweet memories to hold on to, no more whispered prayers that he would return. He was here, holding her, and if she had her way, they had a lifetime of sweet moments together.

The Sweet End...for now...until you begin Sweet Dreams (turn the page)

A Note From Steena...

Dear Reader;

Thank you for reading Sweet Memories. I first wrote this book early on in my writing career, when my heart was full of excitement and I had so many stories to tell...which, still sounds like me even now, even after all these years!

I loved setting this book in Banff. It's only an hour drive from my home and whenever we're in the mood for a drive, we always end up there, grabbing a beaver tail from the Main Street.

What's a beaver tail? For all my non-canadian readers, it's a delicious pastry that's drenched in butter and smothered in toppings. My favorite is cinnamon sugar, but you could put icing and Skor bits or...well, anything really! Trust me when I say you'll have to try one!

I love to create reader trips and so far we've gone to Holland and Paris, but one day I'm going to create a trip to my neck of the woods and if you join me, you can taste on for yourself!

Interested in knowing more about my reader trips? Check out my website and click on the **LET'S TRAVEL TOGETHER** tab!

I hope you enjoy a sweet life full of chocolate, happiness and peace.

Steena

A LOVE SO SWEET
NOVELLA

sweet

DREAMS

STEENA MARIE HOLMES

New York Times Best Selling Author

Sweet Dreams

Since chocolate couldn't cure her broken heart, creating the finest macarons and croissants this side of Paris would have to do.

Who needs love anyway?

Opening up Sweet Treats could have been the answer to all her problems - except all the problems she'd ran away from in Paris followed after her, via a first class ticket and wore rugged jeans.

It didn't help he made the best chocolates she'd ever tasted, either.

What's a girl to do when the only man she'd ever loved was willing to give their love another try - even when she'd been the one to betray it by keeping a secret from him that could destroy all their future dreams?

Chapter One

THE EARLY MORNING fog barely gave way to show the pavement beneath her feet, but that was okay. For a few minutes each morning, Lexi was able to pretend she was still in Paris.

She imagined the fog covered a cobblestone pathway leading to the backdoor of her patisserie, that Claude's old pickup idled out front as he unloaded a crate full of fresh cream, butter, and eggs, and that the cool, crisp air that kissed her cheese was not fresh mountain air.

She really needed to get over her homesickness.

Lexi leaned against the Ford Escape she had just leased and stared at the storefront on the other side of the street. Decadent Sweets, her new store. It was boxy and modern, completely unappealing in her opinion, but it was now home.

For now, at least. She didn't plan to stay long.

She had dreams and goals, and she didn't leave Paris, her heart, to waste her creativity in a town full of skiing and hiking enthusiasts. She needed to be surrounded by like-minded individuals who saw chocolate as a passion, a way of life—not a temptation best left untouched.

Beside her store was Decadent Events, the event planning party her sister Ellie helped run with her best friend, Tessa.

When Lexi first arrived, Tessa sat her down and explained her vision for Decadent Sweets. In Lexi's opinion, Tessa was small-minded and didn't see the big picture. Or rather, Lexi's big picture. A few battles of the wills escalated before Ellie stepped in. If it weren't for Ellie, Lexi wouldn't be here.

And it was only because of Ellie that she remained.

"How are you not freezing our tush off right now? Who needs a freezer when you live in the North Pole?" Lexi rubbed her hands over her arms and shuddered while she eyed her sister, who only wore a heavy sweater, scarf, and no gloves on her hands.

"You think this is cold?"

Yes, Lexi considered this cold. She was bundled up in a down-filled winter jacket, a knitted scarf wrapped around her neck, and her hands were covered with mitts to match the scarf.

And it wasn't even winter.

Why do people live in places that are colder than her freezer? This is ridiculous.

"Oh, hey," Ellie glances over her shoulder at her with a mischievous glint in her eye. "I hope you're not too busy Friday night." She grabbed a bag from the trunk of the car.

"Why?"

"Because I set you up with our neighbor. He moved here a few months ago and hasn't really met too many people, so I suggested the two of you should go out one night. That night happens to be Friday." Ellie smiled at her before she crossed the street.

Lexi lingered behind, shocked that her sister would do something like that. She knew better. Or she had. They had a code, not to hook each other up with anyone. Not even friends of friends, or in this case...neighbors.

"You're not allowed to do that. We promised. Remember?" Lexi said, following behind her.

"Yeah, but that was back then. After...everything. It's time to move on. Live a little. Have fun and just be...free. Come on. It's just for coffee down at the coffee shop on the corner. I'll even swing by if you want, to make sure things are working out okay."

Lexi shook her head. "No. You'll have to cancel."

"I'm not canceling. You're going. Ever since you moved here, all you've done is focus on helping us to get this up and running. It's only an hour, tops. Besides, the guy is out on some back trails taking photos, and he won't be back until Friday anyways."

"Oh great. You've set me up with a bushman. Just what I need," Lexi muttered under her breath.

"He is not. He's quite handsome, actually. Sexy even, with his tousled hair and ripped jeans. Your type."

"How do you know what my type is?" But Ellie was right. That was her type, all right.

But there was only one man...no, she wasn't going there. Not now. Not when she had work to do.

"You play dirty, you know that, right?"

"Does this mean you'll go?" Lexi couldn't ignore the twinkle in Ellie's gaze.

She groaned. "It means I'm going for coffee. That's it. And you had better show up within the first thirty minutes, or I won't make you waffles on my day off."

Ellie's eyes widened. She held up her hands in mock surrender. "I promise. Tell you what, I'll get some coffee started while you do your"—she waved her hands in the air—"thing." Ellie gestured towards the back, to the kitchen. She then pulled out bowls of fresh fruit she'd prepared last night for their breakfast.

Lexi smiled and headed towards the back, to her retreat.

The kitchen was a baker's dream come true, and she had no doubt Sean had his hand in this. He'd asked Lexi during their first meeting what she needed in a kitchen, and she'd given him her wish list, never expecting to have it come true. But it did, and he managed to make it look like one of those million-dollar kitchens found on the cover of a fancy home magazine.

With a touch of a few buttons, she had her ovens preheating and then reached for her apron.

"All right, what can I do to help?" Ellie pushed open the doors and barreled through. She already had her apron on and her hair pulled back, and she rubbed her hands together in anticipation.

"Coffee. That's all I need." Lexi hated to burst her bubble, but she didn't need or want any help.

"It's on. Come on, you promised you would teach me how to make croissants."

"Girl, we're not doing that today, especially today of all days." It was opening day, and the last thing she wanted to do was to give a baking lesson.

"Why not today?"

"For one thing, you slept in, remember? I wanted to be here before now. A baker has early hours, or did you forget that? No sleeping in, *thank-you-very-much*."

Ellie's eyes narrowed as if she could read her thoughts. "You're not serious. It's not even four in the morning. You have to get up earlier?"

"Dead. Serious." No one said pursuing a dream wouldn't be easy. She was used to the hours by now, but even she had to admit in the beginning, it had been tough.

Lexi reached up for a stack of bowls off a shelf.

"You know, Sean and I were talking..." Ellie's voice drifted off, but Lexi caught the sly tone and knew she was about to get hit with some harebrained idea.

"Whatever it is, run it by Tessa first." Lexi arranged the bowls on the large table in the middle of the kitchen and then headed into the pantry. She'd spent enough evenings with Ellie and Sean to know that Tessa was the grounding partner in that threesome. She'd learned her lesson early on that Tessa had the final say.

"Oh, but we did. And she loved it. As long as you were on board."

Lexi turned to see a huge smile stretched across her sister's face. *Oh boy*.

"Trust me, I think you'll love it. And it wouldn't just benefit us, but it would help you as well."

"How?" Lexi crossed her arms over her small chest and sighed. She needed to get to work on her dough—every minute counted—but she had a feeling whatever Ellie was about to say required her full attention otherwise, she'd end up agreeing to do something stupid, like start teaching pastry classes or something.

She tried that once, at the request of her mentor, back in Paris a few years ago, and it had been a disaster.

She was not a people person and having to walk through every minute detail of how to make pain au chocolat with people who had no idea how to bake had been pure torture.

She'd ended up calling her mentor in to help her end the class, and he'd somehow managed to save her by offering a chocolate tutorial along with some homemade chocolates. The class ended up being a success, amazingly.

Her skills were best behind the kitchen door. Away from people. And she was happy with that.

"Well…it would help get your name out there. More than just being the caterer for our events." Ellie's gaze darted all over the room.

"Catering and this shop are all I need. You know that.

Besides, we have that big event coming up, the Summer Arts Festival, right?"

The festival was the perfect venue for her to make her name. Sean had managed to book Lexi into several events throughout the city and then a large exclusive party held at the Banff Springs Hotel. Lexi was very excited about the event. She already had her menu planned to showcase her chocolate talents that night.

If everything went the way she hoped it would, after that, her name would be known within the Canadian foodie community, which was a start.

"Right, but we have a few weeks yet for that."

Lexi's stomach dropped. *What did her sister have in mind?*

"Ellie, I really need to get started on my pastry." She wasn't sure she wanted to hear whatever scatterbrained idea her sister had come up with now.

"Oh, go ahead. I won't stop you. Let me grab us some coffee, and then I'll tell you all about it." Ellie disappeared into the front, and Lexi breathed a sigh of relief. At least she would have a few moments to herself now. It was only four in the morning; this was way too early for her brain to focus on anything but her pastry.

Her baking in the mornings was routine, a mindless act that she could do half asleep. She only used the simplest of ingredients, farm fresh was preferred, but the process itself took time.

Besides, croissants weren't all they would be offering. She needed to make buns, muffins, and danishes all before the store opened. And then it would be cupcakes, brownies, cookies, and more throughout the day. Her ovens would shut off by late afternoon if she were lucky.

Eventually, she would need to hire some helpers, but not until the store proved to be a success.

That was one of Tessa's stipulations.

Lexi figured it would take a week before Tessa gave in and hired some help. Until then, Lexi planned to use both Ellie and Tessa after her morning baking was completed. Two could play this game.

With the industrial-sized mixer kneading the dough together, Lexi didn't notice Ellie's return. She did, however, smell the coffee.

She breathed in deeply, reaching for the large mug Ellie placed beside a bowl of fruit.

"Thank you." She took a sip. You'd think she'd be used to the early mornings by now, but it usually took at least two to three cups of coffee before her brain woke up enough.

"Can I get started on the muffins?"

Lexi hesitated. It made sense to utilize Ellie to help her, but she had a hard time giving up control to someone lacking in experience. Sister or not.

"Seriously, Lex, I promise to follow your recipes word by word." Ellie reached for the binder Lexi had placed on the table and went to the muffin section of the book. "How many did you have on your list to make?"

"Five." Lexi pulled out her notebook from her apron's front pocket.

"So, can I get started? At least with the base mix?"

At Lexi's hesitation, Ellie threw her hands up in the air.

"Oh, for Pete's sake, Lex. It's not like I don't know what I'm doing. Who do you think taught you to bake in the first place?"

"Fine. Just...please be sure to follow the recipe the way I wrote it. Please?" She had fine-tuned that base recipe until it was just about perfect and she kept it well guarded, even from the other bakers at the patisserie back in Paris.

As the two worked in silence, Lexi's thoughts went back to her last day in Paris, and the sense of loss she felt back then filled her anew.

She'd told everyone her flight left the day before it truly did. She wanted to be able to say goodbye to the city of her heart in a way that would leave fond memories and not be full of tearful goodbyes from her friends.

She spent the day walking along the streets, stopped in at the various churches she loved to visit, and basked in the quietness she found within those hallowed walls.

Towards the end of the evening, she found herself in a section of the city she promised herself never to visit again. Instead of turning around and heading home, she tortured herself with glimpses into a future that would never be hers.

Truth be told, that was the hardest part about leaving Paris. Her heart was there, and she'd never get it back.

"I can't wait to have my first real Parisian breakfast." Ellie threw her a smile.

"For it to be a true Parisian breakfast, we need to be in Paris. But I'll do my best." That included adding freshly squeezed orange juice to the menu. She eyed the crate of oranges on the back shelf and was thankful Ellie had convinced Sean to come in and squeeze those for them.

"So...my news...Tessa managed to convince her chocolate guy to sell his product here."

"Chocolate guy?" Lexi's brow rose. "A chocolatier, you mean."

Ellie shrugged. "Same diff, right? Anyway, she's pretty stoked because up till the other day, he'd all but refused. And trust me, she harangued him forever about it."

"There's a huge difference." Lexi learned a long time ago that it did matter. "A *chocolate guy* makes chocolate from cocoa beans. A *chocolatier* takes that chocolate and makes it into the stuff people are willing to spend fortunes on." She'd met many chocolatiers in Paris. She doubted whomever it was Tessa had contacted was even half as good as those she knew.

Being a chocolatier was a passion. A calling. It took years of training to become a master at it, a distinction many endeavored to obtain but few achieved.

She knew one of the best.

Had loved one of the best.

If she were being honest, she still loved him.

"Anyway," Ellie continued as if the difference didn't mean anything to her, which it probably didn't. "Tessa thinks you might know the guy. He's from Paris."

That piqued Lexi's interest. She tried to think about the dozen of people she knew who would fit the category and who might be interested in selling their product in her store. There weren't many, though. A few, when she'd said her goodbyes, had expressed interest in coming to Banff, but only for a holiday.

"Really?"

Ellie nodded. The smile on her face stretched across her fine cheekbones and lit her whole face on fire with happiness.

"Are you going to tell me who?"

When Ellie shook her head, Lexi all but rolled her eyes. *Figures.* If there was one thing her sister loved, it was secrets.

"When will I find out who this guy is who I might know?"

Ellie quirked her lips and glanced at the clock. "In a few hours. Tessa should be getting ready to leave to pick him up in Calgary."

"She's picking him up? Instead of being here?"

"She's a huge fan of his. Remember that ring box I told you about when Jude proposed?"

Lexi's heart sank. No, there was no way *he* would be coming here. Not now, not after...her hands shook slightly as she hit the lever on the mixer to shut it off, hoping Ellie hadn't noticed.

"You don't mean Paul Ormand, do you?" She struggled to keep her voice steady, to not show her growing panic.

Her sister had no idea about the past between her and Paul. She wanted to keep it that way, too.

"That's the one. You know, it was really strange." Ellie paused as she pulled out a stack of muffin tins from beneath the counter. "It wasn't until I mentioned you were the one to help open up this bakery that he agreed to come and check it out. That's what made Tessa think you might know him."

Lexi just shrugged. She concentrated on lifting the large mixing bowl out of its holder and setting it on the counter, where she carefully worked the dough.

Paul was coming here. *Here.* Waves of panic flowed through her until she gripped the edge of the counter to keep from falling to her knees.

She'd left Paris knowing she was leaving Paul behind forever. She never expected to see him again. Coming here had been the only way she knew to salvage her tattered heart.

Damn it. Why did he have to come? Why couldn't he leave well enough alone? What did he hope to accomplish? He'd been the one to call it off, to break their engagement.

How was she supposed to get through this?

She hadn't seen him since that fateful day over a year ago.

Could she handle seeing him again without falling to her knees and begging him to take her back?

Chapter Two

Wind whipped through Paul's hair as he followed behind Tessa and her husband outside. He hunched his shoulders a bit against the cold to protect his neck as they exited the airport.

"I thought it was almost summer, no?" Paul mumbled as he pulled his suitcase behind him.

His voice must have carried on the wind as Tessa laughed.

"Don't worry. Calgary tends to have a mind of its own, but I promise, Banff is beautiful. It'll be shorts and sandals weather in no time, just like I promised."

Paul glanced down at his jeans and quirked his brow. He didn't do shorts. Never had. Sandals, yes. Torn and dirty jeans, yes. Shorts? No. He wouldn't be caught dead looking like a tourist, even if he was one.

The niggling of a memory played with his mind, of a laughter that made his heart ache.

Lexi used to love playing tourist; she'd buy the most outrageous clothing for them to wear and then walk along the Seine, mingle with the crowds, and wait to see whether a pickpocket would dare to come too close to them.

Would she have that same laugh when he arrived this afternoon? He doubted it.

He took a big chance by coming, but this past year made him realize one thing.

He lived a year with a hole in his heart and he couldn't live like that anymore. Losing Lexi was like losing a part of himself.

"If I remember correctly, it was a little cool the last time I was here, too." He handed off his luggage to Jude as they stopped at a truck parked close to the walkway from the airport entrance. He watched as Tessa placed the box he'd brought in the back and then went and picked it up. That one stayed with him, it was precious cargo and needed to remain intact.

"I'm just so glad you came. You didn't have to, you know." Tessa climbed into the back of the truck, leaving the front for him. One look inside the truck interior and he was thankful. There was no way he could fold his long frame in that back seat.

"Does everyone living in the mountains have a truck? I thought only cowboys drove these things." Despite the teasing in his voice, hew as somewhat serious.

"This old thing? Nah. The only livestock we have is a dog who likes to sit in the back there. But it sure comes in handy on the back roads in the winter. Besides, it was either this or my bike and with your luggage..."

Paul nodded. He had a bike Paris, so he understood.

"Are you still at the wondrous hotel?"

The one and only time he'd been in Banff had been a few years ago for their local chocolate festival.

He'd been in a lull with his designs, tired of creating the same old but missing the passion to think of anything new.

When he'd been invited to Banff as a guest presenter, he'd hoped that maybe that would spark something inside him, and he'd been right.

He'd stumbled upon Jude at the Banff Springs Hotel where

he'd been staying and they'd had drinks a few times at the bar after Jude's shift. He liked the man, liked him, even more, when he discovered he was going to propose and his girlfriend loved chocolate.

Paul had given him some VIP tickets to his session and created the little box Jude ended up using as a ring holder. The project had been fun and revved up his creative juices so that by the time he returned to Paris, he was ready for the magic to begin.

That's when he'd met Lexi.

Sweet Lexi. Full of life and wonder.

Did her skin still smell and taste like strawberries and vanilla? Did her head still tilt to the side while she worked through a joke, did her face still light up when she smiled?

That smile of hers was magical. It would draw you in, wrap you in a hug, and leave you feeling like you'd been let in on the worlds biggest secret.

Would she smile at him, smile like that, when she saw him?

If he was lucky, maybe.

"Paul?"

He twisted in his seat to find Tessa with a questioning look on her face.

"I'm sorry. I was lost in my thoughts for a moment."

She patted his shoulder. "It's okay. I only asked if you were able to sleep on the plane and if it felt good to be back in Canada?"

Did it feel good to be back? Yes and no.

"I did. Thank you. I'm sure by tonight, I'll be exhausted, but for now, I feel good. Have you ever been to Paris?"

Tessa shook her head.

"You need to come, as my guests, one day. I'll be your tour guide and introduce you to the finest chocolates and wine France has to offer."

"One day. Lexi has told us so many stories that we were just saying we would need to go."

Paul struggled to keep his face calm, to not show any interest at the mention of Lexi's name.

"Let's discuss this idea of yours for me to personalize my chocolate to your brand." He changed the subject, hoping it wasn't too noticeable.

Tessa clapped her hands together, and Paul caught the wink Jude gave him.

"Are you sure you are ready for this? Why not just enjoy the scenery? Once Tessa gets talking about her ideas, nothing will shut her up." Jude reached back across the seats and entwined his fingers in with his wife's.

Paul's heart twisted at the obvious signs of love. He was glad things worked out for the two of them.

"What can I say? Decadent Events is my baby. My passion. And I want to see it grow, expand. Ellie—she helped to arrange your travel—is the one with the big ideas."

"Bigger than having my chocolate linked with your name?"

She nodded. He wasn't sure whether he should be offended or not. In Paris, he was a major player in the chocolate industry. There weren't that many *master chocolatiers* with his clout and fame.

"She wants to link us up with this company called Bella Dia but—"

"The travel concierge?" Paul interrupted her.

"You've heard of it? It's run by a friend of hers from college, and someone has convinced them we would be an excellent addition to the services they offer."

"It's an elite company. I've used them many times. That's a great connection to have." He was impressed. Maybe Tessa's small company wasn't so small after all.

Until he'd heard Lexi's name when Ellie had called one day,

he hadn't been interested in linking them together. His life was in Paris. His brand was in Paris. If he had wanted to expand, it would be New York, not Banff, Canada.

"You think so?" He heard the uncertainty in Tessa's voice.

"I do. Their clientele is very exclusive, and their level of service is one of the best in the world..." His voice drifted off as the view of the Rocky Mountains came into view. They were breathtaking. Their snowcapped mountaintops rose high into the clouds, and he could only stare at them.

"Quite the thing to be driving into, isn't it?"

"Honestly, I couldn't imagine living in them. There's still snow on them."

He much preferred his wobbly cobblestones and narrow streets in the arrondissement where he lived.

This past winter had been their warmest yet, with barely any snow and he much preferred that. He remembered too vividly his childhood winters in northern Ontario, where even bundled in a thick coat, mitts, and hat, he still froze.

"I couldn't imagine living anywhere else." Tessa sighed.

Paul settled back in his seat and watched the countryside pass them by. If he remembered correctly, they had a good hour before they entered Banff. An hour to prepare himself.

How would Lexi react when he walked into her store? How would he react when he saw her?

He'd walked away from her once, and it had been the hardest thing he'd ever done. At the time, it had been the right thing, but he thought...he'd thought she would come back to him.

Never had he been so wrong.

"I can't wait for you to meet the team." Tessa's voice jolted him back to reality.

"And that's Ellie and Lexi, right?"

"Don't forget Sean," Jude added.

"Of course not. Who do you think is hosting tonight's dinner?"

Paul's stomach rumbled at the thought. The fare on the plane was barely tolerable.

"Lexi mentioned you normally eat late in France, but since you have to deal with jet lag, I'm hoping you don't mind if we eat a little early? Jude reserved a private room for us at the Banff Springs Hotel, where you'll be staying again."

Paul glanced at his watch. It was almost three o'clock in the afternoon. If he remembered correctly from the last time he was here, by nine o'clock, he'd been dead on his feet. He was an early riser, a habit he learned early in his days of confectionary training.

"Of course not."

"Good." There was a loud chirp, and Tessa pulled out her cell phone. "Change of plans. Ellie says they're swamped and not to come by. So..." Her voice trailed off as her fingers danced along the screen.

"Why don't we drop Paul off at the hotel so he can relax a bit?" Jude suggested.

Paul's heart sank. He'd hoped to see Lexi today. That was the whole reason he was there. For her.

"Great idea. We can all meet at the hotel later for dinner. Oh...how about cocktails first?"

Jude smiled while Paul watched the two of them share a look through the rearview mirror. He must be missing something...

"The bartender there has this special drink he named after Tessa."

"Really?" Paul feigned interest when really, all he could think about was the fact he had three hours until he saw Lexi.

"You wouldn't know it, but Tess is a bit picky when it comes to food and drink. Tessa issued the bartender a challenge and what he came up with was out of this world."

"It wasn't a challenge per se. Rather a question," Tessa said.

"Right." Jude snorted. "Anyway, she asked him if he'd ever heard of Cointreau caviar, and before the poor guy could respond, she gave him a lesson on how it's made and what it should taste like."

"Not everyone knows, you know. You didn't." She smacked Jude on the shoulder.

"So what happened?" Paul rather enjoyed the way the two teased each other.

"This is the best part. While she was giving him a lesson, he was busy behind the bar putting a drink together. Before she was even finished, he'd set it in front of her and waited for her to notice."

"What did he make?"

"The best drink I've ever tasted." Tessa sighed.

"Champagne, these bubble things, and some Blue Curacao. It reminds me of her eyes every time." Jude's cheeks flushed as he glanced over at Paul before he focused on the road ahead of him. Up ahead, cars had slowed to an almost standstill.

Tessa leaned forward. "Those goats are *still* there?" She sighed in frustration. "We caught them coming down the hill earlier but thought for sure they'd be out of the way by now." She leaned back, crossed her arms, and frowned. "I hate goats," she muttered.

Paul waited for the explanation he knew was about to come.

"They like to eat her flowers." Jude threw him an apologetic look.

Paul stopped himself from rolling his eyes at the last minute but knew he'd been caught by Jude, who only shook his head. *Goats eating flowers? What, did they live in the country?*

To keep himself occupied, he pulled out the notebook he carried in his jacket and worked on a few ideas he had for Tessa's company. He liked to draw images of his designs, to see how they might look. Since he'd made that first box for Jude a few years ago, he'd gone on to make several hundreds, if not thousands more.

It was now one of his signature creations.

He'd been stuck in a rut for the past year, though. Unable to design anything new. His inspiration had left him the moment he knew he couldn't marry Lexi.

She was his muse.

Maybe being back here, in Banff, with her, would bring it back?

"What are you...drawing?" Tessa peeked over his shoulder.

Paul glanced down, and his face flushed red. On the paper he'd drawn an etched box, but inside of it he'd written one word. *Lexi.*

Now, how did he explain that?

Chapter Three

Lexi leaned against the counter and savored the stillness in the shop for a moment.

Opening day was a success. She knew it would be. If only Tessa had been here and she could have proved it in person.

When she'd first arrived, there had been a lot of tension between the two of them, tension Lexi hadn't understood until she'd had a very frank conversation with Tessa one night without Ellie around.

They were more alike than either one of them wanted to accept. Tessa didn't like change, not fast change anyway, and assumed with Lexi leaving her whole life in Paris that, she thrived on it.

That was so far from the truth, it was laughable. Lexi knew Ellie had painted her as the younger, carefree sister who lived her life on the fly, but that was only because that's what Lexi wanted her sister to believe.

She didn't want Ellie worrying about her.

After a few shots of whiskey and a solid frank conversation, the two of them managed to create a foundation for a solid working relationship.

Not only that, she ended the evening with admiration for the woman. Tessa wasn't competition or a block to her future, she was a partner, a partner she could work with.

The front display was almost sold out of everything she'd made throughout the day, which was worth celebrating. The notebook behind her was full of orders for the next few days and weeks, and Ellie had promised to twist Tessa's arm into hiring someone to help her after they'd received a stack of resumes as people waited in line to buy their pastries and bread.

Contentment and a sense of peace filled her heart.

This could work. It really could work.

"I don't know how you do this, day in and day out. I'm exhausted." Ellie walked out into the main area and sat down at a table.

"It'll become a routine, eventually." Lexi smiled at her older sister. "It also helps when there are more than two people working."

It had been really nice to work alongside her sister. It had been a long time since they'd' spent some quality time together, and she missed Ellie. Like, really missed her.

They'd been best friends growing up, leaning on one another especially after their father had died, leaving their mom to work insane hours just to make ends meet.

"Lexi, I love you, but I do not want this to become my routine." Ellie leaned her head back, closed her eyes, and groaned as she stretched the muscles in her neck. "I think I'm going to need a hot bath and a massage tonight."

"Did someone say massage?" Sean peeked through the partly opened door between Decadent Sweets and Decadent Events. He winked at Lexi at first, but then his sole focus was on Ellie.

Lexi thought it cute, the level of attraction between the two of them. Something neither one seemed willing to admit. Yet.

"Massage. Hot bath. Maybe some ice cream. Not necessarily in that order." Ellie opened her eyes and smiled up at Sean, who towered over her. "Hi."

"Hi, back. Lean forward, and I'll see if I can help with one of those requests."

Lexi watched the two of them and struggled to squash the sadness that hit her heart hard. Once, she'd had her person, the one to rub her shoulders, walk in the rain together, laugh at silly jokes no one else understood.

She'd had her person. Then she lost him, and it was her own fault.

She turned around and made herself busy tidying up the counter behind her. Watching them, seeing them dance around the beginning stages of open flirting...it reminded her of Paul too much. Of the happiness she'd felt as they first got to know each other and then later as they fell in love.

Paul. He was coming here, and she was scared, nervous, terrified, and giddy all at the same time.

Would he look the same? Older but still youthful? Was he still wearing jeans and a t-shirt, or would he have dressed up to impress Tessa? Did his eyes still twinkle with his deadpan sarcasm?

She couldn't believe he was coming here. Here. Back to Canada, for her.

Or maybe she was overthinking things. It was all she could think about throughout the day: why he was coming, why he'd changed his mind once he knew she was here. Why now when he had so many opportunities in the past?

She was the one who had made the mistake, who held herself aloof too much, who kept placing barriers around her heart and never gave him the chance to break them all down. Maybe if she had, maybe if she hadn't kept her secrets so close, he wouldn't have felt as if there was no hope for them.

She'd like to imagine that m, just maybe, his arrival meant she had a chance to redo things, a chance for her own happily-ever-after.

"Today was a good day, wasn't it?"

Lexi turned and plastered a smile on her face. "It was. Thank you for helping this morning with the juices."

Sean shrugged while he continued to rub Ellie's shoulders. "Do you plan on doing that every day?"

"Every morning. There's nothing better than freshly squeezed orange juice. Things will slow down to a more...manageable pace, and it won't be as rushed as today."

Ellie groaned. "Please tell me that day will be tomorrow?"

Sean laughed. "I hope not. We don't want things slowing down too fast. We've got something good going here. Just wait till Tessa sees the sales numbers."

"Starting next week, we'll go down to the regular hours I had talked about, only being open until two in the afternoon." Lexi knew this was a sore spot with Sean, who didn't understand why she was so adamant about closing early each day. He saw the loss of sales while she saw the increase in hours to do other things.

"Right. Then you'll focus on helping us build the catering side to Decadent Events," Ellie mentioned.

"Exactly. I have a few ideas too, but," she shook her head at Sean, who looked up at her with sparked interest, "that's for another day. I need to start cleaning up if you want me to be at this dinner tonight." She grabbed a few empty trays from the display case and made her way into the back.

"You have to be there, Lex. You're the reason this chocolate guy is coming here in the first place."

"Chocolatier, Lexi. Please don't call him the *chocolate guy* to his face, okay?" She pushed the swinging door open and set the trays down on the counter. She glanced behind her through the window and watched the soft smile her sister gave Sean as he took the chair beside her and casually leaned back.

"She seems pretty sensitive to the whole name thing," Lexi heard Ellie mutter.

A quick glance at the clock forced her to stop dawdling and get a move on. She could walk away from things and deal with it in the morning, but then she'd just be behind schedule...so why leave a job undone? That was something her mom used to always say. *Finish today so tomorrow can be fresh.*

She filled the large sink with hot, sudsy water and added the trays. Maybe some mindless cleaning would do her some good: work out the kinks in her neck and shoulders and give her time to get ready for Paul.

Who was she kidding?

She'd never be ready for him.

She'd honestly thought that part of her life was over.

When she left Paris, she walked away knowing there was no going back, no second chances, no way for her to make right something she'd ruined by keeping quiet.

She'd thought about that moment every single day since it happened. Thought about what she could have done differently, and how she could have stopped it from happening. But she knew. She knew there was nothing she could have done to change what happened.

As she scrubbed the trays, a wave of guilt hit her hard. The way their relationship dissolved, all the hurt...it was all her fault.

Her secret was something she hadn't wanted anyone to know. Anyone. Not even Ellie, her sister who thought she knew everything.

Foolishly, she thought she could keep her secret from even Paul, the one and only man she ever thought she could trust.

She should have known better.

"Need any help?"

Lexi dipped the pan she'd been scrubbing into the hot water in the second sink before setting it down to dry. She breathed in deep and twisted enough to see Sean standing off to the side.

"Almost done." She gave him the barest hint of a smile before she grabbed another pan and sunk it down in the hot water.

"I can dry, if you'd like?"

Lexi shook her head. What she wanted was to be left alone.

"I locked up already. Hope that was okay?"

"Thanks." She scrubbed the dried chocolate off another pan. She waited for Sean to leave, but for some insane reason, he didn't.

"Do you want to talk about it?"

The pan slipped from her soapy hands as his question startled her.

"Talk about..." Had she been that obvious about her reaction to Paul? Did they know something? Had Paul slipped and mentioned their past? Her cheeks flamed at the thought. Ellie would kill her for this. *Kill. Her.*

Sean sighed, and Lexi glanced over at him. He leaned against the counter, his arms crossed over his chest, but the look on his face, the way his gaze fidgeted around the kitchen, the steady tap of his fingers against his arms...

She grabbed a dry rag, and wiped her hands.

"Are you sure you want to talk about this...now?" She still hedged, unsure whether he was talking about what she thought he was talking about.

"Now's as good a time as any. Does Ellie know? Have you told her anything?"

He knew. How did he find out? What did he plan on doing with the news? Knowing Sean, he'd figure out a way to use it to his advantage. She might not have known him for long, but that much she did know.

"Ellie…" Her voice trailed off. If he knew, he knew, and there was no sense in hiding it. It was just a matter of finding out how much he knew about her past with Paul. "No, she has no idea."

The look of instant relief on Sean's face confused her.

"Thank God. I was afraid… it was too soon. If she knew, she'd have doubts…and I want to do this right. You know?"

Did she know what? What was he talking about? What doubts would Ellie possibly have?

"You have no idea what I'm talking about, do you?"

Lexi slowly shook her head.

Sean ran his fingers through his hair then pushed himself up from the counter. It looked as if he had something to say but then changed his mind. His shoulder dropped, and he turned to leave.

"I know you're in love with her." Her words tumbled out. "I know you love her, and that's okay with me."

"Are you sure?" He didn't turn, but Lexi could hear the hope in his voice.

"I'm sure." Why wouldn't she be?

"It doesn't mean I want to take her from you." He turned then, to face her, and she read the honesty in his eyes.

"Why would it?" She wanted her sister to be happy. Why would he be worried…unless…

"Well…" Now it was his turn to hedge, and Lexi found it quite appealing. She could see why her sister had fallen for the man. "She might have mentioned…nothing." He blew out a long breath and groaned. "I should have just kept my mouth shut."

"Let me guess. She told you that I needed her right now, right?" Classic Ellie. She didn't want to get hurt, and so she'd protect herself before anything could even happen.

Ellie had thought Sean was in love with Tessa, and it had been hard to know her sister had to struggle to protect her heart.

Since coming to Banff, it had been clear that Sean only had eyes for Ellie. How come her sister couldn't see it?

Unless she did but chose to ignore it. Was that why she was using her move here as a crutch? To protect herself?

Sean shrugged. "Listen, I shouldn't have said anything. I just..."

"Want to do a do-over?" She was the queen of do-overs.

"A do-over?"

"Yeah. You know...when you can take back a whole conversation and start fresh? Like...I'll pretend you didn't say anything, and we can tell Ellie we were talking about..." Her voice trailed off as she tried to think about a topic.

"About tonight," Sean answered. "Which is a good idea, by the way. Tessa is very excited about this guy from Paris being here, and it's my goal to make sure he agrees to create chocolate for the Decadent brand. You must have heard of him in Paris? He's the golden ticket for us, for Tessa."

"You don't need me to be there, though, tonight? Right?" She would give anything not to have to see Paul again in such a public setting. Maybe she could leave a note for him at the hotel, to meet her for coffee later.

"What? Of course, I do. It's because of you that he's even coming. You must know him."

Lexi shrugged and turned back to the pans in the sink.

"Lexi? Is there something you're not telling me? Something I need to be aware of before it all explodes in my face?"

Suddenly, Sean stood beside her, with his hand on her shoulder. She shook her head, unable to say anything. There was no sense in denying it, not when everyone would know in a few short hours.

"Just...be prepared for anything, okay? Yes, I know him. But please don't ask me any more than that. Please."

Sean pondered her words. "Might I suggest a *before-dinner*

drink with him then? He's staying at Banff Springs Hotel. Play nice and if that doesn't work, send me a text. If you're not there for dinner, I can make your excuses. But I'd rather not have an awkward dinner if it can be helped."

He squeezed her shoulder and then stepped away. Lexi nodded her head, thankful for his pragmatic attitude in this. That would work. She could do a drink in the bar. She could talk to him, apologize and see whether he forgave her. She wouldn't beg, though. She couldn't.

Lexi let a slow breath as Sean left the room. She came here, to Banff, for a fresh start. There was no going back, no turning back the clock or praying for a second chance.

She still loved Paul with every fiber of her being, but...her secret had destroyed what bound them together, and it had been all her fault.

There was no going back after that.

Chapter Four

PAUL DUG through his suitcase and almost panicked when he couldn't find the goofy tie he'd planned to wear tonight.

He hated ties. Hated wearing them. Hated them for the faked social importance it gave him when he was out at parties.

He typically refused to wear one. He was known for his bad boy look: his faded and ripped jeans, black shirts, and messy hair.

He didn't do ties. Until he'd won the World Master's Final for the second year in a row and Lexi had bought him a goofy tie as a dare.

The night of the competition, after he'd cleaned up from his session and went to change, she'd been there and tried to talk him out of wearing it. She didn't want to embarrass him, not in front of his peers and the press, but he knew that if he did wear it, she would have that smile on her face that he could never resist.

She was his happiness, his joy, and when he joined her at the table wearing that silly tie she'd bought him, she'd stood up and kissed him in front of everyone.

It was a memory he would always cherish.

When he found it, he tossed it onto the bed and sat down in the chair. No way he was lying down. The moment he stepped into the room, exhaustion hit him, and he knew he'd fall asleep and wouldn't wake until the early morning hours.

No way would he miss seeing Lexi tonight. No way.

When he arrived at the hotel, apparently someone recognized him, and they upgraded his room to the Vice Regal suite. He appreciated the upgrade, having the room to spread out and relax instead of being crammed into one of their well-known smaller rooms.

Rather than sleep, he called room service and ordered a pot of coffee and a cheese plate. His notepad sat out on the small table, and he worked on some designs he'd thought would work.

He would need a kitchen to test them out, but Tessa had already promised him the kitchen at Decadent Sweets.

He got up at the knock at the door, and went to let in the room service. The aroma of fresh coffee teased his senses and perked him up. He had an hour until dinner, more than enough time to get caffeinated, have a shower, and get dressed.

An hour until he saw Lexi again. His palms tingled at the thought.

He didn't want to imagine how this meeting would go. Knowing Lexi, it would be anything other than what he expected. She could still be upset, hurt, indifferent, or maybe happy. He had no idea.

He'd rehearsed what he would say, how he would say it a million times, but he knew, in that moment, it would be worthless.

He couldn't wait to see her again. If he'd been smart, he would have told her he was coming and arranged to meet up first, alone. But he didn't want to give her the chance to turn him down, to say no.

He wouldn't let her say no.

An envelope rested on the tray with his coffee and platter. He poured himself a coffee before he opened it, but once he did, he sat down and reread the message.

She wanted to meet for drinks before dinner.

Lexi. Wanted to meet with him. *Alone.* He glanced at the clock and saw he had only half an hour before she would be downstairs, waiting for him.

He gulped the steaming hot coffee without a second thought and headed into the bathroom for a quick shower.

He wanted to be down there early, before she arrived. He wanted to see her first, to see her face, the look in her eyes when she saw him. Then he'd know.

He'd know whether he'd been a fool for coming. He'd know whether she was as nervous as he was. He'd know whether there was a second chance for them.

Chapter Five

HER BED WAS CLUTTERED with clothes she'd flung down from her closet. She had nothing to wear. Nothing.

She hadn't gone shopping since she'd arrived in Banff and her lackluster closet showed it. She needed an outfit hot enough to make Paul's jaw drop but subtle enough to say she'd moved on. And she had nothing like that.

"Hey, I was wondering if I could borrow that cute little purple dress..." Ellie's voice trailed off as she stepped into Lexi's room and caught the mounds of clothes on her bed.

"You okay?"

Lexi was holding a dress she'd found at the back of her closet and hugged it tight to her body. She loved this dress, but she wouldn't be able to wear it. It was what she wore the first night she'd met Paul. It had been at an evening hosted at the Louvre, and they'd bumped into each other while they stood at the dessert table.

"Lex?"

"I don't know what to wear." She hung the dress back up in the closet, pushed the clothes out of the way on her bed, and sat down.

"What was wrong with that dress? Or this one?" Ellie pulled a black dress off the top of the pile and held it out. "I haven't seen this one on you."

Lexi shrugged. She'd bought that for a party Paul had wanted to take her to...except she'd never worn it because they ended their engagement.

"Do we need to have a chat? We're overdue, you know."

"No. Well...yes, we probably should. We actually haven't had a night to just sit and talk, have we?" She sorted through the clothes, not really looking at them but needing an excuse not to look at her sister.

They'd both been busy ever since Lexi had moved into Ellie's small two-bedroom condo.

"Are you nervous about tonight?"

Lexi's head shot up. "No, why would I be? It's just a dinner. Only a dinner. I actually thought I might leave early. You know, with tomorrow and all. I'm sure we'll be busy, just like today, and—" She rambled on. She wanted to stop talking, knew she needed to stop talking, and yet she couldn't.

Ellie just sat there, her brows raised high.

"I'm not nervous," Lexi attempted to reiterate.

"Right. And I'm getting married tomorrow."

Lexi's shoulders slumped.

"What's going on? Is there...do we need to talk about something? Anything?"

Lexi shook her head. But then nodded.

"It's about Sean, isn't it?"

Her sister's voice was laced with myriad emotions. Disappointment. Sadness. Hurt. Forced acceptance.

"What about Sean?" Lexi felt lost. *What did Sean have to do with any of this?* Why would she think he had anything to do with this?

"I kind of...saw you. In the kitchen."

"Okay. And...?" She still didn't understand.

Ellie lay down on the bed and stretched her arms over her head. "You've been so quiet about your life in Paris and we've been so busy since you moved in...but I just wanted you to know that if there is something going on between you and Sean that I, well...I get it."

Lexi pushed her clothing out of the way and leaned down. "Get what?"

"You know." Ellie's words were weighted down with disappointment.

Lexi thought she understood. Ellie must have seen where Sean had his hand on her shoulder. But that didn't explain why she thought something was going on between them. She hardly knew the man, and it was obvious to everyone around them that sparks flew between him and Ellie.

"No, Ellie, I don't. I don't know how you could think that there is anything going on between me and him. You should know me better than that." She touched her sister's arm and smiled.

Ellie shook her head. "I don't know you—that's the problem. I thought I did. I knew the girl you had been before you left for Paris. You were happy. Joyful. You knew what you wanted, but you'd decided to have fun at the same time. But now...you're serious. There's no sparkle in your eyes. It's almost like..."

"Like?" Hearing this hurt. She could only imagine what else Ellie would say.

"Almost like before."

Those words stuck a knife through Lexi's heart.

"It's not like that." She would never go back to being like that. *Ever.* It bothered her that Ellie would think that.

That time had been the darkest in her life, and the only one who had been there for her was her sister.

It was Ellie who had found her, lying in the alley after

having been badly beaten by boys from their high school. It had been Ellie who had lied for her to her parents, the teachers...to everyone. Ellie, who had taken care of her, protected her from the rumors that swirled around their school, and then later, that summer, when she'd realized she was pregnant, it had been Ellie who found someone who would help her with an abortion, had taken care of all the details while Lexi had just laid there, frozen to everything that had happened.

But not even Ellie knew the complete truth. She had no idea about afterward, the things the doctor had said, the horror of having to deal with the pain that ripped through her body for the weeks that followed the procedure. Nor had Ellie been there, to help her or protect her, when years later, she found out from her own doctor that her body was so damaged from that abortion that she would never be able to have children.

"Are you sure?" Ellie reached across and grabbed Lexi's hand. "Because if being with Sean would bring that sparkle back, then..."

"Then what?" She forced those memories behind her. "You'd give up your own happiness? You would forget you love the man and have been in love with him for years now?"

When Ellie didn't say anything, Lexi had her answer.

She tore her hand away from Ellie's and sat up. "You've always been there for me. You've always made the sacrifices, told the lies...to protect me. But," she turned, tears gathered in her eyes as she looked down at her sister, "you don't need to do that anymore. I'm okay."

She'd thought she'd been able to hide her pain, to hide her broken heart...but apparently, she hadn't done a good enough job.

"You're not okay, and that's what worries me. If it's not Sean...then who? I've never heard you talk about any other guy...is there one? Was there one?"

Lexi jumped up off the bed. "You wanted the purple dress, right? It should be here in this pile, somewhere." She rummaged through the dresses, tops, and skirts and found the dress Ellie had asked for at the very bottom. "Here." She held it up. "It will look amazing on you."

"Thanks." She reached for the dress. "But you didn't answer my question."

"It's not Sean. Trust me on that, okay? Besides, it's so obvious that he only has eyes for you."

Ellie's cheeks bloomed a gorgeous shade of rose, and she ducked her face. "Do you think so?"

Lexi snorted. "Do you really need me to answer that?"

"Sometimes I wonder."

"And that makes you afraid. But, what if you're missing out on someone really special?"

Ellie stared at her, and Lexi felt a twinge of discomfort. "You're sure there's nothing going on between the two of you?"

Lexi walked over to her sister and held out her pinkie finger. "I promise." She hooked her finger with Ellie's, something they used to do as children when they'd made promises to each other. "Sean is a nice guy, but I'm not really into nice. He's safe, and I like my men to live on the edge a little."

Ellie rolled her eyes. "Yeah right. What men? When was the last time you had a serious relationship, let alone dated? If you want to use Sean as that bridge...just let me know, okay? I need to be prepared to nurse his broken heart once you start running." She left the room, dress in hand, while Lexi just stood there, gaping.

Run? Sean? Use him...what was she talking about? Why didn't she believe her? She had no interest in Sean. None.

She should tell her about Paul. She knew she should. But yet...she couldn't.

All she needed to do was meet with him tonight, convince him to keep their past a secret, and all would be well.

Right?

Chapter Six

Pulling up to the Banff Springs Hotel, Lexi almost had a panic attack and was about to drive past the attendants until she saw Sean. He waved at her and approached her vehicle as she pulled over to the side.

"Glad to see you took my advice." He opened her door and held out his hand.

"How did you know I'd be here this early?" She let him help her out and adjusted the dress she'd chosen at the last minute to wear.

"I didn't. I hoped you would, though."

Sean held on to her hand as they walked through the front doors, as if worried she might bolt.

"Have you met him yet?"

Sean shook his head. "No, but I had the most interesting conversation with Tessa earlier after they dropped him off."

That piqued her interest. "Really?"

"Have you been here before?"

It irritated her that Sean didn't elaborate, but she wasn't about to pry. She'd ask Paul herself.

"The hotel? Once or twice. Ellie brought me here for drinks one night and showed me the view from out back. It's gorgeous."

"Where are you meeting him?" They stood in the middle of the spacious lobby.

"The Ramsay Lounge. I remember Tessa telling me about the bartender here."

Sean laughed. "She likes having a drink named after her, that's for sure. Did you know the hotel is said to be haunted?"

"Right." Lexi didn't believe in that stuff.

"I'm serious. There's a staircase, somewhere in the hotel, where apparently a bride's dress caught on fire and she ended up tripping down the stairs to her death. And a few of the rooms are said to be haunted."

"Let me guess, with star-crossed lovers?"

He shook his head. "Murders."

"And you know this how?" She searched for the small gold plaque that would lead the way to the lounge where she would meet Paul. She was early and wanted to get settled, have a drink or two before he showed up.

"I used to work here as a teenager. Jude tells the stories better than I do, though. Maybe we can convince him tonight to share." He led her up an ornate staircase and down a hallway with plush carpeting.

"You're nervous, aren't you?" Sean asked.

"I'm fine." She lied.

They stood just outside the doorway, and Lexi peered inside. The room was virtually empty, from what she could see.

Sean reached for her other hand and held both between his. He stared at her, a soft smile on his face, and once again, Lexi could understand why Ellie had fallen so hard for him. He had a way of calming a person without saying a word.

She took a deep breath, straightened her shoulders, and smiled.

She could do this. She would do this without breaking. Her heart might be fragile, but that didn't mean she would fall apart.

Yes, she loved Paul. She always would. But, she understood her betrayal, her secrets, had destroyed any hope of a life together.

She would find a way to put their past behind her and work with him on a professional level in order to further her own dreams. Hers and Tessa's. Decadent Sweets would be a success, and she would find a way to make a life here without him in it.

"Thank you for being here."

Sean shrugged. "I figured you would need moral support, and I have a feeling Ellie has no idea, right?"

Lexi shook her head. "I just told her I'd meet her here, that I had some things to do beforehand."

"You know, she was so excited to have you move here. She really missed you. In all the years I've known her, she always claimed a part of her was missing with you being across the ocean."

Lexi wasn't sure what to say to that. The best thing she had done for them was move away. It was too hard on Ellie to keep her secret, no matter how much she claimed otherwise.

She'd made some foolish decisions, and when she tried to rectify them, she paid a price that had been too high. Life wasn't fair sometimes.

"I wouldn't be where I am today if it weren't for her. I owe her everything. And I'll do anything for her."

She pulled her hands from Sean's grasp and turned.

"Then be honest with her." Sean's words stopped her.

She nodded before she walked towards the bar and smiled at the bartender. She clasped her purse tightly in her hand and took a few deep breaths.

Paul would be here soon. She hoped. She never gave him the opportunity to decline, just asked him to meet her down here by the bar. She went to pull out a stool and then thought better of it. Privacy would be better, and a few tables in the corners were a bit more secluded.

"What can I get for you?"

"A glass of white wine, please." She could have gone for something a bit stronger, but Paul knew her too well. A stronger drink meant she was on edge, and she didn't want him to know that.

She eyed the gin on the shelf behind the bar and sighed. Something stronger would definitely be nice right about now.

She handed the bartender money for the drink, but he pushed the bill back to her. "It's already taken care of."

"I'm sorry?" She glanced around, but there was no one close enough to pay for her drink.

"He's over there." He pointed towards a booth in the corner, partly hidden by a plant, but in front of the large picture windows that overlooked the mountain range.

She stepped to the side, and that's when she saw him. He'd been hidden by that darn plant.

Paul was already here.

Chapter Seven

A LIGHT JAZZ band played over the speakers as Paul arrived at the Ramsay Lounge. A quick scan of the room confirmed he'd arrived early enough.

"What can I get for you?"

"Whatever you have on draft. It's been awhile since I've had a good Canadian beer."

"Is that right? Where are you from?" The bartender grabbed a glass and filled it. *Rickers Red. Hopefully it tasted good.*

"France. Paris, specifically."

"Rien ne vaut une bière Canadienne." *Nothing beats a Canadian lager.*

"Précisément."

Paul watched as the bartender knifed off a portion of the foam from the top before it was handed over to him. He took a long drink and savored the barley taste. He'd grabbed a Molson from the airport lounge when he first arrived, but this was just as good.

"I'm meeting someone in a few minutes. She's tall, brown hair, and will probably be wearing a killer dress. Will you pour her a glass of your Piesporter?"

"She likes her white, does she?"

Paul shrugged. "She prefers gin, but she'll pick the wine." She'd want to prove a point. "Bring over a tall gin and gingerale, though, along with another of these ten minutes after she arrives, if you could." He hoped it wouldn't take her that long to relax, but it might.

"You got it."

Paul took his drink and headed over to the corner booth in front of a bay of windows. He sat in the corner, his presence hidden by a large plant, leaving him an open view of both the doorway and bar. She should arrive soon. If he knew her, she'd want to get here before him.

His phone vibrated with a text message.

So?

Paul shook his head. Leave it to Marc, his best friend, to expect miracles right away.

Patience, he wrote back.

What's taking so long? Cold feet?

You do realize the time change, right? Marc was a fellow Canadian, from Montreal.

If you screw this up again, don't come home. I can't put up with your sorry ass another day.

Paul didn't bother to respond. Instead, he took a photo of his beer and sent it to him with one word. *Jealous?*

Insanely. I knew I should have come. Why didn't I?

Why? Because Paul didn't need any distractions or help from his friend. Marc and Lexi had a great friendship, and he didn't need that getting in the way.

He caught movement out of the corner of his eye by the doorway. She was here. He sat forward, and pushed his glass of out of the way to watch her.

Her beauty took his breath away.

He knew she'd wear a dress. She once told him she felt more

in control, more feminine, and self-assured when she was dressed up. He told her she was a goddess in a dress and should wear one all the time.

She wore them more often after that.

The thu-thump of his racing heartbeat was almost too much. He wanted to get up, to go and meet her, to forget all about his plans of softly leading her along until he could tell her he made a mistake and loved her no matter what, but then he realized she held hands with someone.

Not her sister.

He took another long drink of his beer and watched while his blood boiled. That was his woman. His heart. What gave that guy the right to hold her hands like that? Who was he? And why was he here, with her, when she'd asked Paul to meet her here?

That's when everything stopped. His heart. His breathing. Everything. Every expectation he'd had, every dream...it all stopped dead.

She must be in love. That must be why she wasn't alone and why she asked to meet him early. Why she held hands with someone other than him.

She'd moved on.

The idea left him cold. His heart sank, and he drained the last of his glass. He held his hand up to the bartender for another drink. Screw the dinner meeting. Screw Tessa and Jude and their chocolate branding idea. Screw everything. The only thing he wanted—no, the only thing he needed—right now was to get drunk and go back home.

It's over. He texted Marc. *I'll be on the next flight. Once I sober up.*

After one drink? What did you do?

Paul's fingers hovered over the keyboard on his phone.

Tell me you didn't know. If you knew...just tell me you

didn't. So help him, if Marc had any inkling of this guy she held hands with...

What?

Paul glanced up and saw her walk towards the bar. Alone. She was alone. He leaned back in the seat with a swoosh. Okay, so maybe he overreacted.

She came in alone, but she sure as hell wasn't leaving that way, and he'd do everything to make sure the next hand she held was his.

Chapter Eight

LEXI STRUGGLED to keep her walk steady. Her knees quaked, her ankles wobbled, and she could hardly see, thanks to the tears that blurred her vision.

She almost hated the influence Paul still had over her.

Almost.

She knew she needed to be strong, but all she wanted to do was melt against him, feel his arms around her and just surrender her heart once again.

Who was she kidding? He already owned her heart.

She approached the booth and stood there as the bartender set down their drinks. She studied Paul's face, the way his gaze held steady with hers, how he reclined there, as if at ease.

How could he be so relaxed when her body felt like a firework waiting to be lit?

She placed her purse on her lap, moved it beside her on the seat, and then on top of the table. She fiddled with the strap before she placed it back down beside her. She must look like a fool, sitting there, unable to meet Paul's gaze.

"I don't think I've ever seen you look more beautiful." His

voice, husky with the tinge of an accent, brushed across her skin like a soft feather.

She glanced up and smiled. "And you're still as cocky as ever."

It was his shrug, the way his shoulder lifted slightly, that she knew this was as hard on him as it was on her. He struggled with his emotions as much as she did.

He reached for her hand, his fingers gently gliding over her skin.

She was putty and unable to do anything but let him touch her.

"I'm glad you suggested this, us getting together before the dinner party. We have a lot to talk about."

Lexi tried to read into his words, to catch whatever nuances he threw out at her. *What did they have to discuss? Their past? How to work together and not divulge their history?*

"I'm actually surprised you are here." She swallowed and sucked in a deep breath. She withdrew her hands from his and reached for her wine.

"Why wouldn't I be?"

"Banff is a long way from Paris."

"If you hadn't left, I wouldn't have had to come." His shoulder lifted in that singular shrug of his that said *it is what it is, let's move on.*

"Why did you leave?" His lips pursed after asking her that all important question, the one question she really didn't want to answer, not right now.

Her fingers wrapped around the stem of her glass, her grip as taunt as her shoulder muscles.

"That's what you want to talk about?" *Why did she leave? That's what he wanted to talk about?*

"Yes. You never told me. There were no goodbyes." His gaze remained steady with hers, and she found it very hard to look away. But she did it. She stared out the large bay windows, out into the gorgeous scenery of the Rocky Mountains.

"We already said our goodbyes," she whispered. She didn't want to remember that day.

"Oh, Lexi," the way he said her name, she wanted to melt, "that wasn't a goodbye, love."

Her resolve almost broke then. She stared at one area on the mountain ahead of her, determined to remain calm, to not let him see all the emotions she felt at that moment.

What was she feeling?

Seeing him, she knew he was everything she wanted and needed.

He was her heart. Her soul.

The slime of self-disgust was still there, a sickening realization that she'd ruined everything good between them. She would have done anything to turn back time, to redo things between them, to be honest with him, if she could.

But that was one thing she knew for sure. There was no going back. That's why she came to Banff.

"What was it then? Because it sure felt like it to me." Not just goodbye. It felt like death. And it almost killed her.

When he didn't answer right away, Lexi tore her gaze from the serene scene outside and into his stormy gaze.

"That was a tearing of hearts." His voice lowered until it was so low, she knew if her head had been on his chest, the rumble would have vibrated through his body.

Her heart lurched at his words.

"My heart didn't just tear, Paul. It crumbled to pieces." She blinked away the visceral tell the softening of his gaze elicited from her.

She readied herself for his touch, with every nerve in her body ready to feel his skin upon hers, even if it was only briefly.

And then his stupid phone rang.

He hesitated, for oh so brief a moment, but then that moment was gone.

"This had better be good," he growled into the phone. Lexi smiled inside, happy to know he'd felt the connection between them.

After a brief moment, he held the phone out to her. "It's Marc." The scowl on his face had her smiling as she reached for the phone.

She loved Marc, like a brother. He knew how to lift her spirits, how to calm her down, and just what to say at the right time.

He also knew Paul inside and out and had been a good buffer between the two of them when things fell apart.

Leaving him behind had been equally hard.

"You're not going to yell at me, are you? I planned to call."

"When, chérie? When? You can't run from me, nor should you." Marc's smooth voice drawled on the phone. If she hadn't fallen in love with Paul, it wouldn't have taken much for her to look at Marc as a possible love interest. He was safe, and comfortable.

Not exactly the love affair she had with Paul, but it would have worked.

"Soon. Things just got busy..." She knew that was a thin excuse.

"No excuses. No lies. Not between us."

Lexi winced. Would he, too, turn away if he knew? Would he look at her with sympathy and pity, view her differently once he knew the truth?

Of course, he would have. It was one reason why she never told anyone.

She'd assumed Paul had kept her secret as well. At least, she hoped he hadn't.

"Now, tell me,..." he said, "have you kissed and made up with Paul, or are you making the man beg like he should?"

She glanced over at Paul, who scowled. She could only imagine the thoughts going through his head.

"Or something..."

"Lexi." There was a warning tone to Marc's voice. "I love you, girl, but you can be stubborn as a mule. Let it go. Whatever happened between you two, let it go, okay? Come home. Please?"

She sighed. "You know I can't."

"But you want to."

"Don't make me answer that. Not right now." To admit it, and agree to it, meant only one thing. Heartache. Because what she wanted and what would actually happen were two different things.

"This isn't his time." Paul caught her attention. She raised her brow, and challenged him to repeat himself.

Paul only rolled his eyes. "We don't have much time, love, before everyone else is here for dinner. I'm a very jealous man, it seems."

"Since when?" The words tumbled out without thought.

"Oh, he's become a very different man since you left," Marc said on the phone.

"I'm a different girl, too," she said quietly.

"Just give him a chance, okay? Listen to him. Open yourself up. Promise me," Marc insisted.

"Okay, okay."

"Good girl. And call me before you go to bed, chérie. I miss our nightly chats."

Lexi smiled. She missed their nightly talks when she was in Paris too. Since she'd come to Banff, they hadn't had one.

The few times he'd text her, she used the time change as an excuse. But, it had also helped to rebuild her relationship with her sister. Instead of talking with Marc about pastry, shopping, and other trivial things, she would crawl into bed with Ellie, and they'd tell stories, reminisce about the good memories from their past, and talk about the shop.

It wasn't the same, but it was just as good.

"I'll call with a new bedtime story, just for you," she promised while she winked at Paul. Immediately her cheeks flamed. *What was she doing?*

She didn't look Paul in the eye as she handed him back his phone. He ended the call without a word and reached for her hand, not giving her any time to prepare herself.

Her skin tingled while a light flush grew in all the right places. It was dangerous how much he still affected her. She needed to take control of whatever was going on, before Ellie and Tessa, and Sean arrived.

"Paul, I...thank you, for coming and meeting me here, before everyone else."

His fingers rubbed against her skin. There was a light roughness to his fingers, calluses that she wasn't used to.

"I was trying to figure out a way to get you to meet me privately, after our dinner."

She looked him in the eye. "You were?"

"There's a lot we need to talk about. Us. Our past. This partnership with Tessa and Jude."

And how to make it work, she added silently.

"Why did you agree to come? From what Ellie told me, you continually declined until you found out I was here." She'd wondered about that ever since Ellie told her. *Why?*

"You're the only reason I'm here."

Lexi's heart melted at that. *He came for her.* She dipped her head as she tried to hide how much his words affected her.

"I don't understand."

"You left me, without telling me goodbye. Without warning me, either."

She raised her gaze to his. "I left because there was no reason anymore for me to stay."

His soft brown eyes almost killed her. She was too afraid to read what he was trying to say.

"I am sorry," was all he said.

"I wanted to say goodbye, to tell you I was leaving, but..." How did she say she'd been too afraid to?

"I was selfish, love. I turned you away out of hurt and my pride, and it took you leaving for me to admit it. I was and am a fool." The sincerity in his voice, the look of contrition in his gaze...she believed him, and her heart started to hope. To really hope.

"Come back home," he said. "Come back to your life there, and let's rebuild what we lost."

Home. Paris wasn't home anymore. Banff was.

She was here to rebuild her life here, without him. She couldn't leave Decadent Sweets behind. She couldn't walk away from her sister, not again.

"How can you rebuild something that isn't there?" She hated that the words came out from her mouth, from her heart, but there they were. *Trust.* There was no trust between them. Paul made that very clear to her.

"We both made mistakes. But we can move on from that. Build the future we want, together."

She shook her head. "No. We can't. It's taken me a long time to realize that." Regret, guilt, shame, and grief welled up inside. Regret for being the reason they were broken. Guilt for not trusting him enough. Shame for what happened to her - something she will never be able to surrender. Grief...grief for the children she could never have, the relationship that could have been, the girl she used to be but would never be again. It was all there, always there, beneath the surface.

"You were right, Paul. I destroyed whatever trust there was

between us," —she struggled to swallow and forced the words to come out, no matter how hard it was to do so—"by living a lie, by not telling you the truth, by thinking that you didn't need to know."

The way the lines of his mouth tightened, she knew.

That's all it took, one small tell, one she knew he tried to hide. It still ate at him, her lie.

Before they'd met, Paul had been engaged and dreamed of having a family, his own family for years, only to find out that his fiancée didn't want children and had chosen to have two abortions without his knowledge. That was a betrayal to him, to his dreams and their future. She knew that going in and yet... yet, she'd hoped her past wouldn't be the dynamite to destroy their future.

She'd been wrong.

"That doesn't matter now. Not anymore." He leaned forward as if to emphasize his words.

Tears she hadn't wanted to shed blurred her vision. "How can you say that? Of course, it matters. I knew I couldn't have children. I knew how important it was for you to have your own natural child. You were right when you accused me of purposely keeping my lie. You were right." And she'd been so wrong. "I thought that you didn't need to know, not right then. One day I would have told you. You would have found out, and I knew that. But—"

"You didn't trust me enough to tell me then. I get it, love. I do. What you went through was so horrific, it wasn't fair of me to expect you to relive that, to go through it all again, just so that I would understand." His voice broke as he squeezed her hand.

She shook her head, in an attempt to push the memories aside, but it didn't work. It never did. The memory of the abortion, of the terror and pain afterward, the voice of the doctor who didn't care that he'd just ruined her life...it was still there.

All of it. A haunting both when awake and when asleep.

"This is my home now." Even she heard the weakness in her voice. But it was true. And she needed to remind herself of it.

"Is it? Honestly? Have you built up such a life that you won't come back with me? For me?"

Lexi shook her head. There was nothing to go back to. She gave up her job. Gave up her flat. Gave up everything in order to rebuild it all here. And she was. Little by little. The shop was open now, and it would only be a matter of time before she built up her reputation here.

"What about your dreams? Of children? I can't give that to you." Those hurtful words he'd said to her that night when her truth had been exposed, still hurt.

They'd been out at a function, something so insignificant now, yet it had been so important then. She'd had a little too much to drink at the after-party, and when one of Paul's colleagues had come up and casually mentioned how amazing adorable their children would be, Lexi had blurted out she couldn't have kids.

"*I lost the ability to have my own children years ago, poor Paul.*" She would have done anything to stop the flow of words from pouring out of her mouth, anything to not have seen the look of dismay, or regret in Paul's gaze. That look haunted her still.

"Then we adopt. Or we don't."

Everything inside her wanted to believe him. She needed to. His words were a balm to her tattered soul, but they weren't enough.

She still could hear the words he'd said as he flung the ring she'd taken off her finger to the ground. *When there is no trust, there is no future. You didn't break my trust—you destroyed it.*

"What we had was a...fairytale, Paul. It wasn't real. You said so yourself. Please," she looked him in the eye, savored the sight of him and burned it into her memory, "let's find a way to move past it—"

"Exactly!" Paul interrupted her. "That's why I came. Because it doesn't matter. I realized that after you'd left. I need you. You are my heart. Everything else doesn't matter, not without you."

"And find a way to make this partnership with Tessa work." She ignored his words, although they tore through her heart.

"You don't mean that." Paul withdrew his hands and sat back. Lexi clutched at her purse and nodded. She had to mean it. She needed to.

"This is my life now. Here. I can make a name for myself."

"You had a name in Paris."

She shook her head. "Not really. I was associated with you and with Jean, who trained me. Here, I can make my own name."

"That's important to you then?" She caught a note of something in his voice, a deceptive calm.

She nodded. *Let him think it was. Let him think that it was all that mattered to her.*

"You're as stubborn as ever, love." He checked his watch and sighed. "This changes things then."

She sat up. "How? What would it change?"

Paul stood up, took another drink of his beer, and emptied it before taking her hand.

"Before we head into dinner, does everyone know about us?"

She shook her head. "No. They're curious, but they don't know about—"

"About our past? I see. Not even your sister?"

He must have read the answer in her face. "Are you that ashamed of me, of our love, that you would hide it?"

"Not ashamed. Destroyed," she admitted. "It's the only way I could move on."

He stared down at her, and the briefest of smiles settled on his lips before he leaned down and gently kissed her.

She didn't move. She couldn't. She breathed it all in—his scent, his taste as his lips moved over hers—and memorized this moment.

He lifted his head, and his tongue snaked out of his lips. "You still taste the same, like chocolate infused with a hint of berry, sweet and intoxicating."

She swallowed, unable to reply. His hand rested on her cheek, and his thumb outlined her lips.

"I learned early in my training that chocolate is a finicky love. You have to be gentle with it, treasure it, and be willing to make mistakes before you make a masterpiece." His voice was husky, his smile soft but his gaze was determined.

"You can't woo me by comparing me to chocolate. That won't work a second time." She lied. It totally did work, and he probably knew that.

He only smiled.

Lexi reached for her purse. "Everyone should be here by now."

He nodded. "You go ahead. I'll catch up in a few minutes." He reached for his phone.

As she headed back towards the entrance, she peeked a glance over her shoulder. He sat back down in the booth, his phone up to his ear. No doubt he called Marc back.

They never did discuss how to handle everything tonight. And what did he mean by saying this changed things? How?

A seed of worry niggled at her heart. Was he getting Marc to change his return flight home?

Had she just ruined everything for Tessa and Ellie?

Chapter Nine

HE WATCHED her walk away from him, and instead of feeling demolished by her rejection, there was a sense of rejuvenation, of excitement.

He should have known it wouldn't be easy.

Nothing about Lexi said easy.

Yes, he might have wooed her successfully at first, but he'd had to fight to keep her, to earn her trust, to see her smile on a regular basis with him. That's what had hurt the most—finding out it had all been a lie, that he'd never fully earned her trust, never really got to know her.

He'd been a fool to let her walk away.

No, that was wrong. He'd walked away.

He'd accepted his ring back and stomped on her heart, wanted—no, needed—her to feel the hurt that he experienced. Twice he'd been burned, twice he'd given his heart to someone who didn't trust him in return...twice he'd been made a fool of.

His pride had been wounded, and he let that cloud everything else.

But no more.

The moment Marc told him she'd left Paris, everything else

that had mattered vanished. He had no idea where she was headed. Neither had Marc. So he'd waited.

He'd searched the Internet for her name, called all his friends and contacts to see whether they knew where she was headed, and came up empty.

Until Ellie.

He had a special gift for Ellie tonight, a way to say thank you. It had been her who let it slip that Lexi was there in Banff.

If Lexi needed to make a name for herself, he understood that. He'd been there, done that. But he didn't get the feeling that she was married to the idea of needing to stay in Banff to do that. Whether she realized it or not, Lexi had earned herself a reputation in Paris as one of the best up-and-coming pastry chefs.

There had to be a way to convince her to come back, or...an idea churned in his head.

He dialed a number on his phone and watched as the woman of his heart walked away from him, knowing that it wouldn't be for long.

Chapter Ten

HER HANDS SHOOK as she walked away from Paul. She should be happy: she'd stood her ground, she'd kept herself in check instead of allowing herself to be swept away by Paul's sweet smile, soft touch, and seductive words.

There was an ache in her soul for him, and she knew there always would be. She was worried she'd ruined things for Tessa, but she could fix that. She had to.

She knew people, others who, although not as gifted as Paul, would jump at the chance to do this—to create a signature brand for Tessa's company and add it to their portfolio.

It might be better all around. She just needed to warn not only Ellie but Sean too.

She headed down the hallway and stood in front of the doors to the Bow Valley Grill, where they had the dinner reservation. She looked around but didn't see anyone, and after a quick check with the front waitstaff, no one had arrived. She wasn't sure she wanted Paul to find her standing there, so she headed out towards the stairs and waited.

Sean was the first to climb the stairs, and he must have caught a look on her face to know things didn't go well.

"So it's damage control mode, is it? Shoot. I was hoping for better news. What happened?"

She shrugged. Honestly, she wasn't sure what had changed Paul's mind, other than her refusal to return to Paris.

"Don't tell me this was all a ruse to get you to go back?"

Her eyes widened in shock. How much did Sean know?

"Oh come on, Lexi. I'm surprised Tessa or Ellie haven't figured it out. The guy had no interest in even listening to Tessa's proposal until Ellie mentioned your name. It was easy to put two and two together, not to mention I did a quick online search and found a few photos of you both together."

Lexi sighed. "I'm sorry, Sean. I really am."

Sean reached for her hands and held them. "Tessa might not be pleased, but we'll deal with it."

She smiled up at him, thankful he didn't ask any probing questions.

"Paul might be a no, but I have enough contacts in Paris that I'm sure I can find someone else."

Sean winked. "That's a girl." He let go of her hands and reached for his phone. "I need to give Tessa and your sister a heads-up, so they're prepared. Give me a second." He turned and stopped.

Ellie, with Tessa and Jude close behind, came up the stairs. But the look on Ellie's face wasn't a very happy one. As if the night couldn't get any worse. Lexi had a feeling she probably saw Sean hold her hands and assumed the worst.

Lovely. Just lovely.

She plastered a warm smile on her face and hoped her sister would see she had nothing to worry about, but unfortunately, Ellie wouldn't look at her.

Instead, she stepped to the side and waited for Tessa to join her. The two spoke quietly to each other before Ellie walked down the stairs.

Oh no. Lexi could only imagine what was going on. No doubt Ellie was convinced something was going on between her and Sean despite what she'd said earlier and headed home to nurse her broken heart.

Lexi rushed after her, ignored Tessa as she called her name, and hurried to catch Ellie before it was too late.

"Wait," she called out, just as Ellie pushed open one of the front doors to the hotel. Thankfully, she stopped and turned.

"It's okay. I promise. I just...need some time, okay?"

Lexi hated that she'd been the cause of the pained look on her sister's face. "It's not what you think. I promise."

Ellie snorted. "Really? 'Cause what I think and what I saw seem to be very similar."

"Remember when I first arrived and was about to meet Sean? You told me two things. He'd loved Tessa forever, and he was a very friendly guy, so don't take anything personal. Remember? And when he hugged me and then kept reaching for my hand, no matter how many times I'd pull away, you kept reminding me he meant no harm. Right?"

Ellie slowly nodded, but Lexi could see the tension in her shoulders lighten.

"That's all that was. I promise."

"But why?"

Lexi knew it was time to be honest, to tell her sister the truth about Paul. And so she did.

She led her over to a plush red bench in front of large ornate windows and told her every little detail about her time in Paris, how she'd met Paul, fallen in love, and then eventually ran away with a broken heart. True to fashion, Ellie went from swooning over the love story to righteous anger over the betrayal from Paul and then to confusion when she told her about their talk upstairs.

"I don't understand. It sounds like the guy is still in love with you. And it's obvious you love him."

"Sometimes you can never go back." Why did it sound like she was trying hard to find any excuse to protect her heart?

"But it doesn't sound like what he wants is to go back to the way things were." Ellie leaned forward and hugged her. "It sounds like you just don't want to get hurt again," she whispered into her ear.

"Do you blame me?" Lexi asked.

Ellie shook her head. "How can I when I'm doing the exact same thing?"

Lexi pondered on that and realized her sister was right. They were both trying to protect their hearts from getting hurt again.

She reached for Ellie's hand and held fast. "At least we've got each other."

Ellie stood up and pulled Lexi along with her. "Sis, I love you, but if I have to spend forever with you, I'll go stir crazy. There's a man upstairs I aim to catch, and to be honest, I'm tired of being afraid to be loved. Aren't you?"

Lexi held back, unsure whether heading back up was the right thing to do.

"I was loved, and I proved I wasn't worth it." There it was—the absolute honest truth of the matter. She self-sabotaged her present and future because of the one simple truth she'd held deep in her soul since a teenager. She wasn't worth it.

Ellie's arms wrapped around her and pulled her tight. It took a few moments before Lexi could reciprocate the hug. She rested her head on her sister's shoulder and let herself be hugged.

"You are worth it, and that man upstairs knows it. Yes, he was a jerk in not seeing it from the beginning, but he does now, and that's what matters, right? That he realized *his* mistake?"

Lexi nodded. Ellie was right.

"But I'm here now. This is where my life is, my home. Not in Paris. It's too late for any second chances." She pulled away and smoothed her dress.

"Okay, okay...so the schematics aren't in your favor. But we'll figure it out."

A loud whistle came from above, and Jude waved his arms at them. He pointed to his watch, indicating they were late.

They made their way to the stairs and began to climb when Ellie's phone rang.

"It's Lauren. Hang on one sec."

Lexi stood there while Ellie answered the phone. Lauren Summers was one of Ellie's best friends from college. She ran the elite travel agency Bella Dia, and from what Lexi understood, they were in the midst of attempting to link both Bella Dia and Decadent Events together.

"Hey, girl, what's up? I was just about to go have dinner with that chocolate guy from Paris." She winked at Lexi, who only shook her head.

Lexi headed up the stairs to give her sister space to chat with her friend and met Tessa and Jude in the hallway. Paul, off to the side, talked with Sean. His arms loose at his side, he gave her a smile. She nodded back and then half turned, so she didn't face him anymore.

Okay, yes, she was still in love with him.

Yes, she was hurt.

Yes, she placed the blame on herself, and yes, she would jump at any second chance offered from him.

But, the reality of their situation was that she now lived in Banff, while his life was in Paris. She wasn't up to the whole long-distance relationship thing. Then there was the whole trust issue...would he really trust her again, or would he always harbor a little bit of doubt?

It was better to keep her distance and guard her heart. It was safer that way.

"Sean filled us in already," Tessa told her.

Lexi winced. "I'm sorry. I know how important this was to you."

Tessa shrugged as Jude placed his arm around her shoulder. "We'll figure it out. We always do."

Lexi watched as the two exchanged a shared glance between them, and she longed for someone to be there, by her side, like them. She knew things hadn't been easy between them. Ellie had told her about their separation. But true love always finds a way, right?

She caught herself wanting to look over her shoulder at Paul.

"Oh my...oh my...Tessa, have I got news or what!" Ellie climbed the stairs, a large smile across her face. "I just spoke to Lauren from Bella Dia and she has a client wanting to get married here next year. I told you this would work for us!"

Tessa's eyes lit up, and she reached across to hug Ellie.

"When you say here, you mean..."

"Here here. This hotel. This location. And in exactly one year. The bride is insistent on the date, but I told Lauren we're her miracle drug. We'll get it done." Ellie stepped to the side and spoke into her phone, and made notes to herself for what they needed to do.

"Oh," she paused, "and get this. The bride then wants to go on a chocolate tour of Europe for their honeymoon and needs a guide." Her gaze twinkled as she looked from Lexi to Tessa and back to Lexi.

"Lauren will handle that, right?" Tessa said.

Ellie shook her head. "Nope. I told her I had the perfect person for that."

Lexi held her hands up. "You did not. Oh no, you did not.

I'm not good at that, Ellie...promise me you didn't give her my name."

"I sure did. And you'd be perfect for it! You could create a one-of-a-kind tour because you know so many people there. Think about it, Lexi. *THINK* about it." The emphasis was quite pronounced, so much so that Tessa's gaze sharpened on her and Ellie.

"Do I need to be worried that I'm about to lose my pastry chef?"

"No."

"Maybe."

Both Ellie and Lexi replied at the same time.

Tessa palmed her forehead. "Let's just get through this dinner, and then we can discuss this over drinks. Okay?"

She turned just as Sean and Paul approached them.

Lexi watched the exchange of pleasantries between them all and didn't say a word. Instead, she thought about Ellie's phone call. *A tour guide. Her?* She was the wrong person for the job. Sure, once upon a time she'd thought about doing that for a career but then she realized she had a gift for baking. Let's not forget those cooking classes she'd attempted once-upon-a-time had been dismal failures, too. She just wasn't good with people, with large crowds. Why would Ellie suggest her? Why?

That's when it hit her. It would give her a way to go back to Paris. Maybe not full-time, but one step at a time. Hope bloomed in her heart. Had her sister just given her a lifeline back to that happy-ever-after she'd always dreamed about?

When Ellie's arm snaked around her waist, Lexi leaned over and kissed her cheek. "You're meddling," she accused.

"I know," Ellie answered. "But you love it."

Lexi caught Paul's gaze and held it. There was something there, something in his gaze that he was trying to say to her.

Once upon a time, they could look at each other in a crowded room and know exactly what the other thought. She missed that. Missed having that connection with him, missed sharing something so intimate with someone who knew her better than anyone else.

And that's when it hit her.

He knew her. Inside and out. And loved her. Still, despite all the ugliness there in her heart, the insecurities, the shame. Loved her and wanted to give their love another chance.

He used to tell her that she was his sweet dream come true...she used to laugh when he said that, not daring to believe him. But now she did. She could see it in his face, in his eyes. In his smile.

She walked towards him, her footsteps slow and steady. Paul remained where he was, waiting for her.

"You play for keeps, don't you?" she said to him. The moment Ellie had said Bella Dia, Lexi knew. It was too coincidental.

"Always."

"Who did you call? The bride or Lauren?"

Paul held out his hand and Lexi took it. "I'm making the bride's cake, but I knew she'd talked with Lauren about coming here. So I just helped to make it happen."

"Helped, my foot." She let go of her inhibitions and fears. "I promised Tessa a year," she said.

"I know."

"And I can't just take time off to visit you whenever I want," she continued.

"I know that too." Paul took her other hand and a warmth spread through her body at his touch.

"And we both said a long time ago that we didn't believe in long-distance relationships."

This time he pulled her close until there was no space left between them.

"But you don't care, do you?"

His reply was to lower his head until their lips barely touched.

"No," he whispered. And then he kissed her.

A note from Steena

Dear Reader;

Thank you for reading Sweet Dreams. I first wrote this book early on in my writing career, when my heart was full of excitement and I had so many stories to tell...which, still sounds like me even now, even after all these years!

Banff, and specifically Banff Springs Hotel, are special to me. Over the years, I've spent Mother's Day, Valentine's Day, just because days there and I hope to one day see one of my daughters get married there (sentimental and a mother's wish...).

I love the idea of second chances, of couples destined to be together but make silly mistakes along the way, of watching them realize they weren't made to be alone...and I love when I can add in my love for chocolate, travel and especially Paris!

Speaking of Paris...if you've ever wanted to join me on a reader trip to Paris...I'd love to have you come with me! Upcoming tours are on my website and I promise to bring you on a trip that feels decadent and delightful at the same time! Check out my website and click on the **LET'S TRAVEL TOGETHER** tab!

I hope you enjoy a sweet life full of chocolate, happiness and peace.

Steena

A LOVE SO
SWEET NOVELLA

sweet
RETURN

STEENA MARIE HOLMES

New York Times Best Selling Author

Sweet Return

Stable. Dependable. Gets things done. Those are three ways to describe Lauren Summers, and she's tired of it.

Why can't she be exciting? Adventurous? Maybe even a little mysterious? She knows why...for one, someone needs to run their family tour company while her sister explores new destinations to add to their tour schedule, and two, she's nursing a love she lost six years ago and is too afraid to step out of her comfort zone.

She's been telling herself that one day she would try something new and that time is now, except while she'd planned a nice weekend away at a resort for massages and mai tai's, she's being whisked away to a mysterious island she's never even heard of. After being pampered with luxury, massages, and the best chocolate a girl could taste, she starts to realize that it's time she left the past behind and moved forward with life, and maybe with love.

What she doesn't know, is that someone from her past has other ideas...

WARNING: This is a SWEET ROMANCE novella full of love, laughter, soul mates and chocolate.

Chapter One

A DELICIOUS BOX of handmade chocolates from one of the best chocolatiers in the world sat on her desk.

They were his latest creation and he wanted her to taste test them for him. Damn that man. Paul Ormand, her friend from her college days and now a world—renowned chocolatier, knew she was trying to lose weight.

He did this on purpose. Women didn't belong on diets, he once told her. They should love their bodies in all forms, and accept for who they are, instead of trying to be someone they weren't.

"A sweet thank-you for all you do, my foot," she muttered to herself. He'd called in a favor a few months ago, and she'd been able to help him.

When he'd asked what he could do to repay the favor, she'd jokingly suggested chocolate but then told him she was still on her diet, and if he sent any, she'd make him pay.

She should have known better.

The tantalizing aroma from the opened box tempted her, and it was all she could do not to try one. The smart thing would be to close the box, put it away in a drawer, and attempt to forget about them.

"Oh, what do you have there?" Melanie, her sister, peered over her shoulder and went to reach for one of the decadent pieces of heaven.

"Hands off." She slapped the offending hand away and glared up at her sister, who smirked and stuck her tongue out at her.

"I do just as much for the man, and he doesn't send me chocolates." Melanie pulled a chair up to Lauren's desk.

"He loves me more," Lauren teased.

"That's only because he met you first."

"Or maybe he still remembers you trying to fool him into thinking you were me?"

Lauren was the oldest of triplets, and despite having the same facial features as both her sisters, Melanie was the only one who had the same body type, or close to it. Jessica, the youngest of the three, could pass for a model.

Melanie shrugged before she reached over and snagged a chocolate despite Lauren's glare.

"Are you or are you not a diet?"

"I am," Lauren grumbled.

"Well then," she popped the chocolate into her mouth, "conshider jist my way of helfing," Melanie said with a full mouth.

Lauren shook her head before she inhaled the decadent smell that came from the box. Somehow she managed to replace the lid and move the box out of reach...but it was difficult.

One chocolate wouldn't hurt, but she'd been so good lately and was down twelve pounds. Just another twenty or so to go, and she'd maybe go swimsuit shopping.

Maybe.

"Have you heard from Jess today?" Melanie licked the

162

chocolate off her fingers before she leaned back in her chair and crossed her legs.

"Not yet." Lauren checked the time. "She said she'll call when she gets to her room tonight."

"What venue was she checking out today?"

Lauren grabbed a notebook from the side of her desk and thumbed through the pages until she found the itinerary she'd written out.

"Today was that surprise day Lexi and Paul asked to have free." She had some ideas where they were headed, hints Paul had given her on the phone.

"And she comes home when, again?" Melanie pulled out her phone.

"Two more days. Haven't you booked her return flight yet?"

Melanie's lips pursed. "No, and I'm starting to get a little worried. Not only is the flight more expensive now, but she hasn't responded to any of my emails or texts in the past few days."

Lauren's chest tightened for a brief moment until she remembered something. "She's using a credit, right? She'll probably just book the return flight at the airport. You got that email when I gave her the return options, right?" When Melanie nodded, Lauren smiled. "Nothing to worry about then."

"We're talking about Jess, right? Our baby sister who tends to leave things to the last minute? The one who misses flights all the time? Who only thinks of herself at the best of times?"

"The same one who is the most adventurous, who can sweet-talk her way out of any situation, and always finds the most amazing deals for us. Yes, that one." Lauren preferred to give Jess the benefit of the doubt. It was easier on her nerves.

Melanie leaned forward. "Do you know for sure she's with Lexi and Paul? For sure, sure? Remember that time she ditched the tour guide, paid him to lie to us, and took off for a week, suntanning on some beach?"

Lauren winced. "Yeah, but the Jennings loved that trip afterward, didn't they? If it hadn't been for her doing that, we never would have found that secluded beach."

Melanie shook her head in disgust, but Lauren attempted to ignore it.

"At least this chocolate tour will be what our happy bride is looking for." Melanie reached for a stack of mail Lauren had dropped into a basket and flipped through it.

Lauren almost groaned. In the five years of operating Bella Dia as an exclusive travel concierge, they'd seen a lot. Their clientele were the elite, the rich, and extremely privileged for the most part. Lauren and her sisters were known for performing miracles for those with high demands.

They currently worked with a bride and her soon-to-be husband: a wedding in Banff, Canada, nestled among the mountains, and then a honeymoon in Europe, where they wanted to take an exclusive and private chocolate tour. But not just any tour, one that was tailored exclusively to them.

That's where Paul and Lexi came in. Paul and Lexi had connections to the best chocolatiers and pastry chefs in Europe, and despite Lexi leaving Paris due to a broken heart, Lauren had worked her magic to bring the two lovers back together.

Lexi was one of her best friends, and she would move heaven and earth to see her back together with Paul, another good friend of hers.

It was a win-win situation. The two were back together, and Lauren had a tour guide for her bride. Now, if she could only ensure the wedding went off without a hitch.

That's where Melanie and Tessa came in.

"Have you heard back from Tessa regarding the guest list issues?"

Melanie tossed some fliers into the garbage. "I have a call scheduled in an hour."

"How many guests are we over?"

"We managed to get Ellen to narrow down her guest list by five. We're still ten over our limit, and the hotel isn't budging."

"So we go to Plan B?" Ellen, the bride, wasn't too accommodating when it came to paring down her guest list. Everyone was crucial to her happiness, it seemed. Which meant if they couldn't get the hotel to overlook the five guests who may not arrive despite being invited, they had to either find a different venue or plan an outdoor wedding on the grounds of the Banff Springs Hotel.

"Plan B it is. You know, when I finally get married, I want a very quiet wedding in Mom and Dad's backyard. No fuss. No drama." Melanie leaned forward, and Lauren noticed an envelope she held in her hands.

"You say that now, but when your big day comes, you can't tell me you won't want to say your vows on the beach of your favorite resort?" She glanced over at Melanie's office, where she had a wall plastered with all the locations they used for their company that she was determined to vacation at. The ones she'd visited all had postcards attached to them.

"For the honeymoon, sure. I know Jess would rather elope, but you want the intimate wedding too, right?"

Lauren shrugged. She'd never really thought much about her own wedding. Six years ago, she'd met her soul mate while on a life-changing trip to Europe, only to come home brokenhearted.

If there was one thing Lauren believed in with her whole heart, it was soul mates. Her parents were the perfect examples of this to her, and she wasn't willing to settle for anything less.

Even if it meant she remained single for the rest of her long and lonely life.

"In Mom and Dad's backyard and have to compete with you? Not on your life," Lauren teased. "We had another inquiry today, did you see it?" Lauren tried to get Melanie off the topic of their own weddings.

The anniversary of when she first met Marc was coming up in a few days, and like every other year, she was feeling a tad bit emotional.

Normally she went away for a few days around this time, to reflect, to remember, but this year with Jess gone, she didn't want to leave Melanie all alone to deal with Ellen.

The thought of Marc and when she'd first met him hit her hard, and she bent down in a pretence to pick up her purse but, in reality, blinked her eyes to stop the tears from being noticeable.

She hated how much it hit her, still, after all this time. The ache in her heart, the memory of his smile, and the way she felt when she'd been in his arms...she only allowed herself to dwell on the memories of that intense love once a year.

"A new one? Can we handle it? I thought we'd discussed taking a month off after Ellen's wedding?" Melanie toyed with the envelope in her hand before she handed it to Lauren.

"If I was to tell you it was one of the biggest stars in Hollywood, would you say no?"

With the envelope in her hands, she fingered the linen paper and knew it was of high quality. There was no return information, just LS embossed in gold lettering. She turned it over in her hands and looked at Melanie.

"Who is this from?"

Melanie shrugged. "You got me. It's your initials though, I think. That L could be a J too...open it up and check."

Lauren set the envelope back down. If it was for Jess, she didn't want to intrude. But there was something familiar about the envelope, something she'd seen somewhere.

She filtered through the various magazines she'd read, and online sites she visited on a regular basis, and that's when it hit her.

On one site's private email group she was in, a travel agent had mentioned a client receiving an envelope similar to what she held in her hand.

"Oh sweet..." She reached for Melanie's hand and held tight. "This is an invite to Eden," she said.

Melanie sat up straight.

Eden was a destination they'd talked about in the quiet morning hours as the place they would go to if they could, as the one location they wouldn't ever share with their clients...it was their nirvana, their heaven...their genie in a bottle.

Invitations to the island were rarely issued, so the fact Lauren held one in her hands was a miracle in itself.

"What did Jess do to get this?" Lauren mumbled. Part of her was amazed that her sister would get the hallowed invite, but then there was another part of her that was jealous...when would it be her turn?

While her sisters traveled the world and fell in and out of love, Lauren was here, in this office, behind this desk, and worked to ensure everyone else's dreams came true but her own.

She reached for the box of chocolates she'd resisted earlier.

Life sucked sometimes.

Chapter Two

Marc paced the room, from one end to the other. Nervous energy coursed through his body.

"If you don't sit down, we're going to leave."

Marc glared at Paul, who sat off in the corner with Lexi. They snuggled together on a large love seat, totally immersed in themselves while he sweated buckets as he waited, no, needed confirmation that everything was in place.

"Why haven't we heard yet? Are you sure it's all going to work out? Why hasn't he—" Marc was in a panic but stopped what he was about to say when he caught the glare coming from Paul.

"It's all taken care of. You need to relax."

Marc sat down on a chair and leaned forward. His elbows rested on knees that bounced.

"You asked, I delivered. My...friend...assured me the invitation would be delivered, today."

Lexi sighed. "And when he says delivered, he means we've already gotten the text that it arrived and Lauren has it. You just need to get ready for your flight and stop worrying."

Marc ran his hands through his already messy hair. His

teeth ground as he swallowed back his frustration. Stop worrying? Like that would happen.

Six years ago, he'd made the biggest mistake of his life and had spent years trying to mask that pain by playing the role of a playboy—a role he played quite well if he were honest.

He'd almost forgotten about her, forgotten why that hole in his heart remained until Lexi showed him a photo.

That's when he knew...fate had given him a second chance at love, and it was out of his hands.

And he was to stop worrying?

"What if she doesn't read the invitation in time? What if she doesn't get on the plane? What if all of this has been for nothing?" He jumped to his feet and paced in a circle, the worry too much for him to handle.

"It's all taken care of," Paul said.

Marc turned. "But how? How have you taken care of it? I need to know. Who is this friend of yours with such pull? How does he even have an island I've never heard of before and we've never been?"

Paul shrugged. "The guy has a lot of money and asked me to keep quiet. And we haven't been because we don't need to. When and if we do, we will." When he turned his attention away from Marc to Lexi and stared into her eyes, Marc almost wanted to gag.

He was happy the two lovebirds were back together. It made his life so much easier. It had been hell to have his two best friends so at odds. Things weren't perfect yet—Lexi refused to move back to Paris—but he knew Paul would wear her down. That or he'd move to Banff, some godforsaken beautiful backwoods town, just to make her happy.

Marc was okay with that, except, Canadian winters, especially when living in a mountain town like Banff, were cold, and he didn't do cold.

"But what's his name? I'd rather not be made to look the fool when I arrive and don't even recognize him." Marc glanced at his watch. He had an hour before he needed to leave for his transatlantic flight.

"Oh, you won't meet him." Paul stood from the couch. "He's an old friend from school and I haven't even seen him in...way too many years. We talk via email or text only. And if anything, you'll hear people refer to the Master, instead of his real name. He's, well, he's a bit eccentric."

Marc slapped his forehead. "He's the dude you've been sending boxes of chocolates to every month? The one in our system labelled Eden Master? I thought that was for accounting, but it's just his name."

Paul smiled. "He loves the chocolate and places it in some of the guests' bedrooms when they first arrive."

"He must love them. It's not every day you grant exclusivity to one of your best-selling products." Marc glanced at his watch again.

"Come on." Paul must have noticed. "Let's get you to the airport."

"Just think, Marc. In a few short hours, you'll see Lauren again." Lexi stepped to his side and reached for his hands. "I just wish I had put two and two together earlier. Imagine, my best friend in the States and my best friend in Paris...I'm so happy for you guys!"

"Don't pop the bubbly, just yet," Marc grumbled. "If she doesn't get on that plane and come to the island, I'm not sure what I'll do."

"Of course you do. You'll go to the States and show up at her office. I'll even take you there myself." Lexi grabbed him in a hug. "Now, stop worrying, you big lug, and grab your luggage."

Marc already had his bag by the front door, so he waited for

Lexi to grab her purse. Paul held the door open and sneaked in a kiss as Lexi passed by him.

"So, the Master, huh?" Seemed like an odd name to be called. "Master of what?"

"Just go with it. It started out as a nickname between him and his pilot and then it just caught on."

"So he's not into any of that kinky sex stuff, right?"

The look on Paul's face said it all.

"Seriously, dude?"

Paul pushed him out the door. "Are you going there to reconnect with Lauren or are you wanting to be introduced to the man in charge? You can't have both."

Marc didn't bother to reply. They both knew the answer to that.

He still couldn't believe it had taken him this long to put two and two together.

Paul had mentioned Lauren numerous times to him in their meetings regarding events that were coming up. At the time, all Marc had known was that Lauren was an old friend and she tended to call in favors here and there for her company. She would always call Paul directly if she had clients coming to Paris, and Marc never thought to ask for more in-depth information about the woman.

Until Paul came home with Lexi in tow, and they showed him pictures.

Before coming back to Paris, they'd flown to the States to meet with Lauren personally to discuss this new venture for Lexi. Apparently, Lauren and Lexi were best friends, which boggled his mind. Paul and Lexi were his best friends, Lauren his soul mate and yet they'd never crossed paths in the past six years.

The moment he'd seen the image of Lexi and Lauren together on a beach, it was as if he'd been punched in the gut.

Lauren, his Lauren, stole his breath away in that image. She'd been beautiful six years ago when they were both too stupid to know better, but now, she was breathtaking.

And the moment he'd seen her, all those emotions he'd bottled away came back with a force that left him reeling.

He'd convinced himself she was married with a family, that she was happy and satisfied, that she'd moved on from him...but she hadn't. And it was that knowledge—she hadn't forgotten him—that forced him to move.

It was Paul's idea to surprise her with a trip to Eden after Lexi confirmed Lauren was a workaholic who never left the office. He found that hard to believe since that wasn't the woman he knew.

When they'd been together, she had a passion for traveling; it was the main reason she'd left him behind—to do what he couldn't. Back then, he'd had to stay close to home, close to his ill parents. They'd made a pact to reunite, to meet up and not let what was happening between them fizzle, but that's exactly what they'd done.

Well, to be fair, that's what he'd done.

The fact they lost touch was all his fault. He'd been the one to get scared. He just hoped he could make it up to her.

Six years wasn't a long time, really. Right?

He'd made the wrong choice back then, but now he had the opportunity to correct it. And she would forgive him; she had to.

At least, he hoped she would.

But, there was one thing he'd learned about Lauren: expect the unexpected.

Chapter Three

EDEN. That hallowed island all covet to visit. And her sister was the one who ended up invited. Her sister.

It makes sense since she's the one who does the most traveling lately, but still...she picked up another piece of chocolate and popped it in her mouth.

Life wasn't fair sometimes. Of all people to get an invitation to Eden and it goes to the one who gets to test out the luxurious life events they offer to their clients. What about the ones who are left behind, sitting at the desks, staring at all the photos their sister posted on social media?

She really shouldn't be upset. She's not. She's jealous, but that was her own fault.

When they started Bella Dia, they'd all agreed upon their own roles. Lauren was the one with the best organizational skills, so it only made sense she stayed in the office and ran the day-to-day schedule.

Melanie was the creative and most business-oriented one, so she handled the contracts, the payments, and other stuff that crept up.

And Jessica, baby Jessica, was the bubbly one with a thirst for adventure that outdrove Lauren's own passion.

Jess hated being in the office: she was happier to travel, visit the sites, and create relationships with the owners, the clients, and everyone else who ended up loving her and signing with them.

Their team dynamic made sense, even if Lauren grumbled about it. She'd made the decision to squash that travel bug. Her sacrifice had been worth it, especially considering where they were compared to where they'd been. They regularly ran a profit in the millions, had the cream of the crop when it came to clients, and were known as *the* travel concierge.

Exactly what they'd set out to accomplish.

Lauren stood, invite in hand, and went to place it in Jessica's inbox on her desk when Melanie stopped her.

"What are you doing?"

"Leaving it for Jess. Why?"

Melanie stood. "You have to open it."

"No, I don't."

"Yes, yes, you do." Melanie came over and grabbed the invite out of her hands. Lauren snatched it back. They played a game of tug-of-war with the invitation until Lauren gave up.

"You have to open it, Lauren," Melanie insisted. She shoved the invite into Lauren's face.

"I'm not opening Jess's invite." She took the paper and set it down in her box, and walked away.

"What if it's time-sensitive? We've both heard the rumors."

Lauren stopped and slowly turned. A sick twist in her stomach forced her to head back to Jess's desk. Rumors were that the invites were for a specific time and date, and that was it. No second chances and no re-invites.

She'd really hate for Jess to miss this chance all because they never opened the invite.

"Okay, we'll open it and then send her a text to let her know when she has to be home by, deal?"

Melanie shrugged. "If she'll even check her messages, but sure."

Lauren reached for her letter opener and carefully slid it along the edge. She didn't want to destroy the envelope. This was something they'd keep, maybe mount on their wall as proof that not only did Eden exist but that Bella Dia was invited.

Melanie leaned over her as she slowly slid out the parchment paper inside and read the words imprinted on the page. She had to read them a few more times before she handed it over to Melanie.

"That says today, right?" She had to have read it wrong. She must have read it wrong. There was no way the elegant and flowy script on that paper said to meet the pilot at their small coastal airport within the hour.

"Lauren, the plane is leaving in forty-five minutes." There was a weird look in Melanie's gaze, and Lauren didn't like it. She'd seen that look far too many times.

"No. No. You are not going to pretend you're Jess and go in her place. You can't." Lauren snatched the invite out of Melanie's fingers.

"They're never going to know," Melanie hedged. A sly smile crept along her face, and she took a step towards Lauren, who promptly took a step backward.

"I'll know. You'll know. Jess will know when she gets back. You can't do it. You just can't." She shook her head and clutched the invite tight to her chest.

Every time one of them attempted to swap places with another, it always ended up in ruins. Always. Although their facial features were similar, their body figures were not. And even though the pilot wouldn't know who was who—Lauren would know.

"Well, of course, I can't. I'm too busy here in the office. But you could."

Everything in Lauren screeched to a halt at her sister's words. She could? Of course, she couldn't. She didn't do that. She never did that.

The last time she'd pretended to be Melanie, she'd got caught red-handed by Melanie's date and felt like a fool. Of course, she wouldn't do it.

"I'm too busy as well." Her chin lifted as if to emphasize her words.

Melanie only laughed at her.

"Chicken."

Lauren's eyes widened. "Am not."

"Are too. You hide behind your desk day in, day out, year after year, and barely live your life the way you used to." Melanie took another step. "You deserve some time away. Relax and enjoy yourself for once. It's Eden. The one place we've always wanted to go...no one will even know you."

Lauren shook her head. "I do, too live my life," she protested. She did. She ran a successful company with her sisters, and she went for long walks along the beach at night.

Okay, so maybe she walked that shoreline alone but still—at least she went. And she volunteered on the weekends when they didn't have any client emergencies at the local retirement home. She had a life. And was quite happy with it.

"Neither one of us is going." Lauren put her foot down.

"What about the pilot?" Melanie asked.

"What about him?"

Melanie reread the invitation. "Says here the pilot will be waiting."

"So?"

"So, we can't just let them sit there, wondering if Jess will ever show up or not."

"Why not?" That's exactly what Lauren had planned to do. The airport was on the other side of town, and she had emails to respond to.

"Seriously, Lauren? What does that say about Bella Dia? At least go out to the airport and explain the situation. Maybe Jess will get re-invited." Melanie leaned against Lauren's desk, folded her arms, and stared at her.

Melanie really expected her to go. Why?

"I'm a little busy today. Why don't you go?"

Melanie grinned. "Sure. I can do that. No promises I'll come straight back, though. A weekend away on an exotic island sounds like—"

"Fine," Lauren interrupted her. "I'll go." She caught the satisfied gleam in her sister's eye. "On second thought, we'll both go." For some reason, she didn't trust Melanie and would rather have her by her side than be left alone to her own devices. Who knows what she'd do while Lauren was out of the office.

"Fine by me." Melanie pulled her car keys out of her pocket, looped them around her finger, and headed towards the main door. "If we leave now, we'll have time to stop for a coffee. The least we can do is buy one for the pilot for his return flight home."

Lauren grabbed her purse, turned off her monitor, and followed after Melanie.

At the door, she stopped and checked to make sure she had the invitation with her before she locked the doors behind them.

She had a feeling they wouldn't be coming back anytime soon.

Chapter Four

A SINGLE CHARTER plane sat on the tarmac with its side door open.

As they drove closer, someone jumped out of the plane and waited on the tarmac.

"See, I told you they would be waiting." Melanie smiled in satisfaction as they pulled up to a stop. Lauren just rolled her eyes.

The whole ride out here, Melanie went on and on about how she couldn't believe someone from Bella Dia actually received an invite and how they shouldn't pass up the opportunity, and Lauren continued to remind her that what she suggested would not happen.

Would not. End of story.

"Why don't you wait here, and I'll take the coffee over and explain everything." Melanie winked at her from the driver's seat.

"Are you kidding me?"

"What?"

Lauren shook her head, knowing full well Melanie knew

exactly what she meant. Her sister would do it. She'd get in that plane and go to the island without any qualms.

"I'll go." She reached for the coffee and pushed open her door.

"Make sure to take your purse." Melanie leaned over and grabbed the handle of her bag, and held it up. Lauren snatched it, flung it over her shoulder, and closed the door. She started across the pavement when Melanie called out to her to come back.

She lifted her gaze to the sky. Lauren pivoted in her heels and marched back to the car, all as she muttered foul words beneath her breath.

"What?"

"You forgot your coffee." Melanie smiled up at her sweetly.

Lauren didn't say a word as her coffee was shoved into her hands. She just turned and walked away, but not before she looked over her shoulder and childishly stuck her tongue out at Melanie.

She caught the grin and fought not to smile back. As much as her sister annoyed her, she loved her and knew they'd laugh about all this on the way back to the office later.

Maybe she'd prove her sister wrong about not living her life and suggest they drive into the city for a girl's night out. Rent a hotel room at the small boutique they both loved, go to dinner at the new French restaurant that recently opened, and watch a new movie in an actual theatre rather than at home.

"You must be Ms. Summers." The pilot walked towards her, a smile on her face, and held out her hand to shake.

Lauren handed her the coffee instead.

"I'm one of them, but not the one you're here for."

"Is that right?" The female pilot looked her up and down and then pulled out a photo from her breast pocket and examined it. "I'm pretty sure this is you." She turned the photo around, and Lauren stared back at herself.

That didn't make sense. The invitation was for Jessica. Not her.

"You're here for Jessica, my younger sister. There's been a mix-up. We're—"

"Triplets. Yep, I know. I'm Joely, your pilot, and we're on a bit of a schedule, so if you wouldn't mind hopping on board, we can get going." Joely turned and held the door to the plane open for her.

"But I...no, there's been a mistake."

"No, ma'am. The Master doesn't make mistakes." Joely took a sip of her coffee. "Now, this is good. Thank you for bringing me one. The owner inside," she pointed to the small office far off in the field, "offered me a cup of what they had, but I swear it was sludge." She wrinkled her nose in disgust. "There's nothing worse than bad coffee."

Lauren took a sip of her own and had to agree. When Jess was in the office, she wasn't allowed near the coffee machine.

Wait. "The Master?" Was that rumor true as well? Apparently, there was this man no one ever saw who ran Eden.

"The one and only. If you've got an issue, he's the one to talk with. Come on, I've got some frozen items in the coolers in the back that will melt if we don't get up in the air." Joely held her hand out to help Lauren up into the plane, and without protesting, Lauren got in. It wasn't until she was inside that she realized what she'd done.

"Wait, I can't go. Can't you just tell him yourself?" She waited until Joely was in the cockpit.

"Nope. No can do. Don't worry. I have a trip back to the mainland in a few days, so I can bring you back home."

A few days?

"I can't wait a few days." She glanced out the window at

Melanie and waved for help. Melanie only waved back, and then Lauren watched in horror as her sister turned the car around and drove away.

"Wait," she called out. She could hardly hear herself over the roar of the engines and had to cover her ears to block out the noise. "This can't be happening," she yelled.

Headphones were shoved at her, and Joely indicated she was to wear them. Lauren put them on and breathed a sigh of relief when the loudness of the plane dimmed.

"Can you hear me okay?" Joely's voice came through the speakers.

Lauren nodded.

"You have the wrong sister." Lauren attempted to make Joely understand, but the woman shook her head.

"Lauren Summer?"

Lauren nodded.

"Then I have the right one."

"But how..." Lauren tried to process this all the while she watched her sister's car fade into the distance. How could this be happening to her? It was all a mistake.

She should have just stuck a return to sender sticker on the invitation and placed it back in the mail. This was ridiculous. She didn't even have a change of clothing with her.

"If you're worried about your clothing, don't be. Your sister packed a bag for you, and it's in the back." Joely smiled at her before she taxied down the runway.

In the back? Her sister? A bag? What? Lauren rubbed her face as she tried to assimilate all of this and then pulled out her phone.

There was a text from Melanie.

Relax. I've got you covered. Go and enjoy some time away. You deserve it. And yes, this trip is meant for you.

Lauren's body shook as the realization of what her sister's words meant.

This had been planned. She was going to the island. To Eden. To the paradise she'd always dreamed of.

Alone.

Her heart sped up until it hurt to breathe, and she knew she was in the midst of a panic attack. She clutched at the armrests until her fingers turned white.

"Close your eyes and count to one hundred." Joely's soothing voice calmed her, and she did as was suggested.

One. Two. Three areyoufreakingkiddingme. Four. Five. Six ohmygodImgoingtodie. Seven. Eight. Nine. Ten. Twenty thisisnotworkingandImgoingtokillMelanie...

"Look, we're up in the air now. Take a deep breath. Your sister didn't tell me you hated flying."

"I don't."

Joely's laughter was soft. "Could have fooled me."

Lauren listened to the woman talk as she told Lauren what to expect on their two-hour flight, how she normally flew from Miami to the island, but since they were only a bit north of Miami, this worked just as well.

As Joely talked, Lauren calmed until she could stare out the window into the crystal-blue waters below and not freak out.

She was going to Eden. To the island. Her. Not Jessica.

A tiny bubble of excitement welled up inside at the idea. The last time she'd actually gone away for a vacation was...well...six years ago when she toured Europe. She'd kind of lost her passion after getting her heart broken. For her, in her head and heart, Europe contained the memories of Marc and a love so pure she knew there would never be another.

Not only that, it carried the weight of a heart decimated by that love, and she'd yet to heal.

Thankfully, Eden wasn't Europe.

Maybe this year, she'd be able to put her memories to rest, say goodbye to the past, and move forward. Maybe this year, she wouldn't mourn a love lost but celebrate something new.

Maybe this year would be the start of an annual vacation where she celebrated a lighter heart full of life and happiness.

Maybe. She just needed to get past this year's anniversary first. The weight of that thought hurt, and a tear trickled down her cheek before she could wipe it away. She rested her head back against the seat and closed her eyes. She didn't want to do this, not here. She was on her first trip in what seemed like forever, and if Eden was everything she anticipated it to be...she wasn't going to ruin this experience with the memories of a broken heart.

Who knows, maybe this trip was the start to healing her heart. Maybe it was time.

Chapter Five

"Wake up, sleepyhead," Joely said.

Lauren rolled her neck, slowly, to get the kink out from sleeping on an angle. When she opened her eyes, she gasped, amazed at the view out the window.

"Pretty awesome, right? It never gets old, trust me." Joely chuckled while Lauren leaned forward to get a better view.

Crystal-clear blue waters lapped against the beach shoreline of Eden, the white-capped waves mesmerizing until Lauren's gaze moved from the exotic beach to the castle more inland.

"Oh my..."

"Yep."

"Is that...that's not—" Lauren wished for a pair of binoculars for a better look.

"A castle? Yep." Joely's voice was full with laughter. "In the flesh, so to speak. Beautiful, isn't it? But that's not where you'll be staying."

Disappointment clouded Lauren's gaze for a brief moment until she saw the water bungalows like in the Maldives she routinely booked for clients.

"I can handle those." She pointed to the white roofs and smiled.

Joely shook her head. "Sorry, you won't be staying there either."

Lauren kept her gaze fixated on the island. If she wasn't staying in that amazing castle, or in those luxurious water bungalows, where was she staying?

Please don't say a tent in the jungle located in the middle of the island. Anything but that. Just the idea of all the bugs set her skin crawling.

The plane angled to the left as they circled around and lowered until they were low enough to the water that Lauren could have jumped out if she'd wanted.

"There." Joely pointed ahead.

If the castle and the bungalows had made her gasp for air, where she would be staying took it away.

She couldn't believe what she was looking at. White cottages led from out over the water, trailed down the sparking white beach, and then inwards.

One cottage stood out from the rest, however. It sat out in the middle of the ocean, on its own little island, and as they neared it, she could see that there were in fact, two cottages on the tiny island with a shared pool between them. A wood deck connected the cottages to the mainland, but Lauren could only imagine the peaceful retreat it must portray.

What she wouldn't give to stay in one of those cottages away from the others. It looked like pure heaven.

She must have sighed loud enough for Joely to hear because the woman chuckled before maneuvering the plane to land in the water and then taxi up to the dock.

Lauren grabbed her bag and jumped out as soon as her door was open. She wobbled a bit on the wooden dock as it swayed beneath her and smiled in thanks as the pilot reached out to steady her.

"So now what?" Lauren looked around her and took it all in: the way the wind played with her hair, the sound of the water as it slapped against the wooden dock beside her yet caressed the sand ahead of her, the chirping of the birds off in the distant trees. But most importantly, she breathed in the air and let it cleanse her lungs.

She was here. Really here. In Eden. And it was nothing like she'd ever imagined it would be. She pinched the inside of her wrist to make sure she wasn't dreaming.

"Now, you wait for those Greek gods to come out and escort you to your home away from home. Now, you learn to relax and just soak up Eden. Let it heal you."

Those words, let it heal you, rang in Lauren's ears as Joely jumped back in the plane and taxied it away from the dock.

"Where are you going?" Lauren called out.

"Gotta drop the supplies off. The Master gets a bit cranky without his trail-mix." Joely winked and waved goodbye.

Lauren turned and noticed the men Joely had called Greek gods and had to admit, the girl was right. Even from a distance, the way the men moved...she enjoyed the view. The closer they came, the better it was.

"Ms. Summers, we're glad you were able to make it. I'm Trevor, and this is Tyler." Trevor, the more muscular of the two, which really didn't say much as they both had arms the size of tree trunks, and their pectoral muscles were clearly defined even through their shirts, pointed to Tyler.

Lauren smiled. They were identical twins. Closely cropped dark hair, sea green eyes, and a smile to melt a heart, the only difference she could see between the two were their tattoos that covered their arms.

Tyler held out his arm and waited for Lauren to attempt to wrap her arm around it. She failed miserably.

"If you're ready, we'll escort you to your cabin. Our brother, Leon, is there making sure everything is ready."

"Leon?" Lauren laughed. "Let me guess, younger or older?"

"Middle," both men said at the same time.

"Triplets?"

They nodded. "Dad couldn't think of a name starting in U, so he went with T again," Trevor explained.

"I'm a triplet as well, the oldest. But my parents picked our names out of a hat." Her dad used to tell the story every year at their birthday, how they couldn't agree on names, and so Mom wrote a bunch out that they'd written down and tossed them all in her dad's baseball hat and made their doctor pick out the names.

"Out of a hat, huh? That's got to be the best name story I've heard this week," Tyler said.

"This week?"

They walked down the pier; the guys' flip-flops smacked against the boards while she wore heels that clicked.

"There's a triplet gathering happening up in the main castle. You'll have to check it out if you have time," Tyler explained.

Lauren could only see the tall piers of the castle in the distance.

"Don't worry, one of us will escort you. It's a small island, but it's easy to get lost. One of us will always be close by to make sure everything runs smoothly for you."

Lauren liked the sound of that.

"So, in other words, I can leave everything in your capable hands?" Meaning, for once, she didn't have to plan anything out, prepare anything for anybody or...

"You leave everything up to us. And the Master, of course.

This is your time to relax and enjoy. There's healing here and," Trevor leaned down close to her ear, "your heart needs it."

She glanced up at him, wondering how he knew. Just like Joely.

"Is that why I'm here?" She knew people were only invited to Eden for a reason, or at least, it's what she'd heard. Was she here to heal her broken heart?

She couldn't think of a better way to do that. Not with the Greek gods by her side.

She couldn't stop smiling as they turned the corner and headed towards the large cottage off in the water. She hadn't wanted to hope, but this was the only path out there.

"Is that where I'm staying?" She breathed in deeply and held her breath.

"Only the best. Those were our orders."

The best? Only the best? The exact phrase she used with her clients. Only the best from Bella Dia. Except, for once, instead of ensuring her clients were treated in this fashion, it was her.

She could get used to this.

As she walked between her two Greek gods—and she loved how she thought of them as hers—she wished her sisters were here with her to experience this. They worked just as hard as she did, and she felt a little bit guilty for not being able to share it with them.

But when she saw Leon step out of the door to her cottage, that guilt flew away.

Every once in a while, a girl deserved to be pampered, and now it was her turn.

Thank the good Lord above.

Chapter Six

MARC WAITED on the tarmac for what he assumed was his charter plane to taxi down the runway.

There'd been a text on his phone to let him know his pilot would be late, which was a good thing since his own flight had been behind schedule.

The air sweltered around him and he tugged at his t-shirt, which was already plastered to his chest.

He'd take a Parisian summer over this Miami heat any day.

When the plane stopped, he reached for his bag and jogged the remaining distance between him and the pilot, who'd just stepped down.

He almost did a double take. This small thing was his pilot? Could she even see over the dashboard?

"Dude, if you give me that look one more time, you're not getting in. Got it?" The sprout had her arms crossed over her chest and frowned up at him. He would have smiled, but for some reason, he had a nagging suspicion she was serious.

"Sorry." If he said anything else, it would be too incriminating.

"Hope you weren't waiting too long." She grabbed his bag and hoisted it up into the back of the plane.

"My flight was delayed, so only a few minutes." He stuck out his hand. "I'm Marc."

"Joely." Her grip was firm. "Would love to chitchat, but I need to get fuel and then up in the air. We're behind schedule and there's a storm brewing." She waited for him to climb aboard and then slammed the door behind him.

The whole time they taxied down to get gas and then as they waited in line to depart, Joely had muttered beneath her breath things he was sure he wasn't supposed to have heard. The message was clear—she was in a bad mood—so he waited until they were up in the air before he attempted to strike up a conversation.

"Think we'll beat the storm?" he asked.

Joely sighed. "We'd better. If we'd left twenty minutes later, we might not have. I'd prefer to be on the ground when those clouds break." She pointed towards the almost black clouds off in the distance.

"Will it hit the island?" He didn't anticipate experiencing his first tropical storm on his first night in Eden.

"Not where I'm staying, it won't. And that's all that matters to me. You should be wishing the same, if I were in your shoes."

Marc nodded, not really sure what she meant by that, but something told him not to ask either.

He pulled out a book he'd wanted to read for ages and opened it, but he couldn't focus on the words. Instead, all he thought about was Lauren. She would be there by now. Did she get his box of chocolates? Would she understand the message?

"Oh, before I forget. Here's a message from the big guy." She reached back to hand him a folded note.

All is as planned. You've got a good friend in Paul.

Don't mess it up.

Don't mess it up. What the...seriously?

"I can tell by the look on your face, you're not happy," Joely said. "Don't shoot the messenger, or in this case, the pilot. The Master has a way of—"

"Rubbing people the wrong way?" Marc interrupted her.

Her sigh was more than audible in his ears through the headphones. "He just doesn't mince his words. And he's got a special interest in your girl."

He what? "My girl. You know Lauren?"

"No. But I am the only pilot who flies the guests to the island. Guess who was my guest earlier today?"

Marc hadn't thought of that, and for some reason, the idea left him anxious.

"Was she okay? Did she come willingly? Did she seem excited, worried? Did she have any idea why she was invited?" He paused. "And what do you mean, he's got a special interest in her?" He really didn't like that part.

"Whoa, dude, enough with the questions. You'll find out soon enough. And I didn't mean it the way you think. All I know is that your buddy told him she was special and to make sure she got the royal treatment. Not many get that, and if they do, there's a specific reason." Joely looked back at him and smiled.

Marc hated that smile. It seemed to be the universal look all women gave men when they were keeping a man in the dark about something. He hated it.

He turned away and looked down at the ocean and let his

thoughts drift back to the last day he'd seen Lauren, exactly six years ago to the day, this weekend.

They'd met for breakfast at a local boulangerie down the street from where she was staying and lingered over their baguette and orange juice, not wanting to admit that they would soon be parting ways.

Marc had loved how Lauren would reach across the table, almost without thought, and entwine her fingers with his. She was headed to Belgium, to do a chocolate tour through the small country, and then to Germany before stopping in Tuscany. She promised she would come back to him, to Paris, and she did. But he stood her up.

He'd been a boy in a man's body and made the worst mistake of his life. He only hoped she would understand when he tried to explain it to her.

She'd stolen his heart right from the very beginning, and it wasn't until after she'd left, to complete her traveling, that the idea of a soul mate, of true love, really scared him. He knew what it meant. Knew how it would shape his life and he'd been afraid he'd have no life afterward.

What a fool.

He would never forget the day they'd first met. There'd been an instant connection, a spark that grew quickly into a flame. She'd been standing in the line to go into the Musée d'Orsay and he'd bumped into her after he snuck in to meet his friends.

Throughout the day, they continued to run into each other at various collections until they both sat down on a bench and decided to introduce themselves.

From that moment on, they'd been inseparable, and Marc had fallen hard. She was his everything, and he thought she felt the same way.

It had been six years, and he knew he sounded like a fool,

but there was something still there, deep in his soul, for her. No one else came close to touching him the way she had.

He'd tried to ignore it, played the ladies' man, was seen all over town, in the magazines, on the entertainment channels, and even Lexi had tried to set him up with her friends, but it hadn't mattered. No matter what he'd done, or whom he'd dated...that connection hadn't been there.

No one could compare to Lauren.

Don't mess it up.

Those words irked him. He had no plans to mess it up. He'd go on bended knee to apologize and make things right if he needed to.

Everything was in place, and his girl was about to get swept off her feet, one tiny toe at a time. And he was determined she wasn't going to slip away from him again.

He needed her in his life, even after all this time.

Chapter Seven

AN HOUR HAD PASSED and so far, Lauren hadn't moved from the hammock strung across a corner in the more than spacious room. She was in heaven and wasn't ready to leave, no matter what the urgent knocking from her door meant.

The breeze had picked up from the open windows and with the white curtains blowing with the wind, Lauren was in her happy place. Nothing to distract her but the peace and quiet. She loved it.

Well, nothing but the constant vibration of her phone. She'd been texting Melanie since the moment she arrived.

What are you doing now?

Lauren smiled. She'd taken numerous photos of her room, the ocean, and her hammock and shown them all to her sister.

Lying in the hammock. We need one of these at home.

Get out in the sun, woman!

"Ms. Summers?" There was a knock on the door, but she couldn't get up. Funny how lethargic her body became once she crawled into the hammock. She never wanted to leave.

The door opened, and one of her Greek gods entered. She waved her hand and caught the slight shake to his head.

"I'm sorry to disturb you." Tyler came over to her and smiled down.

"I don't think I can get up." She laughed as she struggled to sit up.

Tyler reached out his hand. "There's a secret to these things, trust me. You want to keep the stool close, swing your legs out, and then tilt."

Lauren reached for his hands and let him pull her out of the hammock. Out of the three brothers, Tyler was the only one who didn't wear a wedding ring. Which was perfectly fine with her.

There'd been a small card resting on her bed earlier that said

The Island Knows What You Need

Well, if the island decided she needed Tyler—then she was fine with it.

"Not sure if you noticed, but there's a storm brewing." Tyler closed all the windows in her cabin. "I need to take you to the mainland for a bit."

Lauren pulled a curtain aside and looked out. "How long will it last?" The sky was almost black, and what she'd thought were soft waves hitting the posts of her cabin were actually large white caps that slammed into a barrier just out a way.

She'd grown up with storms coming off the ocean and knew this didn't look good.

"It should pass us by in a few hours. Enough time for you to have a massage and then dinner."

Her ears perked up at that. "Massage?"

"You're booked in with one of the best."

It had been ages since Lauren had last had a good massage.

> I'm going for a massage!!

"And then dinner is in a little private area where you can stay relaxed. From what I hear, there's even been a special chocolate dessert prepared for you."

> And there'll be chocolate at the end!

Her sister was going to be so jealous by the time her Eden vacation was over.

"Am I alone, or would you be able to join me?" She smiled up at him. "I'd be more than happy to share my chocolate with you."

Amazed at her own boldness, she couldn't keep the blush from showing on her cheeks, so she went into her bedroom area to grab a bag she'd found packed for her on the bed earlier. Inside were flip-flops and a book she'd wanted to read.

It amazed her how well her room had been prepared, especially considering she brought no luggage with her.

When she'd first arrived, she'd found a stack of clothing on the bed and then a closet full of sundresses and cocktail dresses in her size and comfy clothing she couldn't wait to try.

She wasn't sure how long she was staying, but by the look of the outfits that filled her closet, she could stay for a few weeks and not have to do laundry.

Right now, she wore cream pants that hung perfectly over

her slightly rounded hips and thighs and the softest black blouse that hugged her in all the right places.

"Should I change?" she called out.

"All women are the same, aren't they? You look amazing, and it's a massage." Tyler poked his head in her room and grinned. "Just bring your book, and you'll be set to go."

"Are you married?"

"Why do you ask?"

She liked the twinkle in his gaze.

"'Cause you sure know what to say and what not to say," Lauren teased.

Tyler laughed. "I've watched my brothers long enough with their wives to know when to shut up." Lauren grabbed one of the sundresses from the closet and stuffed it in her bag, just in case, and was about to join Tyler when she caught sight of a gold box that sat on the table beside her bed.

She didn't remember seeing that before, and she knew she wouldn't have missed this box for anything.

She knew exactly what this box was.

These were Paul's signature chocolates that were no longer available. She knew they were exclusive to someone else now, but hadn't realized it was for Eden.

She grabbed the box, smiled, and then snapped a photo of it.

Sure enough, there was something written on the box. Paul used to send these to her with simple messages, like smile, laugh, just one word to let her know he was thinking of her.

She missed those packages from him.

But the word written on this box to her didn't make sense. No one, other than her sister, knew she was here. Right?

Dream.

What did that mean? Dream what? Sweet dreams? Dream of a future? What? And why?

"Are you ready?"

Lauren held up the box. "Did you bring this?"

"Are there any chocolates missing?"

Lauren opened the box and held it up for him to see.

"If they're all there, then no, I didn't bring it. You can't trust me around chocolate, I'll warn you now." He winked at her while he approached, his hand out as if to grab the box.

She hid it behind her back and shook her head. "Hands off. I won't be sharing these."

"What? You just said you'd share your chocolate with me! You can't take that back." He pouted before he shook his head. "I can't believe you got a box. Those are pretty special, and only handed out to really special guests."

Lauren nodded. Special didn't adequately describe this box of chocolates.

"My friend is the chocolatier who makes them. They're one-of-a-kind and exclusive. I just didn't realize how exclusive."

"There is a small chocolate shop in the castle where there is a box of those behind lock and key. There was no price, and when I asked about buying one once, I was offered a different box, one that wasn't behind that glass."

Her brows rose at that. What kind of markup did they put on them?

"Oh, don't look like that. They only meant that the Master reserves these and makes them available to purchase extras before they leave. But...if you ever feel like sharing..."

"Hands off, buddy. I'll be savoring these babies for a long time to come." She longed to enjoy a small piece now, but decided to wait until later, when she could really savor the taste.

She placed them in the small fridge in her room and heard Tyler's sigh.

"I really thought you would share at least one," he said as she turned around and then grabbed the bag off her bed.

She laughed at him.

"Not these. You'd have to be...Mr. Perfect for me to give one of these babies up."

"Give me a chance? I'd do just about anything for one of those boxes." Tyler held the door open, and as he did so, a gust of wind blew in. "Come on, let's get you to the mainland while we can."

On the dock, Lauren glanced over at the other cottage that was linked to hers. There was a light on in one of the rooms, and she caught the brief outline of someone as they stood at the window. She had the vague feeling that she was being watched.

"What about them?" she asked Tyler.

She caught sight of a small smile on his face. "Your neighbor? I'm sure you'll meet up with him soon enough. Leon is there with him now."

Him?

"He's alone too?"

Tyler shook his head. "He came to reconnect with his soul mate. It's a touching story, actually."

The world soul mate hit her hard and reminded her what this weekend was really about.

"That's nice." She held on to the bag in her hand as she followed Tyler down the wooden dock and onto the beach. The warm wind blew her hair until it was all tangled, and she had to shield her eyes from the sand as it kicked up.

An enclosed white golf cart waited for them at the end of the dock. Lauren had to stifle her laughter as she watched Tyler try to climb inside. The man was a giant.

"Go ahead and laugh at my expense. Everyone else does too," Tyler muttered.

"What is it you do here?" Lauren asked as they made their

way towards a small path nestled in among the bushes. It was so well hidden that she wouldn't have seen it if it weren't for being in the cart.

"A bit of this and a bit of that. Whatever the Master asks, basically."

"And how long have you and your brothers worked here?"

Tyler shrugged. "A few years now. It's not a bad gig."

Lauren thought about their wives and children. "Do you live here year-round?"

He shook his head. "Some do, but not us. We have a complex on the mainland that we all share. We take shifts here, get weeks off at a time. It's not bad."

"What did you used to do before?" Lauren thought he'd probably been a bodybuilder.

"The army. All of us were. Leon just got out, a couple months ago, whereas Trev and I have been out a few years now."

"It must be nice to have your family back together. I think I would be lost without mine so close."

"Are you close with your sisters?"

Lauren nodded. "So close, we started our own company together. The youngest one does a lot of traveling, though, so I don't see her as much as I would like to."

Tyler stopped the vehicle by a set of doors and hopped out. Before Lauren could unbuckle her seatbelt, he was at her side and held his hand out for her to hold.

"You'll have to make sure you all join us next year for our triplets get-together," he said as they headed inside the main building.

Before Lauren could respond, she took a look around her, and her jaw dropped.

If she'd thought her little cottage was a dream come true, this place was a fairy tale. From the tall ceilings and chandeliers to the warm island pictures that lined the walls, everything about the entrance embraced her as warm and welcoming. She loved it.

If this was the side entrance, she couldn't wait to see what the main entrance looked like.

Tyler led her down a hallway and stopped at a door with an ornate sign that indicated they were entering the spa area.

"This is as far as I go." Tyler held the door open for her and waited for her to walk past him.

"Before I leave, this is for you." Tyler grabbed a box off a side table from inside the room and handed it to her. It was a beautiful gold box wrapped with a soft chocolate brown ribbon. "Don't open it until you are inside, though."

She held it up and jiggled it a little, to see if she could guess what was inside.

"Do you know what it is?" she asked him.

Tyler shook his head. "Not a clue. Whatever it is, I'm sure you'll enjoy it! The Master does love his surprises, so be warned." He gave her a smile and then closed the door behind him.

Surprises? How many more were there?

Today had been all about surprises, and the feeling was a bit overwhelming. Within a space of six hours, she'd been whisked away to a private island she'd always dreamed of visiting, fell asleep in a hammock in the most amazing cottage she'd ever stayed at, found the best chocolates she'd ever tasted beside her bed waiting for her, and was now about to be spoiled for an evening with a massage and private dinner.

Could this evening get any better?

Chapter Eight

SHE SMILED AT HIM.

Well, not at him, but towards him. At least, he thought it was towards him. It could have been directed at the man who stood beside her, but he preferred to think the smile was meant for him.

Except, she didn't know he was there.

He itched to send a text to Paul, to ask for his advice on what to do next, but every time he went to send his message, he would delete it instead. He needed to man up and just do what needed to be done, follow his plan and not freak out. But when he saw her there, steps away from him...everything fell to pieces.

His plan. His goal. His heart.

After six long years of only remembering her smile, to see it again...she took his breath away. He knew he was being sappy, but damn it, he didn't care.

"You're a lucky man," Leon said.

Leon had met him at the dock earlier when he'd landed and was here to bring him inland, thanks to the storm.

"I hope so," Marc said.

"Everything is all set for tonight. She's on her way to a

massage and then will meet you for dinner." Leon slapped him on the back and Marc winced from the impact. Compared to Leon, Marc was a bean pole. His six-foot muscular frame had nothing on Leon, or his brothers, from what he'd seen earlier.

"Thanks for doing that," Marc said.

"Dude, I didn't do anything. I'm just the messenger here." Leon stood by the front door. "And we need to leave. I really don't want to get caught when the rain hits."

Marc followed him out the front door and down the dock.

"Where are we headed, anyways?" he asked.

"It's tacky games night tonight, and I figured you needed something to keep your mind off the time until dinner."

"Games night?"

Leon nodded. "It's fun, and guests usually love it. Tonight it's staff against guests and winners get a fondue party. I'm under strict orders to make sure we win, too."

The look on Leon's face made him laugh. "Strict orders? From who?"

"My pregnant wife. She's been craving chocolate fondue for the past couple days now."

Marc climbed into the golf cart that waited at the end of the dock. He was amazed at how quickly the wind had picked up.

"I thought Joely had said the storm shouldn't hit the island?" Marc complained. He'd hoped to have dinner outside on the dock between both his and Lauren's cottage. There was a nice little area behind them but the storm had kiboshed that idea.

Leon shrugged. "Looks like it's only hitting this side, which is odd since it's not a large island. But...you never know what will happen here."

"What does that mean?" He'd heard that saying a few times now, or something similar.

"The island knows what you need. Don't you feel it? The way it pulses around you? Almost like it's alive."

Marc raised his brows at that. Alive? The island? It was a landmass stuck in the middle of a large body of water. How would it know what he wanted or even needed?

"Don't doubt, man. Don't doubt. I've seen things happen here that wouldn't—couldn't—happen anywhere else. Trust me. The storm is here for a reason."

"It had better be a good one. I had plans that involved dinner and watching the sunset right on that dock behind us." Marc scoffed.

Leon only shook his head. "If tonight doesn't work out better than you originally planned, I'll..."

"Buy me a drink?" Marc guessed.

Leon chuckled. "Sure, if that works." He pulled up to a side entrance of the massive castle and parked the cart. "We'll go in this way, a lot faster and less chance of running into a certain somebody too early." He winked at Marc before he led the way.

His body was a bundle of nerves, but he attempted to keep his cool. It was difficult, though. In a little over an hour, he'd be face to face with Lauren, the girl his heart couldn't let go.

He followed Leon down a hallway and out into a sheltered courtyard, and couldn't get over the amount of people there. For some reason, he'd been under the impression the island wasn't that busy this weekend but he should have known better.

"Crazy, right? With the storm, everyone is coming up to the mainland. Give it another hour or so and you won't be able to grab a seat." Leon led him over to a large table where his other brother and two women—he assumed the wives—all sat.

"Marc, this is Trev, and Tyler..." he glanced around and then shrugged, "will be here shortly."

"He's with Lauren still," Trevor said. He stuck his hand out to Marc. "Good to meet you.

Marc looked from Leon to Trevor and back to Leon and caught the faint look of disapproval in Leon's gaze.

"You've only got a little over an hour, so what do you say we get the games started?" Leon rubbed his hands together and looked about the room. "Ping-pong. Let's go!"

Marc watched as Leon took off and shook his head. Ping-pong? Really?

"Be warned, he's a fanatic when it comes to that ball and paddle," Trevor said.

"How fanatic?" A man and his sport was never to be trifled with. Personally, he preferred rugby.

"Won state championship in high school and got a team started while stationed overseas a few years ago. The group is still going strong."

Marc groaned. "What's with guys and little balls? Give me a big one any day." The moment he said it, he knew it came out wrong. "Rugby, dude. Rugby."

Trevor slapped him on the back before he pushed him along to follow after Leon.

Marc was itching to do anything other than play Ping-pong, but it would probably be a good way to vent some steam, release some energy and waste time until after Lauren's massage.

He checked over his shoulder to see whether Tyler had come in but he didn't see the guy yet. Which worried him. They all knew the reason she was here, right? For him? Which meant, hands off, right?

But the thing was...Lauren didn't know that. A sinking feeling hit him then. What if he were too late?

Maybe the massage had been a bad idea. Maybe he should have been the one to meet her when she first arrived? What had he been thinking? Why had he let Lexi and Paul talk him into spoiling her for a bit before he revealed himself?

How could he have been so stupid?

Chapter Nine

SHE COULDN'T MOVE. She was literally glued to the bed and there was no way on God's green earth she was moving from this spot.

The massage therapist had golden hands and knew all the right spots to work. She couldn't believe how tense and tight she'd been and how amazing she felt right now. She tried to move her legs to the side but they were loose jelly. A giggle escaped before she could stop it.

Maybe she shouldn't have had that extra glass of wine before the massage? She peeked at her fingers and smiled. That wine had been worth it because it meant she now had the prettiest shade of coral pink on both her fingers and toes.

"Do you need some help, ma'am?" There was a knock on the door.

"I can't seem to get up," Lauren called out. She giggled again. She knew how silly she must look but she didn't care.

"This has been the best day of my life in a long, long time." She smiled up at her miracle worker, who only shook her head, helped to adjust the sheet around her body, and then pulled her up to a sitting position.

"Make sure you hydrate a lot before bed, and tomorrow will be just as good."

"Water. Right. I'm sorry we went over the allotted time." Her pretty nails were worth it, though.

"Don't you worry about it. You are my last client of the day and honestly, probably my most fun." Her miracle worker smiled before she stepped back out into the hallway. "Oh, I placed some warmed up towels outside the shower doors for you. Enjoy your shower."

Lauren sat there, hunched over, not really wanting to move any more than she had to, but then her stomach grumbled, and she knew if she didn't eat something soon, she'd pay for it later.

The small plate of cheese she'd munched on earlier with her wine really hadn't cut it, and considering she hadn't had much to eat all day...no wonder the wine went straight to her head.

She hopped off the bed, and the sheet pooled at her feet before she headed into the shower just off the room. The hot water rained down over her relaxed muscles. She leaned up against the tiled walls and let out a long breath.

How was she supposed to get out of there and make it to dinner?

It took a while, but she managed to crawl her way out of the shower and get dressed. She was thankful that the summer dress she'd thrown into the bag fit her properly.

How they managed to find her clothes that fit her hourglass figure was beyond her. She normally had a hard enough time trying to find something to fit her hips and thighs while accommodating her larger-than-preferred chest.

"I hear you're all done." Tyler's voice was on the other side of the door, and Lauren's stomach flip-flopped at his voice. She stuck her feet in her sandals and opened the door, a huge smile on her face.

"That was amazing." She leaned against the wall.

"You look amazing," was all Tyler said. He held out his arm, and she reached for it. "Ready for dinner?"

Her stomach growled loud enough for him to hear.

"I'll take that as a yes."

"I've been looking forward to this meal since you mentioned it." The only question, in her mind, was whether she would be eating alone or with a certain muscular Greek god that could take her mind off what this whole weekend was about.

She preferred option two.

She didn't want to think about Marc. Not anymore. It was time to let him go, time to move past the hope she harbored deep inside.

Who was she kidding?

Despite the sweet smiles, and the feel of his muscular arms beneath her hand, she'd trade this hunk for Marc any day. If the island really knew what she needed, it would have brought Marc to her.

"Why the frown?" Tyler stopped outside a set of white French doors. A warm glow emanated from behind the soft white curtains that covered the glass on the other side.

She shrugged. "No reason, other than this dinner signifies the end of an amazing day."

"What if it wasn't the end, but rather the beginning of something you've always dreamed about?"

Lauren just looked at him, not bothering to respond.

"The island knows what you want and need..."

She laughed. "Then the island should know I'm wanting something chocolate for dessert and then a warm breeze while I lay in the hammock tonight."

"Just wait and see." He leaned down and placed a soft kiss on her cheek. "Leave your heart open, okay?"

Puzzled, Lauren watched Tyler as he walked away from

her. She was really going to have dinner by herself, on this island where supposedly her dreams were to come true? Really?

Whoever planned this day for her forgot one tiny tidbit of information. She hated eating alone. There was nothing worse than being alone at a table surrounded by couples who whispered sweet promises to each other.

She had half a mind to walk away and find her own way down to her cottage for the night when she remembered the promise of chocolate. And the fact she wasn't sure how to navigate the maze Tyler had walked her into.

With a sigh, she turned the knob on the door and pushed it open.

The warm glow in the room surrounded her, the soft music that played danced around her, but it was the sight in front of her, or rather the person, that made her already weak knees give out until she crumpled to the floor in a heap.

Marc was here. He couldn't be. That couldn't be him. Could it?

Whomever it was, he rushed over to her and knelt down.

Neither one said anything. Lauren couldn't. Her mouth had gone dry, and all she could think was why. Why?

"Hello, beautiful," Marc said to her.

Marc. It was really him. She would know his voice anywhere, because it still whispered to her in the middle of the night, even now, after six years of believing she wasn't enough for him.

She smiled and raised her hand to gently stroke his cheek. It was really him.

"I've missed you," Lauren whispered. She swallowed past the lump in her throat and then struggled to get up.

With her hands firmly enclosed in Marc's, he helped her up off the ground, and they both stood there, their hands clasped, small smiles on their faces as they stared at each other.

"I take everything back that I thought about this island. I love it," Lauren said.

Marc's eyes lit up, and he pulled her close. "I can't believe you're here. Really here." His gaze traveled over her face, and she loved the way he appeared to be memorizing everything about her.

It had been six years. She wasn't as young, or as skinny as she had been back then. There were a few wrinkles at the corner of her eyes, and her skin didn't glow like it used to. Did he notice?

"I..." they both said at the same time, stopped, and then said it again before they laughed.

"You go," Lauren said.

Marc shook his head. "No, you."

They were at a stalemate, and Lauren loved it. Happiness flooded her soul, and she couldn't believe he was here, in the flesh. That it was his skin touching hers, his presence that filled her up...him.

Her hungry stomach beat them both as it growled loud enough to fill the room. Lauren winced before she looked behind Marc at the table and noticed the basket of bread there.

"Are you here to have dinner with me?" What a silly question, and yet...she was afraid to take anything for granted right now. It felt like a dream come true, having him here. But not all dreams ended with a happy ending.

"I thought that would be a nice way to end your day, if that's okay?"

She felt a bit tongue-tied. What was she to say? Ask him how he'd been? Why he'd been silent for six years? Why he stood her up and never contacted her? Why he was here, now?

"I'd love that," was all she said.

Marc pulled out a chair for her, and she caught the brief scent of his aftershave. Still smelled the same. When he sat beside her, there was a brief lull between them that carried a sense of awkwardness.

She watched him, as he buttered his bread, poured their wine, and did anything else at the table that would normally be considered mundane.

She memorized the way he moved, the way he held his knife, cocked his head, and even the way he smiled at her. She memorized everything she would need to get her through the next six years.

As much as this seemed like a dream come true, even she knew princesses woke up from their slumber. If they'd ended right there and then, with things being on the surface between them, she could have gone back to her room in a state of bliss, excited about what tomorrow would bring.

But then Marc had to ruin it.

"I couldn't believe it when Lexi showed me a photo of the two of you on the beach."

Lauren almost sputtered the wine she'd just sipped and ended up coughing instead.

"You know Lexi?" she managed to squeak out after her extreme coughing fit.

She asked the question again, despite his nod. It wasn't possible. How could he know her best friend? How?

"I've known her for a few years now. Since she started to date Paul."

Her heart sunk. He knew both her best friends. How, in God's green earth, could they have gone six years and never once mentioned Marc to her?

"They never mentioned me before?"

He shook his head and then shrugged. His posture was suddenly rigid, and he pulled away from her a bit.

It was only a slight tilt, but it spoke volumes.

"I don't understand. They're *my* best friends." Marc heard

the solid emphasis on *my*. "Lauren and I went to school together, and I met Paul during my trip to Europe, after..."

Marc nodded. "After you left me in Paris. I know. He told me all about it."

"Paul told you...when? When did he tell you all about it?"

"Last week."

"Last..." He'd only found out about her last week? She'd talked to Lexi a few times during the week, and there'd been a flurry of text messages between her and Paul yesterday over the wedding cake he was making for her client.

Marc nodded, a somber look in his eyes. "I wish I had known years ago...so close and yet, so far apart."

Lauren let out a haggard breath and felt as if everything inside her was being wrenched apart. Lexi and Paul had been in her life forever. How could Marc's name never come up? How? She shook her head and rubbed her neck as she racked her brain to remember whether he'd ever been mentioned. He must have.

"What is Paul to you?" Maybe they were just passing friends. That would explain it. And she'd never really told Lexi about Marc, never had to. They both nursed their broken hearts in private, knowing there'd been a connection between them but never needing to explore the reason behind it.

"He's my best friend and business partner."

Her head whipped up. "What?" She pushed aside her half-eaten dinner and reached for her glass of wine.

"I know. How have we never crossed paths before? How?" He shook his head but then reached his hand over to touch hers.

She moved hers away.

She wasn't sure how to react, how to respond, or even what to do. This was crazy. Crazy.

There had to be something he wasn't telling her. Something he was hiding from her. She pushed her chair back and guzzled her wine, not taking the time to savor it as it slid down her throat.

"I'm sorry. I mourned you. Mourned you for six years. I thought I'd lost you forever...why didn't you come and meet me?" She reached for the wine bottle; she poured the liquid into her glass and then gulped it back again.

Did she really want to know the answer? Wasn't it better to live in her dream world, with all the scenarios she'd built up for herself?

"I mean, I know your parents were ill," she stared down at her wine and swirled it in the cup, "so I just assumed something happened, and that's why you never showed up." She lifted her gaze, but he stared down at the table. That didn't look good.

She needed to get drunk and fast. Maybe then her mind would be able to process this and stop her heart from breaking apart again.

"You never called me. Never said goodbye." She hiccupped. She wanted to die from embarrassment. This was her tell, or so her sisters said, for when she was upset. "Never explained why," hiccup, "you weren't there when I," hiccup, "returned."

All the tears she'd cried in secret, all the whispered longings, the questions she'd never been able to share with anyone poured out of her, and the only thing she now felt was relief.

Relief to let it all out.

"I've loved you forever." She took a deep breath, calmer now. "I loved you until there was nothing left inside me, and you didn't care. You tossed me aside, like I wasn't worth anything, and moved on."

She wiped at the tears before she pushed her chair back even farther. Her legs wobbled as she stood there, and she was suddenly nervous that she'd fall down again, at his feet.

Oh God. She wanted him to deny it, to give her an explanation that made perfect sense, one she could easily forgive and understand. Like his mom was on her deathbed, or an emergency had come up, and he'd tried to get there, but... all he did was sit there, his gaze downward, as if he were too embarrassed by her reactions.

"I'm sorry," he finally said.

She waited for something else, for an explanation, but he just sat there. And the longer he sat there, the more her ire picked up until she wasn't embarrassed but rather angry with him and his lack of response.

"I'm sorry? That's all you have to say?"

He finally looked up then, and in that moment, she knew, no matter what he said, she would rather have lived with not knowing.

"We were just kids."

Lauren took another drink of her wine and sputtered at that.

"Just kids? It was only six years ago, Marc. I'm almost thirty now. I think I was more than just a kid." If he dared to use that as an excuse...

"I'm sorry. That came out wrong." Marc sighed and ran his fingers through his hair. She could tell he was nervous.

"I made a mistake. One I've regretted every day since."

She swallowed hard. She wanted to stop him, to tell him to stop, but she couldn't. She knew, though, that she would hate everything he was about to tell her. Everything she'd worried about but never wanted to admit.

"You never came, did you?" she said.

He shook his head. "I couldn't."

She almost sighed with relief. He didn't come because his mother was sick. That had to be it.

"I was scared."

"Scared of what?"

"Of our future." He stared at her, a plea in his gaze, and she tried so hard to be understanding.

"What about the stories you told me of your parents? How they were soul mates and how you wanted a love like that. How we could have a love like that. Did you lie to me?"

Marc reached out to her, but she stepped out of his reach.

"I didn't lie. But once you were gone, reality sunk in, and I...I wasn't ready. Lauren, I wasn't ready for what love really meant."

That hit her in the gut, hard. "What did you think it meant? That it would ruin your life?" By the look on his face, that's exactly what he'd thought.

After six years of wondering why he never showed up, never contacted her...now she knew, and it wasn't what her dreams had been made of.

"Reality sucks, sometimes," she whispered. "I've held you up to a high standard. I loved you. Loved you. But I never really knew you, did I?" Her nostrils flared as she struggled not to cry.

She needed to get out of here, away from him. But he stepped towards her and reached out. She smacked his hand away, wishing it had been his face or chest she'd hit instead. "Leave me alone."

She rushed through the door, not caring that she'd just left her heart broken on the floor behind her, and ran down the hall-way. She almost tripped over Tyler, who stood there at the end.

"Whoa, slow down." Tyler's grip on her arms soothed her. She sank into him and let the feel of his arms around her comfort her.

"Can you take me back, please?" Her voice was muffled against his shirt.

"Lauren." Marc called her name.

She raised her head and looked up at Tyler. "Please?" she repeated.

She read the concern in his gaze and breathed a sigh of relief at his nod. He turned them both and went down a short hallway until they exited through a door, down another hallway, and then out into the night.

Lauren tilted her head back as a warm breeze wrapped itself around her.

"Looks like the storm ended, just in time," Tyler said. He led her to a cart, helped her in, and then drove down a pathway. Lauren had no idea where they were, but she knew they were headed toward the water. The sound of the surf crashing upon the sand welcomed her as they pulled up to the wood deck.

Without a word, Tyler helped her out of the cart and walked with her up to the cottage. The lights were on, candles aflame all around the room, and the tears welled up again.

"Are you going to be okay?" Tyler asked.

She nodded, not trusting herself to speak before she shook her head. No, she wasn't going to be okay. She was confused. More than confused. Hurt and even a little angry, but she wasn't sure who to blame.

"Do you...would you like some company?" Tyler asked her.

Lauren let out a small laugh, which turned into a cry. She sat down on the couch and sobbed into her hands. Tyler joined her and pulled her into his arms, giving her refuge while she continued to cry.

Eventually, she sat up and patted at his now-wet chest. She took the tissue he held out to her and wiped her eyes and nose. She wasn't a pretty crier; she knew her face would be all blotchy, her nose swollen, and her eyes bright red, so she attempted to hide her face from him.

Tyler scooted to the edge of the couch and briefly touched her knee. "How about some chocolate?" he asked.

She laughed, and when she realized it sounded like a croak, she laughed again.

"I never did get dessert," she said.

His eyes widened. "We need to fix that, then. Why don't

you go have a hot bath and relax, and I'll make sure you get some of that dessert I heard was being made for you tonight. Okay?"

She pulled her knees up to her chest and nodded.

"Are you going to be okay?" He asked.

She attempted a small smile. "I'll be fine after that chocolate." Chocolate was always the answer, no matter the situation.

"I'll come by in the morning and take you for breakfast, okay?"

"You won't be back?" The minute she asked, she knew she'd been a fool. Of course, he wouldn't be. He wasn't the reason she was here, and it wasn't fair of her to lean on him right now.

"Forget it—silly question." She let out a long sigh. "See you tomorrow." She rubbed her face, sniffled a bit, and rested her head back on the couch while Tyler left.

Now what? What was she supposed to do? Marc was here. HERE. She'd envisioned this night for years, working through scenarios if she ever met him again. Never had she thought of this one.

She jumped up from the couch and headed into the bedroom, where her phone rested on the nightstand. She picked it up and checked to ensure there was a signal. There was one person she wanted to hear from, one person who needed to give her an answer.

Lexi.

Tell me you didn't know.

While she waited for a response, she headed into the bathroom, where a large, two-person claw tub sat. A long soak was exactly what she needed right now.

Thirty minutes later, her phone buzzed.

Give him a chance

Lauren couldn't believe what she read. Lexi had known. She'd known and not said anything.

Give him a chance? Are you kidding me? How could you? You should have told me. Given me a heads-up at least.

I'm sorry.

So am I.

Lauren had no idea what to do now.

He loves you.

Lauren snorted at that.

So much, that he stood me up six years ago and never looked back.

Let him explain. Please.

Explain? What could he possibly say?

No. She thought she'd been in love with a man, but all she'd been in love with was a memory.

That hurt more than anything else, and she had no idea how to move past something like that.

Chapter Ten

He'd paced his cottage all night and waited for the lights in her room to go out. It had taken everything inside him to leave her alone, to not go to her and try to explain.

Last night had been a disaster.

He'd almost been out the door when the light in her room finally went out. He could have kicked himself for chickening out, for not manning up and going after her.

What had he been thinking?

He'd finally sent Paul a text and Lexi her own separate one and realized what an ass he'd been. Give her time, was their advice. But he knew better. He'd known better. She'd already had six years—why had he allowed another minute to go by? Why?

He checked the time and hoped he'd given her more than enough time to get up and get dressed. He wasn't willing to waste another minute without her by his side. He didn't care whether she was angry or sad or...no, he lied. He did care. He cared more than he thought possible.

Watching her run from him last night just about killed him. But to see her in another man's arms destroyed him.

He reached for the bag she'd left behind last night and left his small cottage. The moment he stepped outside, the bright glare from the sun blinded him, and despite lowering his sunglasses, it took a few seconds for him to see that he wasn't alone on the deck.

Lauren was there, outside his door. Waiting for him.

"Hi, neighbor," she said. Her voice was low, a bit hesitant, but it warmed him like the sun couldn't.

He swallowed.

"Hi, back." Hi back? That's what he said? Honestly? He joined her at the railing, where she was half-leaning, and handed her the bag in his hands.

"Thanks." She set the bag down and leaned her elbows on the wood rail to stare out over the ocean.

He couldn't take his gaze off her. She was beautiful. Her dark brown hair shimmered in the sunlight; the length of it rested on her shoulders and curled down around the tops of her arms. She wore a beautiful white sundress with soft pink sandals, and her skin glowed.

She was a goddess, and he so much wanted to kiss her.

He turned and stared out over the water as well, hoping to find something there to hold his attention, but there was nothing. Just...water. So he turned back to her, not caring if she noticed.

"Have you had breakfast?" he asked. They could talk about why she took off last night later. Right now, all he wanted was to spend time with her. He realized last night that he needed to try a different tactic with her.

Six years ago, there had been an instant connection. He needed to prove to her that it was still there. He'd seen it last night between them before everything had fallen apart. He planned to go slow, to show her that he was still the same guy she'd fallen in love with in Paris.

"Not yet. I was...I was going to see if you wanted to join me?" A brief smile kissed her lips, and his heart swelled.

"Funny, I was about to do the same. I figured if this island is as magical as it's made out to be, we should be able to find a proper croissant or baguette somewhere, right?"

Lauren groaned. "I would kill for a Parisian baguette right about now. American bread just isn't the same."

His brow lifted. "Is that right? Well then, let's go find one, shall we?" He held out his hand and caught the way she hesitated before she reached out and placed her hand in his.

"We need to talk—" she began, but he cut her off.

"Breakfast first. We can talk about last night later. There's no rush, okay?" He needed her relaxed, not all tense and apprehensive.

"Okay." Her shoulders relaxed, and when she took in a deep breath and then let it out, he knew there was a chance.

"Let me just put this bag back inside." She glanced down inside the bag and hesitated. "I forgot about this." She pulled out a box with a brown colored bow and held it up. "Tyler gave this to me last night, and I was going to open it after my massage."

Marc stilled...he knew what was in the box, and he wasn't sure if he wanted her to open it right now.

"Oh, I wonder if it's more chocolates." She bit her lip as she played with the brown ribbon. "Although, more chocolates would be a bit of a letdown, especially after getting Paul's gold-boxed chocolates."

"You got one of those?" Who would have given them to her? Paul? The guy who owned the island? What was written on it?

Her face lit up. "I did. And I'm not sharing." Her eyes twinkled, and he was reminded of her love for chocolate. "Unless...any way you could convince Paul to send me more of those boxes?"

Marc took his time answering that. His friendship with Paul was the reason she took off last night.

"I can't even get them." He decided to be honest.

She scrunched up her nose at that, but when her stomach grumbled, she placed the box back in the bag. "I'll worry about this after breakfast."

Marc waited for her to open her cottage door and slip the bag inside.

"How did you know where I was staying?" he asked.

She lifted her shoulder. "I had a hunch after something Tyler said last night."

"What was that?"

She looked as if she were about to answer but then stopped. There was something in her gaze, mischievous but happy. Satisfied even. He knew he could prod but didn't want to. She'd tell him eventually. He hoped.

They walked down the boardwalk and made their way along the beach. More buildings were off in the distance. Not in a rush, Marc made sure his pace was slow to match Lauren's. He asked her a few questions about her flight to the island and whether she'd done any exploring so far.

"I thought maybe today, I would. There was a pamphlet in the room detailing today's activities. Did you know there is a sunken ship somewhere close by?" Lauren said.

"Do you snorkel?" He hoped she said no.

"I love it. You?"

As much as he hated to admit it, he shook his head and gazed out at the water. "I can't swim."

He'd only admitted that to a few people. He loved the beach, the feel of the sand beneath his feet and thoroughly enjoyed visiting the coast during the weekend with Paul and playing a round of beach volleyball. But other than playing around in the water close to the shoreline in France, he never went any farther than his chest.

Paul knew he couldn't swim and made fun of him on a constant basis. Only Lexi knew why.

He expected to see pity or sadness in Lauren's gaze but what he didn't expect was for her to reach out and touch him. She laid her hand on his arm and squeezed.

"Then snorkling is out of the question."

He smiled down at her, thankful for her understanding. That's when it hit him, a memory from when they'd first met.

She'd wanted to go to the top of the Eiffel Tower and had tried to coax him into going up with her. When he'd finally confessed his fear of heights, going to the top of the tower wasn't a goal for her anymore. Just like that. No pouting, no guilt trips. Just acceptance.

Even then, she'd been an angel.

They rounded a corner and came upon what looked like a beach cafe, complete with outdoor tables and umbrellas. To the side was a lounge area with wicker furniture all situated so you could sit and watch the water.

"Let's stop here," Lauren said. She headed to a table, sat down, leaned back, and smiled with contentment. She looked happy, which made him happy. And sappy.

He couldn't believe how sappy he felt. Paul would rib him for sure.

"Do you think they'll have baguettes and hand-squeezed orange juice?" she asked him as he sat down beside her.

"If the island is as magical as I'm told it is, they should."

"Should we test it?" Her eyes twinkled.

"How?" He was game.

"What's something you've craved for breakfast but can never find?"

Marc thought about that. Since his parents' passing, he'd

missed his mom's shirred eggs. She would add homegrown herbs from her window box, some mushroom, ham, and serve it for breakfast on the weekends.

"It would be sweet if they had oeuf cocotte." He wondered whether she would know what that meant.

She cocked her head and stared up at him. "That means shirred egg, right?"

"Oui. Très bon."

He felt as if he'd just won a lifetime of eggs from the way she smiled up at him.

"The last time Jess came home from one of her trips to France, she only spoke French to us for a month." She shook her head.

"She did that because..."

Lauren groaned. "She thought it would add a new component to our company if we could speak in different languages. As much as I hated her for it at the time, it's worked to our advantage over and over. We now all take classes in different languages."

"How many languages can you speak?"

"Not as many as you'd think. French and a bit of German. That's it. I'm to start a new class next month to improve my German. It's a nine-week course, and I promised myself if I got an A, then I would plan a trip there."

"Impressive. German's an easy language to learn. It's been a while since I was last there."

She narrowed her gaze at him. "Don't tell me you're fluent."

His reply was to shrug his shoulder.

"Marc." She sighed. "Is there anything you can't do?"

"I can't speak Korean. Or Japanese. Or Chinese. Or snorkel."

"True. Okay, I can handle that. So you're not perfect. Good

to know." Her cheeks blushed, and she lowered her gaze to the table.

Just then, someone Marc only assumed was the waiter came out and handed them menus. The kid looked like someone who should be on a surfboard and not serving tables.

"Question," Marc asked the guy. "Do you have fresh baguettes, fresh squeezed orange juice and—"

"It's all in the menu, dude."

"Excuse me?" Lauren said. She sat up in her chair and frowned.

"I'm just filling in. I work in the surf shop but something's going on over at the mainland, and I was sent here." The kid shrugged and crossed his arms.

"Do you know what?" Marc asked.

"Nope."

"Okay then." Marc looked over the menu and found exactly what he'd been hoping to find.

"I'll have the Parisian special number five."

"And I'll have the number two," Lauren said.

Marc glanced over down to see what Lauren had ordered and smiled. Two hard boiled eggs, half a baguette with homemade jam, and freshly squeezed orange juice.

Exactly what she'd wanted.

They handed the kid their menus.

"So there may be a little bit of magic after all," Lauren said.

"We'll see if the eggs are as good as my mom's." Marc winked at her.

"How are your parents?"

Marc glanced away. He stared out into the ocean and watched the way the waves gently rolled onto the shore and thought about his mom and how she'd loved the trips to the ocean when he was a child.

"They passed away about a year ago," he said.

"Both of them?"

He nodded and swallowed, hard. "Mom passed away first. She just died in her sleep one night. Dad..." He swallowed again and shifted in his seat. "Dad went shortly after. I think it was too much for him, being alone after so long. He told me his place was with my mom, that he was only half the man he used to be, and a few days later, he was gone."

Lauren leaned forward and grabbed his hand. "I'm so sorry."

Marc nodded but didn't say anything. He still choked up when he thought of it. Of them. Of their love. It was because of his parents that he believed in soul mates and true love and love at first sight. Because he knew it was real.

"They loved each other with a passion I've never seen before. I...I can only hope to love as hard as my father did. Mom was his life." He smiled and stared down into Lauren's eyes. "She was his heart and soul, and he knew it from the moment they first met." He didn't look away, just prayed that she understood what he tried to say.

"I think I would be lost without my parents. I know how important they were to you. I'm sorry."

The silence grew between them at that.

Their server came back out with some cups and a canister of coffee. He set it down and attempted to pour until Lauren reached out and helped him. She steadied the coffee cups and took the cream and sugar from his tray, and set it down on the table.

"Sorry," the guy mumbled under his breath before he headed back into the cafe.

"Poor kid." Lauren poured him a cup of coffee before she filled her own cup. Marc drank his black, but if his memory was right, Lauren needed both sugar and cream in hers.

"Black?" he said, a bit surprised.

226

She brought the cup up close to her mouth and inhaled. "It took me a bit, but it was either drink coffee black or give up chocolate."

"What?"

"A bet between me and Melanie. I lost."

"Do I even dare to ask?" From the look on her face, she didn't seem too bothered to have lost.

She laughed, took a sip of her coffee, and set it down.

"It was silly. She said I couldn't go a week without chocolate, and I said I could do a month."

"You? Give up chocolate? Even I would know that was crazy."

She shrugged. "I don't like being so predictable. But, yeah, kind of silly." She leaned back and sighed. "I've kind of grown to enjoy the taste of coffee now that it's not covered up in cream."

"I wish they were here." Lauren cleared her throat and leaned forward. "Melanie and I have had a long fascination with Eden, and we've often fantasized about what it would be like here. She would love it. The calmness, how serene it is. Although...it might be too tame for her." There was a faraway look in her gaze, and for a moment he felt jealous of her relationship with her sisters. He wanted her focus to be on the here and now, on him.

"Is it for you?" He wanted her to walk away from this with a heart full of memories, and hopefully, love. For him.

"Too tame?" When he nodded, she shook her head. "Not at all. This is exactly what I always dreamed of. The quiet. Listening to the waves, knowing there was no schedule, no appointments, no clients I needed to take care of."

"You take care of a lot of people in your life, don't you?"

She nodded. "That's my job. Bella Dia is...well, it's my life. We all have a role in the company, my sisters and I, but mine is exactly that—taking care of things, for our clients. Ensuring their every need is met. Jessica finds all the amazing locations, Melanie takes care of the practicalities, and I...I take care of my clients." Her shoulders slumped, and she leaned back in her chair. For a moment, Marc caught the look of exhaustion on her face, and he heard the words she didn't say.

"But who takes care of you?" He couldn't help himself. He touched her hand and threaded his fingers through hers.

"I don't really need to be taken care of. I'm okay."

Marc just raised his brows. Even he heard the lackluster in her voice. She needed to be taken care of, and he needed to be the one to do it. He felt it, deep inside.

"Will you let me?" He hadn't meant to ask her. Hadn't meant to say the words out loud. But he did, and now his world rested on her answer.

"Don't answer that." He wasn't sure he could handle knowing. Not yet. It was too early, too soon. There was more to be done, more that he needed to do, to show. There was something there between them, something that went beyond physical attraction, although he could see it in the way she subconsciously leaned towards him while they walked side by side, and, even now, how she was angled towards him. He knew body language, and he could read hers loud and clear.

There was more between them, though. It was in the silence, the peace. He just needed her to realize it, to believe in it. To believe in him and what they have.

He needed to prove to her that they had more than just a memory of love.

Chapter Eleven

WOULD SHE LET HIM? Her heart basically melted the moment he asked. She almost said yes before he stopped her.

He stopped her. Why? Why would he do that? Was he unsure? Did he regret asking?

All morning, all she'd wanted to do was lean into him and wrap her arms around his waist and feel him, his strength. She wanted to have the feel of his arms around her and to know it wasn't all in her memory.

And he'd stopped her. Maybe it was for the best.

Last night, she'd gone to bed with a plan. She'd been pissed. Well, more than a little pissed. But once she calmed down and really thought about what he'd said...she couldn't fault him for being scared six years ago.

She did blame him for how he reacted—standing her up was not okay, but if he asked her to forgive him, she would. It was in the past.

She'd realized last night that she had a choice.

It was obvious he wanted a second chance, so the ball was in her court. She'd held on to the memory of them for so long...was she willing to give it up all because he made a mistake?

Her pride said yes...that he wasn't worth her heart, but her heart...her heart said differently.

Today was a new day. A new chance. And she was going to do everything she could to give whatever they had between them that chance.

She'd thought he wanted the same, except now it didn't sound as if he was too sure.

They ate their breakfast in silence. There was so much she wanted to say, but the words were never there.

Yes, there was a connection between them. The past years seemed to just melt away, but that didn't negate the fact that for years he'd given up on them.

"Answer me one question." She decided to dare it. To bring it up and see what he had to say.

"Anything."

"Why couldn't you tell me how you felt? Why did you think standing me up and then remaining silent for six years was the right thing to do? After all, you had my information."

The look on Marc's face gave her pause. As if he couldn't believe she asked him that.

"You didn't leave me your contacts. I went back, a few days afterward, hoping maybe you'd left a message, but there'd been nothing. I blamed myself. You were probably mad at me for not showing up, for not being there." His voice remained calm, at ease, but the way the veins in his neck stood out and how tight he gripped his fork...he was anything but calm.

"I was," she admitted. She leaned forward and rested her elbow on the table. "So much happened at once. My parents had been in a car accident, and I couldn't stay, then someone stole my phone at the airport so I couldn't get in touch with anyone. But, I'd left you a note at the restaurant we were to meet with my email and even the home number. I'm guessing you didn't get it. "

"You did?"

She nodded.

"You left me a letter. There was nothing there. Not even when I spoke to one of the waiters when I..." The tone in his voice was a mixture of bewilderment and disbelief. Didn't he believe her?

"You went back?"

He nodded. "I realized I'd been a fool and thought that maybe, if you had left me something...that was a sign. But you didn't, or I assumed you didn't..."

"But I did. I swear I did." There was a sick twist in her gut, and she needed to move, to walk, to be anywhere but in this chair.

"Where are you going?" Marc wiped his mouth with the napkin.

Lauren's chest was tight, and she knew she was about to have one of her classic panic attacks when things were out of her control.

"I need to walk." She struggled to breathe in deeply. "I just need to walk." She left him standing there and took off, almost running until she was down by the water. She took off her sandals and looked back to see that Marc spoke with the waiter.

She felt bad for leaving him like that, but she had no choice.

Her thoughts went round and round, like one of those horses on a merry-go-round. She left him a note, which he obviously never got. That would explain why he never wrote her, never contacted her. For years, she'd wondered, but the owner had promised her Marc would get it.

Promised her.

He'd stood her up, but then he'd gone back...that said something. That told her that he'd been able to move past his fear...but it had still been too late. Inside, she was unsettled. She wasn't sure how she was supposed to feel: Angry? Sad? Confused? All of those?

The water lapped the shoreline and caressed her toes. It was warm and felt refreshing, so she stepped farther in until her ankles were submerged. She stood there and watched the way the sun danced along the water, sparkling like diamonds, and hugged herself as Marc stood at her side.

"It almost feels like we were doomed from the start, doesn't it?" She whispered into the soft gentle wind.

"No, love. Not doomed. We just weren't ready."

She shook her head. "The owner promised me you'd get the letter. She promised. I always wondered...thought that maybe you hadn't gotten it, but then I would remember the way you'd talk with the owner, how friendly you were, and that she was a friend of your parents."

It was why she left the note in the first place, confident he'd get it.

One look at him, though confirmed something that niggled at the back of her mind, a comment he'd made out of the blue.

"She never gave it to you, because..."

He turned to her and placed his hands on her shoulders. "Because she knew my mother wouldn't understand my being in love with a foreigner." The way he said it, so sad and forlorn, told her more than she probably wanted to know.

She sighed, and in that release of breath, she let out everything that she'd kept bottled up inside her. All the pain of the past six years, of feeling unloved, neglected, unworthy. The sadness of knowing that what they had wasn't real. The heaviness of wondering whether she'd done something, anything, to cause his silence.

"And if you'd gotten the letter...would you have contacted me? Or would you have left things alone and been a good

French boy who listened to his mother? Would you have kept running?"

"I would have written you. Emailed you. I would have begged for your forgiveness for not being there and for being so foolish. And then I would have done anything and everything to make it work."

She closed her eyes at his words.

"But in the end, we both would have known it couldn't have."

"Could you have left your parents?"

She shook her head. "The accident was rough. Dad was in a coma for weeks. Mom broke both her legs and hip. I couldn't have left them."

"Family is the most important thing in our lives. Without them, we are lost."

Lauren reached her hand up and gently touched his cheek. She stroked his unshaven jawline and memorized every subtle change from what she'd remembered.

"Our hearts would have been broken, no matter what. We both would have chosen our families over our love."

Marc nodded while he stepped towards her. He took the shoes from her hand and threw them back on the beach, and then pulled her close.

"But what we have...it's more than just a memory of a love."

She loved being in his arms. It was everything she'd remembered it to be. But...even though this is what she'd wanted, what she'd hoped would happen, why did it feel wrong? Like it wasn't meant to be?

There was a sadness in her heart that surprised her.

"I'm not sure if it is." She hated the words as she spoke them, but she knew, in her heart, it was the truth.

"If there is one thing that I've learned about myself, it is that my heart is never wrong. Ever. I loved you. I loved everything

233

about you, or what I thought I knew about you. And I held that close. It's what got me through these past six years. The memory of what we had. The memory of our love. And it was enough. More than enough. But, that's all it was—"

"Don't say it." Marc shook his head but wouldn't look her in the eyes.

She ran her fingers over his jawline and then touched his lips.

"It was just a memory." She stood on her tiptoes and kissed him. A gentle touch of her lips against his.

A goodbye.

"It wasn't just a memory. What we had was real," Marc argued.

She stepped out of his arms. "It was real. Then. But for the past six years...it's just been a memory. We're not the same people we were then. We've grown up, changed...but we're still very much apart."

"We don't have to be, though." Marc stuck his hands in his pockets. "You've given up on us, on the idea of us. I can hear it in your voice."

Lauren didn't say anything. What could she say?

"This weekend wasn't meant for us to say goodbye. It was to give us a second chance. Sure, there are obstacles...but I knew the moment Lexi showed me your picture that we'd been given a second chance."

"Don't you think that's a sign, though? That we share best friends, and yet, in all those years, we've never crossed each other's path? Marc, I deal with your company on a regular basis, and we never put two and two together. Doesn't that say something?"

For two heartbeats, there was silence. Lauren could have sworn that time stopped between them as she waited for him to answer.

"It means we weren't ready."

She heard the hope in his voice, the belief, and tears pricked her eyes. She turned from him and stared out over the water. She tilted her head back and stared up into the cloudless sky before she closed her eyes.

"Every year, on the weekend of when I last saw you, I hide away so that I can remember you. Every other day of the year, I've forced myself to move on, to forget you, but once a year, I remember what we had. I remember what it was like to feel loved, to be in your arms, to believe in a future together despite all the odds. I try to recreate our meals. I write you letters...I fall in love with you all over again."

His arms encircled around her, and she leaned back into his chest. She rested her head on his shoulder and breathed in deep, letting this moment envelop her.

"Don't forget about me, please," Marc whispered in her ear.

"I need to let you go, to move on. I can't keep living in the shadows of the past." Her voice broke against her own whispered words, and Marc's arms tightened around her.

"I'm not letting you go," he said. "Ever again."

"But what if I want you to?" It was hard to say the words, to admit them. Her heart broke a little, and the tears flowed down her cheeks. But she couldn't take them back.

Marc laid a kiss on the top of her head and then rested his cheek there.

They stood there, for what seemed like hours, but was probably only minutes. Lauren revealed in each second and knew she would always remember this moment. She would hold it close to her heart and think of how it felt to have his arms around her once more, when she lay in bed at night, alone.

"You are my soul mate, Lauren Summer," Marc whispered. "That will never change. There will never be another in my heart. But if you want to walk away, if you need to say goodbye to me, to us..." his voice faltered, "then I will not stop you."

She turned in his arms then, not believing what he'd just said. She'd thought...she thought he would have fought harder for her. For them. But he wasn't. And she wanted him to. Needed him to...except, wasn't that what she'd said earlier?

"I will always be here. Always. But I will not force you to do anything you are not ready to do. Yet. I've lost six years without you in my life, but I will gladly lose another six if it means you will keep thinking of me, knowing that I haven't walked away." He leaned down and placed a kiss on her forehead, then on her closed eyes, and then on her lips, where he stayed, his lips moving over hers in a silent plea.

"Just promise me you will never forget about me." He breathed the words into her mouth as he laid one final kiss on her lips and then stepped away.

She was so confused. What just happened?

She wiped at the tears that lingered on her cheeks and shook her head, not sure what to say or what to do. So she did the only thing she knew...she ran.

Chapter Twelve

MARC WATCHED Lauren run from him. As difficult as it was for him to stand still, he did it.

He knew this is what she needed to do.

They'd have to work on this habit, though; it wasn't going to go well if she continually ran from him when she was confused.

He moved upwards, away from the water, and sat down in the sand. He wasn't sure how long he would have to wait for her to come back, so he might as well do what he wanted for a bit.

And right now, sitting on the beach, soaking in the sun, was exactly what he wanted.

"Is Eden still the paradise you pictured it to be?" Someone stepped over him and blocked out the sun.

Marc turned. His hand shielded his eyes and he glared up at the man standing before him.

"Mind if I join you?" Leon asked as he sat down beside him. "Saw Lauren running. All okay?"

Marc shrugged. "She's got to work things out, but she'll be back. Hopefully."

"I don't know, man. That's twice she's run from you in a

matter of days. Hours, actually. I'd be a bit worried, if I were in your shoes."

Marc leaned back on his elbows and smiled. "She'll come back." He knew she would. He wasn't too worried. He didn't know why...but there was a sense of...peace about all of this.

"My brothers and I are going to get a game of beach volleyball going. You want in?" Leon pushed himself up to his feet.

There was nothing Marc liked better than a good game of volleyball on the beach, but not today.

"I told her I'd be here, waiting. Don't want to break my promise."

Leon reached his hand down and Marc grabbed hold of it and shook it. "You're a good man. We're all rooting for you," Leon said.

"Even Tyler?"

"Well," Leon grinned, "Tyler's rooting for Lauren. Can't blame the guy either."

Marc laughed as Leon left. No, he couldn't blame the guy at all.

Chapter Thirteen

Lauren could barely see where she was going from the steady stream of tears in her eyes. She was a fool. Again.

Why was the first thing she thought to do was to run? Why? She wasn't a runner—in life or in character—so why did she take off from Marc instead of facing things like a grown woman would do?

Soul mates. The word bloomed in her heart while at the same time planted a seed of fear.

Up ahead she could see some activity. There were tables, chairs, umbrellas, hammocks, a game of volleyball and little cabanas all over the place.

She slowed and wiped her face. She hoped she didn't look like the ugly crying fool she was.

She couldn't believe she ran. Again. He was bound to think her emotionally unstable and he'd be right.

She needed to get a hold of herself and stop reacting when what she should do is live. Live in the moment. Trust her heart, herself. This wasn't like her and if Melanie were here, she'd probably get a stern talking-to and the chocolate back in her room would be hijacked.

She made her way past all the groups that stood there and tried to hide her smile as she saw the obvious triplets in the crowds.

For the umpteenth time, she wished her sisters were here with her. She needed to remember to get the info for this triplet group from Tyler before she left. Wouldn't it be amazing to come back, all three of them, together?

Ahead of her was a small cabana-like building where there were. Back at home, she'd never drink until at least mid-afternoon, but here, she honestly couldn't care less. Maybe it would help her calm down, and soothe her soul.

Maybe.

She couldn't stop her smile as she read over the list on the chalkboard. Jamaican Me Crazy? She needed to get that for Marc. Then she spotted it—Eden's Miracle Cure. That's exactly what she needed—a miracle. And it came with chocolate!

Lauren stood next to a woman who looked at the list as well.

"A chocolate drink?" Lauren said under her breath.

"I know." The woman laughed. "I just ordered it. I mean, how can it be bad?"

Lauren liked how this woman thought. "I know, right?"

She watched as the woman beside her raised her hand to the bartender and asked him to make a second before she turned to Lauren.

"I'm Carissa."

"Lauren."

The two women shook hands, and then grinned gleefully when the bartender set their drinks down in front of them. Tapping glasses in unspoken cheers, they each took a sip.

Lauren sighed. The tension left her body as the smooth, sweet chocolate slid down her throat with a trail of delicious heat in its wake.

"Oh my..." she managed to say while at the same time Carissa muttered, "Thank God."

"That bad?" Lauren set her drink down on the counter.

Carissa shrugged. "I'm here on a platonic vacation with my best friend. Problem is he wants to delete the platonic part and turn this week into forever."

"Wow." At least she wasn't the only one here not finding Eden to be the promised land of paradise right now.

"Yeah."

"And I gather you're not interested in him romantically?"

Carissa took another sip of her drink. "Truthfully, I...well...I mean..."

"Ah. So you are." She took back her earlier thought.

Carissa nodded. "I think I am. But he's never glanced my way once back home in all the years we've been friends. I'm afraid it's the romantic atmosphere of this island that's got him all hot and bothered. What if I give in, then we go home, and he realizes I'm not the woman of his dreams after all?"

"Do you really think that's what will happen?"

"No," Carissa admitted, "I don't."

The thought of love, romance, and going home forced Lauren to reach for her glass and take a gulp of her drink.

"Looks like I'm not the only one freaking out," Carissa said softly.

Lauren gave her a rueful grin. "You're not. Do you believe in soul mates?"

Without giving Carissa a chance to respond, Lauren took another gulp of her drink, and then set it down.

"I do. Or did. Or do."

"Which is it?" Carissa asked.

"I do." Lauren shrugged. She could be honest here. What did it matter? "I'm here because the guy who I believe is my soul mate wants to reconnect."

241

"And that's a bad thing?"

"No, well...maybe?" Lauren shook her head. "I don't know. Honestly, I'm so confused at this point. I mean, I've been in love with this guy for six years, but what if I've only been pining after a memory? Is that even possible? He seems to be too good to be real."

"Is it possible that it is real?"

Lauren quirked her lips and glanced behind her.

"That's what scares me," she admitted. "I came here to say goodbye, but I find myself falling head over heels again, just like before." She finished the last of her drink and pushed the glass forward.

"If my sisters were here, you know what they'd tell me?"

Carissa shook her head, but Lauren could tell she was interested.

"They'd tell me to take a chance. To trust in love."

"Sounds like good advice."

Lauren turned around and rested her elbows on the back of the bar while she looked up into the clear blue sky. She wished they were here, to help her, to give her confidence.

"Tell you what. Pretend I'm one of your sisters. But instead of telling you to trust in love, I'm going to tell you to trust your heart."

Lauren turned her head and smiled at Carissa. She liked her.

"Then I'm going to do the same. Trust your own heart and see what happens." Lauren pushed herself away from the bar. "Hopefully, we'll run into each other again," she said before she walked back to where she'd left Marc.

Trust her heart. Nothing scared her more while exciting her at the same time.

What was her heart telling her?

She thought back to how comfortable she felt in his presence, how all she could think about was Marc's arms around her, how light her heart felt when she'd made the decision late last night to give their love a second chance.

There were so many obstacles, so many reasons this couldn't work, why it wouldn't...but was she willing to go through another year, two, or even another six, wondering what if? What if she'd given it a try? What if it had worked?

She made her way back down the beach and couldn't believe that Marc was still there, where she'd left him.

He must have noticed her approach because, by the time she was even remotely close to him, he was waiting for her.

"Are you done running, love?"

"How long would you have waited for me?" Her heart pounded in her chest, and she wasn't sure whether she could wait for his answer.

"However long you needed." He reached for her hands and pulled her close until there was barely any space left between them.

"I shouldn't have run, again."

He only smiled at her, but his eyes were a brilliant green, and the message in them told her everything she needed to know.

"You live on the other side of the ocean." There were so many obstacles between them.

"I do." He nodded.

"And I don't travel much with my job, so it's not like I could just take off to come and see you."

"I understand. Paul also likes to keep me chained to my desk, running his company for him."

"Long-distance relationships don't always work..." Her voice drifted off as she realized how futile her arguments really were.

"Did you say that to Lexi when she gave you the same argu-

Steena Marie Holmes

ments between her and Paul?" Marc had a teasing glint in his gaze.

She shook her head. "You know I didn't."

"Then give us a chance. That's all I ask. Just a chance." His grip tightened against hers.

"And if it doesn't work?" That was her biggest fear.

He pulled her close. "It will. I haven't waited six years for it not to work."

She gazed into his eyes and knew, in that moment, that she could not only trust her heart, but she could trust him with it.

"Okay," she said.

"Okay?" He sounded surprised.

"I'm willing if you are."

A huge grin spread across his face at her words and he pulled her in tight and held her close.

"I have a surprise for you," he whispered into her ear.

"I like surprises," she said.

"I know." He let go of her and started to walk, pulling her along with him.

"Where are we going?" She almost had to run, which was difficult to do in the sand.

"If I told you, then it wouldn't be a surprise, would it?"

"Can you give me a hint, at least?"

Marc stopped suddenly, and she almost collided with his back. "Do you trust me?"

She nodded.

He turned and waved his arm at one of the brothers who sat in a golf cart up on the path. The brother waved back, and Marc turned to her.

"Let's go." He had a huge smile on his face.

She followed along, unsure of what the plan was, but once they reached the cart, Trevor hopped out so there was room for both her and Marc in the front.

"Everything is set up," Trevor said.

"Thanks. Any special requests?"

Trevor shook his head. "Any will do."

Lauren sat there, confused but before she could ask any questions, Marc started the golf cart and drove.

He reached across and held her hand and that's how they sat, for the next ten minutes, until they drove up to the main door of the castle. The whole trip, as the building loomed ahead, Lauren's mouth dropped and she couldn't believe what she saw.

"It's amazing, isn't it?" Marc helped her out of the cart and they walked up the stone steps that led to the main door.

"Breathtaking," she replied. She couldn't get over the expansive size of the building.

The massive wood door to the castle opened up as they climbed to the top of the stairs and Marc led her inside. She smiled at a staff member who stood there as they passed by.

"Where are we going?"

"Just wait and see."

Lauren barely had time to see all the wondrous sights around her, from the marbled floor to the vases that overflowed with fresh flowers. They stopped in front of a set of elevator doors and Marc pushed the button.

"I need you to close your eyes."

"I'm sorry?"

The boyish grin on Marc's face grew. "Will you close your eyes, please?"

Lauren slowly closed her eyes and heard the ding of doors as they opened. He led her inside and put his arms around her so that she could lean back against him.

"I hope you like my surprise," he whispered in her ear.

"Can I open my eyes now?"

"No." He chuckled.

They stood there and listened to the soft elevator music. Lauren couldn't help but wonder where they were going.

At last the elevator doors opened and Marc led her out and then they walked, and walked. Marc was gentle as he instructed her to climb a few stairs, to watch out for a table or two but the whole time he wouldn't let her open her eyes.

Finally they stopped. A soft breeze billowed around her and caressed her skin.

"Okay, you can open them now."

When she did, she was breathless. They stood high up on a balcony and overlooked the island below. Soft white clouds floated in the distance over the ocean and the trees swayed in the wind.

And Marc stood at her side, taking it all in.

"The heights—are you okay?" She knew he was afraid of heights and couldn't believe he stood there, at the edge of the balcony, with her.

He squeezed her hand and leaned forward, until his elbows rested on the railing. "It's beautiful, isn't it?"

"It's amazing. But..."

He turned and looked at her. "You had wanted to climb to the top of the Eiffel Tower so badly but didn't because I was too afraid to. After you left, I made myself a promise to never to do that to you again...so I faced my fear. It took me awhile, but the next time you come to Paris, I'll climb those stairs with you."

Lauren blinked away tears she hadn't realized gathered in her eyes.

"I...I..." She sighed, unable to form words to describe what she felt. Overwhelmed at the beauty before them, amazed at the strength of the man in front of her, honored that he would do something like that for her...and thrilled that he'd done all this for her.

"I wanted this weekend to be about you. A time where you

felt spoiled and loved. A time when you could relax and let others take care of you rather than you taking care of others. I wanted..." Marc paused and looked out over the view. "I wanted to show you that you deserve all this and so much more."

He wiped the tears that fell along her skin and then bent down to kiss her. It was soft, full of promise and love, and it was enough. Enough for her, for her heart.

"I have one more surprise, when you are ready to leave this gorgeous view."

Lauren laughed. "I'm not sure I'll ever want to leave this. It's breathtaking."

Marc rolled his eyes. "What if I said we could come back and have dinner here, on the balcony, and watch the sun set?"

"That would be perfect." It sounded amazing and very romantic.

"Good." He bent down and kissed her again. "We need to go back to our rooms. That box you were given last night— you're going to need it for my next surprise."

Chapter Fourteen

FORGET the hammocks and the massages and all the amazing clothes in her closet.

Forget even the fact that this whole weekend was all because of Marc.

This moment was something she would never forget.

Her. Marc. Hands covered in chocolate.

Thank goodness she'd changed before coming. Marc wouldn't let her open the box from last night until almost the last second.

Inside the box was a brown apron with an adorable chocolate saying embroidered on it.

All you need is love, but a little chocolate now and then doesn't hurt.

She loved it.

He'd arranged a private chocolate-making afternoon with the island's own private chocolatier.

"I still can't believe Paul gave his best-selling chocolates to this Master dude as exclusives when he's got his own chocolatier on the island," Marc grumbled as he poured his chocolate into small molds.

"I can't believe I've got two of those boxes now in my room."

Marc's head lifted. "Pardon?"

"I've got two boxes of those chocolates in my room," she repeated.

"Well, that little..." Marc's lips thinned and he shook his head.

"Let me guess." Lauren tapped her mold tray to get rid of any little bubbles. "You didn't get any."

She smiled and knew she'd need to thank Paul when she got back home.

"Will you share?" There was a hopeful note in Marc's voice.

"Um, hello? You work for the guy. Can't you get your own?"

"Trust me, I've tried. Paul hand-makes each box himself before he seals them and gets me to print a shipping label. I don't even get the throwaways."

"Paul Ormand is a master all on his own," their chocolatier said as he cleaned up the workspace. "I had the opportunity to watch him once...it's why I am in this profession today."

Marc took both his and her trays to the fridge section and set them inside. "Any way you can get your hands on one of his gold boxes?"

"Oh, leave him alone, Marc. I happen to have a box that's meant for the both of us anyway." She gave him a wink before she headed to the sink to wash her hands. As she watched the chocolate melt away under the hot water, she thought about the box she'd found on her bedside table earlier.

It was the message written on it, specifically, that made her smile.

Share

After an afternoon of surprises and laughter, while they created their own chocolates, Lauren had no problem sharing that box of chocolates with Marc.

Lauren wasn't sure how much time she had left on the island, but she wasn't sure she even wanted to leave. This was the perfect place for her and Marc to reconnect, to get to know each other all over again, and to build something that could last.

Last a lifetime.

Wouldn't that be nice? She knew it would take some work—okay, it would take a lot of work—but it would be worth it. She'd rather try to build something with him over spending another month, week, or even day without him in her life.

It was amazing really. They'd met six years ago and over a week, they knew they had something special. Something so special that it was like a seed, fermented in their heart, and waited for the right moment to sprout and bloom.

Arms wrapped around her waist and she smiled.

"So you'll share, huh?" Marc placed a small kiss on her cheek.

"I might," she gave a little shrug, "if you're nice."

"We made chocolate together, we're about to have dinner watching the sunset, and we can sit in front of the fire tonight making s'mores with the chocolate bars we made today. Isn't that nice enough?" Marc nuzzled the side of her neck and tickled her.

"And to think I almost didn't come."

"What?"

"When the invitation arrived, I thought it was meant for Jessica. I told Joely that the invitation needed to be returned."

"Your sister knew, though."

"I still can't believe you set this all up."

"I had some help. We have some great friends who believe in the power of love."

Lauren smiled. "I'm so happy they're back together. Their's is a love meant to last a lifetime."

"They're not the only one." Marc turned her around and kissed her with a passion she knew she'd never forget.

A Note From Steena...

Dear Reader;

Thank you for reading Sweet Return.

The main idea for this story came from a series I co-wrote with some other amazing authors - Island of Eden series. That book was a lot 'steamier' than this one...but I like this sweet romance, don't you?

Feels like I have a thing for Paris and chocolate...those seem to be a theme entwined throughout this series. I think that's because when I first wrote the first book - Sweet Memories, I'd been planning my first trip to Paris, and when I wrote Sweet Dreams, I'd just returned!

I still have that passion for the city of love - it's probably why I love doing my Sweet Tours there with my amazing readers. I hope one day you'll join me!

Upcoming tours are on my website and I promise to bring you on a trip that feels decadent and delightful at the same time! Check out my website and click on the **LET'S TRAVEL TOGETHER** tab!

I hope you enjoy a sweet life full of chocolate, happiness and peace.

Ps...turn the page for the first chapter of Sweet Retreat, the next book in the series!

Steena

A LOVE SO SWEET
NOVELLA

sweet
RETREAT

STEENA MARIE HOLMES
New York Times Best Selling Author

Sweet Retreat

Must love long walks, fresh coffee, romance, and know how to schedule a day planner. That wasn't asking too much when it came to dating, was it?

Kerrie was done with swiping right, trying to find love through apps, and always ending the first date early. Where had all the good men gone?

After being gifted a weekend in a mountain chalet as a bonus for winning a recent case for her firm, the only plans Kerrie has is to soak in a hot tub, get a massage and eat some delicious Canadian fudge. So why did she let her best friend set her up with a blind date?

Mr. Mountain Man is everything she'd ever wanted except for one thing: he's opinionated and difficult and yet somehow seems to know not only all her desires but all her needs too.

Can Ms. Sophistication fall in love with Mr. Mountain Man? They live in two different worlds, or do they?

WARNING: This is a SWEET ROMANCE novella full of love, chocolate and a little bit of passion.

Chapter One

THE IDYLLIC SCENE on the flyer of a rustic cabin nestled at the foot of the Rocky Mountains promised a weekend Kerrie had needed for a very, very long time.

Fingers crossed. After the hell she'd just gone through to get to where she was today, she needed — no, deserved this trip to a five star resort while seeing if her dreams would come true.

The partners at her firm could have given this trip to any other lawyer in her firm, but they gave it to her...and she was going to enjoy every single moment of it too.

She might even bring home some Canadian maple syrup for the rest of the team.

So why, for a trip that was so perfect and needed, did it send shivers of anxiety through her body?

I'm not sure this is a good idea." Kerrie sat down in the plush chair, shucked off her heels, and dug her toes into the fluffy carpet.

"Cold feet?" Sandra Mark, Kerrie's best friend, sitting in the seat facing her, leaned back and crossed her slender legs.

"No..." This was so out of character for her. When she called the receptionist an hour ago and explained why she had to see

Sandra immediately, she'd almost had a panic attack. She'd totally forgotten that Sandra was about to leave for the weekend as well.

"Then what's the problem?" The corner of Sandra's mouth lifted as she folded her hands together on her lap. There were drawbacks to having a therapist for a best friend.

"Is this the right thing to do? It's so--" Kerrie struggled to admit what she was afraid of.

"Not part of your plan?"

Kerrie nodded her head. She was a stickler for plans. Without them, she wasn't in control. And being in control was necessary.

By the time she was forty years old, not only did she want to be named partner in the firm, but she wanted to buy a little cabin in the mountains. A place for her to escape to.

She also wanted a husband to escape with, but that wasn't about to happen. Her life wasn't made for marriage or children. She was okay with that.

What she wasn't okay with was deviating from her plan.

"Kerrie, it's okay to go outside the plan every so often." Sandra leaned forward. "We've already discussed this. You've weighed all the pros and cons. You're going away for a weekend to a resort in the Canadian Rockies. Relax. Enjoy yourself. Besides, everything's already arranged, and you can't back out now." Sandra's eyes twinkled as she pulled out her notebook and started to write.

"Who says I can't?" She crossed her arms in defiance but then dropped her head back and sighed. "I can't believe I let you talk me into this. I'm going there to relax, focus and recharge. I don't need to go on a date, especially in a town where there's no backup for me in case anything goes wrong?"

She turned the pamphlet over. The trip had been set up by a tour company called Bella Dia, and apparently, every woman in her firm was insanely jealous she'd won the trip and not them.

This company was known for creating one-of-a-kind trips that were exclusive and costly...maybe she should give it to Ashley, her paralegal, instead?

"This isn't like me. You know that. I'm a disaster when it comes to dating. You know how many times I've been told I'm too cold for love? I should just give up."

"You're not a disaster, nor are you too cold. You just haven't found the right man." Sandra says. She glances at the clock, and her lips turn into a slight frown. "You're going, there's no ifs, ands, or buts."

"No, I do have a but," Kerrie lifted up a finger. "What if he's into kink or is a member of a cult located high in the mountains and kidnaps me?" Kerrie leaned forward in her chair. "Who's going to rescue me if I need help?"

Sandra shook her head. "A cult? Seriously?"

Kerrie shrugged. "Don't you remember that one case from a few years ago...it could happen."

"You're forgetting I know the guy. He's...basically family. If he's into kink, I'd be very surprised, and I know for a fact he doesn't belong to a cult. He was burned by his ex-wife and wants nothing to do with relationships, commitment, or anything else that could hurt him. Besides, he's lonely. He needs this just as much as you do." Sandra glanced at her watch and sighed. "I'll call Tessa at her bakery. Why don't you stop there first. Maybe pick up some sweets or chocolates she gets delivered from Paris and give her the interrogation. She knows him too."

"Bakery? What's it called?" Kerrie perked up.

Sandra shrugged. "Decadent Treats or something...I don't know. It's basically new. She runs an event planning company called Decadent Events, and this is an add-on to her company.

Knowing Tessa, it will rival anything you can find here in the city. Their baker is from Paris."

"I'll stop at the bakery, but I'm not so sure about this guy." Kerrie frowned.

Sandra leaned forward in her chair. "No wonder you're still single. You can't keep running away like this. Go out for dinner, is that too much to ask? It's not like you need to sleep with him or anything. Besides, I think you'll really like him." A frown marred Sandra's face as she rose from her seat. "Kerrie, honey, you need to relax. Go buy that cabin so we can spend Christmas up there together as we'd planned. Just enjoy yourself for once. Please."

Kerrie grabbed her purse and stood. "But San--"

Sandra shook her head. "No. You are not getting out of this. Sorry, but as your best friend, I'm declaring a coup on your inhibitions. This is what you need, Kerrie: a weekend that is for you. One hundred percent. Find your log cabin where you can escape and write your story. Come back a rejuvenated woman. Go out for dinner with a man who will leave you breathless."

Kerrie closed her eyes and took a deep breath. Her best friend was right. This was exactly what she needed. A weekend where it was all about her and not about the firm. Finding a place where she could escape to and write that novel she's always wanted to write.

Any hesitation she'd felt at walking out that door and heading to the airport evaporated. This was the first vacation in a long time that wasn't work-related. She needed to stop being so scared of stepping outside of the lines and learn to enjoy life.

Except, Kerrie was a black-and-white type of girl. She knew where the lines were drawn and never stepped outside them unless it would advance her goals. This wasn't a line she'd drawn, however. It wasn't even one she could see. And that scared the living daylights out of her.

Chapter Two

DYLAN READ the email for the umpteenth time.

This woman had serious control issues.

What did Sandra think sending him on a blind date with her psychotic best friend?

It was one thing to offer to show her around town, he did that all the time with clients, but to take her out for dinner, a dinner that was so obviously a date? Did she think he was so blind he didn't see what she was doing?

This was a setup, pure and simple.

Although, when it came to Sandra, he shouldn't be surprised. She had set him up on a blind date with his ex-wife. Look how that all turned out.

No thanks.

He was tired of his friends thinking there was something wrong with him. His life wasn't lacking. He was perfectly happy, thank-you-very-much. He didn't have time for this.

He looked at the requests Sandra had in her email.

Woo her. Make her feel sexy and wanted. Keep his identity a secret until the last minute. Utter a specific phrase to let her know who he was after he bought her a drink.

What did this woman think?

Him, of all people Andrea knew, did not need a list of instructions on how to meet a woman.

And what type of person was this Kerrie who needed a list like this?

Control freak. Doesn't know how to relax. Needs to be swept off her feet. Sandra had added to the email.

Swept off her feet. A smile crossed Dylan's face. Hmm... maybe this could be interesting.

The more he thought on it, the more the idea held a specific appeal. He did owe Sandra one, and with this ask, they could consider their score settled.

Fine. He'd do it. He knew exactly what he was going to do.

What this woman needed was a night where someone else was in control.

Dylan threw the list of instructions down on his kitchen table and shoved his chair back. She wanted to be wooed. She wanted to feel beautiful - every woman wanted that. He could do that.

She didn't want to know who he was until the very last minute. Fine. He memorized the phrase he was to utter after he bought her a drink, even though he thought it was the silliest thing he'd ever heard.

At the end of her email, Sandra added a little tidbit she thought he might be interested in.

Her idyllic life would be living in a log cabin writing romance novels.

Log cabin and romance novels, huh? For some odd reason, Dylan got the feeling Sandra was leaving a heck of a lot out.

What does a hotshot female lawyer whose last boyfriend was over a decade ago know about romance?

She obviously dreamed about being swept off her feet and finding the love of her life. So she couldn't be all that bad. Right?

He was about to find out. First, he had a cabin to finish building.

A smile crossed Dylan's face.

He knew exactly what he was going to do.

Chapter Three

IF EVER THERE had been a perfect day, this would have been it. She found the log cabin of her dreams.

A recent show home built by a local designer, it was a two-story log house nestled at the foot of Cascade Mountain outside of Banff. She'd fallen in love immediately.

With the open concept of a loft as a bedroom, Kerrie knew this would be the perfect place for her to escape and write her novel.

And the town was amazing. The images on the pamphlet were nothing compared to the actual view.

A small mountain town full of promise.

Her favorite part of the day was walking down the main street, a cup of hot chocolate in her hands, and having a mountain right in front of her. Literally. And the shops. Who would have thought a year-round Christmas store would hold so much appeal?

Her favorite was the little chocolate shop nestled on a side street she almost missed. The one Sandra mentioned. Sweet Treats.

She loved not only the name of the bakery but everything

inside the shop too. The macarons and chocolate truffles had sealed the deal for her. Her little mini fridge up in her room was full of all the decadent treats she'd found.

She hadn't met Tessa, Sandra's friend, but she had been introduced to Lexi, the one who made all the delicious treats. Lexi had a note for her from Tessa, and it contained two sentences.

He's a good guy with a broken heart. Treat him like gold - please.

Lexi told her the guy was a regular in the shop, and that he had a weakness for her french macarons, so Kerrie bought a box for him as a thank-you gift.

Unfortunately, it had been the last box available, but Lexi had a few single cookies left over that Kerrie snagged. They were amazing.

In fact, everything about this town was amazing.

Kerrie leaned back in her chair and smiled. From the moment she stepped off the plane and drove toward the mountains, she knew she was home.

And finding her log cabin? That confirmed the feeling.

Coming here on weekends might prove too difficult. What if she were to live here full-time?

"Excuse me, miss?"

Kerrie looked up at the server from the chalet restaurant holding out a glass of white wine.

"The gentleman over at the bar asked me to bring this to you."

A warm flush burned across Kerrie's cheeks as she took the offered wine. The man at the bar smiled at her. She smiled back before turning her attention to the fire.

Was that him? With his broad shoulders and dark hair, she wouldn't mind if it was. But he was too early.

Her hand shook so hard the wine sloshed around in the glass. Kerrie took a sip and willed herself to relax. She counted to five as she enjoyed the taste of the liquid gold in her mouth.

Feeling a tad more courageous, she half turned in her chair and was about to wave at the man, but he'd already turned his back and was talking to someone else.

Her face burned as she realized she'd almost made a fool of herself.

Of course, he wouldn't be here yet. They weren't to meet until seven.

Kerrie swallowed back a groan. Why on earth did she allow Sandra to talk her into this? She didn't need a man in her life, in fact, that was the last thing she needed.

Who was she kidding? She'd already made a fool of herself. She couldn't move out here. That was totally out of character and not part of her plan.

She needed to stop indulging in fantasies and concentrate on her goals. The log cabin was perfect for a weekend getaway and for holidays. Now she'd have no excuse not to take them.

Moving here was impulsive.

She'd be stupid to jump ship now all because she fell in love with a town and a log cabin. Kerrie shook her head. No. Impulse decisions led to poor futures.

She needed to think about this. Weigh the pros and cons. It would mean leaving her old life behind and starting new. Fresh.

The thought scared her...which wasn't much of a surprise. Kerrie glanced at her watch. There was still plenty of time to cancel her dinner date, soak in a hot bath, and head home tomorrow.

The log cabin could wait.

Kerrie pulled out her phone to send Sandra a text, only to find one already waiting for her.

> Don't even think about asking me to cancel your date. Have fun. Relax and enjoy.
>
> And yes, you are making the right decision.

Kerrie closed her eyes after reading the message. Okay. Maybe Sandra was right. She had an hour before her mysterious date would appear. Plenty of time to relax. Have some wine. Look through a magazine or two. She would do this.

Oh my god. She couldn't believe she was doing this.

Kerrie pursed her lips. No, it was time to stop lying to herself. She couldn't be talked into anything she didn't want to do.

But it had to be on her terms.

Was it so wrong to want to feel wanted? To be desired? To hope that her date would be slightly interested in her?

She didn't want it to be awkward or even forced. If he followed her steps, then at least he'd be able to walk away if that's what he wanted without her knowing it was him.

No harm, no foul. Right?

As long as he didn't utter her phrase.

For years she'd put romance, falling in love, and dreams of the future in a box that was sealed shut and tied with a bow, then locked away in a safe hidden in the farther corner of her heart.

It was better that way. She'd refused to be one of those, in her career, who slept their way to the top, which meant she hadn't had a relationship or even been on a date in forever.

She never knew who she could trust, and the only men she ever met were lawyers or clients.

Sure, she had offers. With her looks and smarts, the men she worked with weren't stupid. But she knew too many colleagues with ruined careers because they let their hearts get in the way of their goals.

Not her.

Kerrie set the glass of wine down on the table coffee table beside her and picked up the brochure she'd taken from the show home. It shared more information about the builder.

While the handsome realtor she'd flirted with all afternoon did up the paperwork, she wanted to do some homework on the company that built her dream home.

"Is this seat taken?"

She glanced up at the most incredible grey eyes she'd ever seen. Her gaze traveled down the length of his muscular body and stopped at his tapered waist. She gulped. The black t-shirt he wore hid nothing.

"No, feel free." She waved the brochure in her hand toward the chair beside her.

She sipped her wine as she watched him out of the corner of her eye. When he leaned back, his shirt pulled across his chest, and every indent from his muscles could be seen. Kerrie sighed before she closed her eyes.

"Have you taken a tour of the log homes?"

Kerrie's eyes popped open. There was something oddly familiar with the timbre of his voice. Where had she heard it before?

She glanced down at the brochure in her hand. A soft smile settled on her face. She still couldn't believe her luck. First place she looked at, and it was love at first sight.

"I take from that smile that you have. They're something else, aren't they?"

When she turned to look at him, her breath caught. The dimple in his cheek when he smiled gave him the look of a little boy. With his short-cropped hair, grey eyes, and rock-hard body, Kerrie was in heaven.

This was a man who knew nothing about ties and court-rooms. She stole a glance at his shoes. Rugged brown cowboy boots. Sweet Jesus. This man had probably never had his shoes shined, or his ties pressed.

"I fell in love," Kerrie admitted.

"With the town or the agent?"

Kerrie lifted her gaze to his face. The hint of laughter in his voice threw her for a loop until she thought about Sean, the real estate agent. She smiled before she glanced down at the pamphlet.

"I imagine every single woman in this town loves Sean."

"Not just single women. I doubt there's a woman he can't win over when he needs to. It's what makes him good at his job and the number one real estate agent in Banff."

Kerrie nodded. It made sense. He'd certainly won her over, and she'd seen through his witty sales remarks after five minutes.

"I'm Dylan, by the way." He reached across the small table between them and held out his hand.

Kerrie reached across and placed her hand in his. "Kerrie." His grip was firm, strong, and amazingly warm.

"Whoa, your hand is cold," Dylan squeezed her hand before turning in his chair and placing his other hand on top of hers. His thumb rubbed across her palm and sent a tingling sensation through her body.

Kerrie's first instinct was to pull her hand away. Perhaps it was the wine, the place, or just Dylan, but she didn't want him to stop touching her. If his hands were that warm, what about the rest of his body? She squirmed in her seat thinking about it.

"If you're considering buying a home here, you'll need to be prepared for the cold winters." Dylan let go of her hand and waved down a waiter who walked past.

Kerrie glanced at her watch again while he ordered a beer. There was still a half hour before her date was to arrive. A nervous flutter settled in her stomach as she thought about her night and what it would entail.

Giving up control was a hard thing for Kerrie to do. But she realized she needed there to be an area in her life where she didn't have to be on guard at all times. She needed to relax, to let go.

She'd found the home where she could do that -- relax. Maybe after that, other things could happen...like falling in love.

"Are you expecting someone?"

Kerrie took a sip of her wine and enjoyed the sweet and crisp nectar until it was gone. With regret, she set the cup down on the table beside them and was surprised to see another wine glass, this one full already. She raised her brow as she glanced up at Dylan.

"I hope it wasn't too presumptuous of me?"

Kerrie shook her head. She made it a rule to never accept more than one drink from any given man unless she was interested in him. Unfortunately, it meant she rarely accepted any drinks.

"Not at all. I'm just not accustomed to someone else buying me drinks." She picked up the glass and held it high. "Thank you."

Dylan's brow lifted. "I find that hard to believe."

The sincerity in Dylan's voice surprised her. The warmth in his eyes and the way his lips curled into a smile just about melted her heart.

For once, being hit on wasn't so bad. He'd been sitting there for almost thirty minutes, and he'd yet to suggest they go somewhere private or mention he could take her home, for a small fee. There was no reason why she couldn't relax and just enjoy the attention.

"It was the house," she mumbled under her breath.

"I'm sorry?" Dylan leaned closer to her. She caught a whiff of his aftershave. Mint, with a hint of an outdoor wood smell. Kerrie breathed in deep. It reminded her of the cabin.

"With the house. I fell in love with the house. Or cabin. I never expected to, not like this."

A knowing smile grew on Dylan's face. The way his eyes twinkled, it was as if he knew a secret she was only about to find out.

"City girl at heart?"

Kerrie shrugged. "I thought so. Now, not so much. I thought I wanted a place to come to on weekends or holidays, but after being here, I can see it being full-time."

"And what do you do full-time now that the lure of the log home is pulling you away?"

Kerrie tipped her head to the side. Should she tell him?

From the look of him, he was a hands-on type of person. Living in the mountains, no doubt he breathed the outdoor life on a daily basis. This was her chance to be someone else. To forget about the stress of her daily life. She could be anyone. And yet...

"I'm a lawyer." Something in Dylan's eyes told her honesty was crucial to him.

Kerrie noticed the way his shoulders relaxed.

"Do you think you could adjust to the snail's pace a quiet town life Banff offers after living the high life? The only fast pace you'll find here is on the ski slopes eight months of the year." Dylan chuckled.

Kerrie rubbed her hands together, the tips of her fingers tingling with cold. "Surely winter doesn't last that long?" She hated the cold.

"When you live in the mountains, you need to be prepared for anything. In the higher altitudes, sometimes the snow doesn't go away." He stood to his feet and extended his hand to her.

Kerrie hesitated before reaching her hand out. Was he leaving? Was it something she said?

"You look cold. There's a room off to the side with two fireplaces and comfortable chairs to sit in. Come join me. Please?"

The moment his fingers curled over her palm, a heated sensation jolted through her. She glanced at the clock. Her date should be arriving any minute.

"I'll let the concierge know where you'll be in case someone comes looking for you. Don't worry. There's a clear line of sight from where we'll be sitting to the front desk." He pulled her up out of the chair and placed his hand on the small curve of her back to steady her.

She stood in front of the fire while Dylan crossed the room and spoke to the concierge. A gust of cold wind curled around her shoulders, and she glanced over at the front door expectantly.

A group of women entered. Not her mystery date.

It was now seven o'clock. Where was the man Sandra had promised would sweep her off her feet? Why wasn't he here already? What kind of man waited till the last minute to arrive at a date?

Damn it. She shouldn't have made Sandra promise not to tell her his name.

What a fool she'd been. If it wasn't for the fact she found the log cabin of her dreams, this trip would have been such a waste. She should have known better.

She should have insisted on sticking to her plan instead of letting Sandra arrange this stupid blind date. So much for letting go and letting someone else be in control.

Kerrie watched Dylan cross the room. Maybe she didn't need to have someone else set up a date for her. She seemed to be doing fine all on her own. Maybe all she needed was a different setting. A new location away from her regular bars and restaurants.

She was.... good-looking. Maybe not sexy in the model sense, but attractive. Tall with long legs, hair with just enough wave in it to add volume, and a chest most women paid a fortune to have.

She knew there was nothing wrong with her looks. So it must be her personality. Or the way she came across. She couldn't let her guard down, for not one minute.

Except here, in this small town nestled high in the mountains. She didn't even have her guard up. And look at what happened. Drinks paid for by a handsome man.

Maybe not having her blind date show up was a good thing.

Chapter Four

DYLAN PAUSED at the front desk to catch his breath. She was more than he expected. What kind of game was Sandra playing? He knew she'd left some details out of the email, and he had a feeling she'd done that on purpose.

Dylan watched Kerrie as she stood by the fire.

The way the blaze lit up her body and cast a glow on her face made her to be the most beautiful woman in the room.

The photo Sandra had forwarded him earlier today with Kerrie dressed up in a power suit did little justice to the woman he'd met tonight.

In the photo, her hair was slicked back off her face and in a bun, and she wore a black business suit with a skirt that ended at her knees and black pumps with heels that screamed money.

Tonight though, her hair hung down over her shoulders and framed her face. Her kissable lips begged to be touched by his own and the way her eyelashes swept over her high cheekbones when she realized he'd caught her staring had him smiling.

She was gorgeous, and had no idea how much she affected him.

"The room's ready. Are you going to share what this is all about?"

Dylan turned and winked at John, his best friend and current head director of the Banff Springs Hotel.

"Not really." Dylan turned his back to John and continued to watch Kerrie. He enjoyed the way her silhouette looked alive against the fire's glow.

"Why haven't you ever mentioned her? For you to book the best suite in the house means serious cash. Even with the discount I'm giving you."

Dylan glanced over his shoulder at John and frowned. "I haven't mentioned her 'cause she's none of your business, and don't you dare tell your wife about her. If I get grilled tomorrow during the house tour, I'll delay your move-in date by at least another month."

The way John shut his mouth meant he'd gotten the message. As a special favor, Dylan made a log chalet for John as an anniversary gift. Tomorrow was the big reveal. It had taken a year, but John wanted to make sure this cabin was perfect. John and Amanda were the only family he had left other than Sandra.

"She deserves the room, even if for only one night, and you are paying for it. I'm just adding the price into the cabin."

John shook his head as he leaned his elbows down on the counter. "So, who is she?"

Dylan pushed himself away from the desk when he caught Kerrie looking his way. "She's a lawyer in love with my cabin." He started to cross the floor before John's laughter stopped him.

"Is there a problem?"

"Karma's a bitch, my friend. Karma's a bitch." John chuckled before he turned and headed into the office behind him.

Dylan shook his head. Karma was a bitch, and her name was Sandra. She knew exactly what she was doing when she asked him to be nice to her friend. Why did he never put two and two together? He should have known better.

He pulled out his phone to send a quick email, letting her know exactly what he thought. He'd follow through, but damn if he ever did that crazy woman another favor. Imagine his surprise when he found an email from her instead.

"Settle down. It's not as bad as you think it is. Kerrie is a little pearl waiting to be discovered. Crack the shell. You'll be amazed by what you discover. And yes, I promise never to ask you to do this again. Now shut up and have a good night."

Dylan laughed. If he didn't love her so much...a soft smile settled over his face. Sandra was the first woman to steal his heart. Didn't matter they'd been only kids. He'd be lost without her today. She was like his little sister. And he'd do anything for her.

Dylan crossed the floor and held out his hand to Kerrie, waiting to see if she would take it.

So far, he liked what he'd seen of her. There was a self-confidence he knew had been cultivated in the courtroom. There was also an ease, as if she knew who she was and she didn't need anyone to remind her of it, which he liked.

That was a quality he'd rarely seen when he'd been a lawyer with his own firm. The female lawyers he'd met all felt they had to prove something. They'd use their bodies if they knew how, or they'd shove the feminist movement in his face if he even dared to open a door for them.

He'd been a little hesitant when Sandra mentioned she was a lawyer. His ex had been one as well - a cold-hearted witch who knew exactly where to hit when it counted.

The timid smile on Kerrie's face as she gently laid her palm in his did something to his heart. John was right. It had been a long time. Too long.

Maybe tonight was the start of something special.

But then, maybe it wasn't. She was a lawyer, after all.

The last thing he needed or wanted was to lose his heart to another woman who would only stomp on it the moment she realized the lure of riches and power was stronger than the love he could offer.

As Dylan led Kerrie into the small room off to the side, he reminded himself that tonight was all about Kerrie. It wasn't so much that she wanted to lose control but more that she needed to know she was wanted as a woman.

That much he could do.

Chapter Five

KERRIE FOLLOWED Dylan as he led her into the secluded side room. She glanced around at the bookshelves full of leather bound books and inhaled. The faint musty smell reminded her of her father's old study where she used to curl up with a book and watch him pore over accounting ledgers.

The roaring fires cast a warm glow around the room and the Tiffany style lamps along the walls only added to the cozy ambiance. She checked, and even with the door partially closed to keep in the heat and block out the noise, she had a clear view of the front door and desk. If her date ever showed up.

"You keep looking at the door."

Kerrie turned to find Dylan right in front of her.

"I'm...waiting for someone." Seems like she was always waiting. For someone or something to happen. She glanced behind her and knew right then that she really didn't want her date to show up.

"Male or female? Perhaps I could help you?"

Kerrie whipped her head back. That was the phrase her date was supposed to utter so she would know it was him. A smile bloomed on her lips. She'd worried that she wouldn't be physically attracted to her date, but with Dylan, she didn't have to worry about that at all.

"Excuse me?" She took a step towards him. He was supposed to have said it within minutes of them meeting. Not almost an hour later.

Dylan gestured to the door. "If I knew who you were looking for, perhaps I could help. Leave a name at the front desk or keep an eye out." He shrugged.

Kerrie swallowed back her disappointment and struggled to keep the smile on her lips. Of course he wouldn't be her date. She should have known better.

"I'm not sure of the name. He knows how to find me though. I think." She stepped towards the door and looked out. While the hotel lobby was full, there weren't any single males wandering about looking for a woman wearing a soft grey sweater with a black scarf.

The sound of a chair being dragged across the hardwood floor made her turn. Dylan was repositioning the chairs in front of the fire so that they would have a clear view of the door.

She smiled at his thoughtfulness before giving off a little sigh. It really was too bad he wasn't her date for the night.

"Now you'll be able to see whoever it is you're expecting." He looked up, and her heart almost stopped. "Although why you're waiting for someone who should already be here is another question."

Kerrie raised her brow. True enough. But there was a part of her that feared if she didn't wait and give the guy a chance, she'd never have another one. Not like this.

All she desired was to be wanted for herself. Not for her brains, or for the career advancement men mistakenly assumed she could help with, but for her. Was that too much to ask?

"Good question." She took a step toward Dylan and smiled. The look of surprise in his eyes spread a warmth through her body. His gaze heated when she stopped and stood right in front of him. A flash of fire sizzled through her blood.

He found her attractive. Her. She needed to be careful...she had a feeling this man could sweep her off her feet before she could stop him. But then, she had a feeling she wouldn't want to. Stop him, that is.

She could feel the heat radiate off Dylan as she stood mere inches from him. A frown whisked across his lips before he leaned down. Kerrie held her breath as she lifted her face. Her eyelashes fluttered closed as the briefest touch of his lips brushed against hers.

She couldn't believe she was letting him kiss her, but then, she couldn't stop herself from leaning in if she'd wanted to.

He had the softest lips she'd ever kissed. Ever. The caress of his breath against her skin made her want more. She brushed her lips against his, and when his hand touched the arch of her back, Kerrie couldn't help herself. She molded her body against his and angled her face to deepen their kiss.

A knock on the door stopped her.

She froze for a moment before opening her eyes and found herself staring at Dylan's perfectly sculpted lips. She swallowed a moan. She prayed to God that he would think it was the heat of the fire that made her cheeks all flushed.

"Excuse me. I hate to interrupt but--"

The creak of the door opening reminded Kerrie that they stood in plain sight of a room full of people. She stepped to the side and kept her back to the door. She took a deep breath before turning towards the man who interrupted the hottest kiss she'd had in a long time.

She couldn't believe she'd let herself go like that. She didn't even know the man.

"Is there something we can help you with?"

Kerrie cocked her head at Dylan's tone. There was something about it, something off. She slowly angled her body away from the fire until she faced both Dylan and the man at the door.

What she saw shocked her. Dressed in a white puffed ski jacket that did little to hide his wide girth, and wearing a knitted red hat, the man looked like he should be on his way to the North Pole.

"I'm looking for someone..." the man's voice drifted off as his gaze settled on Kerrie's scarf.

She gulped before bringing her hand up to finger the fabric around her neck. She was mortified. What if this was her date? She couldn't believe what she'd just done. She took a step forward and struggled to find the words to somehow apologize, only to have Dylan block her.

"Male or female?" Dylan asked.

The man blinked a few times behind his horn-rimmed glasses. The way his eyes widened reminded Kerrie of an owl. And she hated owls with a passion. Please God, don't let this be her blind date.

"Female."

Kerrie's eyes widened. No way. There's no way this would be her blind date. She gave specific details on what she found attractive in a man. Tall. Broad shouldered with dark wavy hair. Athletic. Someone like Dylan.

Someone exactly like Dylan.

Kerrie unwound her scarf from her neck and tossed it on the chair to the side. She placed her hand on Dylan's back and waited for him to move slightly to the side so she could stand beside him.

"Perhaps she's waiting for you at the bar?" Kerrie smiled up at Dylan and melted a little inside when he smiled back.

"Um, yeah, the bar. Sorry for..." The man waved his hand in

the air, "...interrupting." He ducked his head, readjusted his glasses as they slipped off his nose, and retreated.

A smile bloomed on Kerrie's face as she watched him turn around and smack headfirst into a woman wearing a grey ski jacket and a scarf the same color as her own.

"Guess he found who he was looking for," Dylan said as he stepped away and headed closer to the fire.

"Guess so." Kerrie rubbed her hands together before crossing them over her chest. "About what just happened..." She stopped as Dylan picked up her discarded scarf and held it out to her.

"The blue strands in your scarf match your eyes. I like it." His eyes twinkled as she rewound it around her neck. "Let me guess, this mystery man will recognize your scarf."

Kerrie shrugged her shoulders. "Something like that. Not that it matters. Now." She hoped she'd placed enough emphasis that he understood what she was saying.

This was not like her. She didn't just meet strange men in the foyer of a hotel and let him kiss her. She had requirements, and standards.

No kissing on the first date. Maybe on the second. But never within mere minutes of meeting one another.

Dylan held out his hand to her. She took it and watched as his fingers wove through her own. The feel of his skin against hers warmed her from the tips of her toes to the top of her head. Even the hairs on her arms tingled. He had the hands of someone who knew the power of hard work. They weren't soft, silky, and manicured like most lawyers she knew. His finger pads were callused, scratched, and rough.

She never did ask him what he did for a living. In fact, she knew nothing about him. So why did she feel so safe with him?

"Why is that?" The huskiness of Dylan's voice caught her attention. She glanced up and blushed. His irises had darkened to an almost dark grey color.

She took a deep breath. She could almost hear Sandra whispering in her ear to *relax and enjoy* life. Maybe she should.

She could analyze her reactions now and possibly spend the rest of the night alone wondering why her date never showed up. She would dwell on how she could be so stupid to let the sexiest man she'd ever met slip through her fingers, or she could take the plunge and experience a night she would never forget.

Dylan's brow rose as he waited for her answer.

"I'm tired of waiting."

Chapter Six

THE LOOK in her eyes did it. They sucked him in, spit him out, and tore his heart to pieces all at the same time.

I'm tired of waiting. It wasn't what she'd said, but how she'd said it. The quirk in her full lips. The seductive look in her eyes. Damn Sandra.

Since when did his friend think she could play matchmaker and him not get burned? If he wasn't careful, his heart would end up tattered and bruised by the end of all this. And that was not an acceptable loss in his books. Not by a long shot.

Time to get his head back in the game. Otherwise, he might as well head back home, grab a case of beer, and drown his lonely sorrows while watching the latest superhero movie. Such a hard decision.

One night with a beautiful woman who would soon hate his guts when she found out about his lies or a night alone wishing he was back here, with her.

He needed to tell her about tomorrow, about who he was because if he didn't, she'd find out soon enough and would think he was a liar.

He'd worry about that tomorrow though. Tonight, he just

wanted to let go and see where they were headed. He wasn't the romantic type normally, not one to woo a girl with flowers and chocolate and whisper sweet nothings in her ear. He had a feeling that while she might enjoy it, it wasn't really what she needed.

Sandra told her Kerrie was a woman who didn't know what it was like to give up and give in, especially when it came to love.

Maybe he was the one to show her how.

Chapter Seven

THE WAY his lips turned up should have warned her, but she let out a small gasp as his arm wound around her waist and she was pulled tighter against him.

Tilting her head up, he took her mouth in a hard show of possession. His tongue darted out and licked at the seam of her lips, demanding she open to him.

Kerrie had no choice. She submitted. And it excited her. For once, she didn't have to take control, someone else was. As soon as her lips parted, Dylan took advantage and delved in.

His hands were everywhere. They slid down her back until they rested in the cradle of her back. She almost expected his hands to go lower and was impressed with his restraint.

Kerrie raised her hands and slid her fingers through the strands of his silky hair. Dylan's tongue continued to play with hers, darting in and out, teasing her. Pulling back, breathing hard, Kerrie moaned, "I can't believe I'm doing this."

Dylan placed his index finger to her lips and murmured, "You're thinking too much. Stop." He traced her lips with his finger, then slid it over her throat, down her collarbone.

Muffled laughter from out in the lobby filled the small room.

Kerrie took a step back and bit her lip. Never one for public displays of affection of any sort, this experience took her completely out of her comfort zone. Something no doubt Sandra would love right about now.

"Dylan, there's no question that I find you..." Kerrie straightened her shoulders as a gleam entered Dylan's eyes. "Attractive. But I don't know you, and this," she waved her hands in the air, "is not like me at all."

As Dylan took a step toward her, Kerrie took a step backward.

"You're saying you're not the type to pick up a stranger at a hotel and make out with him?"

Kerrie nodded. "Right." Dylan took another step, forcing her to retreat further.

"Since you didn't pick me up and I'm not a complete stranger, we're okay then." The smile on his face just about turned her legs into jelly as she backed up into the wall behind her.

She nodded again. Right. That made sense. Kind of.

"But I agree. We don't know each other well enough to make out in this tiny room, full of spectators. Unless you're into that?"

Kerrie shook her head. Voyeurism? Not in this lifetime.

By now, Dylan stood in front of her. He leaned in and placed his hands on the wall beside her head.

"I happen to know the manager here. Their exclusive loft room is available, and the food I ordered should be ready by now. How about we go get a bite to eat and get better acquainted?"

Chapter Eight

W<small>HAT WAS SHE THINKING</small>?

Kerrie stood outside the door to the loft room and stared in amazement at the spacious interior as Dylan walked inside. From the little she could see, this wasn't just any room.

Dylan turned, leaned against the wall, and waited for her. Her stomach clenched as she watched the way his muscles bulged under his sweater. Was this really happening? To her?

How would she explain this to Sandra? Yeah, um, sorry, but I ditched your friend for some sexy local I picked up?

She couldn't believe the connection between them. It was surreal and unbelievable and yet...so clearly there.

What if her date had shown up and saw her lips locked with Dylan? She almost cringed at the text message Sandra would send once she found out. Would it be worth it?

Absolutely.

Thoughts of those lips sent a floodgate of warm tingles flowing through her body. She focused her gaze on Dylan's lips and imagined the feel of his touch as it traveled down her body and over her curves--

"Do you need help, Kerrie?" The way his voice drawled

when he said her name sent shivers of excitement down her back.

About to take a step into the room, she stopped and blinked. *Help.* A word he seemed to favor. A word she'd specifically asked her blind date to say. Could it be? Could Dylan actually be her date?

A smile grew on her face.

Of course, he was. It all made sense.

Of course, he would have been there early; Kerrie had mentioned punctuality was important to her, and she knew Sandra had relayed her message.

Everything he'd done so far was for her benefit. He'd taken charge from the moment she'd met him, bought her a drink, led her to the study where she could get warm, and even arranged this gorgeous room...

She couldn't catch her breath. This room was meant for seduction--oh my.

So far, everything he'd done had been to sweep her off her feet, and if truth be told...he'd done just that.

Good job Sandra. Good job.

"Kerrie?" Dylan took a step towards her, a questioning look in his eyes.

"I do need help, Dylan," she whispered. Kerrie stepped into the room and closed the door behind her. She hid her hands behind her back to hide just how much she shook from her revelation.

"I've never done this before," she admitted.

"What? Enjoy a meal with someone you've just met?" Dylan reached for her hand and led her into the beautiful room.

It was gorgeous and spacious. Her whole apartment would fit in this space. Leather furniture that cost more than all her furniture combined surrounded a fireplace that sat in the middle of the room. A spiral wood staircase wound its way to the open loft to the right of the room. In front of the staircase was a wall of glass, featuring the most beautiful sight of the Rocky Mountains illuminated with flood lights.

"Breathtaking," she whispered. This was a sight she could get used to falling asleep to, instead of the three-level outdoor parkade located beside her downtown condo.

"I hope you're hungry."

Kerrie turned from the window and watched Dylan lift lids off of plates set on a gorgeous cherry wood table covered in lit tapered candles. Her stomach rumbled as bowls of creamy pasta were uncovered.

Dylan glanced over his shoulder and winked while she blushed with embarrassment.

"A little."

Dylan pulled out a chair for her. "Don't eat too much. I believe there's chocolate cake for dessert."

Kerrie licked. "How about we eat dessert first?" She breathed in the tantalizing aroma of chocolate icing as he lifted off the lid covering the decadent cake.

"Ah, a girl after my own heart." The smile on his face took Kerrie's breath away. She couldn't believe that this man was attracted to her. Sure, now that she knew he wasn't just some random stranger changed things.

The fact he had yet to confess who he really was meant one of two things. He either wanted a way out, just in case things didn't work out between them, or he was genuinely attracted to her, and he wanted this to be more than a one-night stand.

Kerrie prayed it was the latter.

She noticed a small box on the table and thought about a similar box in her purse, a box meant as a gift, for him. She couldn't keep the smile off her face.

While she was looking at the box from Sweet Treats, Dylan picked it up and held it out to her.

"I have a special treat for you, I hope you don't mind."

She chuckled and reached for her own purse, pulling out a similar box.

"I knew there was something about you I liked." Dylan laid his box back down on the table, took the one she held out for him, and then brought her hands up to his mouth and placed a kiss on her fingers. One at a time.

"Did you meet Lexi? I once told her the woman of my dreams would bring me a box of her macarons, and here you are." He stared deep into her eyes, and the warm heat she felt bloom inside her turned up a few notches.

Oh boy, she was in trouble.

From the way, he smiled at her, she knew she'd said that last thought out loud. Her cheeks blazed bright red as the look on his face distilled the nervous flutter of excitement lodged deep in her chest.

When his hand tenderly cupped her cheek, Kerrie couldn't breathe. This was so surreal, so not her. And yet, everything about tonight felt natural, as if it was meant to happen.

For a moment, she forgot how she ended up here, in this room. She forgot that it was her best friend who arranged this meeting. That if this night hadn't been scheduled, she would be in her own apartment lying in bed reading the latest romance novel she'd recently bought about a <u>cowboy</u> from an author she'd just discovered - Daire St. Denis.

"I'm going to kiss you again." The huskiness in his voice told her he was just as affected as she was. With a slow nod of her head, she lowered her lashes as his lips hovered over her own.

The gentle pressure of his mouth before his tongue traced the outline of her lips brought Kerrie to her tiptoes as she wound her hands around Dylan's neck. She couldn't get over this feeling, this connection between them. It was everything from those spicy romance novels she devoured night after night. The heat from his body torched hers until she felt like she was fire. Their kiss deepened as their tongues danced to a tune their bodies instinctively knew.

When Dylan pulled away, Kerrie struggled to catch her breath. She leaned her forehead against his and took a deep breath. This was exactly like her romance novels.

Chapter Nine

Dᴙʟᴀɴ ᴏᴘᴇɴᴇᴅ his eyes and stared at the woman before him. She was amazing, so much more than what he thought.

How did she know about the cookies?

Well, he knew how, Lexi probably blabbed about his love of them, but why would she buy them for him?

Girls don't normally buy guys gifts, especially not when set up on a blind date, right?

She did something to him and balanced on the fine line of being scared yet wanting to dive head first into whatever this was.

As much as she wanted to be wooed, to be romanced, and known she was wanted - he had those same needs. To be wanted for who he was, not for what he could offer. Not for his money, or his skills, or for some sorry excuse for a promotion. For himself.

Part of him was afraid that when Kerrie found out who he was, things would change. That the intensity between them would change, and become forced.

"You are so beautiful," he whispered. He watched as her

gaze lowered and her cheeks bloomed. She had the natural intensity of a siren, and he doubted she even realized it.

"You don't have to sweet talk me with words, you know. The chocolate cake did all the work for you." When she smiled up at him his heart jumped, and he pulled back for a moment.

He could tell by the look on her face she was confused by his response, but he ignored it. It had been years since he'd felt connected to someone and the fact he hardly knew the woman before him...well, it scared it to be honest.

What was he doing? Was this a one-night stand or a let's see where it leads type of encounter?

If all she wanted was a one-night stand, then he needed to leave. His heart couldn't handle it - he knew that.

He swallowed hard and was about to say exactly that when she laid her hand on his arm.

"You feel it too, don't you? This connection between us. It's like...it's like I've known you forever even though we just met."

Dylan breathed in deep and focused on the way her thumb lightly stroked his arm.

"Whatever is happening," she said, "let's just let it...happen. Naturally. Okay?" A smile played with her lips, and he covered her hand with his own.

"I like that idea." Letting it happen naturally, that he could do. "So tell me, are you the dessert-first kind of girl?"

Her eyes lit up.

"Then let's take this cake upstairs, shall we?"

Chapter Ten

KERRIE CLIMBED the circular stairs and gasped as she took in the loft.

A four-poster bed, shrouded in sheer white drapes, sat in the middle of the vast room full of old-world wonder.

The room was beyond description. With its soft grey walls, antique furniture, and luxurious feel, it would fit between the folds of a design magazine.

A multitude of candles filled the room with a soft yellow glow. Kerrie turned and faced Dylan who climbed the stairs behind her.

"How did you...?" She turned back to the bed and took in the scattered rose petals on the floor in front of the bed.

"How did I what? Arrange this? Know you love roses and candles, or figure out that you are a woman who deserves to be romanced?"

Kerrie stood still at the top of the stairs as Dylan walked past her and placed the cake down on a table that held two glasses and a bottle of wine in a sterling silver bucket. She was stunned.

He'd planned all this, down to the very last detail without really knowing who she was.

"The room is yours for the night. I wanted you to feel pampered, spoiled...I can leave you, and you can have a bubble bath, watch a romantic movie and then sleep alone in that bed," he pointed towards the canopied bed, "or I could stay and we can get to know one another and see where this leads us."

Kerrie swallowed hard.

"While you are a woman who needs to feel in control, you are also a woman who needs to know there is someone else who can take care of you and your needs. Even if it's just for one night, I want to be that man."

Kerrie gulped as Dylan came towards her. She didn't say anything as he took her hands and led her over to the bed.

"From the moment I saw you sitting downstairs, I knew that I wanted to be that man. Even if it's just for now, just for tonight or the weekend, or until whatever this is between us runs its course. What do you say?"

Something akin to butterflies took flight in her belly. She saw the honesty in his eyes and knew he spoke the truth. She searched for any hidden motives in his gaze, his words, but she didn't see any.

He wanted her. Just her.

She let out a long sigh and smiled. From the blaze burning in his eyes, she had a feeling that tonight was going to be a night she would never forget.

Dylan cupped her face, and his lips touched hers with a light, feathery kiss. Soft, slow, and seductive. He deepened the kiss and threaded his fingers through her hair, massaging her scalp and neck. Then the kiss became sensual, a wide-open, mouth-to-mouth exchange of breath.

Kerrie groaned and wrapped her arms around his broad shoulders. He tasted so good. Like bourbon.

This is what she wanted and what she craved yet was too

afraid to admit. To be wanted. Desired. There was no going back. No second thoughts.

Chapter Eleven

SHE TASTED of warm milk chocolate with a hint of vanilla.

Dylan traced her lips with the tip of his tongue and tried very hard not to moan. She felt like heaven in his arms, hot, soft, and full of a world one only imagined. Her soft moans whispered their way through his body and into his heart.

There was something about this woman that grabbed hold of his attention and refused to let go. Which was going to be difficult come tomorrow morning.

Her kisses fed his starved soul, and he didn't understand what was happening to them or why but he wasn't about to kick a gift horse in the mouth.

Especially when it involved her mouth.

If he wasn't careful, this night was soon to be all about sex, and that's not what he wanted. For some reason, he knew this woman meant something to him, and he didn't want to screw it up over something so physical as sex.

"How do you like your coffee?" He pulled his lips from hers and asked as his hands traveled down her body on their own accord even though he meant to only mold his palms of the curves of her waist.

"Coffee?" She pulled back and gave him a strange look.

"Coffee." He couldn't stop looking at her flush, kissable lips.

Her lips quirked in a smile. "Little bit of cream and sugar. And you?"

"Black and strong."

It didn't make sense. Why did she need Sandra to find her a blind date? There should be a man already at home, waiting for her. A low growl rumbled in his chest. He wanted to be that man.

"Why?" She asked him, and it took a second for him to remember his original question.

"Coffee is important to me. First thing I drink in the morning, and there's always a pot on."

"I can't seem to survive without it," she admitted. "Now, is there anything else you need to know before..." her voice trailed off as her face lit up with a smile that illuminated everything about her.

"Before...?" What were they talking about?

Kerrie glanced over his shoulder. "Cake. That's why we're up here, isn't it?"

He heard the teasing in her voice and saw the laughter in her eyes. That's fine. Two could play that game.

He leaned forward and kissed her once more before pulling back and stepping away.

"Cake." Dylan cleared his throat. "Why is it women desire chocolate over everything else?"

"Why is it men don't?"

He shrugged. "As long as that chocolate covered the things I desire most, I'm all in."

She laughed then, the sound of her happiness filled the room and his heart. "According to Lexi, the things you desire most are in her store. Cookies, fudge, her chocolates but don't forget—"

"Her hot chocolate. Did you try it?" Dylan sighed. "It's heaven. I've never tasted a drink like it. She calls it drinking chocolate, something she learned to make in Paris."

"I tried and fell in love. I want to grab a cup before I leave tomorrow." Her eyes shuttered the moment she spoke of leaving.

"Do you have to?" She'd already fallen in love with his cabin. All he needed was time for her to fall in love with him... what was he thinking? Love?

"This weekend was only meant for relaxation and to find my dream vacation home. Although, between you and me, I think I've fallen in love with the area and can't see myself going back to life in the city." There was a faraway look in her eyes.

"Then don't." He meant it the moment he said it. Don't go. Stay. Stay here with me and see where this leads us.

He hadn't meant to say that out loud, but he must have. The way her gaze softened as she looked at him, the sweet smile on her face...he knew she felt it too.

"I think I need you in my life." He uttered the most honest words he could ever have said.

She didn't say anything, just looked at him, assessing him as if she were back in her courtroom and viewing a witness on the stand. Did he measure up? Did she hear the truth in his voice?

Instead of telling him what she thought or felt, she did the one thing that told him both.

Sweet fire burned in her eyes as she unwound the scarf from around her neck and went to toss it to the side, but Dylan stopped her. He had plans for that scarf. He took the dangling scarf out of her hands and tucked it into the back pocket of his jeans.

He only smiled as a puzzled look swept over Kerrie's face. He knew she was trying to figure out why he'd kept the scarf. She'd find out - eventually.

"Let's see where this leads us, then," Kerrie whispered.

Chapter Twelve

FOR JUST A MOMENT, Kerrie thought last night had been a dream, chapters from her romance novels come to life, her fantasies all meshed into one.

But the tenderness in every muscle throughout her body told her otherwise, and she couldn't stop the smile from spreading across her face.

She placed her feet on the floor and ran her toes along something silky and soft. She leaned down and picked up her scarf. She knew a blush bloomed across her face as she thought about what Dylan had done with it. She doubted she'd be able to wear it again without thinking of how it was used.

She laid it down on her pillow, beside Dylan as he slept. Maybe they could find another use for the scarf this morning before they had to leave.

The clock on the bedside table told her she had a few hours until her scheduled walkthrough with the builder of her dream cabin. She reached for a robe that had been flung over a chair off to the side and tried to muffle her footsteps as she walked down the steps.

She didn't want to wake Dylan from his sleep.

With quiet efficiency, Kerrie prepared coffee, hoping the aroma would wake the sleeping giant upstairs and perhaps he'd join her in the shower.

As she turned on the water in the spacious shower and waited for the steam to rise from the water, she hummed a little tune beneath her breath. There was a happiness in her heart today that could only be explained by one simple name.

Dylan.

She pushed away the thought that what she was feeling was love. It wasn't possible. Right? Not after one night. That only happened in romance novels and fairy tales.

But she had to admit she felt something. She wasn't the same. The woman she'd been last night sitting in the lobby chair waiting for her blind date to show up wasn't the woman she was now. Something had changed.

Someone had changed her.

A new sense of freedom enveloped her as she dropped her robe and stepped under the water. As the hot water covered her body like a silk drape, Kerrie sighed.

Her body was bruised and used, and had never felt so good in her life. Muscles she never knew she had ached. The steady beads of the shower head massaged life back into her tight body.

While she lathered with soft scented soap and washed her hair, she waited for Dylan to join her. After what seemed like forever, she turned off the water and reached for the towel, a small part of her wished that it were Dylan who was drying her off.

She was quiet as she picked up her robe and stepped out of the spacious bathroom. The delicious aroma of coffee filled the air.

The thought of her lover waiting for her with a cup of coffee sent a shiver of anticipation through her body, but when she turned the corner, the only thing awaiting her was a piece of paper beside an empty cup of coffee and a slice of chocolate cake on a plate.

Kerrie stopped and listened. She stepped over to the curved staircase that led up to the loft and placed her hand on the railing. She could have climbed them, but she had a feeling she knew what would greet her. An empty room.

Kerrie closed her eyes and braced herself. She took a deep breath.

So was everything he'd said last night a lie?

What about the connection between them? She realized neither one had spoken of what would happen in the morning, but...surely this was more than just a one-night stand?

It had to be.

She wanted it to be.

Stifling the disappointment, Kerrie took her hand off the railing, tightened the tie on her robe, and headed back to the kitchen. After pouring herself a steaming cup of coffee and adding some creamer to it, Kerrie took her fork, slid it into the decadent cake, and enjoyed a mouthful.

She glanced over at the table filled with dirty dishes. In between rounds of fabulous sex, they had made their way through their dinner. She smiled as she took in how the dishes had been shoved to one side of the table and felt herself go wet as she remembered lying on the other side while Dylan made love to her with his tongue.

If anything, she was able to walk away with wonderful memories.

She picked up the card and read the sparse words Dylan had written.

It takes an amazing woman to make a man realize needs he'd never wanted. Thank you.

It takes an even stronger man to give a woman what she both wants and needs. A smile bloomed on her face. Who knows, Banff was a small town. She had no doubt she'd see him again.

And considering they had not only a friend in common but now also a bakery...Kerrie knew their paths would cross again, and if she had anything to say about it, she'd make sure it was sooner rather than later.

Chapter Thirteen

DYLAN GROANED as he pulled up to the new home he'd built for John as an anniversary gift to his wife. He was late.

He'd wanted to be there, to see Amanda's expression when she saw the red bow on the front door and discovered the chalet was for her.

The front door had been left open and Dylan had no doubt John was following after his wife as she toured through each room. They were family to him and after so many years of listening to suggestions Amanda would make about the many homes he'd sketch out, he knew exactly what she would like.

He glanced at the clock on his truck dashboard. He had an hour before he was to meet Kerrie at the cabin she was about to buy. He wondered what her reaction would be when she realized he was the man behind the scenes.

Would she be angry at his lack of honesty last night? He knew he should have admitted who he was when he saw the brochure he'd made up in her hands. He'd had ample opportunity to come clean.

Maybe she'd be okay with it. Relieved even. Maybe she'd forgive him for walking out this morning without saying a word.

He glanced over at the scarf sitting on the seat beside him. What would she think when she couldn't find it and realized he'd taken it?

He had an hour before he'd find out. An hour to figure out how to explain to his best friends how he'd given his heart away to a woman who might not want it. A lump grew in his throat as he thought about what he'd just admitted.

He didn't believe in love at first sight. But he'd be damned if he didn't admit that's where he could see himself heading if Kerrie forgave him for his small oversight.

He reached across and ran his fingers along the silky scarf. Hopefully, she'd give him the chance to apologize.

As he stepped out of his truck and headed toward the house, he couldn't help but wish she'd let him show her just how sorry he was.

He thought about the bag sitting on the passenger seat. He couldn't resist when he saw the light blue scarf draped across the mannequin's neck in the store window this morning.

He pictured it wrapped around Kerrie's slender neck, highlighting her baby blue eyes and the twinkle in her eyes as smiled up at him. If she smiled at him once she saw him again.

Dylan smiled when John stepped through the door and stood on the front porch.

"You are a miracle worker. She loves it. Do me a favor though - go away. This is a party for two. Only."

Dylan stopped at the foot of the steps and laughed. "There's a bottle of champagne in the fridge. Happy anniversary." He took a quick look at his watch.

Just enough time to plan his own party of two.

Chapter Fourteen

THE BELL over the door of Sweet Treats tinkled as she opened it and Kerrie was amazed to find the bakery practically empty.

Lexi walked through the swinging door from the kitchen, wiping her hands on a cloth she then threw over her shoulder and smiled.

"Welcome back. I was hoping you'd come in before heading out of town."

"Oh really?" Kerrie couldn't resist glancing at the fresh baked scones and croissants on the shelves in front of her.

"I have a package for you to give to Sandra, if you don't mind from Tessa?" She reached down and pulled out a little red and brown tote. "I hope you have room. I tried to remind Tessa you were flying out but she didn't really listen. I also placed a few treats in there for you to enjoy, as a thank you." Lexi handed the bag over the counter.

Kerrie didn't take a look inside the bag, in fact, she couldn't take her gaze off of the chocolate croissant in front on her. Lexi must have noticed because before Lexi could say anything, she pulled the tray out and handed her the decadent pastry.

"Pain au chocolat, my favorite morning treat. Did you know

in Paris, there's a specific skill required for making these? Not everyone can and in fact, a lot of the pattisseries you find in Paris serve frozen croissants now? It's a shame, really. There's only a few left in the city that make them fresh from scratch."

Kerrie listened in while she took a bite and could barely contain her moan. She'd never tasted anything like it before. If she thought those frozen croissants she used to make were good, she know knew she'd been sorely mistaken.

"It's okay. The less you say while eating tells me the most. Enjoy." Lexi turned away and began to wipe down the counter behind her.

"I actually came in for a cup of your hot chocolate," Kerrie managed to wrap the words around her tongue after she ate the last bite of her croissant.

Lexi's eyes lit up. "Well then, you'll like what I placed in the bag for you."

When Kerrie looked, she noticed a bar of chocolate wrapped with ribbon and a sticker on the back. *Melting chocolate - combine in a sauce pan with 250 ml of heavy cream.*

"Will it taste the same as yours, though?" Kerrie asked.

"If you make it right and take your time, otherwise you'll burn the chocolate and cream. Stir it often and then enjoy with a dollop of whipped cream if you want."

"Good to know. I'll have to try it. Thank you."

She reached for the hot cup Lexi handed her and breathed in the decadent chocolate aroma.

"How did your date go last night?"

Kerrie knew her cheeks flushed. "It was...a good night." She knew her smile told spoke more than her words, and she was okay with that.

She didn't really feel comfortable giving too many details to a woman she'd just met last night.

"Good." The bell over the door rang, and a crowd of five

women entered, all ablaze with wonder at the delicacies in front of them.

"Make sure you come back," Lexi said to her after Kerrie paid for her treats.

"Oh, you can count on it." Kerrie had no doubts she'd be back. No doubts at all. Especially since she planned on buying her dream log cabin in...oh, just under an hour from now.

Kerrie pulled up to the quaint log cabin and parked out front. Her fingers tapped on the steering wheel. She was actually doing it. She was actually going to buy her dream cabin and make her dreams reality.

She could hardly believe it.

She slowly opened the door of the rented SUV. The only sound she heard was the squeak of the door. No car horns. No sirens blaring. Nothing but blissful silence. Nature at its best. She loved it. She could come out here and lose herself. Or find herself.

A quiver of excitement filled her heart, and a smile stretched across her face. She knew she was early, but she planned that on purpose. She wanted to spend some time here, alone, before the builder arrived. She had a decision she needed to make.

Kerrie walked across the gravel driveway and placed one foot on the step leading to the porch. As her hand gripped the stair rail, she couldn't help but think that this was her first step into her new home.

She imaged white wicker chairs with red cushions and big potted geraniums lining the porch. For years she'd dreamed of sitting in one of the chairs with pad of paper and a cup of coffee.

She wanted to make that dream a reality.

A gust of cool wind whisked across her face. She clutched

the lapels of her jacket together to cover her throat, missing her scarf more than ever.

Why did she bring only one scarf on this trip? With drawers of rolled scarves in her closet, why would she assume only one multi-colored scarf would be enough?

She breathed in the fresh, clean air and took her time letting it out. A cleansing breath. Out with the old, in with the new.

She was doing this.

She thought back to her conversation with Sandra this morning while she drank her coffee after realizing Dylan had left.

Sandra wasn't the least bit surprised at her decision to want to move here. In fact, she'd already emailed her a listing for a firm with an opening. She couldn't imagine the billed hours or lack of them out here, away from the city. But she didn't imagine she would need them either. She had enough of a nest egg saved that she could afford to take a year or two off and not have it hurt.

Kerrie bit her lip. A year to write.

She shook her head at the thought. She had enough romance stories started, she'd have no excuse not to finish them. Who knows, maybe this would be her year to get published. And find her own romance.

She was determined to track down Dylan and give him a piece of her mind for leaving like he did - right before she threw herself in his arms and prayed to God that he would catch her.

All she knew was that she wasn't leaving town without seeing Dylan again.

Standing in front of the wooden door, Kerrie took a deep breath and placed her hand on the doorknob. She slowly turned until she heard the quiet click of the lock releasing. She wanted to remember this day, every sound, every sensation. She knew it would be a day forever branded on her heart.

She had every expectation of walking into the cabin and memorizing every minute detail of the place before the owner showed up to fill in the details.

What she didn't expect was to find Dylan standing in the middle of the great room, holding a plate with a piece of chocolate cake on it.

She leaned against the door as it closed behind her and folded her arms. "Is that your way of saying sorry?" She struggled to keep the smile off her face as she watched him bite his lip.

He had to be the sexiest man she'd ever laid eyes on. Despite the plaid green shirt he wore, she could see the outlines of his muscular arms as he held the cake.

She could also see the determination in his gaze as he took a step toward her.

"No. This is me enjoying some cake. I have a sudden fondness for a chocolate treat. Angel food cake used to be my favorite, but I think devil's food is worthy of its name."

She caught his wink before he picked up the fork that rested on the plate and sliced into it before bringing it to his lips.

"I could share, if you wanted a piece." As he slid the fork past his lips, Kerrie swallowed. As much as she loved cake, she loved the way this man could use his lips more.

Kerrie pushed herself off from the door and met Dylan in the middle of the room. "Why would I share when I can have a piece of my own?" She smiled before side-stepping him and walked into the kitchen. She'd spied the plate with another piece of cake on the island behind him. A shiver ran over her body as she heard him chuckle behind her.

"So, let me get this straight. The reason why you know the builder so well is because...you're the builder?" She pierced him with the best lawyer gaze she could conjure while sinking her own fork into the decadent cake.

The sheepish look on his face confirmed her suspicions.

"Why the secrecy? Why not just tell me who you were yesterday when you saw the brochure in my hand? Why lie by omission?"

"Fear. Plain and simple. The moment I saw you, I knew I didn't want to ruin what turned out to be—" he shrugged his shoulders and his gaze flittered throughout the room. She could see his mind trying to find an adequate word. That or find the right lie to tell.

"A great night of sex?" If that's all it was to him, then she'd lock her heart in box, throw away the key, sign the damn papers and kick him out of her new home. She wouldn't erase the memory of what happened between them, but she sure could erase her feelings for him.

She wasn't called the ice queen at the firm for nothing.

"Magical. It turned out to be magic." He stepped closer to her, laid his plate down on the wood table, took hold of her own plate, and placed it down beside his. Mere inches separated them.

"Magical, huh? So magical that you left without saying good-bye?" Her voice hitched at the end.

Dylan ran his hands up her arms until they rested on her shoulder. His touch was electrifying. His thumb drew circles against the sensitive area of skin just at the base of her neck.

"So magical that I was afraid to ruin it all. I was a jerk, and I'm sorry."

Kerrie melted inside. She wasn't sure if she could continue the charade. All she wanted to do was throw her arms around his neck, press her body up against his, and kiss him until he begged her to never leave.

He must have been able to read that in her gaze because that sexy smile of his appeared, along with a twinkle in his eye. His face lowered until his breath teased her lips.

And yet he didn't kiss her.

"Let me make it up to you." His lips hovered over hers, while his one hand cupped the back of her neck.

She arched her brow. "Oh yeah? How?" She wasn't going to kiss him. She wasn't.

"Let me give you a personal tour of your new home." The way his lips curved, she knew he had a secret. "There's one room I especially want you to see."

When he straightened, Kerrie struggled not to reach out and grab him and demand he kiss her. Instead, she feigned indifference. Or tried to.

"I haven't signed on the dotted line yet." She shrugged her shoulder. "Technically, it's not my home."

Dylan reached for her hand and walked out of the kitchen. "We both know that's just a legality."

A heat radiated from his touch, and when he squeezed her hand, she knew he felt it too.

Kerrie had a hard time listening to the small details, the very details she couldn't wait to hear earlier. Instead, she found herself watching the expressions on his face, the way his biceps bulged as he pointed out things she would never have noticed otherwise.

It became evident that he loved this house.

"It was hard to give this one up."

Kerrie glanced around the room but didn't see anything in the bathroom that he could have been talking about. Sure, the claw tub and bay window looking over the mountains was gorgeous, but...

"What do you mean?"

Dylan pulled her out of the bathroom and into the upstairs hallway. They stood in front of a door, the last door to a room they had yet to explore. With his hand on the knob, he turned to face her. A serious look covered his face.

"You mentioned last night that you were thinking of moving here, full-time. Instead of using this place as a holiday home. Is that still true?"

Kerrie cocked her head. She couldn't read whatever message he was trying to convey. But the seriousness of his tone convinced her that it was time to stop playing games.

"I can't imagine not living here full time. It's a complete overhaul of all my goals, but I know it's what I want to do. I'm not one for sudden game changes but this..." Kerrie shrugged her shoulders. "I know this is the right move for me." Saying the words out loud, admitting what she knew to be true, was right. It was good. She let out a deep breath.

"This is home. My home. What that means, I have no idea —" She glanced down at her hand as Dylan held it. He squeezed it gently before pulling her close. Kerrie went willingly.

She wanted to be in his arms again. She liked being here. It amazed her, but this felt right. Everything about this felt right.

"I built this cabin a long time ago. I've held off on selling it because...well, I needed to make sure the right person wanted this place. Not some executive looking for a weekend palace. But someone who could...call it home." His voice grew gruff.

Kerrie rose up on her tiptoes and placed a gentle kiss on Dylan's oh-so-kissable lips. "This is home," she whispered. Dylan growled and pulled her closer, slanting his lips, so they covered hers.

"So what's inside?" she murmured. She opened her eyes in time to see a smile grace his lips before his hand covered her eyes.

"I wanted to save this room for last. My way of apologizing for leaving this morning without saying goodbye. I hope you'll forgive me."

There was a slight squeak of the door as it opened. A waft of vanilla welcomed Kerrie as Dylan slowly pulled her into the room. A quiver of excitement settled in her stomach as she waited to open her eyes. Why the secrecy? What was so special about this room?

"Dylan?"

The squeeze to her hand and he pulled her further into the room didn't do much to calm her. She bit her lip. Vanilla scented candles. She loved the smell, and he knew it. When his hand lifted off her face, and she opened her eyes, the only thing she could do was gasp.

It was beautiful. Almost as beautiful as the loft bedroom last night.

He'd saved the best room for last. Her bedroom.

A gorgeous white iron bed filled up most of the room. But it was the sight beyond the bed that took her breath away. A large bay window trimmed with bookshelves both above and down the sides caught her attention. A bench in front of the window with soft white cushions beckoned her to sit there. She imagined herself sitting here in the early mornings with a cup of coffee while watching the sun rise over the mountains in her backyard.

"This is beautiful," she whispered. She turned toward Dylan and couldn't keep the smile off her face. This was perfect. Everything about this house was perfect.

"Why hasn't it sold before now?" She wound her fingers through his before turning to the bed and sitting down.

"It was the first cabin I had ever built." Dylan shrugged. "It was meant to be a home, my home with my ex-wife. But it was too small. She wanted something larger. More grand." Dylan sat down beside her and placed their joined hands in his lap. "So I built another cabin and kept this one as a personal retreat. Until you came along yesterday."

Kerrie thought back to yesterday. She didn't remember meeting him as she walked through the house. Yet, the sound of his voice when she first met him at the hotel sounded so familiar—

"I was in the kitchen talking to Mark while you were exploring on your own. You muttered a few phrases that caught my attention."

Kerrie tilted her head and struggled to remember what she'd said. Or didn't say. The moment she walked into the cabin, she'd fallen in love. Normally one who kept her thoughts to herself, yesterday she couldn't.

"Something along the lines of '*this is where I will write my story*'. If you could picture yourself writing here, then I knew you could see yourself living here full time."

A smile bloomed across her face. She knew exactly where she would sit when writing her story. She had an old secretary desk handed down from her mother that would sit in front of the window.

Warmth spread through Kerrie's body. She threw herself back and spread her arms out along the bed.

"I want it. All of it. Everything this house has to offer, I want it."

She smiled when Dylan stretched himself out beside her. Her breath caught at the teasing glint in his eye as he propped his head in his hand and stared down at her.

"All of it?" He leaned down and paused, his lips mere inches away.

"All of it." She meant it. This was his house. His retreat. And yet he was going to offer it. To her.

The least she could do was take it and offer something of hers in return.

"I have an offer for you," she whispered just as his tongue traced the outline of her lips.

"Is that right?" He pulled away and reached behind him.

Kerrie lifted herself up to see he was doing. He reached beneath the pillows and pulled out a long cloth.

She smiled. She knew exactly what that was. The scarf from the hotel gift shop. A hot flash of desire swept over her. If he had it hiding beneath the pillows that only meant one thing.

"How about we do a little bit of negotiating? I've heard that for some lawyers, it can be a form of foreplay." He let the scarf dangle from his fingers as a wicked glint filled his gaze.

Kerrie bit her lip. Foreplay indeed. "I'm sure I could be persuaded. Hey, whatever happened to my scarf from last night?"

Dylan chuckled. "Finder's keepers."

Kerrie smiled. Who knew this trip would hold so much promise?

For once in her life, Kerrie finally believed in the 'happily ever after'.

A Note From Steena...

Dear Reader;

Thank you for reading Sweet Retreat!

I know it's a little short, but it was cute, right? All the romance, with a touch of passion...who doesn't dream about meeting someone and fall in love with them right away?

I first wrote this book early on in my writing career, when my heart was full of excitement, and I had so many stories to tell...which, still sounds like me even now, even after all these years!

I loved setting this book in Banff. It's only an hour drive from my home and whenever we're in the mood for a drive, we always end up there, grabbing a beaver tail from the Main Street.

What's a beaver tail? For all my non-Canadian readers, it's a delicious pastry that's drenched in butter and smothered in toppings. My favorite is cinnamon sugar, but you could put icing and Skor bits or...well, anything really! Trust me when I say you'll have to try one!

I love to create reader trips and so far we've gone to Holland

and Paris, but one day I'm going to create a trip to my neck of the woods and if you join me, you can taste one for yourself!

Interested in knowing more about my reader trips? Check out my website and click on the **LET'S TRAVEL TOGETHER** tab!

I hope you enjoy a sweet life full of chocolate, happiness and peace.

Steena

A LOVE SO
SWEET NOVELLA

sweet
RENEWAL

STEENA MARIE HOLMES

New York Times Best Selling Author

Sweet Renewal

Seline Cook is focused on one thing, and one thing only — making sure her best friend Bex, otherwise known as Rebecca Teague, who months ago almost died, has the wedding of her dreams. Sounds easy, right?

What she doesn't expect is for Bex to go behind her back and ensure Seline is has her own dream come true.

Over a year ago, Seline ended her own engagement because she lost faith in Ethan James, her soul mate. In the past year, she's tried hard to move on: she started her own pastry photography company and is finally happy, or so she thinks.

Thrown together with Ethan as part of the wedding party, Seline has to fight against the pull in her heart to reconnect with Ethan. But since he's determined to win back her heart...is she strong enough to resist or is it already too late for her?

During Bex's bachelorette party, a game of Truth or Dare is played. Rather than face the truth, Seline takes a dare...and kisses the first man she sees.

Guess who that is?

Dear Reader...

By now you know I love sweets, right? Chocolate. Pastries. Cookies...all of it. In another life, I like to think I was a chocolatier, or...like in this book, a food photographer.

Welcome to my world of chocolate, mountains, romance, and wanderlust. The Love So Sweet series captures all the things I love the most - like second chances, believing in oneself, delicious chocolate and baked pastries, and of course...sweet romance that stands the test of time.

Each of the books in this series are short but sweet reads, stories you can read before bed or while sitting at the doctor's office or even while waiting for your plane to take off.

I have a few hopes for this series...that you enjoy them, that you want to travel to the settings I've placed them in, and that you wish you had a piece of chocolate in your hand as you read.

From my happy heart to yours...

HAPPY READING!

Chapter One

GRITTING her teeth while swallowing her growl of frustration, Seline Cook juggled the box of cupcakes in one hand, her heavy camera bag in the other, as her boots made a heavy thud-thud-thud sound as they connected to her steel condo door.

Inside her apartment, music blared, which only added to her frustration.

All she wanted was to climb into a hot bath, sip on a glass of wine and enjoy the delectable chocolate cupcake her client had given her today.

Was that too much to ask?

By the time she finagled the door open and set her camera bag down, she was ready to toss the cupcakes at her roommate, regardless of how amazing they looked and how delicious they tasted.

Bex, otherwise known as Rebecca, her roommate, and best friend, danced with abandonment to the music, back toward the door.

There was only one problem.

Seline stood off to the side, where Bex could see her, which she would have if her eyes were open.

So picked up a piece of paper off the kitchen table, crumpled it in her hand, and threw it at her friend, hitting her directly in the chest.

"What the..." Bex jumped and whirled in a circle, her hands covering her exposed chest in surprise.

"I didn't expect you home so soon." Bex's chest heaved before she reached for her phone and turned down the volume.

"I can see that."

She wasn't sure how she felt about what she saw. Her best friend stood there wearing her wedding gown. HER wedding gown. The one stuffed at the back of Seline's closet, never-to-see-the-light-of-day wedding gown.

Bex's gaze went downward, her hands danced with ease along the satin fabric, her smile almost angelic.

"What. Are. You. Wearing?" As if the answer wasn't obvious.

"Um..." Bex's eyes widened, her smile faltered for a moment before she gave her that you-caught-me-oops type of smile she was known for.

"What's in the box?" Bex totally ignored the obvious as she reached for the box of cupcakes Seline still held.

"Rebecca Eleanor Teague..." Seline struggled to keep her voice stern when in fact, the feeling she felt more than anything was shock.

"Why are you wearing my wedding dress and...and..." she inhaled, counted to three, then slowly exhaled, "why does it look better on you than it did on me?"

That last little bit just came out. The sly snake of insecurity mixed with jealousy bit hard, and the poison worked its way to her already tattered heart.

Bex was gorgeous. Drop-dead-with-no-clue type gorgeous, and there were days, usually most days, when it didn't bother Seline. But today was not that day.

Her best friend stood there, her long blond hair curled around her shoulders, the ends barely touching the material of the strapless gown.

Seline knew even without looking that Bex wasn't even wearing a push-up bra, unlike herself when she'd bought the gown, and she couldn't help but admit that it draped over Bex's body as if it belonged there, again, unlike herself.

Not fair. Not fair at all.

"I hate you," Seline muttered, unsure whether she meant the words or not.

Bex turned, her eyes wide and full of tears before she ran towards Seline and wrapped her arms around her.

"You don't mean that. I know you don't. Please tell me you don't," Bex begged as she held on tight.

Biting her lip until she was sure she'd broken skin, Seline forced her arms around her roommate, hating the feel of the wedding dress against her palms, and looked up at the ceiling, as if it could give her the help she needed.

"Of course, I don't mean that." There was no way anyone could hate someone as sweet as Bex. "I brought home cupcakes from my latest shoot, and I think you need to eat them all." She suppressed the grin that threatened to fill her face as Bex leaned back with a look of horror in her eyes.

"I can't do that. You know it. My wedding is next week, and if I ate them all, I would never fit into my dress." She recoiled in horror but Seline caught the way she gazed longingly at the box on the table.

"One isn't going to hurt. You probably only ate spinach and cucumbers all day anyways, right?"

"I was told today I can't make any more adjustments to the dress, so don't you dare tempt me."

Seline shook her head. "You changed the beading design again? Again, Bex? What was wrong with what you had?"

Seline made her way to the fridge and pulled out the jug of cold herbal tea she'd made this morning.

"I decided the beaded pattern looked too much like a woman's hooha and that wouldn't do."

"A woman's hoowhat?"

Bex's face flushed. "You know…"

Seline filled her cup as she struggled not to laugh. Bex's skin turned blazed a fiery red with embarrassment.

"It has an actual name, you know." Seline winked at her friend. "Have you told Brian? Considering he picked the design?" Which made the whole situation even more laughable. Brian loved to tease his bride; it didn't take much.

Bex's eyes were as wide as the cupcake now in her hand. "You don't think he did that on purpose, do you?"

Seline didn't even bother to smother her laughter. Of course, he did.

"No, of course not," she managed to get out. "He wouldn't do that to you."

Liar. She was such a liar. A good one, too, because Bex believed her.

"No, you're right. He wouldn't do that to me. Of course, he wouldn't. I bet he didn't even know." She perked up at the thought and headed towards her bedroom, cupcake in hand.

"Hey!" Seline called out.

Bex turned. "Oh, right. Thanks for the cupcake!" She blew Seline a kiss and closed her bedroom door.

Seline stood there, dumbfounded, as she watched her roommate walk away from her in her own wedding dress and not even realize it was an issue.

'Cause it was. Right?

If it wasn't…it should be?

Chapter Two

SELINE GRABBED HER ICED TEA, snagged a chocolate cupcake, and headed into the living room.

It was a shock to see her dress, there in all its glory, again. She'd stuffed it in the back of her closet over a year ago, and despite the momentary urges to pull it out, she never did. Because that wasn't her. She didn't wallow. She didn't throw pity parties, and she sure as wasn't one to live in the past.

So why should it matter if her best friend, the one person who should have known what that dress did or did not mean to her, wore it for no reason?

It shouldn't, but it did.

Seline curled her legs beneath her and trailed her finger through the amazing icing, her focus on Bex's door.

When Bex walked back out, a huge smile graced her face. She wore an old pair of Seline's rolled-up sweats and a white tank top with a sparkling crown across her chest. She flopped down on the couch and snuggled up close, rested her head on Seline's shoulder, and sighed.

"What would I do without you?" Her friend's voice was as light as air, as carefree as the wind, and as sweet as a pixie.

Friends since fifth grade, Bex was everything Seline was not. Innocent, joyful, happy, and sweet.

Seline was sweet, when she wanted or needed to be. But joyful? Not on your life. Happy? Only in crowds when she played up her single and loving-it persona.

There wasn't a mean bone in Bex's body, and she viewed everyone as a friend.

There was probably a really innocent reason for Bex to wear the dress she never wanted to see again.

"Well," Seline gave the most dramatic sigh she could muster, "for one, you wouldn't have any clothes to wear. And two, you would be stressing over a wedding that is going to be amazing." It wasn't hard to add a smile to her voice.

"It will be, won't it? I can't believe how easy everything has been, especially after the horror stories we went through with your wedding." She glanced up and frowned. "Oops, sorry. I just broke my promise never to mention your wedding again. Forgive me?"

Seline patted her friend's knee. "Don't' be silly. Now, want to tell me why you were wearing my dress?"

Bex bounced up on the sofa before she snuggled in on the other end.

"I just wanted to feel like a bride tonight. I would have worn my dress if it were here."

Seline leaned her head back on the couch. "Silly, you are a bride. And a very beautiful one."

"You're not mad, are you? I meant to have it off before you came home. But you were early." Bex's eyes narrowed. "Why were you early?"

Seline took a bite of her cupcake. They were part of the perks of her job as a food photographer. Her specialty was with pastry, thus the name of her company *Sweet Clicks,* and thankfully word spread like a wildfire after one of her images graced the cover of a national food magazine.

As for why she was home early...it was all her roommate's fault.

"I heard a rumor today and thought maybe I should hear it from the horse's mouth before I freak out."

Bex's face matched her skin tone from earlier. Beet red.

"You can't be serious?" Seline groaned. She'd really hoped... foolish but there it was, that it wasn't true.

"Bex...we talked about this." As if she needed to remind her friend.

"I know, I know. But...I need you. There's no one else I want. You know that. I've always wanted you to be my maid of honor. You're my best friend and—"

"I can't stand next to *him*, pretending all is okay when it's not."

"You said you were over him." Bex's voice was full of confusion and horror which covered Seline in a huge suffocating wool sweater of regret.

She hated hearing any of those emotions in Bex's voice. She'd sworn once to do everything she could to make sure her friend was always happy.

Except, how could Bex believe she could possible be over him? Seline doubted she ever would be. Ethan James had her heart the moment he'd stolen her fries at the local pub. It didn't matter distance between them, or the amount of hurt, she knew she'd never be over him.

Even if he was over her.

"Bex, that doesn't mean I want to spend the entire night by his side."

In fact, that was the last thing she wanted to. She could think of a number of other things she'd rather be doing...like herding crocodiles or building an igloo in the Arctic.

"Why? You're both adults, and it would mean the world to me."

Seline loved her friend, she really did, but she could be clueless.

"Please tell me you didn't plan this."

Bex reeled back in shock, her eyes wider than a tennis ball "Why would I do that? I've always wanted you to be my maid of honor, you know that, but when you said no, I accepted your decision, even though it hurt." Bex lowered her gaze and her lips trembled as if she were about to cry. "I've always dreamed of this day, and in those dreams, it's always been you who stood beside me."

Now Seline felt like a troll. She'd promised that this would be the wedding of Bex's dreams and she was about to ruin it.

Way to go.

"Lauren is lovely and my favorite cousin, but..." Bex's gaze never quite met Seline's.

"Bex..."

When Bex had originally asked her to be her maid of honor, Seline had almost said yes. Until she found out that Ethan would be flying from England to be the best man. She loved Bex, loved her like a sister, but she couldn't stand there, next to Ethan and remember. Not when she'd tried so hard to forget.

"I need you, Seline. Please?" Bex reached over to give Seline a big hug and squeezed tight before she rested her head on her shoulder.

There was only one thing she could do, no matter how she felt about it.

"You owe me, you realize that."

Bex leaned back, her eyes bright, and smiled. When she smiled, it was hard for Seline to remember why she'd said no in the first place.

"I love you." Bex leaned forward and planted a kiss on her cheek. "And I'll make it up to you, I promise."

By the gleam in Bex's eyes, Seline was either going to love this or hate it.

"Well, silly...instead of giving away that trip to a random guest at our wedding, I'm going to give it to you!"

Seline just sat there in...shock? Amazement? She wasn't quite sure.

Brian, Bex's fiancé, worked for a large corporate firm in Vancouver, British Columbia and one of his clients gave him a trip for two to Bora Bora to use either for their honeymoon or to give away to a guest.

Seline thought the idea a bit...over the top, but understood it was great promo for the client. Bex and Brian couldn't decide how to best give it away until Seline suggested they use it as an auction piece and then give the money to the Canadian Brain Tumor Association, an organization that helped Bex out when she had her brain surgery.

The tumor had a lasting impact on Bex, making her softer, somewhat gullible, and more emotionally unstable than before, but she was alive and healthy and for that, Seline was working with Brian to figure out a way for them to do a yearly fundraiser for the charity.

"You can't do that, Bex. That's a lot of money you could have donated."

She shrugged. "So, we'll find another way."

Seline shook her head. "No, I won't let you. How about you let me pick my own dress?"

"Then I'll pay for it."

"Bex!" Seline shook her head again and got up from the couch. "You are not spending your money on me. Just let me pick my dress. It'll be in the same colors as the others, but I swear…if you make me wear that strapless piece, I'll…I'll object during the ceremony!"

Bex gasped in disbelief before a wide smile filled her face. "Deal. You know I love you, right?"

"I love you too, darlin'." Seline sighed. "You know I'll do anything for you…even this."

Bex stood up and headed into the kitchen where she poured herself a tall glass of milk. "Who knows, maybe you and Ethan will get back together? Then you'll have your dream come true. I know it."

Seline's jaw gapped open and the only sound that made it out of her open mouth sounded like a high pitched squeak.

"Are you okay?" Bex stared at her like she'd sprouted purple wings.

Seline snapped her jaw shut and swallowed hard. "The only dreams I'm interested in coming true are the ones I make happen." She ignored the way Bex's eyes narrowed. "And," she continued, "getting back with Ethan isn't something I want. Not anymore. Besides…with a week until your wedding, we have other things to talk about."

"We do?"

Seline gasped in mock horror. "We do? You even have to ask? Um, bachelorette party…hello?"

Bex threw her arms up in the air and danced in a circle. "I can't wait! My very own bachelorette party! You're the bestest girlfriend ever, you know that, right?"

Bex's dance put a smile in Seline's heart.

"Not only that, but the bestest maid of honor ever." Seline rolled her eyes as at the new title but she was determined to make sure this bachelorette party and wedding went off without a hitch. All for Bex, for her dreams, for what she almost lost.

Even if it meant letting Ethan back into her life.

Chapter Three

"Dude, I'm not wearing that."

No way, no how, was he going to wear the outfit that hung in front of him. The black suit was fine. Even the pink cummerbund he could handle. Real men wore pink; he even had a t-shirt from the Calgary Stampede he attended one year with that saying.

He could do pink, not a problem.

But the tie. That was out of the question.

"What's wrong with it?" Brian asked.

What was wrong with it? Was his friend blind? So blinded by love that he'd do anything, wear anything, be willing to look like a fool for Bex?

Of course, he was. This was Bex, after all.

"It sparkles."

"So?"

"Dude, I love you, you're like a brother to me, but I will not wear a bedazzled pink tie."

"It's sequins, not bedazzled, and Bex made them herself." Brian crossed his arms and smiled like a cat toying with a mouse.

Seriously? Brian was enjoying himself way too much here.

"Mother freakin' Teresa could have made these for orphans in India, and I wouldn't wear it. What's wrong with a bow tie or even a striped tie with pink in it to match?"

Brian shrugged. "Deal with it. It's what she wants. Besides, I've got my revenge."

One word was all it took to ease the guilt Ethan started to feel about hating the tie.

"Revenge?"

Ethan took the beer Brian handed him and twisted the cap off. This had better be good.

"We made a bet, and I lost."

Ethan snickered. "You never lose a bet. Ever." He'd learned long ago never to bet against Brian.

Brian shrugged. "This is Bex we're talking about. She can play...dirty, when she wants to." There was a gleam in his eye when he said it, and Ethan didn't have to ask what he meant by that.

A woman always knew how to win. Always.

"So you have to wear a sparkling tie?"

He shook his head and then nodded. "The deal was if I lost, she got to pick out our ties. Apparently, she didn't like what I'd chosen. And if she lost, then I got to pick out what she has to wear on our wedding night."

"So you lost on purpose?" That didn't make sense at all.

From the smile on his friend's face, Ethan knew there was more to the story.

"You think I really lost? I've already bought the negligée she's going to wear, and I'll give it to her as a gift after the reception."

Ethan glanced at the ties and shook his head. "Not worth it, dude. Not worth it at all. Where does the revenge part come in?"

"I gave the seamstress a design I wanted her to do in those tiny beads on Bex's train."

And now Ethan was lost. He downed his beer, slid the empty bottle across the table and waited for Brian to explain.

"It's a vagina."

"A what?" He couldn't have hard him right.

A devilish grin filled Brian's face. "My sweet bride is going to be walking down the aisle with the outline of a beaded vagina on her train."

A burst of laughter escaped from Ethan's chest as he pictured Bex walking down the aisle. She'd be mortified.

Once he caught his breath, Ethan shook his head in disbelief, but there was no way he could wipe the grin off his face. "No way. You wouldn't do that to her, I know you. She will freak when she finds out."

"Nah. She'll laugh and be all embarrassed, and then your girl will swoop in to save the day by saying it looks like a cal...a callil...one of those flowers in her bouquet."

At the thought of *his girl*, Ethan smiled. He couldn't wait to see her. It was all he thought about on his flight from England. The way her chocolate brown eyes melted when she wanted to be kissed, how perfect she'd felt in his arms the last time he'd held her.

He was determined to win her back, to find out why she'd pulled away from him so quickly, and to put his ring back on her finger.

Those were his goals.

His reasons for coming back home.

Working with Brian was just the excuse.

"A calla lily? Does Seline know about this?"

Brian snorted. "I should probably mention it to her, huh?"

Ethan replied in kind. "Yeah, maybe give her a heads-up."

Although, knowing Seline, she'd do everything she could to help calm Bex and not be too stressed about her dress.

Bex was...a good soul. He'd first met her through Seline. Actually, that's how he'd met both Bex and Brian.

He'd gone with a bunch of friends from college to a local pub to watch a football game. The pub was packed, and he found himself sandwiched between two tables, his own and Seline's.

At the time, Bex had been a ball of fire, whereas Seline had been the calm one. Since Bex's brain tumor, their roles had reversed. From what Brian had told him, Seline did what she could to shelter Bex, and in public settings where Bex used to thrive but now panicked, Seline kept the focus on herself and helped Bex sit in the background, where she wouldn't be noticed too much.

"Have you talked to her yet?"

Ethan shook his head. He wanted to. Hell, he'd dialed her number so many times but always hung up before pushing the last number.

To say he was afraid of her rejecting his overtures was an understatement.

"Don't you think you should?" Brian set another beer down in front of him. "Does she even know you're back for good?"

Ethan decided not to answer that question and focused on his beer and the ugly tie again.

"Do you think she'd be mad if I wore a different tie?"

"You won't." Brian sounded smug about it.

"I will." No way would he wear that thing.

"Dude, it's not your wedding. You'll only need to wear it for a short time, then you can take it off."

Ethan thought about that. As long as he didn't need to wear it for the whole night, he'd suck it up.

"One picture." He'd be sure to pick up a pink tie to swap out. "That's it. One, and then it's off."

Brian raised his bottle. "Deal." He turned on the television and flipped to the sports channel, where they watched the highlights for a few minutes.

"Have I said thank you yet?" Brian asked.

Ethan pulled his gaze from the latest analysis of last night's football game and leaned forward. "For what?"

"For leaving everything and coming here. To work with me."

Ethan stared at his friend, read the emotions behind the words, and gave a stiff nod.

"I should be thanking you." Ethan stared at this beer bottle. He didn't want to get all mushy and stuff, but this needed to be said.

"Investment banking is not for the faint of heart, and honestly, I'm burnt-out. You gave me the excuse I needed."

Burnt-out didn't even begin to describe how he felt.

More like lost. Somehow, in the craziness of his job, which quickly became his life, he'd become someone he didn't like, didn't recognize, and knew if he didn't do something about it, there'd be no turning back.

He'd lost so much to pursue a goal that, in the end, wasn't worth it.

He'd lost the woman he loved, wasn't there for his parents when they needed him, couldn't be there like he'd wanted for Brian when Bex had her surgeries, lost so much time...time he'd planned to use to travel, to see the world, and experience new things.

The only travel he did was for work, and the only new things he experienced were in hotels and airplanes.

It was rare for him to do any type of sightseeing in the amazing countries he visited for work purposes.

That wasn't the life he wanted to live.

Nor did he want to continue living alone.

"If it wasn't for you," Brian leaned forward and slapped Ethan's knee, "I don't think I could get this foundation for Bex running, not the way it needs to. You're a godsend."

Ethan didn't do well with praise. "I know money and how to make it work for you. I'm no miracle worker, trust me."

Brian leaned back in his chair and crossed his legs. "For Bex and me, you are."

Both Brian and Bex came from money, had money, and after Bex's recovery, both decided to use that money to help others. And so Bex's foundation had been created, or rather, was in the midst of being created.

There was a lot of red tape associated with starting a charitable foundation, but between Brian and him, they could do it.

"The fact that you jumped on board so quickly, I'll be honest, surprised me."

Ethan stood up and stretched. "I needed a change, you know that. And I'm glad I can help. I'll always regret not being there, with you, during..." His voice trailed off because he knew the time of Bex's illness...was a rough spot for Brian.

"You were there. Always." Brian stood and placed his hand on Ethan's shoulder. "No, you might not have been there physically, but you answered your phone every time I called. And it was you who found that surgeon for us, the one who saved Bex's life. So, dude, enough already."

It killed Ethan that he hadn't been there.

Brian had been there for him when his parents had passed away, he'd been there when Seline broke off their engagement, and he'd been there as a sounding board whenever he felt as though he was going crazy from his job.

Brian had always been there for him. Like a brother. But when he'd needed Ethan the most...

He should have quit his job last year, when he got news that Bex might not survive. He should have rushed home for his friend instead of taking on that last project at work.

And yet, it was through the connections of that last project that he'd been introduced to Dr. Greary, the man who agreed to operate on Bex's inoperable tumor.

Ethan drew in a deep breath. Enough. He had to stop wallowing in the past. That's not who he was, and moving back here meant getting in touch with that man he used to admire, the man he wanted to become again.

The man worthy of the love of Seline Barr.

Chapter Four

"I'M GOING TO CALL HER." His announcement came out of the blue but Brian obviously had expected it.

"It's about time." He pulled out his phone and glanced down at the screen. "Bex says Seline came home early from her photo shoot. Want me to find an excuse for Bex to leave? Give you guys some privacy?"

"You think she'd actually meet with me? The last time I spoke with her, I was under the impression she never wanted to see me again. Maybe I should start slow..."

Brian's phone buzzed.

"Don't act too slow. The plan worked."

It took a moment for Brian's words to sink in. The plan—their plan: his and Bex's.

"It worked? She agreed?" He couldn't keep the excitement from his voice.

"Bex really didn't give her a chance, I'd imagine. She wanted her to be her maid of honor even more than you did."

A slow grin spread across Ethan's face. When he'd found out about Seline's refusal to be the maid of honor because it meant spending time with him, he'd been hurt. Until he realized all Seline was doing was protecting her heart. If she wasn't still in love with him, if she'd moved on, then it wouldn't have mattered. But the fact she was so adamant about it...it gave him hope.

"Well now...this changes things, doesn't it?"

Ethan didn't bother to wait for Brian to agree with him. He grabbed his phone and pulled up Seline's contact and sent her a text.

It only made sense for the two of them to work together, didn't it? They had parties to plan, a rehearsal dinner to attend... and if that wasn't enough, he'd find more excuses.

"So? Do you?" Brian asked.

"Do...what?"

"Want some privacy with Seline? I have no problem finding an excuse to see my girl again tonight."

Ethan dialed Seline's number but didn't hit the connect button. "Phone call is all I need, but don't let me stop you." He yawned; he hadn't realized just how tired he was. "Besides, I'm pretty wiped from the flight today. I'm going to call it a night."

Once in the spare room Brian offered him until he found his own place, Ethan reclined back on his bed and called Seline. He waited in anticipation to hear her voice.

"Why did I know you were going to call?" Seline sighed into the phone. The sound of it sent shivers along Ethan's body.

"Well, hello to you too, beautiful."

There was a pause on the other end and no doubt she was taking in the word beautiful, something he called her all the time in the past.

"When did you get in?"

Damn, she sounded cold. Detached. Not how he imagined their call to go at all.

"A few hours ago." And it was all he could do not to have called her the moment his flight landed.

"You must be exhausted."

"A little." He lied. He was more than exhausted. Lethargy had set in and he doubted he could get up to change before he crawled beneath the sheets.

There were so many things he wanted to say but didn't, couldn't. He had to take things slow, to not push too hard too fast.

"I've missed you."

And then there was silence. Why did he say it? That wasn't taking it slow. That was rushing it, forcing her to acknowledge emotions she probably hadn't had time to sort through yet.

Good one, duffus.

"Please don't."

He almost missed her whisper-soft words.

"I've never lied to you, Seline. I won't start now. I have missed you."

"Why did you call?" Her voice was a mere whisper.

"Because I couldn't not call." His voice hitched and the silence on the line grew. "We have a wedding to help plan, from what I hear."

"What do you mean by *we*? You're in charge of the bachelor party. That's it."

Not if he had anything to say about it.

"Brian is swamped with getting the foundation set up and asked if I could step in and help out."

"Step...step in? Like with what? The wedding is a week away..." He heard the desperation in her voice and that was good. Very, very good for him.

It meant she still had feelings for him. He knew it.

"There's that meeting with the caterer, the florist, apparently some songs are getting changed, and then there's the rehearsal dinner."

"I've got that all covered." A level of determination mixed with exasperation in Seline's voice.

"I'm sure you do. But I'm here to help lighten the load. Besides, I think we should come up with something really creative for the stag and doe."

"The what?" This time it was Seline's voice that hitched.

"You know, the party where both the bride and groom are together?"

"No. That's...no," Seline sputtered.

Ethan had a hard time not smiling.

"They are separate. Separate parties. No togetherness, not till the wedding," Seline finished.

"Oh, come on, Selly." His nickname for her slipped out. "It would be fun. We can hold our separate parties and then get the whole group together before the night ends. We should all celebrate together, don't you think?"

"Is this what Brian wants? Because Bex hasn't said anything about it to me, and quite frankly, whatever Bex wants, she gets."

"She'll want this." He'd make sure of it.

"She won't. She wants a fun night, focused solely on her."

Ethan heard the lie in Seline's voice.

"Are you sure that's what she wants?" He let the question sink in, letting her know that he was aware of Bex's personality change since her surgery.

"Why don't we get together tomorrow morning for coffee and figure this out?" he suggested. "Let's meet down at Revolver, like we used to," he added before she could say no.

Revolver used to be their favorite coffee joint in the Gastown district. Seline had loved it for the world art made out of nails on the one wall, whereas he loved it for the coffee.

When she sighed, which she seemed to do a lot throughout the call, he knew she wasn't going to say no.

"One hour. That's all you get. I've got a busy day planned and really don't have time for this."

"One hour of planning. Got it." There was so much more he wanted to say. "See you tomorrow."

He knew Seline inside and out, and although this impersonal vibe he got didn't seem like her, it was possible he'd hurt her more than he'd imagined.

And yet...there was still hope. She didn't say no. She didn't argue, much, about them working together, and she didn't seem all that bothered when his little slips about how much he'd missed her came out either.

All in all, a better conversation than he'd expected. Especially considering this was the first time they'd spoken since she'd broken off their engagement.

He needed to plan things right for tomorrow. It was the weekend, so hopefully, that meant she didn't have any photo shoots planned, and if that was the case, then he'd somehow make sure that their day stretched for as long as possible.

He wanted his ring back on her finger by the wedding.

He realized he only had a week but now that all the reasons Seline had used to break off their wedding no longer existed...it shouldn't be that hard to convince her to give them another chance. Right?

Chapter Five

SHE KICKED herself for the umpteenth time for agreeing to this. As much as she enjoyed walking through Gastown, it held too many painful memories for her.

Memories of her and Ethan as they'd explored the boutique shops, drank way too much coffee, and had fallen in love.

She couldn't walk the streets anymore. Not alone. If she had to be in the area for business, she drove or had someone with her and never, never visited any of the places imprinted with their love.

It hurt too much.

It still hurt too much, even today, as she walked along the street, seeing echoes of what once had been her life.

One hour. That's what she'd agreed to, and that's what she could handle.

One hour and her heart stayed intact.

One hour and she could walk away without tears in her eyes.

One hour remembering exactly why she'd broken their engagement to begin with.

She could do this.

She'd tossed and turned last night, barely sleeping, thanks to him.

Every time she'd close her eyes, she'd see him. His face, his eyes, the warmth in his gaze as he held her, a look that quickly turned to hurt and ache as she tore herself out of his arms. Her dreams always left her waking up crying, and last night was no different.

There was a past between them that she wasn't sure they could erase. It wasn't just their broken engagement. He'd broken her trust in a way she wasn't sure she could ever forgive. Ever.

She wanted to be mad at him. She needed to be. That furious rage within her soul fueled her when the memories threatened to drown her.

And yet...the moment she'd heard his voice on the other end of the phone last night, she'd melted into a puddle of wishfulness. It had taken all her strength to be curt and short and not to give in when he'd said he'd missed her.

He'd missed her.

The moment she saw him, she stumbled, stubbed her foot on the sidewalk, and almost fell face-first onto the pavement.

She threw her arms out and knocked the person beside her, who thankfully grabbed on and helped steady her.

"I'm so sorry," she said, suddenly out of breath. She dreaded looking up, embarrassed to have made such a scene.

"Whoa there, Selly-belly."

A voice from the past almost knocked her over again as she took a step backward, bumping into someone else who passed by at the wrong time.

"Sorry." She mumbled before she made herself look up into the eyes of Chad Benson, an old flame from days gone by.

"Just clumsy as usual." She tried to beam a large smile up at the very handsome man who stood before her. But her smile quickly became a grimace as she put her weight on her ankle and realized she'd twisted it a little.

"Are you okay?" Chad's grip on her arm tightened as he looked down at her foot.

Seline sighed. Out of the corner of her eye, she saw Ethan stand there, waiting for her, and she realized her little mishap was a blessing in disguise.

She leaned into her ex-boyfriend and glanced up at him. "Can you help me to the bench over there? I think I twisted my ankle the wrong way."

They made their way over to the bench, and Seline sat down, Chad beside her, a concerned look on his face.

"I was hoping to run into you while I was in town, but not like this." He reached down for her ankle and gently propped it up on his thigh. His fingers rubbed her skin, his touch soft as he checked for swelling.

"How long are you here for? It's been a long time." She angled herself to get comfortable and placed her arm across the back of the bench, her fingers close to his arm.

He looked good. Very good. She could tell he'd been working out from the way his muscles bulged beneath his white top. They hadn't been like that back when they'd dated, but then, as an intern at the San Fran General Hospital, he didn't really have the time either.

"Just the weekend. I'm here speaking at a workshop at the hospital."

"Is Eileen here too?"

Chad shook his head. "She has some critical patients she didn't want to leave."

"That's too bad." Seline really liked Chad's bride of almost one year, who happened to be a surgeon. "I promised her I'd take her on a chocolate tour the next time you guys were here." She couldn't help but look over Chad's shoulder.

Ethan was still there.

Chad's prodding had stopped, and he rested his hand on her ankle. "I think you'll be fine. Go for a nice stroll and stretch it out." He leaned back. "Is that Ethan down there waiting for you?"

Seline had a hard time tearing her gaze away, so she just nodded while she drank in the sight of the man who still haunted her dreams.

"When did he return home?"

She shrugged. "He's here for Bex's wedding." She knew that didn't really answer his question, but it was the best she could do. "You're still coming, right?"

"I wouldn't miss it. Eileen is going to try, too."

His gaze sought hers, and she smiled. She knew that look all too well. Chad worked as a psychologist in Seattle, but while they'd dated, it used to drive her up the wall when he'd attempt to psychoanalyze her.

"I'm fine. We're just meeting for coffee to go over the last-minute wedding details since he's the best man and I'm the maid of honor." Even she heard the lie in her voice.

Sure, that might be the excuse, but deep down, she knew this meeting was about more than just Brian and Bex's wedding.

She caught his glance at her ring finger but didn't say anything.

"You look exhausted," was all he said.

She laughed and ran a hand through her hair. "I'm way past exhausted. I'm running on fumes here and will until Bex is on her honeymoon."

He nodded, as if he understood. And, of course, he would. He'd been the one she called, time in and out, with advice on Bex and how to handle things.

At first, Bex's depression from the meds before her surgery had been manageable, until they found out from the doctor that her tumor was inoperable. And then after—when the change in her best friend was so drastic—Seline had used Chad as a sounding board.

Despite their past, or maybe because of their past, she was so glad they'd remained friends. Chad's hectic schedule at the hospital, combined with her having to take care of her now-deceased mother, left them little time to focus on their relationship. They'd parted ways as better friends than boyfriend and girlfriend.

"How's your business going?"

This time, Seline's smile was genuine. "Really well." She loved Sweet Clicks, her photography company. It was the only thing in her life that was really *hers*. It was there, during the photo shoots and afterward while she worked on the images, that she could lose herself and just *be*.

"Are you taking photos during the wedding?"

She sighed. "I'm supposed to, or I was. But now I've been roped into being the maid of honor, which will make it hard... unless Bex doesn't mind me wearing a camera around my neck most of the day." She shook her head at the thought. No, that wouldn't work. Thankfully she had some favors to call in. She should be able to find a replacement.

"I hate to ask this, but..." Chad gave her one of his *don't-bother-lying-to-me* looks.

She sighed. She had a feeling she knew what he was about to ask and she wasn't sure how she'd answer him.

"Are you making Ethan wait for a reason?"

Chapter Six

THAT WASN'T the question she'd expected him to ask but she felt just as uncomfortable.

Seline tried really hard not to look at Ethan again, but she wasn't that strong. He looked so good, even from a distance.

"Would you believe me if I said no? That I'd forgotten all about him being down there?"

Chad's brow rose. "If you weren't continually trying to sneak peeks at him over my shoulder, then maybe I would."

She blushed. "That obvious, huh?"

He set her foot down on the ground and then reached for her hand to help her up. "Why don't I walk you down to him? The least I can do is say hi."

There was a bit of bad blood between Ethan and Chad. Ethan had always been a bit jealous of their friendship and Chad didn't think he was good enough for her. Turned out he was right.

"Is he back just for the wedding, or is he back for good?"

"No idea. I haven't really asked." She tried really hard to pretend as though it didn't matter, that she'd moved past him... but she could read the pity in Chad's gaze loud and clear.

"For what it's worth, I did like the guy."

She snorted. "You did not."

He shrugged. "I did. I just didn't like where his priorities were. If he'd loved you more, then I would have been okay with him. But he didn't love you enough, not enough to put you first, and that's where you belong. That's the kind of man you deserve. Someone who will put you first for a change, take care of you...instead of you trying to take care of everyone else."

Speechless, Seline didn't know what to say. She'd honestly thought Chad hated Ethan. Her ankle ached for the first little bit, but the more she stretched it as they walked, the better it felt.

"I'm not even sure I would know what to do with that kind of love," she admitted as Ethan headed towards them. Her stomach knotted up the closer they approached.

Chad's hold around her waist tightened. "I know," he said. "But I hope one day you'll find out."

"Not everyone is destined to find the love of their life, you know." She forced her gaze from Ethan's—which was difficult, by the way—and looked up at Chad. "Not like you and Eileen or like Bex and Brian. Some soul mates are never found."

And even when they are, it wasn't as if the universe made it easy for them to be together. But she didn't say that part out loud.

Chad stopped them, mere feet away from Ethan, and leaned down close.

"I have a feeling you've already found your soul mate," he whispered into her ear.

"You talk nonsense quite often, you know that, right?" she whispered back.

Chad just smiled. "Men can be quite stupid, trust me. Eileen tells me that all the time. Sometimes it takes us a bit to grow up."

By now they'd met up with Ethan and any words Seline had

wanted to say were swallowed up as she stared at her ex-fiancé and drank him in.

It had been over a year, fifteen months actually since Seline had last seen him, and he looked good. Decadent-hot-chocolate-with-handmade-chocolate-bark-on-the-side good.

She barely heard the words passed between Chad and Ethan as they shook hands and greeted one another.

He'd lost weight and his shoulders slumped forward more than she remembered. His hair was longer; little curls wrapped around his ears and reached the collar of his shirt.

She wanted to run her fingers through it, to feel what it was like being that long, because he'd always kept it cropped and short for work.

"Seline, are you okay?" Ethan met her glance, and she caught the worried look on his face.

It must have taken her longer than acceptable to answer him because Chad did it for her.

"She just tripped and twisted her ankle the wrong way, but nothing serious."

"Should she be walking on it?" Ethan went to take a step forward but then stopped himself. Seline wondered why, until at that moment, Chad's arm released her and she was left there, standing alone.

"I'm fine." She swallowed and took in a deep breath. "Thankfully, Chad was there to break my fall." She looked up at him and then stared down at the ground, feeling slightly uncomfortable beneath both men's gaze.

The silence between the three was...awkward, to say the least.

"So," Chad was the brave one to speak first, "I'm on my way to meet with another presenter at this conference, so I should be going." He turned to Seline. She had a moment of panic when she realized he was about to leave her. "It was good seeing you."

He leaned down and kissed her cheek. "Save me a dance next week, okay?"

She smiled up at him. "Promise." She watched him walk away and hugged herself, feeling very unsure at the moment about what the next few minutes would entail.

Chapter Seven

S ELINE BREATHED IN DEEP, needing to center herself before she turned her gaze from Chad, her ex-boyfriend, to Ethan, her ex-fiancé.

"Well, should we grab our coffee?" She glanced around and noticed a few empty tables where they could sit and discuss the wedding.

Although, she had everything under control. She'd even said as much to Bex this morning.

"You've carried me and this wedding more than any non-bride should. Let the man help," Bex had said as she pushed her out their apartment door this morning.

"Fine," she'd mumbled beneath her breath.

If Bex wanted Ethan involved, then okay, she could handle it. As long as his involvement didn't mean extra alone time between the two of them.

"Are you sure you're okay?" The concern in Ethan's voice was so evident.

"I'm fine. Honestly. I just..." she glanced around as if trying to find someone, "I can't believe I actually hit someone." Her cheeks blazed and she pretended it was from embarrassment.

"Why don't you sit down and rest that ankle." He indicated towards the one of the tables. "I can grab us a coffee."

Her stomach growled, and the only culprit to blame was herself. The mouth-watering smells from the shop filled the air, and she'd left without eating breakfast.

"And maybe a muffin or two?" Ethan's eyes twinkled, and he reached for her hand.

Without even thinking, Seline entwined her fingers with his. The touch of heat that radiated off him had her pull her hand away, except he wouldn't let her.

She wasn't going to lie. It felt good to hold his hand again, to have their skin touch, to feel connected. But she released his grip a moment later and stuck her hands inside her pockets.

It had been a long fifteen months since she'd last seen Ethan. Fifteen months of being alone, of trying not to feel lonely and missing him more than she ever wanted to admit. Ending their engagement had been the toughest decision she'd ever made, and on the whole, she didn't regret it. But she'd lost a part of herself when she lost him.

Chad was right. Ethan was her soul mate. Unfortunately, being soul mates didn't mean a thing when life got in the way, and decided to play dirty.

She trailed behind Ethan as they made their way to a table and then mentally kicked herself for reacting the way she had as he walked away. If she wasn't careful, she'd let him sweep her off her feet, only to get hurt again—she knew it.

If she were smart, she'd make sure her schedule was booked so that by the time he left to go back to London, she would hardly miss him.

Except, she knew she wasn't that smart.

Her heart skipped a beat as he came her way with a huge smile on his face. He laid the tray down on the table and then took a seat opposite of her. Seline's stomach grumbled again.

"It's not a muffin, but the chocolate croissant is fresh from the oven, same as the cinnamon bun."

Seline leaned in and inhaled the amazing smells of fresh pastry and cinnamon.

"So, where is yours?" She gave a hint of a smile.

Ethan produced a plastic knife. "I figured we could share. I couldn't decide which one I wanted more, although, I'm not sure the chocolate croissant could be better than what I had in Paris." He cut the croissant and cinnamon bun in half and waited for her to pick first.

"Sure, rub it in. I can't wait to go and try one for myself." She picked up her half of the croissant and took a bite.

"You'd love Paris. I can see you walking along the Seine in the early morning, stopping at a cafe for coffee, walking into a patisserie for fresh bread, and then walking along the cobbled streets in search of chocolate."

Seline smiled sadly. It had always been her dream to go, but sadly, she was never able to. They'd planned to honeymoon there, and now, she knew if she ever went, that's all she would think about.

"Maybe one day I'll go," was all she said.

Seline picked away at her croissant and half of the cinnamon bun, enjoying every last bite while she gazed around the area, watched the crowds, and listened to the noise. She loved to take it all in. She reached for the small digital camera she kept in her purse and took photos, wanting—no, needing—to capture the moment. As she sat there, with Ethan, she felt strangely at peace, despite also feeling as if she was on an emotional roller coaster.

"What are you thinking?" Ethan asked her.

She placed the camera down on the table between them and looked Ethan in the eyes.

She reminded herself to stay strong, to remain detached, to remember the reason they weren't together anymore.

And with that thought, she squared her shoulders and met his gaze.

"Why here? Of all places?"

Ethan twisted in his seat and looked around the area. "Whenever I think about coming back, this is the place I think about. There's so much history in this area, memories that I can't let go, and they all center around you."

"There is no us, not anymore, Ethan." It hurt to even say the words.

He nodded his gaze down to his plate. "I know, and that's my fault. I wish...there's a lot of things I wish I had done differently, but losing you is my biggest regret."

She wanted to believe him but couldn't.

"My biggest regret was believing in you in the first place." The words tumbled out of her mouth. The moment she said them, she knew they hurt, that she'd cut deep from the way he recoiled from her.

"And I wish you'd never stopped," he said quietly.

Seline breathed in deep. They were not going to do this, not here, not now. They couldn't.

Maybe after the wedding, after Bex and Brian were off on their honeymoon, when things had calmed down, and no one needed her to be anything but...*her*. Maybe then she could face this issue and relive the past in order to move forward.

But not today.

Chapter Eight

SHE NEEDED to get this conversation back on track. There was no sense rehashing their past or what they should have done or didn't do...all that was in the past.

"You wanted to discuss the wedding plans. I'm not sure what you think it is you need to do, other than plan the bachelor party—"

"Right," Ethan interrupted her. "So that's how we're going to do this?"

"Do what? I thought we were here to discuss—"

"The wedding. I know." Ethan jammed his fingers into his hair and pulled. "I was hoping we could just talk, you know, like two grown adults?"

Cold. She needed to stay cold.

"We are. We're talking. About the wedding. That's the whole reason we're here, remember?" She wasn't sure, though, who needed to be reminded more: her or him.

"Yes, the wedding. Of course. But you haven't asked how I am, or how was London, or even how long I'm here for. We used to be best friends and could talk about anything. Or don't you remember that?" The desperation in his voice snagged a piece of the crumbling brick around her heart and pulled.

She wasn't going to give in. She couldn't. He'd betrayed her in a way she wasn't sure she could ever forgive.

"Used to be, being the keyword there, Ethan. It's been over a year since we last spoke, so I'm not sure exactly what it is you're expecting from me." Other than not being so cold. She knew her words and attitude were hurtful and she hated being like this.

"How about asking me how I am?" Ethan leaned back in his chair and crossed his arms over his chest.

She sighed.

"Fine. You're right. I'm being rude. How are you?"

A grin broke out on his face. "See, that wasn't so hard, was it?"

She only rolled her eyes.

"I'm great, actually. It feels good to be...home." His voice drifted off and she almost wasn't sure she caught that last word.

"Home?" London was his home, not Vancouver. Not anymore.

"Yeah, didn't Bex tell you?"

A pit the size of a golf ball lodged in her stomach. "Tell me what?"

"I quit my job in London and moved back here. I'm staying with Brian for now and then will sublease his place for the rest of his term once they move into their new home."

"Sub...you're...you quit?" Her mind went blank at his words, and she felt lost.

"I quit my job and moved back here," Ethan repeated, but slower this time.

"Yeah, I got that. But why?"

He shrugged. "Brian needed help in running the foundation, so I offered my services."

"You what?"

He what? She couldn't have heard him right. The Ethan she knew wouldn't have quit his job to help run a charitable foundation.

The Ethan she knew didn't care about friends or family.

The Ethan she knew put his career on a pedestal and worshipped the ground it sat on. He wouldn't have quit.

She didn't believe him.

"Brian needed me. And this...this I could do." Something in his voice called out to her. Regret maybe?

No, she didn't believe it.

When his parents had died, he'd flown in on a red-eye to attend their funeral and deal with any last-minute issues and then returned back to London to an account he'd just landed.

When her mom had collapsed, and they found out cancer she'd battled years ago was back and had spread throughout her body, he'd stayed in London because he was on the verge of landing a partnership with his firm.

Then, when her mother died and Bex found out she had an inoperable brain tumor...he hadn't even flown home to be with her or to stand with Brian, who became a nervous wreck.

That's when she'd realized Ethan wasn't the man she thought him to be. And yet, she loved him. Or had. He said all the right things, sent her gifts and love letters, and she pretended that it was enough.

Except it wasn't. And so she'd broken their engagement.

So no, she didn't believe that he would quit his job to come work with Brian.

"Why now?" She didn't even bother to try to hide the anger in her voice.

No, that wasn't right. She wasn't angry. She was furious.

"Don't answer that." She struggled to regain control. "I don't care." She fisted her hands in her lap and dug her fingernails into her palms, relishing the pain from the indents. "You should have moved back a long time ago. Whatever your reasons are now, they don't concern me." She unclenched her hands and glanced down at the deep grooves from her nails with a sense of detachment.

"Let's just talk about the wedding, shall we?" When she finally met his gaze, she prayed he saw the fury in her eyes.

When she got home, she was going to have a little chat with her darling roommate. And this time, she didn't care whether she hurt Bex's feelings. How could Bex have thought to keep this from her?

"Seline..." Ethan's voice died off as she continued to stare directly into his eyes. He sighed and slowly shook his head.

"This isn't how I envisioned today," he mumbled.

She snorted with feigned laughter and then saw the hope die in his eyes.

Unbelievable. What had he expected? That they would gaze into each other's eyes, and the past would be erased? That they'd continue where they left off? That she would forgive him?

"Not how you envisioned today? Please don't tell me you thought we would kiss and make up." She shook her head and glanced away, staring down the street and seeing ghosts of the past. She closed her eyes, the memories too painful.

When he didn't answer, she wasn't surprised.

"You actually did." She said. "Why? Why would you think I could forgive and forget?"

"I made mistakes." He swallowed heavily. "But I'd hoped you had forgiven me by now."

She shook her head in disbelief.

"I forgave you when you couldn't make it to my mother's funeral. Hell, I even forgave you when you kept giving me excuse after excuse for why you had to stay in London. But I will never," she leaned forward in her chair, "ever forgive you for not being there for Brian and Bex when they needed you the most." She spat out the words before she pushed her chair back.

"Do whatever it is you want to do for Brian's party. I don't care. Just take good care of him and make sure he makes it to the church in time. There's nothing else we need to discuss or do together. As far as I'm concerned, I only need to stand opposite you at the wedding—nothing else. Do you understand?"

Ethan hung his head and didn't reply.

She didn't care. She grabbed her purse, stuffed her camera back inside, and turned away from him.

Right now, she was so bloody furious she was tempted to tell Bex to find another maid of honor. As far as she was concerned, she wanted nothing to do with her or Brian right now. How dare they keep something like him moving back for good from her?

She swiped at the tears that fell from her eyes and ignored the soft ache in her heart as she walked away, again, from the man she thought to be her soul mate.

Chapter Nine

"Dude, you've got to tell her." Brian poked Ethan in the chest, hard.

"No." Telling her, looking for a sympathy vote—that wasn't how Ethan wanted to win back Seline.

"She deserves to know."

"No." Ethan wasn't about to budge on this.

"You're impossible!" Brian threw up his hands in exasperation, crossed the room, yanked open a closet door, and threw a luggage bag down at his feet.

"You might as well start packing then because if you're only goal coming here was to win her back, it's not going to happen." With feet planted apart and his arms crossed, the only way Ethan would describe Brian right now was pissed.

"That's not the only reason, and you know it." Ethan rolled his neck to work out the kinks.

"What I know is you're not taking this seriously at all. It's been how many days since she's spoken a word to any of us? You, fine, that's expected. And okay, I get she's angry with me too. But Bex? She hasn't even said a word to her—and they live together for Pete's sake!"

Ethan winced at that. He knew Bex was taking it pretty hard and he only had himself to blame. He was the one who insisted that Seline not know his part.

Call him crazy, but he actually wanted Seline to forgive him and accept she still loved him on her own. He wanted—no, he needed—her to believe in him again without being told she'd been wrong to distrust him in the first place.

Was that so wrong?

"I'm sorry about Bex, but—"

"Don't say it's not your fault. Don't even go there, dude." Brian cut him off. He was back in his face and was about to poke him again in the chest, but Ethan pushed his hand away.

"Knock it off. I wasn't even going to say that." Right? Of course, he wasn't.

It was all his fault, he knew that, but still...Seline should know better. If she was going to be mad at anyone, it should be him. He stared out the window, not really seeing anything.

"Damn right it should be directed to you," Brian muttered.

Surprised, Ethan looked at Brian over his shoulder and realized he'd said that out loud.

"You don't think I don't know that already? Give me a break here, man. Put yourself in my shoes."

The moment he said it, Ethan knew it wasn't a fair question. His road had been nowhere near rough as Brian's.

"Look," he leaned against the wall, "let me figure this out, okay? Give me a few more days at least. I need her...I need her to trust in me again, to believe in me...on her own."

Brian flopped down on the chair and sighed.

"You don't got days. You have hours. Our party is tomorrow night and if you don't have it figured out by then...well, don't make me uninvite you to my wedding."

Ethan pushed himself off the wall. "You can't uninvite me—

I'm the best man." He didn't like where this was going at all. His time was running out and he had no idea how to fix things.

There was a look on Brian's face, a mixture of smugness and pity. "Dude, Bex's already warned me that if there is any sort of awkwardness between the two of you tomorrow...you're the one getting cut loose. Don't make me do that, okay?" He glanced down at his watch and then pushed himself to his feet.

"You going out?" Ethan asked.

"Yeah. You need time to fix this and I need to see my girl."

"You won't..." Ethan stopped himself. It was wrong of him to keep asking his friend to keep his secrets, especially now.

"It doesn't matter anymore, does it? Besides, Bex texted me earlier that Seline was going out on a coffee date."

"A date? With who?"

Brian shrugged. "No clue. But it's time, don't you think? You had over a year to make things right...if you won't man up, then let her move on. She deserves it."

There was nothing for Ethan to say. Brian was right. It was his own damn fault for losing her in the first place.

But he wasn't going to make that mistake again.

Chapter Ten

"You HAVE to talk to me sometime, you know."

Seline barely glanced over at Bex, who sat opposite her at their kitchen table. She flipped various printouts of homes her new real estate agent sent to her earlier, all the while keeping an eye on the time. She needed to head out soon if she was going to get to the coffee shop on time.

"This isn't fair, Seline." Bex pushed her empty wine glass back and forth on the table. "I said I was sorry, like a million times already. Why won't you forgive me?"

With a sigh, Seline set down the papers and slid the newly opened wine bottle over to Bex, who poured herself a glass.

It had been four miserable days since the morning at the coffeeshop when she'd found out that not only had Ethan moved back to the city for good, but that her best friends had already known about it.

Four long days since she'd stormed into their apartment and confronted Bex on holding back things from her. Four awful days of feeling hurt and most of all, betrayed.

"You're family, Bex." Seline finally broke her silence. "All that I have left. When I look at you, I don't just see my best friend, I see my sister."

Bex's eyes welled up with tears.

"You betrayed me. You went behind my back and while I'm sure you had good intentions...you never once thought about me or my feelings. Did you?" Seline didn't yell; she didn't scream or even cry. She kept her voice calm, civilized and at a fairly moderate level.

And yet, Bex still broke apart as if the floodgates had opened and there was no holding back.

So Seline sat there.

Normally she would have gotten up and hugged her friend, said soothing things to help calm her down all the while feeling an enormous amount of guilt for not being considerate of Bex's emotional well-being.

But normally wasn't today. Or yesterday. Or any day since the one when she'd last seen Ethan.

Sure, he'd tried to call and even came over to the apartment to see her. Thankfully, she'd been in the shower and Bex had been out with Brian. The only reason she'd known he was there was the note he'd slid under her front door saying he was sorry.

She ripped it up and threw it in the garbage.

"I didn't mean to." Bex finally managed to calm down. "Brian convinced me that it would be better this way."

"Brian did?" Why did she feel a certain level of skepticism?

"Well...it was my idea first," Bex mumbled beneath her breath.

"What did you say?" Seline heard her quite clearly, but she wanted Bex to own it, to admit her part.

Bex's cheeks blazed bright red. "It was wrong of me, okay? I'll admit it. I thought..." She sighed and drank half the wine in her glass.

"Thought what? That I would be overjoyed to have Ethan

back here? That I would be willing to let my heart be broken again because of his selfishness?" She couldn't contain the bitterness, no matter how much she tried.

"He loves you."

Seline shrugged. "I'm sure he does, in his own way. But he loves himself more."

"I wish you wouldn't see him like that." Bex drank the rest of her wine and went to pour herself another glass, but Seline stopped her.

The medicine she was on didn't go well with too much alcohol, and lately, for Bex, too much was anything more than one glass of white wine.

"I'm a grown woman, Seline." Bex attempted to grab the bottle from Seline's hands. "If I want another glass, then I'll have one."

Seline stood up and carried the bottle of wine over to the kitchen counter. She stuck a stopper in the lid and then placed the bottle in the fridge.

"No, Bex. You won't." She felt like such a parent sometimes. "The last time you drank too much, I ended up having to call the ambulance."

"I've only had one glass." Bex crossed her arms over her chest and pouted.

Seline breathed in deep in an attempt to remain calm but inside she screamed.

She had two options. She could stay and deal with this like she knew she should, or she could leave and arrive at the coffee shop earlier than she needed to.

Before she made her decision, the doorbell rang.

Bex jumped up from her chair and ran to the door. From the smile on her face, Seline had no doubt that it was Brian.

The moment she opened the door, Bex flung herself into

Brian's arms and whispered into his ear while he walked into the apartment with her held tight to his chest.

Seline got the wine back out of the fridge. If anyone needed a drink, it was her.

Wine in hand, she went to scoop up the papers she'd left on the table and take them to her room when Brian stopped her.

"Please, stay." He blocked her path. He glanced down at the printouts and then back up at her. "Looking for a home? I thought you were going to stay here?"

Seline sipped at her wine and stared into Brian's eyes, attempting to read something that just wasn't there. She wanted to be mad at him, needed to be mad at him, but couldn't. He was Ethan's best friend and, therefore, couldn't fault him for keeping secrets from her.

"I decided it was the perfect time for a new start."

"Ahh," was all he said. "Which area of the city are you looking at?"

"No idea." She hadn't really decided on that part yet. She figured maybe she'd take a look at the homes first and see which ones caught her eye and then base the location on that. Not a smart plan, probably, but she was more of a visual person, so it might work.

"Want any help?"

She shook her head. "You've both helped enough, I think." She caught the grimace on Brian's face and instantly regretted her words. "Besides, you have a wedding, honeymoon, and then your own home to think about." She gave them a small smile, a show of willingness to ease the tension between them. "I've got this covered."

The silence in the room seemed to stretch until it became too noticeable. Seline gathered up the papers and her wine and tried to bypass Brian, but he held his ground.

"Please, we all need to talk."

She shook her head. "Really, we don't. Trust me. Besides, I don't have much time." All she wanted to do was get through their wedding, see them off on their honeymoon and then work on letting the anger go. By the time they returned, all would be well. She'd make sure it was. But she needed time.

"Right. Your coffee date. I thought he'd already gone back to Calgary?"

"He did. And now he's back again." Seline crossed her arms. Since when did she need to explain her coming and goings to anyone?

"He can wait, can't he? This is important. We've given you time, and you've done nothing but ignore us. Me, fine—I can handle that. But it's not fair to Bex, especially now. You, of all people, should understand that."

Oh no, he didn't.

She was tired of being second fiddle to everyone else. First, she'd had to put her life on hold because of her mother's illness, then to Ethan, who made it obvious his career was more important, and then to Bex...well, that wasn't fair: Bex didn't have any choice in that matter. But not anymore...Bex was fine, for now at least, and Brian was there to be her strength.

For once, it was time for Seline to put herself first.

And she was going to do exactly that, damn it.

"You can't play the Bex card. Not anymore. You guys are family, my *only* family left. I've done everything"—she was going to cry, and dammit, she did not want to—"and anything that I could to be there for you guys. How dare you throw that back at me?" The tears welled up, and she turned around so they wouldn't notice.

"That's not what he meant," Bex said.

"It's exactly what I meant."

Seline angrily wiped at the tears that pooled beneath her

lashes. "When is it my turn, Brian? When do my feelings matter?" She slowly turned to face them.

"You matter." Brian reached for Bex's hand and pulled her close. "But Bex matters more to me."

Fair enough. He was being honest with her, and she wouldn't expect anything less.

"I'm okay, love." Bex leaned her head down on his shoulder.

Brian shook his head. "No, you're not. All you've done is cry, and I don't like it. I can't do it anymore." He kissed the top of Bex's head, and then turned his attention to Seline.

The level of intensity in his gaze forced her to stare down at the ground.

"I get that you think we betrayed you, but Seline, that's the farthest thing from what we've done. Ethan is my best friend, just like you are Bex's. We love you both, and it's not fair for you to make us choose between the two of you."

"I'm not making you choose. I'm just asking not to be kept in the dark. You could have told me he moved back...that's the least you could have done. I would have prepared myself...but instead, you throw us together and use your wedding as an excuse."

"But you love each other," Bex whispered.

Seline walked over to Bex and reached for her hand. Her anger, although it was still there, wasn't as fresh or even as vibrant as it was before.

"I love you more. When I thought we were going to lose you...so soon after I lost my mom..." she choked up, "Bex, I couldn't handle it. We might not share the same blood, but we are heart sisters. You're my family, and without you...I'm lost. When Ethan didn't—"

"But he did."

"Bex." Brian's voice was low. Both Bex and Seline looked at him at the same time and he only shook his head. "Don't."

"Don't what?" Seline asked. She looked from Brian to Bex, but her friend tightened her lips and turned her head to Brian's shoulder to shield her face.

"What is going on? Don't what? What are you hiding from me?"

When no one answered, she rolled her eyes and moved past Brian towards the living room.

"See, this is what I'm talking about," she complained.

"Sit down, Seline." Brian stopped her before she reached the hallway towards her bedroom. She turned.

"Pardon?"

Brian walked towards the couch and sat down, Bex alongside him. "Please." He pointed to the chair opposite of him.

What was going on?

Seline didn't understand, but she had a funny feeling, whatever it was, she wasn't going to like it.

Chapter Eleven

"You trust me, right?" Brian asked.

Trust? Of course she trusted him.

"You haven't given me a reason not to." Trust was a huge issue in her books but she always gave it until proved otherwise.

"Then please," Brian leaned forward and rested his elbows on his knees, "please trust me on this. Ethan is not the man you think he is."

Seline pushed herself up from her chair. She didn't need this. Besides, it was time to go.

"Wait." Brian held out his hand as if to stop her. "Hear me out, please."

Seline slowly sat back but remained perched on the edge of her seat.

"Yes, he's made plenty of mistakes. But he's also made up for them," Brian said.

"How?"

He shook his head. "I can't say. It's not my place to."

"Really? So you are here to try to what? Change my mind about him? Stop being angry with him? Forgive him? But you won't give me any reasons why?" Her foot mindlessly tapped while some unspoken communication went on between Brian and Bex.

She'd almost thought they'd forgotten about her before Brian spoke up.

"Yes. That's basically what I'm hoping for. The guy hasn't stopped moping about in my apartment, and honestly, it's driving me nuts. I wish I could tell you...but I can't. So instead, can you just trust me...that he's not the bad guy you make him out to be. Please?"

Maybe it was the soft kiss he placed on Bex's head, or the way she looked over at Seline with a pleading gaze, but suddenly something clicked.

"You wouldn't be here today if it wasn't for Ethan, would you?" She directed her question to Bex, carefully worded as the realization grew.

The way Bex smiled at her confirmed it.

She dropped back in her chair with a thud and stared up at her ceiling.

"How?" She wanted to ask so much more but that was all that came out.

When no one responded, she sat back up and glared at them. "Oh no, you're not playing this game with me again."

"He not only found the surgeon but found a donor who covered all the expenses that went along with going to the private clinic." Bex was the one who gave her the answer.

Seline didn't know what to say. She remembered those days, the void she forced herself to go into when they heard the tumor Bex had was inoperable, that the chances of killing her should they even attempt the surgery were so huge that the risk wasn't worth it.

Knowing her best friend was going to die, that she only had a few short months of the life she knew, to live...it killed her inside.

She'd never needed Ethan so much as she did then.

In the midst of still grieving for her mother, she was about to lose Bex...she'd turned to Ethan and begged him to come home, to be with her, to help her remain strong enough for Bex. But he didn't. He said he couldn't and would never give her a reason, other than he had to stay to see a project through, something he'd already given his word on.

That's when she'd broken their engagement off.

She hadn't even given him a chance to explain...she couldn't. In order for her to survive the next few months, she needed to close herself off and remain strong for her friend.

"I thought you found the surgeon?" Brian had given them the good news, that he'd been in touch with someone willing to take the risk and remove Bex's tumor.

"No, it was Ethan." He sighed. "I promised him never to tell anyone. At the time, I didn't think that meant you too, but after, when you broke off your engagement, he asked me to never say anything."

"But it wasn't right," Bex interjected. "I didn't even know till recently and it's been so hard not to say anything, so..." She gave Seline a little smile and shrugged.

Now Seline understood. "So you worked your little magic and made me the maid of honor...but how?"

Bex sat up and grinned. "Oh, that was easy." Her voice was infused with so much joy. "I knew all along that Jordan had this work thing and could never be at the wedding."

"I don't know what to say." She was confounded by her friend's duplicity and frankly, quite surprised.

"Come on, did you really expect me to walk down the aisle without my best friend at my side? There's no way I was getting married without you as my maid of honor."

The glimmer in Bex's eyes warmed Seline's heart. This is what the old Bex would have done—taken matters into her own hands and made it work. Clearly, Seline had underestimated her.

"You and I will discuss this later, but I'd rather talk about Ethan."

Obviously, she said the right words, because the tension from Brian's shoulders eased and he visibly relaxed.

"Are you willing to forgive him?" Brian asked.

She shook her head. "I've been angry with him for so long now, I'm not sure what forgiveness would mean. I need...I need time."

"Fair enough," Brian said.

"I don't understand, though, why he never came. I needed him, but he could never get away from work." If everything Brian and Bex said were true, then there was no reason he had to stay in London. He could have just come back, for them. For her.

"Ask him."

"No. It doesn't matter now. There's too much between us, and honestly, I've moved on. This has helped, though. I wish you'd been honest from the beginning." She gave them a sad smile as the truth of her words settled in her heart.

"Would it have made a difference? Would you have ended your engagement?"

Good question and one she already knew the answer to.

"Probably. We were fractured already. Some people aren't meant for long-distance relationships. But," this was the part that actually freed her heart, "I don't need to be so angry with him anymore."

Bex clapped her hands in delight. She jumped up from the couch and rushed towards Seline and engulfed her in a bear hug.

"This makes me so happy!"

Seline patted her on the back. "You silly goose. Now, I really do need to go. Chad will be waiting."

Bex pulled away but held Seline by the shoulders. "Are we okay now?"

"Of course, we are, silly. I'm sorry for being so..." She tried to find the right word.

"Hurt. It's okay, I understand. Just remember I love you and you have to love me, and we have my bachelorette party tomorrow night, so we need us to be okay. Okay?"

"Okay." Seline nodded, placed a kiss on Bex's cheek, and left the room.

She'd forgotten all about the party tomorrow night. Crap.

She'd booked the Candybar located in the Surrey, a shop they'd discovered quite by accident one night. Candybar was now one of her clients and were more than happy to close for a private event for her.

"Um, Seline?"

She'd made it to the front door but turned when Bex called out to her.

"I, ah...well, the boys are going to join us later in the evening. I hope that's okay?"

No, it wasn't okay, but what was she going to say? Demand that it remain a bachelorette party only? Most of Bex and Brian's friends were couples, so it made sense to join everyone in the evening, but that left her alone. Again.

"You do realize it means less chocolate for us, right?"

Bex hemmed and hawed a little and then smiled. "Not if I already called them and told them about the extra numbers." Even with the distance, Seline could see the twinkle in her eyes.

"Go figure." She'd have to call Gina tomorrow to confirm that everything was okay, especially with Bex going behind her back and inviting Brian's party.

Which also meant...she had to change up her own plans on

how the evening would go. The cute games she'd researched online would need to be done earlier rather than spaced throughout the night...unless...

"Oh, and I have one extra game to play before the boys join us."

There was something in Bex's voice that stopped her. A remnant from the old Bex, the one who loved to be with people, who enjoyed games and laughter and dancing with abandonment.

It was a sound Seline would love to hear more of.

"Bex Stone, you had better promise me right now we are not playing a game of Truth or Dare. Promise me!"

In all the years they'd been friends, that blasted game was one Bex insisted on playing at all parties. Well, she had insisted. This was the first time since her surgery...

Except, Seline hated that game. Hated. It.

Bex giggled. Giggled like a little school girl about to walk hand in hand with her boyfriend.

Seline didn't even give Bex the opportunity to answer. She walked out the door after she gave her friend a dirty look.

Things couldn't get any worse.

Chapter Twelve

With arms full of gift bags, her camera gear, and other fun stuff, Seline waited patiently for Gina, the owner of Candybar, to open the door for her.

"You came early; I'm so glad." Gina grabbed things out of her hands and held the door for her.

"When you mentioned needing more photos, I figured coming early was a good idea."

Seline set everything down on a table and gazed around.

"Wow...you've outdone yourself, Gina."

The place was a candy fairy-tale. The tables along all the walls were full of glass bottles and containers filled with candy and platters of desserts. Candy-decorated centerpieces covered each small table Gina had set up, along with small settings of chocolates.

"Think Bex will like it?" Gina asked. "When you guys arrive tonight, there will be a soft pink glow, fake candles, and some more surprises."

"Who cares about Bex? I love it! Can we do this but with more of a chocolate theme for my wedding whenever I decide to get married?" She walked over to Gina and threw her arms around her, the sudden desire to give her a huge hug over-whelming.

"Would you mind if I took some photos?" Before Gina could respond, Seline had her camera out and added a lens.

"Actually, let's talk about that." Gina sat herself up on a stool and held out a glass of wine to Seline.

With a glance from the wine to Gina's face and back to the wine, Seline set her camera down and slowly took a seat.

"Okay, let's chat. Is there something up?" Seline asked.

"No. Well, yes." Gina took a sip of her wine. "I was hoping we could do a trade, of sorts."

Seline let out the breath she'd been holding. Trades she could handle. For a moment there, she'd been worried.

"I told Bex I'd have to charge her extra for the additional food. I know we'd agreed upon photos of the food in exchange for the food...but that was before the guys were joining you girls."

Seline nodded. "Right. Trust me, I had no idea they were doing that."

Gina waved her hand as if the subject didn't matter. "Oh, I know, they made that very clear to me too. But, I got to think-ing...this could be great publicity for us in some wedding maga-zines and online sites. So, what if you were to take photos of the night—the setting, the food, and some candid shots—and give me exclusive rights over some of them in our promotional kit."

Seline thought this over for a moment. Her shoots weren't cheap and giving away images...that was asking a lot. This was clearly a smart business move on Gina's part. How could Seline say no? Although...both Brian and Bex would really owe her after this.

"How about two exclusive rights and three images for the kit? I can even put it together for you, if you'd like?" She had a great program and was fairly proficient with Photoshop. This was a new package she had added for clients and so far it had worked well.

Happy with the arrangement, Gina held out her glass; they toasted and then Seline got to work. She had less than two hours before she needed to head back home, get dressed and head back here to meet everyone.

Seline made her way throughout the place and if she'd thought Gina had outdone herself in the front, the area in the back was spectacular. Bex was going to love the whole night.

Note to self: make sure Bex uses waterproof makeup because she was going to be crying a lot.

By the time she was done taking photos of the food and rooms, she barely had enough time to make it home to get dressed.

"Go." Gina pushed her out the door. "I'll take care of everything else, including the gifts and the little games you have—which are really cute, by the way."

"Do you think so? I did a lot of searching online and it was tough to find things to suit our bride."

"And yet," Gina wiggled her brows, "I noticed a few things to take her...outside her comfort zone?"

Seline could only laugh as she walked out the door. Although it was true Bex could be somewhat of a prude when it came to sex and any public displays of overt affection from Brian, she would also be the first one to say something shocking in a room full of people.

Or, she had been. Maybe tonight was just what her friend needed to rediscover that part of herself again.

Tonight was going to be fun. She would make sure of it and then by the time Brian and his gang came to the restaurant, she'd sneak away and head home.

Last night, over coffee, she'd had a long talk with Chad

about what she'd learned. She didn't go into specifics, but Chad was smart and figured it out for himself.

He'd asked her one important question: was she willing to let Ethan earn back her trust?

She didn't answer right away, because she couldn't. If she were honest, she still didn't know.

Until she did, she didn't need to muddy the waters by being in the same room with him and making things awkward. Not only for them but for Bex and Brian, whom she knew would be watching them all night.

After the wedding, she wanted to sit down with him and talk. Really talk. She needed to give him the opportunity to be honest with her and then she needed to be honest back.

She called Ethan her soul mate and would even admit to still being in love with him.

But Chad had asked another really good question. How strong was their love if she'd been able to lose faith in him so easily?

That said a lot.

Maybe too much.

Chapter Thirteen

SELINE EYED the last remaining chocolate-covered strawberry on her table and contemplated whether she should eat it or not.

If it wasn't for the fact that she'd eaten almost a dozen of them so far throughout the night, not to mention the cookies, the mini cupcakes, the éclair filled with chocolate mousse, or the uncountable amounts of candy she'd sneaked from various dishes...she would.

But she was stuffed and if the buzz from the sugar high was any indication, she could either eat to maintain the buzz or suffer the crash and burn that was sure to come in less than ten minutes.

"Here. You look like you could use this." Bex slid a martini glass towards her.

"I do, do I?" She leaned forward and looked closely at the drink. It was pink and sparkly and looked dangerously like an alcoholic beverage...the same beverage Seline had been trying very hard not to drink.

Someone needed to keep a clear head and be able to drive home and that someone was her.

"There's no alcohol, I promise. It's a strawberry frizzer. It's good. I've had three so far."

Seline took a sip. There was a hint of strawberry and mint mixed in with club soda.

"You're not going to eat that, are you? I think it's the last one left." Bex pointed towards the strawberry and Seline blushed.

"That's probably because I've eaten the majority of them. I don't know what kind of chocolate they used, but it's good." She licked her lips.

"How many have you had?" Bex snatched the strawberry from the plate and bit into it.

Seline shrugged. "Close to a dozen or so throughout the night." She sighed with regret as she watched her friend enjoy the last one and knew she should have eaten it before Bex came to the table.

"Why do I have a feeling we're all about to have a sugar hangover in the morning?" Bex glanced around the room and smiled. "It sure has been fun, though, hasn't it? Thank you so much for doing this. I love it. Love it all."

That made Seline happy. If Bex was happy, then her job tonight was complete. They'd played all the games but one... apparently Bex had a top-secret game she wanted to play before the men arrived, which should be soon.

"You're still okay with me leaving, right?" She'd mentioned it to Bex earlier but wanted to make sure.

"I don't like it, but I called Brian and told him to wait a bit, giving us more time before they arrive. I'm not ready for you to leave yet." Bex pouted.

"You didn't have to do that." Now Seline felt bad. This was a night for the two of them to celebrate together, and Bex shouldn't have asked Brian to delay coming here tonight.

"It was either that or beg you to stay."

"You could have begged," Seline said.

"Would it have worked?" A hopeful gleam shone from Bex's eyes.

Seline nodded. Of course, it would have worked. She always gave in.

Bex stared at her, and Seline could see the wheels turn in her brain. Should she or shouldn't she beg? Would she or wouldn't she?

"No." Bex shook her head. "You've done more than enough for me, and I will forever love you for it. If you need to leave, then I'm not going to stop you."

Surprised, Seline leaned forward, reached across the small cocktail table and placed a kiss on Bex's forehead.

"But you owe me big time, you do realize that, right?" Bex jumped down from her stool. "And don't think I'm going to forget it." She pulled out her phone and glanced down at it.

"Now..." she gazed around and raised her voice, "are we ready for the last game of the night?"

There were well over a dozen shouts in response. Satisfied, Bex made her way through the crowd to stand somewhat in the middle.

Seline was really happy with the turnout tonight, and never, since Bex's surgery, had Seline caught so many glimpses of the "old" Bex as she had tonight. For the first time in a long time, her best friend was in her element and happy.

Which meant Seline could sit back and be the quiet introvert she really was. It was nice.

It was more than nice. It was refreshing.

"Any idea what this last game is?"

Seline turned to find Gina at her side. She shook her head. Bex had remained tight-lipped about it, no matter how many times she'd asked.

"I haven't seen her this lively in a long time," Gina commented.

"I haven't either, but I'll take it."

The way Gina smiled, Seline had a feeling something was up.

"How many drinks did she have tonight?"

Gina shrugged. "Not many. You warned me about the wine, so I kept anything she asked for fairly light. A lot of wine spritzers, if anything."

"That doesn't sound too bad, then." Something else had to be up. Unless Bex was really just enjoying herself. Then it was possible she'd crash later tonight at home, and if that were the case, both Seline and Brian needed to be ready.

"She probably needed this. I know she's still healing, but she's the type who gets energized by crowds." Gina nodded over to the crowd now gathered around Bex.

Seline watched her friend. Her eyes were bright, albeit a little bit glassy, her shoulders tight and pulled back, her smile ready. She looked tired but Seline wasn't too worried as she knew Brian was on his way over.

"She used to be." She addressed Gina's comment. "But the idea of being in a crowd, of being the center of attention like she used to be, stresses her out too much."

"And yet she doesn't look stressed," Gina mentioned. "In fact, she looks downright giddy, as if she has a trick up her sleeve no one knows about."

Seline narrowed her gaze and caught the smile from Bex as she glanced over. Bex bounced on her toes as she talked with her friends in front of her, and the excitement she exuded was fairly contagious, by the growth of sound in the room.

"Are you sure you have to leave early?" Gina leaned forward and spoke over the noise.

"I'm sure. Crowds like this drain me. Besides, I want to download all the photos I've taken and use some for Bex's photos we're going to show during the reception."

"Are you sure it's not to run away from a certain somebody?"

Seline picked up the drink Bex had brought her and sipped at it, not bothering to reply. Of course, she was running, but she didn't need to admit it. It was bad enough everyone knew it.

"Everyone, come closer. That means you, Seline. Come on!" Bex's voice rang out in the room, and Seline forced a large smile on her face as she set her drink down and stood.

"You're coming with me." She linked arms with Gina and forced her to move closer to the crowd.

Once Seline made her way to Bex's side, Bex linked her arm with Seline's free one, took in a deep breath, and waited for everyone to quiet down.

"Most everyone here knows everyone else...but I want to see how well we really know one another. So we're going to play a game of *Truth or Dare*."

Chapter Fourteen

THERE WERE groans and laughter from the crowd at Bex's announcement, including from Seline.

She hated this game and shouldn't have been surprised that Bex would have picked it.

Every single year for her birthday, Bex would request they play this. She got some perverse pleasure watching her friends squirm as they struggled with picking the lesser of two evils.

"Here are the rules. Since I'm the bride, I get to ask you all one question...Truth or Dare. Once you've picked, I'll then pick a question or an action from one of these two boxes in front of me." Bex pointed to the two pink boxes Seline hadn't noticed before.

"What about you?" someone called out.

"Oh, that's easy. After you're done, you'll come up and write something in this book. You're either going to choose a question you want Brian to ask me or an action you want me to do with Brian. At the end of the night, he'll take this book home, and we'll go through everything, one by one, while on our honeymoon! Doesn't that sound like fun!" Bex blushed at the catcalls and laughter after she explained everything.

Seline found it really interesting that people were able to pick an option. Normally, Bex always picked Dare, while Seline always tried not to be around while the game was being played.

Apparently, she should have left five minutes ago.

"Bex, what are you doing?" she whispered into her friend's ear as she tried to tug her arm out from Bex's hold.

"Having fun! It's been so long since we all played this. And since the boys aren't here yet, it's the perfect time to start, don't you think?" Bex whispered back, not releasing her.

"Be gentle with me, okay?"

Bex's response was to smile. Her eyes twinkled with mischief.

"On that note," Gina whispered into Seline's ear, "I'm out of here. Time to get those gift bags ready."

"Chicken," Seline hissed at Gina's retreating back.

"You know it." Gina glanced over her shoulder and mouthed the words.

Seline took in a deep breath and mentally tried to prepare herself for whatever was about to come her way. What would she pick? Truth or Dare?

Knowing Bex, if she picked Truth, she'd have to admit some deep, dark secret, like she was still in love with Ethan or something else just as dreadful, so she'd be smarter to pick Dare.

There wasn't much Seline wouldn't do. She might not like it, but she was never one to turn down a dare.

She fully expected Bex to pick her first and so she was surprised when Bex started with another girlfriend in the crowd.

One by one, Bex asked the girls who surrounded her whether they wanted Truth or Dare, and to be honest, everyone was having fun. There a lot of laughter, and with Gina behind the counter, shots were being handed out as turns either began or ended, depending on what Bex picked from the hat.

Every so often, Seline caught Bex looking out the front windows, and she knew she was waiting for Brian.

Maybe, if she were lucky, she could head out before it was her turn and before the guys showed up. With that in mind, Seline took tiny steps backward until she was far enough away from the crowd that she was able to grab her purse from behind the counter without anyone noticing.

"Oh, Seline..."

Busted. Seline held her purse tight in her hands and walked forward a few steps once Bex called out her name.

"You called, oh beautiful bride-to-be?" Seline winked at her roommate and prepared herself for what was coming.

"You weren't trying to sneak out of here without having a turn, were you?"

"Would I do that?" Seline pretended to be appalled at the thought. There was no backing out now, so she made her way back toward the crowd and stood in front of the table with the two pink boxes.

"You would, and we all know it. Now, it's your turn to pick. Will it be Truth or Dare?"

Seline looked into Bex's eyes, and concern ate away at her. Bex's gaze was very glassy, and her smile was almost too forced.

"Bex, are you okay?" Seline whispered.

Bex nodded, but Seline knew she was lying. At that moment, Seline knew that she wouldn't leave Bex until Brian came, which should be any moment, or so she prayed.

"You should pick Dare. I know the questions left in the Truth box," Bex staged-whispered.

With a laugh, Seline pointed to the Dare box. Considering the things others had to do tonight, this should be a breeze.

Walking down the street singing a ridiculous song or going up to a stranger and asking for something was mild compared to some of the other games she'd played with Bex over the years.

Bex reached into the box and pulled out a folded note, and read it. She smiled wide as she glanced out the window and then back to her.

"Are you ready for this?" Bex asked.

"Let's just get it over with, please? Before the guys come in?" She forced a smile on her face and pushed back her shoulders. She'd never turned down a dare before, and tonight wasn't going to be the first time.

"You'd better be praying then that you can do this *before* the men arrive." With her voice raised, she held up the note.

"Your Dare, Seline Barr, is to kiss the first man to walk through those doors."

She groaned. Others in the crowd groaned. Bex, on the other hand, laughed.

"What's so funny?" Hands-on her hips, Seline glared at the piece of paper in Bex's hand before she snatched it away. She had to have made that up.

Kiss the first man to walk through the front doors.

She hadn't made that up.

Seline turned the note over, sure that somehow it had been marked for Bex to use especially for her, but there was nothing. Not a secret code, no special mark...nothing. Except, her note had been folded and the remaining ones in the box weren't.

"Bex Stone, if you—" She was stopped by the sound of the low bell that rang when the front door opened.

"Oh look...there's someone now." The widest smile Seline had ever seen appeared on Bex's face.

Even without looking, she knew. Her heart raced, her palms tingled, and despite all the arguments...all Seline could think about was the fact she had to kiss him.

Had to. Of course, she did. It was a dare. And Seline Barr never turned down a dare.

Not when she was dared to walk around the school campus

in a Catwoman outfit, or when she'd been dared to eat chocolate-covered spiders, or even when she'd been dared as a thirteen-year-old girl to kiss Joey Szabo in front of everyone at the beginning of their lunch period.

There was no choice, no option. But Bex had better realize that her ledger was now red.

"Just you wait," Seline whispered to her friend, whose smile faltered slightly at the threat.

There was silence in the room other than the slight shuffle of people behind her. Seline tucked her purse tightly beneath her arm, squared her shoulders, and turned.

The emotional sucker punch to her gut caught her off guard the moment she saw Ethan. His hair was wind-blown, his jaw outlined with the five o'clock shadow she always found sexy, and the look of hope that grew in his gaze as he stared back at her threw her for a loop.

She was over him. She had to be. She needed to be, and yet, she didn't want to be, all at the same time.

Without thinking about her actions, she stepped forward, thankful for the crowd that gave way, and stopped with mere inches to spare between her and Ethan. She reached up with her hand, threaded her fingers through his unruly hair, and brought his head down towards her while she raised herself up on her tiptoes.

The moment her lips met his, she couldn't breathe.

Time stopped as heat rushed through her body as their lips danced to a tune only known to them. There was nothing holding them back from being who they were to each other: soul mates, lovers, and friends.

His head angled to deepen the kiss while his hand cupped the back of her neck. Her body leaned closer, to close the gap between them, and Seline was lost, heart and soul.

"Hello, beautiful," Ethan whispered against her lips.

Seline pulled away, embarrassed at how willing she'd been to lose herself with him, and found herself at a loss for words.

Tears welled up, and before she made more of a fool of herself, she pushed past him, Brian, and the other men who filled up the entryway and dashed out of the restaurant, despite the calls from those behind her to stop.

Seline fled down the street to her parked vehicle, wiping away the tears that ran down her cheeks. She focused her gaze ahead of her, on the pavement illuminated by the vehicle headlights and not on the man who had run outside after her and now stood in the middle of the road, watching her drive away.

Chapter Fifteen

As the lights of her car grew fainter in the distance, Ethan was at a loss of what to do. After that kiss...how could she just leave him?

How could she not?

That kiss was...electrifying, hot, and said everything he knew she wouldn't say with words.

She still loved him. She wouldn't have kissed him like that if she didn't.

So now what? Was he just supposed to let her run away from him, again, and leave her be? Or go after her and fight for what he knew they both wanted, and needed?

"Why haven't you left already?" Bex answered for him.

He turned and found Bex and Brian outside the front door to Candybar, Brian's arm around the woman he loved more than life, and he knew what he had to do.

"I'm going. Is there anywhere else she would have gone other than home?"

Bex shook her head. She fiddled with something inside her purse, and then next thing he knew, a key landed at his feet.

"I'm exhausted, so don't take too long, okay?"

Ethan studied her and realized she leaned on Brian so much that he practically held her up.

"What happened in there?" What he really wanted to know was why she came up and kissed him as she had.

"The less you know, the better. Trust me. But you better make it right, otherwise, she's going to be very mad at me when I get home. And I don't like Seline mad." Bex leaned her head on Brian's shoulder before he whisked her off her feet and held her in his arms.

"You've got this, dude. Make it right. And take your time; this woman is coming home with me tonight." Brian walked back into the restaurant amid loud claps and whistles.

Make it right? He could do that, he hoped. That's all he'd been trying to do, was make things right, and yet, all he'd done was drive the one person he couldn't live without away.

Not again. He needed Seline. Needed her in a way that made his soul at ease, his heart lighter, and his life happier. As mushy as that sounded, it was still the truth.

He thought about what he'd say while he drove to her apartment, but all he could think of was saying *I'm sorry*, over and over again.

And it's what he did say, the moment he knocked on her door, and she opened it. Except, instead of welcoming him in and falling into his arms, she slammed the door in his face.

"Come on, Seline. Help me out here." He leaned his forehead on the door.

"Go away." Her voice, muffled, was clearer than he'd expected. She must have been right on the other side.

"I can't." He watched the shadows beneath her door and knew when she'd slid down and sat on the floor. He joined her, angled so that his shoulder leaned on the door, and he slid his fingers beneath the slight gap between the door and floor.

"I need you to." She was crying, and it broke his heart. She was crying because of him, and there was nothing he could do about it.

"Open the door, Seline. Please?" He waited a few minutes, and when she didn't respond, he decided to try a different approach.

"I'm not going anywhere, so if you want your neighbors to listen to me beg for your forgiveness and my list of all the reasons what we had is worth giving another try..." He let his voice trail off and waited.

"What's your list?" Her tired voice came through loud and clear. She was giving him a chance.

"It's a long one, I'm warning you. You're the only one who gets me, who laughs at my jokes and could finish my sentences. We have the same dreams, same desires. We would be amazing parents. We both love a good chocolate. You light up my heart. I love the way your eyes sparkle moments before you're about to laugh. But most of all...you complete me. There's been something missing inside me, something that leaves me feeling empty, and I don't like it. I don't need you to be a better man, but that's what happens whenever you're around me. You challenge me to do better, to be better."

For a few brief seconds, he felt the touch of her fingers against his before he listened to the sound of her standing up and unlocking the door.

He made his way to his feet, and watched the play of emotions on her face as she looked at him. He could tell she was deciding whether to invite him in or not.

"Should I keep going?" he asked softly.

A small smile played with her lips and it gave him hope.

"I won't hear the end of it from Jonathan," she pointed to the door across from her, "if you keep going." She stepped aside for him to enter and then closed the door behind them.

He tried to ignore the fact that her eyes were red and her

mascara had smudged from her tears, and attempted to give her room. She sat down on the couch and reached for a glass of white wine that was still quite full.

"Help yourself if you want a glass. It's in the kitchen."

Ethan's brow rose at this. Welcoming him to wine meant she expected him to stay. Him staying meant a long talk and possibly—

"It's just wine, Ethan. Just wine. Pour it. Drink it. Then leave. Got it?"

Those might be her terms, but they sure weren't his. He opted for a glass of water instead.

"Why are you here?" Her wine glass now half empty, Ethan returned to the kitchen to retrieve the bottle and placed it on the coffee table in front of her. She was always more honest with her words, when she had a drink or two, as if her internal inhibitions were cast aside.

"You can't kiss me like you did and not expect me to follow you." He sat down beside her on the couch and watched as she scooted towards the far corner, to create more of a distance between them than there already was.

"I sure as hell can."

She was on edge. He could handle that. There were two options in front of him. Keep her on edge until she said something she never would have in a moment of panic, or talk her down, make her feel more safe, at ease and give her a way to take control of the situation.

If he went with option two, he'd leave here, alone and with a broken heart.

That wasn't going to happen.

"No, love. You can't. You said more in that kiss than you have in the year we've been apart."

"Fifteen months, not a year," she corrected him.

"Too long, either way. You can't hide from me now, not after that."

"Who said I was hiding?" She took a sip from her drink. Ethan reached for the bottle and held it.

"You did when you took off." He filled her glass for her and set the bottle back down on the table.

"I didn't...okay, maybe I did. But not because of you. It's been a long day, and I'm exhausted. I wanted a bit of a breather before Bex came home."

She did look exhausted, he'd give her that.

"Bex's staying with Brian tonight, so you don't need to wait up for her."

"Good. You can leave now then, so I can get to bed." She pulled her knees up tight to her chest and rested her head on them.

"Or I can draw you a bath..."

Her head whipped up.

"You are not drawing me a bath, Ethan James." Despite the fierce tone in her voice, he caught the slight play of a smile on her lips.

"I would, if you'd let me." He loved to tease her, to see the way her eyes lit up, to feel that joy back in his heart as she struggled not to smile.

"Please, be serious now. None of that," her fingers did a circle in the air, "is happening right now, and you know it."

Right now. He'd caught that. See...there was hope.

"What do you think is going to happen tonight? Yes, I kissed you and," she sighed, "I shouldn't have, not like that, but it felt good. Too good. But that's it. That's all you're getting. There's nothing else here between us."

Ethan leaned forward. "I hate to break it to you, love, but there's more, and you know it. I'm not ready to give up on you, on us. I made the mistake of not fighting for us before. I'm not going to do it again."

Seline leaned her head against the side of the couch. "Was there really anything for you to fight for? I'm not so sure anymore."

This caught Ethan off guard. What did she mean?

"Of course there was. Is."

When she shook her head, frustration set in. Why couldn't women just say what they meant instead of being so bloody cryptic?

"How can you say that?" he asked.

The saddest smile appeared on Seline's face. "If there really was something there, don't you think we both would have fought harder?"

She'd given up on them, and that wasn't okay with him. Life got messy, for both of them, and yes, they'd made mistakes—

"We weren't perfect, and yes, there was a lot we could have done better and not fighting for you...that was my biggest mistake, my biggest regret."

"It is what it is." She reached her hand out to him, and he grabbed hold as if she'd just given him a lifeline.

"But it doesn't have to be like that, Seline. I love you. I've never stopped loving you." He entwined his fingers with hers, needing her touch.

"I'll always love you, Ethan. I'll always admire you for the man you are, for what we had...but there needs to be more than love to make a relationship work."

The way she said it, with the heartache so evident in her voice, his heart broke. He wanted to reach for her, to pull her into his arms and make her understand how much he loved her, but would it matter?

She'd already given up on them.

Chapter Sixteen

"Love is a decision. A commitment." Seline's voice broke.

"Right." He agreed. "Love," he said, "is in the actions between two people who know they are soul mates. No matter what happens between them, they weather it out, because of that commitment."

The way she looked at him, broke his heart. She was hurting so much, and he didn't know what to do to make it better.

"You've already given up on us, haven't you?" She whispered.

Tears gathered in her eyes, and Ethan leaned forward to wipe them away.

"Oh love," His voice broke. "I've never given up on you."

"But I did." She bowed her head. Her shoulders heaved beneath her silent cries.

Ethan moved forward on the couch and gathered her into his arms. He held her, tight to his chest, and rubbed her hair, and her back, touching her like he'd wanted to for a long time.

Having her in his arms, even if she were crying, was right. This was right.

"I love you. I always will," he whispered before he placed a kiss on her forehead.

He needed her to believe him. To believe in them. Again.

She pulled out of his arms and stood. He watched her as she refilled her glass and then went to stand by the living room window.

"I gave up on you, Ethan. On us. So easily. Doesn't that bother you?" She stared out into the dark night, over the city lights, and Ethan had to force himself to remain on the couch.

"You had your reasons." He didn't know what else to say.

"Did I? Really? I blamed you for not being there for me. For not caring about your friends. For placing your career above everything else in your life. And you never once tried to prove me otherwise, did you? Not in words, anyway." She leaned against the wall, angled away from him, but he watched her reflection in the window.

Not in words. She knew, didn't she? Brian must have told her, even when he'd specifically asked him not to.

"My career was never first. You were. Always." He leaned forward and rested his elbows on his knees.

"But I didn't believe you. In you. Not enough. If I had…" Her voice trailed off.

"What? If you had, what?" He needed to know.

"I don't know."

Ethan jumped up from the couch and paced the small room.

"We would be married by now, that's what. We would still be together, facing things together, as a couple. But instead, you pushed me away—when you needed me, you pushed." He ran his fingers through his hair, frustrated at how things were turning out.

If she wanted to be done, fine. But not until they got all of this out in the open. Not until he tried everything, said

407

anything, to win her back. He was not going down without a fight.

"I didn't mean to." She turned, leaned her back against the wall, and watched him. "I needed you, but I didn't know how to tell you."

"Exactly. I'm not a damn mind reader, Seline. God, you women are so...so...frustrating." He stopped in front of her. "I'm a guy. We don't do well with emotions or mind games. Just tell me what you need, and I'll be there. I'll move heaven and earth to get it for you...but you've got to tell me." He flexed his fingers at his side and regretted his decision not to have a glass of wine.

"What I needed was for you to be there with me. Beside me. Hold my hand while I grieved for my mom and figured out how to handle Bex's diagnosis. That's what I needed." She crossed her arms over her chest but didn't move, didn't try to get away from him.

"Then why didn't you tell me that?"

She shrugged and gave him a half-smile. "Because I'm a girl, and we expect our men to be mind readers."

Ethan laughed and did the one thing he wanted to do more than anything else: he wrapped his arms around the woman he loved and pulled her close.

"I know I'm good at many things, but mind reading isn't one of them," he said.

"Apparently, that's another thing I need. So what are you going to do about it?" Her arms wrapped around his waist, and she laid her head on his chest.

His heart soared, and he couldn't stop smiling.

"There's only one thing I can think of...I'll have to spend lots of time with you, find a way to decipher that gorgeous mind of yours and learn to read between the lines." He pulled away slightly, never relinquishing his hold on her, and looked down into her face.

Her eyes held a glow in them, giving him even more hope.

"Or you could just ask."

Or he could just ask. What a concept.

"Do you promise to always be honest with me then? To share your feelings, your needs with me?"

She shook her head. "No. That's not how women are wired. You should know that by now. But will you promise not to keep things from me?"

Her arms dropped from his body, and he felt the chill of not having her close to him immediately. Funny how that worked.

"I mean it, Ethan." The look in her eyes was hard, reminding him of how she was that day at the wharf.

He believed her.

"I was going to tell you; I had always planned on it. But..." What could he say? He didn't tell her because she ended their engagement and told him she never wanted to see or hear from him again?

"But I wouldn't let you."

He nodded.

"That shouldn't have stopped you, though. Right? So why didn't you?"

Here was the part he was most embarrassed about. The thing that ate away at him over and over whenever Brian asked him what stopped him from winning Seline back.

"I was hurt. My pride was torn apart, and I wanted you to believe in me because of what we had together, not because of what I did for Brian and Bex."

"But it was because of what you did, or what I thought you weren't doing, for them that made me lose my faith in you."

He nodded. "Screwed up, isn't it? But Seline, you'd just told me you could never love a man who placed his own career above the lives of his friends. I wasn't that guy, and I'd thought you would have realized that after everything was said and done. I thought you'd come back to me...that you would see that what I'd done was the exact opposite."

Ethan went to sit back down on the couch and focused his gaze on the floor.

"What did you do? No one has ever really told me, not the whole story."

When Seline came to sit beside him, he didn't really expect her to touch him, let alone place her hand on his knee, but when she did, a warmth spread over his entire body. It gave him the courage to tell her the truth, something he should have done a long time ago.

"Being in London, so far from you and everyone else, it was hard. I wanted to be with you, to get on the plane and tell my boss to shove all the projects he'd just placed on my desk. But Brian told me to wait, that it didn't make sense for me to come home when I was so close to my goal."

"Your goal?"

He swallowed. "I'd applied to a few firms here in Vancouver, and one of the CEOs had a meeting in London, so he scheduled an interview with me. I was going to cancel it, but Brian didn't want me to."

"You were moving back?" He heard the shock in her voice, and noticed the tremor in her hand.

"I wanted to surprise you." He snorted. "But then Brian called and told me about the surgeon's report and how there was no hope. I heard something that day, in his voice, that I never want to hear again. He'd given up and lost faith, and didn't know what to do. I knew my boss had connections—his wife was the top brain surgeon in London—so I asked him for help, for advice. He offered to give me a name, under one condition."

He let out a long breath and worked out a kink in his shoulders. There'd been no choice, no option...she had to see that, understand why he chose to stay in London instead of coming when she needed him.

When he had the courage to look up, he noticed Seline crying. With the pad of his thumb, he gently wiped her tears away, amazed at the look of love in her gaze.

"I think he knew I was looking to leave, so he made me a deal I couldn't refuse. I had to stay with the firm for a year in exchange for him not only giving me the name of the surgeon, but he'd also cover all the costs of the surgery and aftercare."

Seline gasped and covered her mouth with her hand. Ethan's worry that she wouldn't understand disappeared.

"I had no choice, Seline. I couldn't say no, not when it meant possibly saving Bex's life. And I wanted to tell you...I wanted to share it with you, to explain things to you, but that night, when you'd called..."

"I didn't give you the chance." The anguish on her face did it to him; it broke him apart in ways he hadn't expected. He pulled her back into his hold and crushed her tight against his chest.

"It's okay," he whispered moments before he tilted his face down to hers and kissed her brow, her cheek, and then touched her sweet lips with his.

He was lost in that moment. Forever lost. As their kiss deepened, he knew she was still his, that he had her heart just as she had his. Forever.

"You're here now." Seline broke from his kiss, her breath raspy as she gazed up at him.

"I'm not going away again. My life is here, with you. I'll work with Brian and help him get things set up, and then...who knows. Stay with the foundation or create my own company. It doesn't matter, though, as long as you're by my side."

Seline rested her head back on his shoulder, and he'd never

felt so much peace. This woman completed him, in ways he never really thought possible.

He reached inside his pocket and pulled out the one item he'd carried with him ever since his return to the city. He held it out for Seline to see and placed it in the palm of her hand, unable to say the words that needed to be said.

"Ethan." The hesitation in her voice took the breath right out of him. "I love you, I always will...but I need...I'm worried." She swallowed and pulled away from him.

"Do you need time? Do you need me to do something, prove something more to you?" Whatever it was she needed, he would do it. He'd move heaven and earth for her if he could.

She shook her head. "No, you...you don't need to do anything else. You've done it already. I just...I lost faith in you so easily, Ethan, and that—" Her voice broke as she looked down at the engagement ring in the palm of her hand.

He wanted to see it back on her finger, but he knew it had to be her decision.

"You didn't lose faith in me, Seline. You were hurting, and I wasn't there like you needed. Please," he placed his hand over hers, curling her fingers in towards her palm to cover the ring, "sleep on it, think about it. Don't make a decision right now." He couldn't bear it if she gave up on them so easily.

Ethan stood and pulled her along with him.

"Seline Barr, you are an amazing woman, and I will love you to the end of days. Nothing will ever change that. I want to marry you, spend the rest of my life at your side...and I hope you'll want the same thing."

The smile she gave him was bittersweet. Afraid of what she might say, he kissed her. He softly put in every ounce of his feelings into that gentle kiss, and hoped—prayed—she would understand.

"Tomorrow is going to be crazy with all the last-minute

preparations that need to happen, and Brian has me scheduled to meet a fair number of acquaintances of his, so I probably won't see you. But think about us, think about this ring and what it means..." he bent down to kiss her again, "and wear it on your finger as you walk down the aisle if you believe in us as much as I do."

He let go of her then and walked away. He didn't stop until he was at the front door. He wanted to turn around, to beg, plead with her to give them a chance, but he'd said everything he could. Now it was in her hands.

"I thought you were going to draw me a bath?" she said softly a moment before he opened the door.

"Sweetheart, if I draw that bath, I'm not leaving." His grip on the doorknob tightened. If she was asking him what he thought she was asking...

"Didn't you just finish promising to never leave me again?"

Her voice was low, husky, and sweet. He leaned his head against the door and prayed for strength. He didn't want to rush her, to push her, to make her regret any choice she hadn't made on her own.

"Besides, do you really want to go back to Brian's apartment with Bex there?" He heard the laughter in her voice, and he listened to her footsteps as she walked towards him.

The moment her hand landed on his back, he was lost.

Chapter Seventeen

"Psst, Seline!"

With a quick flick of her wrist, Seline hid the small brownie she'd sneaked from the table beneath a napkin and turned to find Bex.

"I need help." Bex bit her lip and glanced around the crowded room.

The wedding had gone off without a hitch. It was a fairy-tale atmosphere for Bex as she walked down the aisle to her Prince Charming.

"What's wrong?" She looked Bex's dress over, worried that maybe she'd spilled a glass of wine or dropped food on her skirt or even ripped a seam.

"I have to pee," Bex leaned forward and whispered.

Seline's brow rose.

"I tried to do it myself, but the skirt," she lifted up the hem a few inches off the ground, "it's too bulky." Bright red dots appeared on Bex's cheeks and Seline laughed.

"I told you to change after the pictures were taken."

"I love my dress." Bex pouted for a few moments. "But I

really have to pee now, so please?" Her nose wrinkled as she glanced towards the small room reserved for the bridal party.

"Why not ask Brian?"

Bex's eyes grew wide. "If I ask him for help, we'll miss the rest of the party, you know that!"

"Just so we're clear, you're not asking me to hold your skirt while you pee, right? 'Cause I think that goes over and above the role of maid of honor." She couldn't stop laughing as the mental image of exactly that played out in her mind. Oh no...no, no, no.

Bex sighed and grabbed Seline's hand. "Just help me get this dress off. Please!"

With one last look at the brownie she'd left behind, Seline trailed after Bex as they wove their way through the crowded dance floor and into the small room where Bex's other dress hung, waiting for her.

"Be quick though, please?" Bex turned her back and stood there, in the middle of the room, while Seline went through the lengthy process of unhooking the back of Bex's beautiful dress.

She sneaked glances into the mirror and watched Bex as she gazed at her wedding ring and smiled. Everything about today had been perfect, and all Bex's dreams about her wedding had come true.

"I'm going to miss you." Seline struggled not to cry as she realized that life as she knew it with Bex was over. She was alone now, without her best friend to keep her company at night, eating brownie ice cream after a photo shoot or laughing together over a bottle of wine while watching their favorite TV show.

She wiped away at the tears that gathered and concentrated on getting her friend out of the dress.

"Nothing has changed. You know that." Bex smiled at her. Tears brimmed in her eyes as well.

"Oh honey, everything has changed. But I'm so happy for you."

There was a brief knock on the door.

"Everything okay in here?" Lauren, Bex's cousin poked her head in. "Oh, do you need help..."

Seline nodded. "I can't stop crying enough to unhook her from her dress, and she has to go to the washroom."

Lauren laughed. "Let me take care of it." She closed the door behind her and gently nudged Seline out of the way. With swift fingers, Bex was soon out of the dress and ran to the washroom located to the side of the room.

"It was pretty magical today, don't you think?" Seline took the dress from Lauren's hands and hung it up. The seamstress told them she would take care of getting it cleaned and delivered to Bex after the wedding, so she didn't bother to zip it up in the protected bag the dress came in.

"I literally haven't stopped crying." Lauren wrinkled her nose. "Every time I see that girl of ours, I can't help but think we almost lost her." Tears welled up again before she fluttered her hands and groaned. "There I go again." She took a tissue from her purse, dapped at her eyes and left, claiming she needed better mascara.

Alone in the room, Seline stood in front of the mirror and looked at herself.

The dress she wore was flattering to her figure, but that wasn't where her attention was focused. It was on her hands.

"That feels so much better!" Bex literally pranced out of the bathroom and threw her arms around Seline. "I will love you forever, that will never change."

"Oh silly girl, I know that." She hugged her friend back. "What am I going to do alone in our apartment, though, and who is going to cook all the meals? You know I tend to burn water."

"That's only because you get so focused on the images you upload on your computer. Besides, you won't be alone for long." Bex winked at her before she reached for her hand and stared at the engagement ring there.

"You have no idea how happy this makes me," Bex said. "I always knew you'd get back together, that nothing could keep you guys apart, but you're just a little stubborn."

"Is that where the Dare idea came from?"

Bex blushed. "I had to do something," she admitted.

"I knew it. The moment I realized mine was the only folded piece of paper, I knew you did that on purpose."

Bex shrugged before she reached for her other dress and put it on. She turned her back for help from Seline in zipping it up.

"Like I said, you're just a little stubborn. But now that's Ethan's problem."

"Did I hear my name?"

Both Seline and Bex whirled around to find Ethan and Brian in the room with them.

Bex ran over to her groom, jumped into his arms and gave him a long kiss.

"Didn't hear you come in," Seline said as Ethan made his way towards her.

Her heart skipped a beat as she took in his sexy smile. The ridiculous sequined pink ties Bex insisted the men all wear was undone and loosely wrapped around his neck.

"We were hoping to catch you both off guard." He held out his arms.

"You almost came to see a nearly naked bride." Seline went willingly into his embrace.

Ethan's eyes widened and then he chuckled. "That's why Brian came in first."

"Good call." She nodded. She let herself relax in his arms,

enjoying the feel of his strength around her, supporting her. Loving her.

"Question. How long do we have to stay?" he whispered into her ear.

"Well, we are the maid of honor and best man. It would probably be polite to wait till everyone else leaves and help clean up a bit." And by clean up, she meant see if there were any desserts left.

"But then I get to whisk you away?"

Now this sounded promising. Whisk her away?

Ethan gave her a kiss and then whispered into her ear. "You know how I won the auction for that trip earlier?"

As planned, they'd held an auction where the money raised would go towards Brian and Bex's foundation for brain tumors. At the last minute, Ethan had outbid everyone else for that secret island vacation that only Brian, Bex, Ethan, and she knew the location.

"Well, I checked ticket prices and I found a last-minute seat sale, but it means we'd leave tonight." He gave her a wink.

"Tonight? Really? You found a seat sale today and we leave tonight?" For some reason, she found that hard to believe.

"What can I say?" The smile on his face said it all.

"Your bag is in the trunk of Ethan's car already. I packed it for you." Overhearing, Bex called out.

Seline laughed. And laughed.

"You planned this, didn't you?" She said her comment loud enough for everyone to hear.

"After everything you've both done for us, did you really think we wouldn't find some way to say thank-you?" Brian released his bride and shook hands with Ethan and then wrapped Seline in a hug, moments before Bex pushed him out of the way and enveloped Seline in another hug.

"Like I'd go away on a dream vacation without you. We always travel together."

"Bex, I am not coming on your honeymoon." Seline couldn't believe what she was hearing.

Ethan wound his arms around her and held the hand where his ring rested.

"Seline, you should know by now, it's useless to argue with Bex. She always gets her way."

Seline gazed down at the ring as well. No, she couldn't argue with that at all.

The End

A Note From Steena...

Dear Reader;

Thank you for reading Sweet Renewal!

If you can't tell by now, I'm a sucker for second chances. Maybe that's because my love and I had our own second chance once and choosing one another and what we had/have, was the best decision I'd ever made.

I really do hope you enjoyed this series and that you'll check out some of my other reads. Whether you like sweet romance, women's fiction or something a little darker...you'll find it under either my Steena Marie Holmes name, or under Steena Holmes.

Have you had the chance to check out any of my reader trips yet? I love traveling with my readers and I would really love to travel with you!

Interested in knowing more about my reader trips? Check out my website and click on the **LET'S TRAVEL TOGETHER** tab!

I hope you enjoy a sweet life full of chocolate, happiness, and peace.

Steena

Secret Info on Steena...

Here's some other fun things about me I bet you didn't know (want to ask me a question...find me on FB and I'll answer):

• I'm afraid of heights
  • Christmas is my favorite season
  • I'm a travelholic
  • spiders/bugs/bees... yep, afraid!
  • HATE mushrooms
  • LOVE the scent of vanilla
  • can't stand anyone to touch my nose
  • I save love notes from my husband
  • I have a stash of chocolate I can't find
  • need silence to write
  • shows I love: HANNIBAL, NCIS, BLACK LIST, BONES, GRIMM, any cookie/chocolate/baking challenge show, X-FILES (the list continues to grow...)
  • favorite movies: MY FAIR LADY, LAKE HOUSE, ANYTHING MARVEL and most Christmas movies...

Other Sweet Reads you may enjoy...

The Promise of Christmas:

For the past two years, Ashley Tanner has been trying to keep her promise to revitalize the small mountain town of Innsbruck, but it's starting to look like she's failing as mayor, and failure is never an option for her.

Second Chances at the Chocolate Blessings Cafe

This was my first published novel from 2005. It's been updated and reissued. Enjoy!

Left at the altar, everyone blaming her for the groom's cold feet, all Wynne can do is place a smile on her face and take one step forward: right into the arms of chocolate, because, chocolate is a jilted bride's best friend, after all.

NEW YORK TIMES & USA TODAY
BESTSELLING AUTHORS

STEENA
HOLMES
and ELENA
AITKEN

HALFWAY
to nowhere

Halfway to Nowhere:

Nikki Landon walked away from her small town, Halfway, Montana, ten years ago, with no intentions of setting foot there again. But, when her mother dies unexpectedly, Nikki has no choice but to return, and this time with a secret she's been hiding.

Halfway in Between:

Secrets in a small town have a way of getting out, and if Melissa and Nikki aren't careful, this is one secret that could destroy everything.

NEW YORK TIMES & USA TODAY
BESTSELLING AUTHORS

STEENA HOLMES
and ELENA AITKEN

HALFWAY
to nowhere

Halfway to Christmas:

A lot has happened in Halfway, and this year the holidays are set to take on a whole new meaning.

LOVE AT THE CHOCOLATE SHOP SERIES:

Book 6: CHARMED BY CHOCOLATE

After a mishap on a hit reality show called Charming, where she earns the name "Lonely Leah", she returns to Marietta to hide, never once dreaming she may find love back home.

Book 11: CAPTURED BY CHOCOLATE

Radio DJ Dylan Morgan enjoys small-town life in Marietta. Unlike his longtime girlfriend and globetrotting photojournalist Casey Michaels, he's never been tempted to spread his wings.

Until an east coast job offer at a major radio station catches his eye. He considers taking the position, but then Casey calls...

She's coming home.

By Steena Holmes

If you enjoyed this story, you might enjoy:

Finding Emma

The Memory Child

Stillwater Rising

The Word Game

Saving Abby

Abby's Journey

The Forgotten Ones

The Patient

The Perfect Secret

Lies We Tell Ourselves

About the Author

STEENA MARIE HOLMES is the sweeter writing of Steena Holmes, a NY Times & USA Today author with over 2 million copies sold. The novels you will read under the name Steena Marie Holmes are heartwarming stories full of sweetness.

Let's Connect!
www.steenaholmes.com
steena@steenaholmes.com